Praise for *Kiss*

"A perfect 10 packed with romance, politics, scandals, and non-stop suspense."

—Laura Wilkinson, Olympic gold medalist
and world champion diver

". . . no less fast-moving than the Christy Award–winning author's solo prose, but also more gripping as it plunges into the life of a woman with frayed and painful family relationships . . ."

—*Publishers Weekly*

"Dekker and Healy form a powerful team in crafting redemptive suspense. *Kiss* is emotionally absorbing and mentally intriguing—don't miss it."

—Lisa T. Bergren, author of *The Blessed*

"The human brain could actually be the real final frontier—we know so little about it and yet it drives the world as we know it. So when authors like Erin and Ted bravely explore these mysterious regions, going into complex places like memory and soul and relationships, I become hooked. The creativity of this suspenseful story is sure to hook other readers as well. Very memorable!"

—Melody Carlson, author of *Finding Alice*
and *The Other Side of Darkness*

"Dekker and Healy prove a winning team in this intriguing, imaginative thriller."

—James Scott Bell,
best-selling author of *Try Darkness*

Kiss

teddekker.com

DEKKER FANTASY

BOOKS OF HISTORY CHRONICLES

THE LOST BOOKS
Chosen
Infidel
Renegade
Chaos
Lunatic
Elyon

THE CIRCLE SERIES
Green
Red
White
Black

THE PARADISE NOVELS
Showdown
Saint
Sinner

Skin
House (with Frank Peretti)

DEKKER MYSTERY

Blink of an Eye

MARTYR'S SONG SERIES
Heaven's Wager
When Heaven Weeps
Thunder of Heaven
The Martyr's Song

THE CALEB BOOKS
Blessed Child
A Man Called Blessed

DEKKER THRILLER

THR3E
Obsessed
Adam

TED DEKkER
& ERIN HEALY

THOMAS NELSON
Since 1798

NASHVILLE DALLAS MEXICO CITY RIO DE JANEIRO BEIJING

Published in Nashville, Tennessee, by Thomas Nelson. Thomas Nelson is a registered trademark of Thomas Nelson, Inc.

Published in association with Thomas Nelson and Creative Trust, Inc., 5141 Virginia Way, Suite 320, Brentwood, TN 37027.

Page design by Mandi Cofer.

Thomas Nelson, Inc., titles may be purchased in bulk for educational, business, fund-raising, or sales promotional use. For information, please e-mail SpecialMarkets@ThomasNelson.com.

Unless otherwise noted, Scripture quotations are taken from The HOLY BIBLE, NEW INTERNATIONAL VERSION®. © 1973, 1978, 1984 by International Bible Society. Used by permission of Zondervan Publishing House. All rights reserved.

ISBN 978-1-59554-819-1 (TP)
ISBN 978-1-59554-583-1 (IE)

Library of Congress Cataloging-in-Publication Data
Dekker, Ted, 1962–
Kiss / Ted Dekker and Erin Healy.
   p. cm.
ISBN 978-1-59554-470-4
1. Coma—Patient—Fiction. 2. Recovered memory—Fiction. I. Healy, Erin M. II. Title.
PS3554.E43K57 2008
813'.54—dc22

2008042009

Printed in the United States of America
09 10 11 12 RRD 7 6 5 4 3 2 1

Whoever said 'Don't look back'? Unblind yourself.
Turn your eyes to the past to find your way forward.

—MIGUEL LOPEZ, *THE LIVES WE SAVE*

Remember that you were slaves in Egypt . . .

—DEUTERONOMY 16:12

prologue

The view from my therapist's window is unremarkable. Four stories down, the parking lot blacktop ripples under waves of Texas's blazing summer heat. I stand here facing the view because it's easier to look at than the two men in the office behind me. There is dear Dr. Ayers, the wisest old soul I have ever met. He might be eighty, judging by that wrinkled cocoa skin and his head of hair whiter than cotton, but he's agile as a fifty-year-old. My beloved brother, Rudy, is also here. He has kept me tethered to my sanity in ways that should earn him sainthood.

Rudy comes to these sessions because he knows I need him to.

I come—have been coming for weeks now—because I am trying to put the past behind me.

But today I am here because tonight I will see my father for the first time in five months. My encounters with Landon are hard enough in the best of circumstances. They always end the same, with flaring tempers and harsh words and fresh wounds. But tonight, I must confront Landon. Not about my past, but about his future.

Yes, I call my father by his first name. The distance it creates between us helps to dull my pain.

"So your dilemma," Dr. Ayers says to my back, "is that you fear the consequences of confronting him could be worse than the consequences of staying silent."

I nod at the pane of glass. "Of course, I'd rather avoid everything. Even Rudy thinks I should wait until I know . . . more. But if I'm right, and I don't speak up now . . ." Why am I here? I have made a mountain out of a molehill and am wasting everyone's time. I should drop this. "Landon probably won't even listen to me. Not the way he listens to you, Rude."

"He listens to you too," Rudy says. Always looking for the positive spin.

The truth is, Landon does not listen to me. But Rudy, who is deputy campaign manager of Senator Landon McAllister's bid for the United States presidency, is following in the man's footsteps and so has his undivided attention. Also, Rudy doesn't look a thing like our mother, as I do. Mama was a Guatemalan beauty with a café-au-lait complexion. I have had her personality and her looks since the day my head of thick black hair came in. Even today, I wear my hair short and windblown, the way she did. I have her leggy height, her long stride, her laugh.

Against all odds, our father's recessive Irish genes won the genetic dispute over Rudy. As for me, I have always believed it is painful for my father to look at me.

"And I don't think she should gloss over this," Rudy says to the therapist. "I think Shauna should step very carefully. Avoid burning more bridges with Dad, if it can be helped. If she's right, God help us all."

I finally turn to look at my brother. "It's not my goal to burn anything, Rudy, even though I'll never have what you have with Landon." This truth pains me more than the truth of what I've learned. And what I've learned, partial though it may be, is monstrous.

The tension headache that has started at the top of my spine spreads its fingers over the back of my head. The sickness I feel right now might come from what I suspect, or it might be rooted in my certainty that he will reject me again tonight.

Yes, I'm pretty sure that I am nauseated by the prospect of another rejection.

I'll never forget the first time my father turned his back on me, though the second time was more painful, and though all the times since have clumped together in a unified throbbing heartache.

Rudy was the unwitting cause of Landon's first abandonment. My brother came into the world when I was seven, and our mother died nineteen minutes after his birth. I remember not being able to breathe when I heard she was gone. I honestly thought that I might die those first few hours, my mother and I both dead in the same day all because of this baby boy.

My father said it was God's fault, though he seemed to blame Mama's passing on me. I guess I was the more tangible target.

After Mama's doctor delivered the crushing news, my father turned away mumbling something about my uncle and carried Rudy out of the hospital without me. Uncle Trent found me two hours later, hiding behind a chair in the waiting room.

Truth not only hurts, it shames: at the time, I wished Rudy were dead. The day I stood at the head of Mama's casket, I wondered what would happen to Rudy if I covered his squalling face tight with that silky blue blanket. Wishing that the balance of the universe might require Mama to come back.

It took just one night for me to understand that Rudy's heart had been broken into more pieces than my own. The tears he cried for Mama came from some well that would not dry up. That night I fed him a bottle of warm milk and took him into my bed, promising to keep Mama's memory alive in this little boy who'd never met her.

I'm twenty-eight now, and I have long since realized that the wounds of rejection do not heal with time. They reopen at the lightest touch, as deep as the first time they were inflicted. The pain is as real as flash floods in the wet season here in Austin, overwhelming and unstoppable.

The pain, even when I can successfully numb it, has kept me at a distance from people and God. Now and then I consider the irony of this: how it came to be that my mother's God, who once seemed so real and comforting to me, managed to die when she did.

So many deaths in one night.

And here I am, expecting yet another tonight. The death of hope. For most of my life, hatred of my father and hope of gaining his affection have lived in stressful coexistence behind my ribs.

I'm crying and didn't even notice I had started.

Dr. Ayers's voice is gentle. "Do you believe your father is culpable in this matter you are investigating?"

The question behind the question stabs at the tender spot in me that longs for Landon's love. *Do you believe your father is guilty of anything more than hurting you? Do you care about truth or only about the past?*

Somehow I care about both. Is that possible?

"I believe he is capable. More than that . . ." I sniff. "I don't know yet. Very soon, though, I will. Very soon."

Dr. Ayers leans back in his leather chair and folds his wrinkled hands across his slender stomach.

"Tell me: what do you want this confrontation to do for you?"

Several possible answers rush me. I want to be wrong, in fact. I want Landon to tell me that none of what I suspect is true. I want my father to reassure me that I have nothing to worry about, that he is an upright man who would never do anything so foolish, so hurtful. Nothing like what he has done—

Rudy's eyes bore into the side of my head, and the truth of what I really want punches me in the stomach. I step to my chair and sit.

"I want to bring him down," I say before I think it through. "I want him to know what betrayal feels like. I want to get him back."

My tears turn into sobs. I can't help it. I can't stop.

Rudy places his hand on my knee. Not to urge me to stop bawling, but to remind me that he is by my side.

Hatred for my father did not become a part of my life until the second time he turned his back on me.

I was eleven. Patrice had been my stepmother for three days when she took over my upbringing, with Landon's permission. He claimed Rudy, and she got me.

Her style of parenting, if it can be called that, involved locking me in closets and burning the scrapbooks my mother had made me and refusing to feed me for a day at a time. As I grew I quit trying to make sense of such behavior and simply became more defiant. She responded by graduating to more extreme measures. There was no hiding our animosity for each other.

I suspect I reminded her, too, of my mother.

When she turned brazen enough to beat and burn me, though, I broke down and told Landon. I showed him the triangular burns on the inside of my left arm, imprinted by Patrice's steam iron for my failure to pull my clean clothes out of the dryer before they wrinkled.

Landon handed me a tube of ointment and turned away, saying, "If you ever go to such lengths to lie about my wife again, I'll bandage those myself. And you won't like my touch."

My wife. He had always called Mama *my love*.

Dr. Ayers makes no attempt to calm me. He has said before that crying is the best balm. Eventually I fumble through my mind for the words to justify what I have said.

"If Landon pays for what he's done, I'll get closure."

"On what?" says Dr. Ayers.

"On my past."

He takes a few moments to respond. Rudy produces a tissue out of thin air and I try to compose myself.

"So you're saying that closing yourself off from your past is what you need in order to move on with your life."

There is more than an attempt at clarity in Dr. Ayers's tone—a challenge perhaps.

"Yes." I swipe at my nose with the tissue. "That's exactly what I'm saying. I want to put the past behind me."

"By inflicting on your father what he has inflicted on you. By betraying him, you said."

"No. By forcing him to remember me."

"Ah! I see. So when he remembers you, then you will have accomplished your goal and can forget your past."

His words fill me with confusion. The way he says it, I have this all wrong. But in my mind, my goal is—was—clear. Isn't that how it works? Deal with the past, get justice, make the pain go away?

"Something like that," I say.

Dr. Ayers nods as if he sees everything clearly now. He rises and comes around the desk, propping himself against the front of it and leaning toward me.

The doctor reaches out with an aging hand and touches my shoulder. "Would you mind if I gave you an alternative theory to consider?"

Honestly, I have no idea.

Dr. Ayers straightens. "It is possible that your plan will only root you more deeply in the pain of your past, not separate you from it."

My confusion mounts. "So how do you suggest I put my past behind me?"

"It is behind you, dear. And that's where it will be forever. You can't make it vanish—"

"But I want to. I believe I can."

"By creating more pain? The mathematics of that isn't logical."

"I can't just ignore it!"

"No, that's true."

"But you think I shouldn't confront Landon."

"Oh, I'm not making any judgment about what you should do, Shauna. I'm only talking about your motivations. What do you *really* want?"

"To *forget*. I want to forget every single, stinging moment that was inflicted on me by people who were supposed to *love* me. I want someone to take these memories away from me."

Dr. Ayers wags a finger in my direction, smiling. "I felt that way once."

I take a steadying breath.

"You know I used be a reverend before I began helping people here?" He gestures to the modest office. "Ministry of a different but no less valuable kind. Got thrown out of my pulpit by some folks who said they loved God but hated his black children. I spent a lot of years feeling the way you do now—that if I looked far and wide enough, I'd find a way to erase both the blight of my memory and the stink of people I held responsible for my pain."

He leans forward again, encroaching on my space. "But I discovered something better. Shauna, your history is no less important to your survival than your ability to breathe. In the end, you can only determine whether to saturate your memories with pain or with perspective. Forgetting is not an option. I tell you the truth now: Pain was not God's plan for this life. It is a reality, but it is not part of the plan."

I exhale. "God and I aren't exactly on speaking terms. Especially not about his plans for my life."

"Pain or perspective, Shauna. That's all that's within your control."

I drop my head into my hands, feeling more certain than ever that absolutely nothing is in my control.

In spite of Dr. Ayers's warning, I decided to talk to Landon tonight. Regardless of the outcome—closure for me or more pain for him—I hoped the truth would count for something.

Instead, when the moment came, I tripped all over my words. Landon's larger-than-life and had the upper hand from the outset. Instead of staying on topic, I took offense at something he said. I can hardly remember now, something about a man's world, and when I tried to set him straight, he cut me to the floor with a few harsh words.

So here I am once again, driving fast through the night on a rain-slicked road, away from yet another argument with Landon. And as he has so many times before, Rudy has come along to calm my explosive temper. He is smiling slightly at my ranting. Sometimes I think he finds me entertaining.

The hum of tires kissing asphalt through water soothes my anxious heart. "I don't know why I let him roll over me like that, Rude."

"You handled yourself just fine. I thought you showed remarkable restraint."

"But not enough."

"Okay, not enough." Truth does not make Rudy flinch. My car follows a downward slope onto a bridge, pointing me east into Austin.

"Underneath it all, Dad worries about you, you know."

I look at Rudy. No, no I didn't know. Just as Rudy doesn't know about my scars from Patrice's iron. I've told Dr. Ayers, but not Rudy. He and Patrice get along.

"What does he worry about?" The relative unsafety of my little car? The condition of my heart?

My heart is even more mangled than the skin under my arms.

So why have I never stopped wishing? Wishing that Landon would only—

"Watch out!"

Rudy's cry comes at the same moment that glaring lights from another vehicle blind me. It all happens so quickly that I don't have time to think about swerving or stopping.

A horn is blaring, and voices are screaming, and then the terrible sound of metal smashing into metal.

Daddy . . .

This is the last plea for help that fills my mind before the world ends.

He shifted his cell phone to the opposite ear and stared at the hospital entrance through the windshield of his car. The parking lot lights were still on, though dawn had broken the horizon behind him.

"She was in surgery six hours," he said. "Internal bleeding."

"Where is she *now*?"

"Private room."

"But still in a coma, correct?"

"Yes." Ironic that Shauna McAllister had dodged death only to end up in a coma. "I can get to her easy enough now. She'll be dead within the hour."

"No. Change of plans. Our hands are being forced. I'll explain later, but for now she stays alive."

"She's too big a risk to just—"

"What's her prognosis?"

"Too early to tell. She could be in a coma for a day or for a year."

"Or forever. Even if she comes out, she could have brain damage."

"Yes, that's possible."

"So she stays alive for now. She's not a threat as long as she's unconscious."

"And when she comes around?"

"With any luck, she'll forget everything."

"I don't do business with luck."

"You will today. Like I said, our hands are being forced in this. Her condition buys us time. I'll call Dr. Carver; he'll have options for us. If we have to change course, we do it later."

"What if she remembers?"

"If she remembers, she dies."

1

Nightmares of death by black water ticked off the hours of the deepest sleep Shauna McAllister had ever experienced. In an eternal loop, she choked and drowned and was somehow resuscitated, only to choke and drown again, and again, in an endless terror. Always the same fight, the same thrashing for air. Always the same intense agony for the same amount of time before the screen of her mind dimmed.

Then it would flicker back to life.

Merciless, exhausting.

Her stomach hurt with the penetration of a hundred slicing knives, cutting her enough to scrape and bleed and sting. The cold water was not a strong enough anesthetic.

She could not remember where she was or how she had come to be here.

Why wasn't her father with her? And where had Rudy gone?

The water closed over her head again. She considered welcoming death and letting her fatigue have its way. She was so tired.

Something touched her. A stable hand, gentle and helpful, grabbed her wrist. In that Herculean grip was all the strength she could not muster. And so it was that at the very moment she resigned herself to drowning, she sensed as she rose through the black waters that maybe she would not die today.

Shauna broke the surface, gasping and flopping like a snagged fish tossed onto the deck of a—

No, she was on a bed, some narrow thing that rattled when she moved.

Her hands hit metal rails and she grabbed hold to avoid sliding back under-water, though some sixth sense told her there was no water. She started coughing and could not stop, as if the oxygen in this place would kill her just as quickly as liquid.

How did she get here?

Someone shoved a pillow under her shoulders. Someone was speaking. Several people were speaking at once, animated and urgent.

She opened her eyes and took her first full lungful of air.

A middle-aged woman in nurse's scrubs stood next to the bed, bright eyes wide and gap-toothed mouth slack. She hit an intercom button in the panel over the bed, punching it so hard the plastic speaker rattled.

Shauna was half-aware of people spilling into the room.

"Dr. Siders," the woman said into the wall. She put a hand over her heart as if to prevent its escape. "We need you here now. She's awake!"

Still disoriented, Shauna lay at the center of the small gathering in the room. Through her mental haze, she locked onto a tall doctor in a white lab coat as he moved to the head of her bed. The man was 80 percent limbs and 20 percent torso, long and wiry and strung taut.

"Hello, Shauna. You can hear me?"

She felt her chin dip a fraction of an inch.

He put his hand on her arm. "I'm Dr. Gary Siders. And you—well let's just say you're one very lucky girl. Without a doubt, the most unusual case I've had in here for a while."

Where was *here*? Where was Rudy?

She tried to remember. Random images collided in her mind in a wreck that could not be construed as an explanation: shopping at an open-air market in Guatemala, congratulating a colleague at the CPA firm where she worked, stir-frying veggies in a wok at her downtown loft.

These stray events seemed disconnected from this white bed, this white room, these people dressed in white. She couldn't remember, and the void was the most disconcerting piece of this white puzzle.

She saw a flash of color. Blue. A blue class ring on a long, angular hand that was supporting a man's chin. A handsome man. He stood under the TV, arms crossed, and his worry-lined forehead tripped some wire in Shauna's brain that said *friendly*. His brown eyes held hers and he smiled almost imperceptibly, hopefully.

Her mind held no recognition. But he was a relief to her senses, a warm, sympathetic object in an unfamiliar, cold room. She smiled back.

On the other side of the bed, her eyes landed on Patrice McAllister.

Shauna shivered involuntarily. How was it possible, after all these years, that the woman could make her feel afraid? Patrice wore her trademark navy blue pantsuit and deadpan expression. She had all of Diane Keaton's good looks, but her heart was a stone.

The scar tissue under Shauna's arm seemed to burn, as always when Patrice stared at her. Shauna looked for her father. No sign of him. No surprise there.

Instead, she saw Uncle Trent standing behind Patrice. A close-cropped layer of white hair covered his sun-spotted head. Trent rested his hand on Patrice's shoulder as if forcing her to stay put. The laugh lines around his eyes eased Shauna's fear.

In these beats of recognition, Shauna felt her body with new awareness, as if her senses had been on vacation and just returned: the stiffness of her limbs, the pain in her stomach, the hardness of her mattress, the discomfort of her itchy sheets. She wanted to get out of bed. Her muscles would not respond.

"Let's sit you up." The doctor reached the controls for the hospital bed, and she rose with a whir. "Better?"

"Where is this?" her vocal cords rasped.

"Hill Country Medical Center."

She'd been in this hospital many times, but never as a patient. Behind him on a counter, old flowers wilted in dirty water. Other empty vases lined up behind these.

"How long?"

"This should only take about five minutes. We'll schedule a complete neuropsychological evaluation when we know you're up for it. That will take a day or two."

"I mean, how long have I been here?"

He hesitated. "Six weeks."

Six *weeks?*

"You've drifted in and out for several days, never fully awake."

"I don't remember any of that."

"Not unusual."

"What day is it?"

He checked his wristwatch. "October 14. Sunday. You came in September 1."

September.

She tried to remember August.

Nothing. July.

Nothing. Farther.

Nothing.

She'd been here six weeks? Her mind didn't want to connect with the idea of it, much less any specific memory.

He flashed a blinding light across her eyes and she winced. The stranger under the TV stepped to the bed and placed a warm hand on her blanketed foot. The gesture gave her courage. Who was this man? Someone she trusted, apparently.

"Follow my fingers," Dr. Siders said. She focused on his sinewy hand, contemplating how so much time could have slipped by without her knowing it. Six weeks from—

From what?

She'd taken her trip to Guatemala. That was when, March?

He lifted the blanket and ran a fingernail along the sole of her other foot. Her reflexes snatched it out of his reach. "You have no respect for the Rancho Levels—if you move through those any faster, I'll have to discharge you this afternoon. The GCS score is useless. Apparently all you're guilty of is a concussion. No TBI. The MRIs and CATs are clear, though they're not the most reliable, considering you're in a drug trial."

She had no idea what he was talking about.

"Can you tell me who's here in the room with us?" he asked her.

Shauna kept her eyes on the doctor. "My father's wife, Patrice McAllister. And Uncle Trent—Trent Wilde, a family friend. He's not actually my uncle."

"And what does Mr. Wilde do?"

The answer came to her without her needing to search for it. This surprised her. "He's the CEO of my father's company. McAllister MediVista."

"Where is that company located?"

"Houston."

"Do you know who he is?" Dr. Siders gestured toward the man whose warm hand still rested on her foot.

She studied him again. High hairline. Color-coordinated waves and eyes. Dark brown sugar. Older than she was, maybe midthirties. Professional. He might be an athlete—a distance runner or a cyclist. As for who he was, she came up empty.

She shook her head. Patrice sighed and tapped her fingers on her crossed arms.

"You have no recollection of Wayne Spade?" the doctor asked. "I understand you two are well acquainted."

"How well?"

Uncle Trent exchanged a glance with Wayne, who averted his eyes and shoved his hands into his pockets.

"Honey," Trent said, "you and Wayne have been close for several months." Embarrassment settled over Shauna. "You don't mean—"

"It's okay, Shauna." Wayne's tone was careful, and his smile covered up what Shauna sensed was disappointment. She heard what he didn't say: they had been more, and he didn't want the truth of it to hurt either one of them. "Take your time."

How could she have forgotten someone so close to her? Distress filled her stomach.

"I'm sorry," she whispered.

Dr. Siders turned back to her. "Wayne saved your life, my dear. He pulled you out of the water and performed CPR until the paramedics arrived."

This man? He saved her life? What water?

The doctor went on. "Where do you live, Shauna?"

"Wha—? Um, Austin."

"What is your father's name?"

"Landon. McAllister."

"And he is presently campaigning for the office of?"

"President," she said. "Where is he?"

"California, I think. Our staff is in the process of contacting him about your status. Can you tell me the outcome of the primary elections in February?"

He won, of course, or else he wouldn't still be campaigning. She had a few questions of her own, but the conversation was moving too quickly for her to articulate the bottom line. Why could she remember her father but not—what was his name? Wayne? Why could she remember last year but not this summer? She stood unbalanced at the edge of a yawning gap filled with nothing but anxiety.

"Can we move it along please?" Patrice asked.

Dr. Siders checked his notes. "Do you remember the accident?"

Wayne seemed to recover from the blow of Shauna's forgetfulness. Touching her ankles, he said, "Is now the best time to bring all this up?"

"The—I was in an accident?"

"Oh, for crying out loud," Patrice murmured.

Wayne frowned at her. "Mrs. McAllister, *please.*"

Shauna could not look at her stepmother, but she caught Uncle Trent's eyes. He shook his head at Shauna. *Let it go.*

"Yes," the doctor said to Shauna. "Do you remember it?"

Shauna looked at Wayne. "You were there? How did you . . . ?"

"He was following you home from my house," Uncle Trent said.

"I don't understand," Shauna said.

"Dr. Siders," Wayne said, "she's so tired."

"She's been sleeping six weeks," Patrice said, standing. "She can stay awake a few more minutes."

"Patrice," Trent said.

"No," she snapped. "Enough of this melodrama. We deserve to know what she knows."

"I don't understand." Shauna gripped the bedsheets in a double fist. "What happened?"

"You tell us, Shauna. I believe you know precisely what I mean. If you're pulling a stunt"—Patrice leaned over the bed—"if I find out you're making a mockery of Rudy and your father with this *act* . . ." She frowned and fumbled for words.

Nothing but Patrice's own twisted view of the world could make sense of such accusations. Shauna's temples throbbed. She looked at Uncle Trent, begging him without words to sort this out for her.

He pulled Patrice away from the bed. "Rudy was with you, honey. You were driving when your car collided with a truck and went off a bridge."

Shauna managed a shallow breath but she couldn't exhale. "Is he okay?"

Wayne's eyes shifted. Dr. Siders appeared as baffled as Shauna felt. Trent looked at Patrice but offered no answer.

"Is Rudy okay?"

Patrice glared at Shauna. "You don't deserve an answer to that. You will tell us exactly what happened. Where you got the drugs. Why you planned to hurt Rudy. I can't believe anyone would go to such lengths. You're a beast. You have nearly ruined your father. It's a wonder he has managed to go on."

Rudy was hurt. Fear injected adrenaline into Shauna's heart.

Drugs?

"Where is he?" she demanded.

"California," Trent said.

"I mean Rudy!" She threw back the covers.

Patrice stepped back into Trent. Dr. Siders snapped out of his gawking. He dropped his charts onto the counter behind him, then leaned across the bed to catch Shauna's arm. "I want you out of here, all of you! We spoke about this."

She slapped Dr. Siders's hands away. "Tell me where Rudy is."

Wayne's face lit up with worry, and he reached for Shauna as she dropped her legs over the edge of the bed. A rolling table stood between them, and he bumped into it.

Her bare feet hit the floor and she tried to stand on her atrophied legs, which resented her demands as much as everyone else in the room apparently did. The blood in her body raced to her feet to be of help, emptying her head. Patrice stood back and watched Shauna fall. She went down before anyone else could catch her, clipping her jaw on the table and clamping down on her tongue. She tasted blood and heard her skull smack the vinyl flooring, then she slipped back into the black waters.

2

Wayne held Shauna's elbow and helped her down the white hallway. She insisted on walking this time, desperate to get out of the wheelchair, and determined to get out of this hospital as quickly as possible. It was already Wednesday.

After a day of fluctuating consciousness followed by two full days of being scanned, tested, poked, quizzed, and studied, she had many more questions than the first time she awoke.

But no more answers. They were all refusing to speak to her about Rudy and it was driving her crazy.

"I can't believe how much progress you've made already," Wayne said as her energy flagged. She paused for a break and leaned against the wall. "You're amazing."

She searched his eyes. "Please, Wayne. Tell me."

"Tell you what?"

"What no one else will. About Rudy."

"We've been over this." His tone reflected sadness rather than impatience. "Shauna, they've told me as much as they've told you. How bad can it be if they've sent him home?"

"This is ridiculous! Why all the secrecy?"

"He's home. And he's got the best care your father's money can buy."

"So for all we know they've sent him home to die?"

Wayne chuckled. "Wow. You really do go to the worst-case scenario, don't you?"

"Don't laugh at me." Shauna started walking again.

He sobered up and stayed by her side. "I only meant that your father wouldn't be on the road if that was the case."

"It's maddening!"

"I'm sure it's for your best. Trent has everything taken care—"

"My father should be the one in that role. But then he never was where he needed to be, was he?"

"He's on his way back."

"So I hear."

Wayne didn't say anything to that. Really, what could he say? Shauna didn't wish her family's dysfunctional dynamics on anyone.

"Thank you for all you've done these last few days."

"You're welcome."

"I feel really bad about . . . about not . . ."

Wayne placed a finger on her lips, giving her a light static shock. She flinched. He looked surprised, then grinned.

"Don't worry about any of that," he said. "We'll figure it out as we go. Right now, you have bigger things to worry about."

He placed his free hand between her shoulder blades and guided her into the office, rubbing her back gently.

Dr. Siders was already there, his gangly body folded into a chair too small for him. The office had been painted uninspiring shades of mauve and green that failed to calm her. The colors clashed with the hyper arrangement of chairs and a chaos of paperwork on every flat surface.

"I'll wait outside," Wayne said.

"You can stay."

"This is your private business," Wayne said. "Tell me as much or as little as you want later. I'll be here for you."

His sensitivity took the edge off her nerves. She would press for information about Rudy until they told her what she wanted to hear or discharged her.

Dr. Millie Harding, a devil-may-care psychiatrist with frizzy red hair and glowing lipstick, crossed paths with Wayne at the door, then greeted Shauna with a kind touch on the shoulder.

Shauna hardly noticed it.

"You promised to tell me about Rudy," she said to Dr. Siders.

"Absolutely, Shauna. But you're our main concern right now. Let us bring you up to speed on our evaluations, and then—"

"I've spent three days imagining the worst."

"You've had a terrible crisis to face," Dr. Harding said. Her gravelly voice suggested she had smoked for decades. "Memory loss is catastrophic enough to process. One thing at a time, dear."

"If someone would just say, 'Rudy's fine,' I would—"

The door opened again and sucked in a rumpled man straight from the eighties. He wore a tan corduroy blazer and sage green tie. His sandy brown hair stood in a wave off his forehead.

Dr. Siders stood. "Rudy's fine. Shauna, allow me to introduce Dr. Will Carver."

"You look remarkable, Ms. McAllister," Dr. Carver said, taking his hands in and out of his trousers' pockets. He did not sit when Dr. Siders did. "We're so pleased."

"Dr. Carver is the clinical sponsor-investigator overseeing the administration of new drugs to you during your coma, Shauna."

"New drugs?"

"From a trial still in its earliest stages. Your father was able to enroll you under expanded-access protocols—"

"My father."

Dr. Carver hesitated.

Dr Siders said, "You realize that this hospital is closely affiliated with McAllister MediVista's research and development."

Shauna had not known this.

"What protocols, again?"

"Expanded-access," Dr. Carver said. "In the simplest terms, these are reserved for exceptional situations in which physicians believe the promise of some experimental drug, even in the earliest stages of development, holds out a patient's only hope of recovery."

"We couldn't explain why you slipped into a coma at all," Dr. Siders said. "You had no evidence of brain injury, and no other explanation for your condition."

"It is possible for a drug overdose to push a person into a coma," Dr. Carver said. Dr. Siders frowned at him.

"Overdose?" Shauna echoed.

"A blood test showed traces of MDMA in your system, enough to make you unsafe on the road—"

"MD what?"

"Ecstasy. It's impossible to know how much you actually had—"

"I never had *any*!" Even though she couldn't remember, Shauna knew in the deepest part of her that she never would have done such a thing. Never. Would she?

"The tests were quite—"

Dr. Siders held up two hands. "Let's slow this train down. No one is being attacked here."

Dr. Carver raised his eyebrows but finally sat and let Dr. Siders take over the explanation.

"When your coma entered its second week, Senator McAllister ordered the pharmaceutical branch of MMV to take your case. Coma patients' chances of full recovery decline sharply after five weeks. Even without a brain injury to worry about, everyone was pressed with the need to bring you around, if we could, before then."

Shauna was sure her father's campaign had applied most of the pressure. MMV would've loved to get their hands on her in the midst of a presidential campaign. It made sense, at least when it came to generating sympathy for the frontrunner. That kind of medical breakthrough in a personal crisis would be huge for soft-hearted voters.

Dr. Carver cleared his throat. "We've been testing the applications of a new drug cocktail in trauma patients, and we believed it might stimulate your brain out of its coma. We theorized that your brain shut down as the result of some kind of overwhelming shock rather than physical injury."

"You're saying my brain couldn't handle a simple car accident?"

"It was hardly simple, Ms. McAllister, but yes. This was the idea anyway."

"And your psychological tests so far have supported this," Dr. Harding said.

Dr. Carver continued. "The cocktail includes a complex combination of antianxiety meds, including propranolol and D-cycloserine—you've heard of these?" Shauna shook her head. "It's got a few other things in there too. These were originally developed to treat conditions like hypertension, but they've been successful in recent years in treating victims of violent crimes, war injuries, that sort of thing. They reduce patients' stress and speed up their recovery time."

"By erasing memories?" she asked.

Dr. Harding shook her head hard enough to give her mass of curls a lift.

"No no no. Though that kind of technology isn't so far out of reach anymore. No, these drugs work by suppressing the intensity of the emotions associated with your memory. Their impact becomes less traumatic over the long term."

Less traumatic than what the last three days had been like?

"And these drugs work two weeks after the event?"

Dr. Carver crossed his arms. "In your case it did, though that was an unknown. MMV's formula is unique in that it also incorporates the latest pharmacogenomics technology." He hesitated, as if explaining it to her might be an insult. She was, after all, the daughter of MMV's founder and president. When she blinked, he continued, "That means we adapt the chemical balance of the drugs to match your personal response to each element—a response determined by your unique genetic code."

Shauna blinked again.

"You messed with my *genes*?"

Dr. Carver chuckled, which Shauna found irritating. "No, we 'messed with' the drugs, based on what we know about your genes."

The weight of her already heavy heart grew. She had taken drugs—unbelievable—and been given drugs, and now her mind was a black hole she might never climb out of. Her hands began to tremble. She wished Wayne had stayed.

"It's complicated, but progressive. We'll keep you on the regimen for several more weeks, then taper it off while we monitor your recovery. It's important that we keep the chemical balance of your brain stable. I'll come by later to go over each medication with you."

"Overall," Dr. Siders said, "your recovery couldn't be going more smoothly. You're already progressing faster than we expected."

"You mean physically."

"You had extremely minor injuries for such a violent accident. Some trauma to your abdomen, glass cuts mostly. We think that happened post-accident, when you escaped the car. But no internal injuries. Not even a broken bone."

"You might have the Ecstasy to thank for that," said Dr. Carver. Shauna's cheeks warmed. Was it possible? Why couldn't she *remember*? Her despair took on the bonus element of frustration.

"What about my mind?"

The men turned to Dr. Harding. "Think of your mind as shielding you from something it knows you can't handle yet," she said.

"You think the trauma of the accident caused my memory loss?"

"It's the most convincing culprit."

"Not all these experimental drugs?"

"Unlikely."

"But when will I remember?"

"When your mind is ready. It's not something you can force or rush."

"How can I . . . help it along?"

"Is that what you want?"

Shauna wasn't sure. But if she had to decide in this moment, she would lean toward the affirmative. She might die by falling into this gaping hole of nothingness. More important, their silence regarding Rudy could only mean that she was responsible for some horrible tragedy, some unspeakable harm she had done to him. She should be punished for it! And if they refused to punish her, she would do it herself by remembering every detail.

"Yes."

Dr. Carver cleared his throat.

Dr. Harding tilted her head to one side and contemplated her answer for several moments.

"For many people, amnesia is traumatic in the beginning, and then they find it to be more of a mercy. I'm not sure how it will be for you, but if you can find a way to embrace this, if you can think of your situation as something not entirely bad, you put yourself in the most positive frame of mind."

"Not entirely bad?"

"A clean slate. A new beginning."

Shauna shook her head, unsure how else to respond. She could imagine how some kind of selective obliteration of certain memories might be merciful. But a gaping hole in the past? That didn't make sense to her.

Dr. Harding seemed to see that Shauna wasn't convinced. The redheaded psychiatrist leaned toward her and spoke more slowly. "Then . . . I suggest you face forward. Look forward down the road of your life rather than over your shoulder. Don't try too hard to remember. Leave the past behind you and let your mind decide when it's ready to revisit your history."

"I should do nothing, you mean."

"Not exactly. Pick up in life wherever it was you remember leaving off. I can help you with this. Let your memory, if it chooses, reconstruct itself in context."

"I don't understand."

"What are some threads that you might be able to hang on to or revisit? A church, a job, a social scene, a hobby, a boyfriend?"

Shauna lifted her hands, at a loss. All her life she had kept herself at a distance from close friendships. Mostly, the choice had been a coping mechanism for her, a way of shielding herself from pain upon pain, a way of conserving her emotional energy. She had reduced her world to a small, manageable size. Now she wished she hadn't.

"I don't . . . I can't . . ." She shook her head. "Wayne Spade?" He was far more a question than an answer in her own mind.

Dr. Harding folded her hands across her lap. "Tell me about Wayne."

"I don't know much to tell."

"Then maybe that's where you should begin."

Maybe. Maybe? Was that all these people were good for, pronouncing one possibility after the other, never certainty? When would she get the answers she needed? The real answers, not these speculations?

She had been patient for long enough now. It would end here, beginning with her most urgent question of all.

"When will I see Rudy?"

Dr. Siders set his charts beside him and leaned forward. "As soon as we know—"

"What is so hard about my questions about my brother? I'm asking for the most basic level of information—"

"Shauna, when you're ready to—"

"I'm ready now! I want to see him *now!*"

Shauna's frustration dissolved into gut-wrenching tears. If only Rudy were here to calm her. Without him, without her memory of that terrible night, she was lost.

"What did I do? What happened that is so awful no one can talk to me about it? I deserve to know the truth!"

She put her hands in her hair and gripped it by the roots. Rudy hadn't come to see her in the days since she'd come out of this coma. That fact alone should have been all the information she needed to confirm the monstrosity of her situation.

She lifted her head and stared at them through blurred eyes. The room tipped. Dr. Harding was shaking her head and saying something, but Shauna could only hear her own guilt, screaming at her. She closed her eyes and saw nothing but Rudy.

In a gasp for air she heard Dr. Siders say, "We've got to sedate her."

She shook her head and moaned. Rudy. Rudy.

When a needle penetrated the thickest muscle in Shauna's upper arm, she welcomed the pain. She allowed it to cover and quiet her grief.

Dr. Harding's coarse voice reached Shauna's ears at the same time the sedative reached her brain. "You're all fools."

Millie Harding barreled down the hall after Will Carver, taking one stride for the pharmacologist's every three.

"What was all that in there?" Millie asked.

Carver pulled up and turned on his heel, saw who it was, then resumed his walk without answering. She caught him in four more strides.

"Were you and Siders planning to tell her everything?"

"I thought that's what you were doing."

Millie got in Carver's way, hands on hips. "What are you talking about?"

"You're going to hand her memory to her on a silver platter?"

"I was perfectly misleading. And I didn't give her any ideas that will actually help her recall what happened."

"I'll be the one to decide that."

"No you won't. *I* don't even get to decide anything except whether I want to get paid at the end of the day."

"We'll all get paid. But only if we behave like professionals."

Millie grabbed the arm of Carver's jacket, stopping him. "You two might want to become better liars."

Carver jerked his sleeve out of Millie's grip. "The only lies that ever really work are the ones that can actually be mistaken for the truth." He stalked off. "Don't question me again."

3

A light touch on her brow stroked away the pounding in Shauna's head. She opened her eyes onto her hospital room, dimmed by evening hours.

Wayne was leaning over her. "Shauna?"

Exhaustion weighed her down.

"They told me what happened." She focused on the face of the man who, so far, had been her only ally. If she committed his high temples, narrow cheeks, and square chin to mind, maybe she would remember him. Maybe she could find her way back to the truth.

There were all those *maybes* again.

"You know, your Uncle Trent was supposed to be the one to explain all this to you."

"All what?"

"Everything about Rudy. Everything that I don't know and the docs won't say."

"Why hasn't he?"

Wayne shrugged. "My guess is he doesn't want you to have to deal with so many issues all at one time."

"And so everyone thinks that it's more beneficial to stew over the grim possibilities rather than face reality?"

Wayne raised his eyebrows as if to say, *It's twisted, I know.*

"We're a backward group, my family."

"Each family is, in its own way."

"Trent Wilde isn't even really my uncle, you know that? He's Landon's best friend."

Wayne nodded. "But he's always proven himself worthy of the endearment."

"Except for instances such as these, yes. I can't hold it against him. He means well."

Shauna shifted in the bed and heard a clank of metal on metal. Something pinched her ankle. What on earth? She lifted her blanket. A leather strap was cinched low on her right leg, and its metal clasp locked onto a bed rail.

A padlock? Was this legal?

She pointed to the strap. "Does this fall into the category of 'so many issues'?"

"We have some business to take care of before you go home."

"What kind of business?"

"Dr. Siders told you about the Ecstasy?"

"Dr. Carver did."

"There was also some in your car. And in your loft."

Her home? Patrice's accusation that she had harmed Rudy intentionally landed on Shauna's mind like a jumping spider.

"How much?"

"Not much, but enough."

"Enough for what?"

"They're charging you with possession and reckless endangerment."

"But they're just now locking me up?"

"You got a little . . . hysterical earlier. They thought it was necessary."

Every revelation was a fresh betrayal, a concussive blow to what she might have believed about herself. How much more was she guilty of?

"What else don't I know?"

"Um . . . there's a guard outside your door."

Shauna's mouth fell open. "What do the charges mean?"

"There will be a trial. You've already been indicted."

She shook her head. "I don't want a trial. I don't even know what I did. I can't even deny anything."

Wayne reached for her hand. He sat on the edge of the bed and pulled her to his shoulder. Her forehead pressed into his cheek, and she was comforted by the warmth of his skin. Resting like this, it wasn't at all hard for her to believe she'd been close to him before.

The cologne he wore was faint and breezy. She couldn't name it.

Shauna closed her eyes. She would stay here as long as he would allow her to, leaning into his warmth . . .

Not warm, hot. His skin was hot, like he had a fever, but dry. Did he notice this heat? Before she could mention it, before she could straighten up, her face seemed to be consumed by a blaze, a flash of energy so hot that she thought her skin had burned.

She gasped and pulled back, touching her forehead. It was cooler than her fingertips.

"What is it?" Wayne asked.

"Didn't you feel that?"

"Feel what?" Wayne's forehead creased.

The blush of embarrassment, not supernatural heat, flushed Shauna's cheeks. She hardly knew what had just happened, though it seemed clear enough that she had experienced it alone. And maybe entirely in her mind.

"It's nothing." She shook her head. "I'm on edge, I guess."

Wayne stood, then moved to the window. "What is this like for you, Shauna? What does it feel like when you try to remember? I've been trying to put myself in your shoes."

The right analogy took several seconds to present itself. "It feels like I'm looking in the index of a textbook and can't find the topic I need, even though I'm pretty sure I've read it in that book before."

"What can I do to help you?"

"You've done so much already."

"Well, I'm not going anywhere anytime soon, so if you have any brilliant ideas . . ."

"You could take me to see Rudy." She said it before she fully contemplated what it would mean—returning to her father's home. Her childhood home.

Patrice's home.

Wayne closed his eyes and sighed. "Shauna."

She said, less confidently, "They have to at least let me out of this thing to use the bathroom, don't they?"

"Shauna, the police have instructed the staff to keep an eye on you."

"They like you, Wayne. They'll believe whatever you tell them."

"If you go now, the authorities will know. They'll take you right away. You might only get minutes with Rudy. In fact—"

"That's all I need. Just long enough for an answer." She looked at the wad of sheets in her hand. "Just long enough to apologize."

Wayne seemed to soften.

"Please, Wayne. Please do this for me. I will do whatever I need to do to make things right, okay? But *first*, I am going to see my brother. You can help me, or I will march out of here on my own and get a taxi. What's it going to be?"

Amusement overtook Wayne's eyes and mouth. "I'd like to see you march, let alone figure out how to pay for the ride," he said.

"Take me. Make my father deal with me to my face. You shouldn't have to be the one in this position."

He leaned against the windowsill and dropped his head. "Please rethink this."

"I have thought it through! Repeatedly. Please help me." She begged with her eyes too. "You're my only friend right now."

Wayne turned toward Shauna and crossed his arms. "And how do you suggest I bust you out of here?"

For the first time since she had awakened in this horrid white room, Shauna was overcome with relief. He would think of something. Wayne wrapped one hand around his chin the way she had seen him the day she awoke. He considered her plea until Shauna's relief turned to worry. Maybe he wouldn't help after all.

She looked away, then he said, "I think I can find a way to get you five minutes with your brother. Ten tops. Can you live with that?"

It was a rhetorical question, right?

4

West Lake bordered the Colorado River in the foothills overlooking the city, one of the many Austin suburbs that considered itself "the gateway to hill country." Wayne drove Shauna there in his wine-red Chevy truck through a weak October drizzle. It was nearly seven o'clock on Wednesday evening.

She fidgeted with her fingers in her lap. "Is Landon back from California yet?"

"Yes. He came in this afternoon."

What would she say to her father? Maybe after she saw Rudy she would be better equipped.

And Patrice . . .

Patrice would be here. Shauna's stomach turned. She hadn't set foot on her father's property since Christmas her senior year of college. She'd tried to keep up the holiday routine for Rudy's sake, but even that had become an impossibility for her. When Rudy told her she didn't need to suffer through Christmas for him—because it made everyone suffer—Shauna finally gave herself permission to avoid the estate completely.

Shauna closed her eyes. *God, please help me.* The spontaneous prayer came from a long abandoned place in her subconscious, and she felt irked that it had popped out unannounced. "You've been a lifesaver to me in so many different ways, Wayne. I never thanked you for pulling me out of the river. For saving my life."

"You actually saved yourself. By the time I got to you, you were out of the car. Scraped your way out of a broken window, I guess. All I did was pull you out of the water. Not exactly Superman."

"I can't begin to imagine how fortunate it was that you were there." There was a time when Shauna would have given God the credit for that kind of a miracle. But now, she wasn't so sure. "Uncle Trent said you were following me home? What was that all about?"

"We were at Trent's place—"

"Which one?"

"The one at Lake Travis. He was having a shindig for a friend of his. You left the party early. I was concerned about you and followed you back to town. You lost control of the car at the bridge on 71. Went over the guardrail. I didn't actually see it happen."

"But you know how."

"There was a truck on the bridge coming the other way. The driver says you swerved into his lane, then overcorrected." He paused. "It was slick. Dark. You were upset."

"Upset?"

"An argument with your dad."

She and Landon were always fighting about something. Even that fact had survived her amnesia. "I try to avoid him when I can. We're just . . . not good together. He never did believe me."

"That's been hard for you, I know." The remark caught Shauna off guard. "I forget that you . . . that you know some of this already. You get along with your dad?"

"Yeah, actually. My mom and I were a different story, though. She's been gone a long time." He reached across the seat to squeeze her hand. "I know that doesn't make you feel better, though."

Tears burned the corners of Shauna's eyes, but she held them back. "How much do you know about my family stuff?"

Wayne chose his words carefully. "You and Patrice are archenemies, and the reason why is off-limits. You and the senator have trouble communicating, among other things. Rudy and you are best friends."

The fact that Wayne understood her situation so simply gave her a surprising measure of security. "I don't know if I can face going home."

He nodded. "We can always turn around, just say the word. I'll be right there with you, okay? I won't leave your side. If anything gets weird, or too intense, I'll take you out of there."

Shauna exhaled and relaxed against the seat.

"What did Landon and I argue about? That night."

"I'm not sure. You didn't fight in public."

Well, that was something to be thankful for.

"And what about us? I feel terrible. I don't understand how a mind can just lose that kind of thing."

"Like I said, we'll figure it out as we go. You haven't kicked me out yet." He grinned at her. "That's a good start."

She laughed. "How did we meet?"

"Our paths crossed a few times—before you resigned—at Harper & Stone."

"I resigned?"

"In July. You told me you needed some time off to plan your next move. Said the CPA life was not working out for you."

Well, that sounded like a brilliant way to advance a career. But more and more it seemed she had fallen into the habit of making foolish choices.

"How far back do you remember?" he asked. "Have you pinpointed that?"

"I remember vacationing in Guatemala in March. After that . . ." She mentally calculated that her memory was blank for the prior five or six months. "If I'm lucky, I haven't forgotten anything of value."

A streetlight flashed over Wayne's face through the wet windshield. He looked away from her.

"Except you, naturally."

He frowned. "Naturally."

Maybe the reason she didn't have many close friends had nothing to do with her avoiding relationships; perhaps everyone saw her for the insensitive clod that she was and went out of their way to avoid her.

"So you're a CPA too?" she asked.

"No. I'm the CFO of McAllister MediVista."

This news startled her. "You work for my father?"

"You always preferred me to say I work for your uncle."

"You must think I'm a silly girl."

Wayne shook his head. "Not at all. You remember that Harper & Stone handles our books."

She nodded. "But Mr. Stone felt I presented a conflict of interest. He kept me off those accounts."

"He did. But you helped me with some fact-finding during the last audit. That would have been May."

She tried to call up the event. Futile. But it was true that when it came to audits and overtime, everyone pitched in.

"So are we . . . what are we, exactly?"

He kept his eyes on the road. "We hadn't landed on an answer to that question. We saw each other socially, went out several times. We liked—I liked your company."

"In a way, that might make things easier," she said. She kept her voice light and hopeful. "To start over, I mean."

Wayne turned his truck in to the McAllisters' private drive. "Yeah. Maybe it will."

The McAllister estate was a gated residence bordered by the Colorado River, a sprawling stucco-and-terra-cotta rancher on ten acres that included a guesthouse, tennis courts, a fitness center, and a small dock, where Landon occasionally anchored his cabin cruiser. Shauna often thought it could easily have been the villa of some Colombian drug lord.

Shauna laid a hand across her roiling stomach. She hated this place and all the memories it housed.

The security detail around her father was higher than usual, with the general elections less than a month away. And yet Wayne passed through without question.

They entered the mansion through a side entrance that led to the McAllisters' casual dining area, located off a sparkling stainless-steel kitchen. Shauna smelled barbeque mesquite and buttered potatoes, which only made her nauseated.

She nodded at a cook she didn't recognize and hurried her pace so as not to fall behind Wayne. He took her hand and paused before the door.

"You okay?"

She nodded, but she didn't feel anything similar to okay.

Shauna pushed the door open and stepped into the dining room.

Landon, Patrice, and another woman sat at an oak pedestal table eating the last bites of their supper. Rudy sat by the window.

The clinking of forks on plates came to an abrupt halt, and the room stilled to complete silence. As one they stared at her.

Landon said something, but Shauna didn't hear his words. She was only aware of Rudy.

Her unstoppable brother, a fit and strong track-and-field champion, had been reduced to a twisted twig, contorted in a wheelchair contraption that looked expensive and custom-fitted to his shriveled body. The tilted chair put him in a reclining position and was jacked up on a frame like a monster truck on small wheels. A bag hung from a pole attached to the side of the chair, and a narrow plastic tube ran from it into Rudy's abdomen.

He must have weighed thirty pounds less than her last memory of him. His wild curls, light brown and thick, had been shaved, and large foam pads braced his fuzzy skull. A scar cut laterally through the new hair growth across the top of his head. "Rudy." His name came out of her lips like a dying breath.

Shauna felt too weak to stand. She groped for a side chair and gripped the back for support. Wayne took her elbow.

"I'm so sorry," he whispered. "I didn't know."

Mind numb, she pulled her arm free.

She couldn't tear her eyes from Rudy's shriveled form. Shauna knew then that she should have died in the river that night. She'd done this . . .

Below his hairline, a dark bruise that had long since gone through its rainbow stages nearly covered his forehead and right eye. His gray eyes—she caught her breath—his gray eyes were watching her.

"Rudy?" And this time his name rode out of her mouth on hope.

"He can see you, but I can't say whether he recognizes you," the woman next to Patrice said. Shauna glanced at the middle-aged woman with over-rouged cheeks and a nose too small for her wide face. She rested an equally small chin on her folded hands. "He is in what we call a minimally conscious state."

Shauna turned back to Rudy. Tears filled her eyes at this unbelievable sight.

"What does *minimally conscious* mean?" Shauna asked.

"That he's got a couple more functioning brain cells than a vegetable," Landon said.

"Mr. McAllister," the woman said gently. "He is aware."

Shauna looked at her father for the first time since coming into the house.

Landon McAllister's voice was as she always remembered it: deep and rich and clear and charismatic, a pied piper voice that anyone would follow. But his normally flashing eyes were flat today. The lines of his wide mouth turned down. A surface vein pulsated at his left temple the way it so often had in the weeks after her mother died.

This man was broken, and Shauna's heart overflowed with a new kind of grief.

He did not hold her eyes for long. Again, he was the first to turn away.

"How aware is he?" Shauna asked. She returned her attention to her brother's eyes.

"We really don't know," the guest said.

"Amazing how little you people do know," Landon muttered.

Patrice spoke to Shauna for the first time, cool and formal: "Shauna, this is Pam Riley, Rudy's live-in nurse. Pam, my husband's daughter and her boyfriend, Wayne. We weren't expecting her tonight, as she is under house arrest at the hospital."

Pam's bright cheeks turned brighter, and Shauna pretended not to hear. Wayne rested his hand on her shoulder.

"So, minimally conscious is good?" Shauna asked Pam. "I mean, there's hope?"

"Hope is a fairy tale for the guilty," Landon said, then threw back the last of his coffee. "So you can get any inspirational sap out of your head right now."

His words stabbed her. She moved her chair closer to Rudy and turned her back toward the table.

"All brain injuries are really uncharted territories," Pam said. "We don't like to make predictions or promises. But we are hardly resigned to Rudy's present condition. There's plenty to do."

Landon rose from the table with his empty plate as if he'd heard this speech a thousand times. His long stride carried him into the kitchen.

"The senator has taken every possible measure to increase the chances of Rudy's recovery. Maybe later I can show you the—"

"Shauna has an appointment with local authorities," Patrice said. "I'm afraid it will have to wait."

Shauna clenched her teeth to prevent herself from snapping back. Not here. Not now.

Pam adjusted. "To answer your question, Shauna, yes, there are documented cases of minimally conscious patients regaining their functions—"

"After more than twenty years," Landon said, returning. "And they call that a miracle. Sure there's hope. I just won't live to see it."

"Rudy's case leaves a lot of possibilities open," Pam continued, unfazed. "His injury was caused by trauma rather than by hypoxia—"

"Which is?"

"Lack of oxygen."

"He didn't drown, then?"

"No. He just got really banged up. Thrown from the car before it hit the water. But he was breathing on his own the whole time."

Rudy had not stopped looking at her. She shivered. "And why is that better than drowning?"

"Hypoxia shuts down the entire brain," Pam said. "Remember Terry Schaivo? That's what happened to her. For Rudy, though, the damage was partial. Devastating, but partial. Some parts of his brain are still functioning fine. It's possible, in time, that these areas will be able to rebuild his lost connections."

Landon moved to stand behind Rudy and placed a gentle hand on his son's head. Rudy kept his eyes on Shauna. Those eyes might have been conveying recognition or fascination. Mercy or accusation. They might have been requesting a key to unlock their prison, or screaming at her to leave. They might be seeing nothing at all.

"In time, Rudy might be able to compensate for his other losses," Pam said.

"There is no compensation for this," her father said.

Paired with her father's words, Shauna believed Rudy's eyes turned hostile. They burned through her, judging her forgetfulness.

"Dad, I'm so sorry. I'm so, so sorry, Rudy. Please forgive me."

She released the chair, crossed to Rudy, and eased herself into a seat close to him. Leaned forward and touched his hand. If she could make all this right she would do it without a second thought. She would sit in that chair and lock herself up in that broken mind so Rudy could come back and be the calm force in the center of this stormy family. What would it take? She would do anything.

"Please. I'm so sorry." His skin felt rubbery and unnatural to her. He did not respond. She squeezed his fingers.

"Stop it, Shauna," Landon said, sending the command like a kick to her heart. She let go of Rudy's hand, a defensive move. Stop what? Touching him? She looked at her father and instantly recognized his anger, which was so familiar to her: taut forehead, flat lips.

Why couldn't she be as familiar with his affection? Just a minute of the hours of love he had poured into Rudy. She didn't need so much from Landon, only a moment, a glance, a smile.

Certainty that he believed her. Trusted her. Protected her.

"Your groveling doesn't help anyone."

"I wish I—"

"This isn't about you, Shauna. This is about Rudy. This is about what you took from us. Rudy won't get to campaign with me. He won't get to attempt a single one of his dreams. For heaven's sake, Shauna, he wasn't even old enough to be disillusioned yet! He wanted to be a *politician!*"

Rudy uttered a moan that sent a chill through Shauna's nerves. She stood, unsure what to do.

"Now I think we'd better all take a deep breath," Pam said, coming around the table. "Let's lower the volume a notch, shall we?"

"Is he okay?" Shauna asked.

"Is he okay?" Patrice mimicked, barely audible. "You are unbelievable."

Shauna eased back into her chair and picked up Rudy's hand again. His head began to hit the pad.

"Sh, Rudy." Shauna stroked his palm. She could not bear the sight of his pain. "Sh." He beat his head more violently, and for the first time, his eyes let go of hers. They slipped upward, back into his head. "Rudy?"

"You let me take care of this," Pam said, preparing to wheel him out of the room. But Shauna could not let her brother go.

Landon leaned over and gripped Shauna's wrist. He drilled his thumb between her small bones and she cried out, dropping Rudy's hand. Her father's eyes were gray like her brother's, but much more clear in what they meant to say.

"I'm sorry."

"Sorry doesn't fix this. You only upset him."

Rudy's moan rose to a shrill pitch as Pam pushed him away from the conflict and down the hall toward his bedroom. Landon released Shauna and turned his back on her to face the window.

"You ought to go now," Patrice said to Shauna, stacking empty plates on the table, making more noise than was necessary. "You upset him."

"I think he's responding to conflict—he senses the stress between us, obviously."

"So we remove the cause, and voilà."

"There's no need to be sarcastic."

"I'm completely serious."

Shauna folded her hands in front of her to prevent them from shaking. She sensed Wayne move to stand behind her. She looked to Landon for defense, but he had removed himself from the exchange.

"I take full responsibility for what happened to Rudy," she said, staring at her thumbs. "And I know there's no way to make up for it, but I'm sure I can help—"

"Shauna, you owe so many people so much that you will *never* be able to make it up to even one of them."

Shauna's first tears finally escaped, and she couldn't say whether they were tears of injustice or anger or agony over the truth of her stepmother's words. She felt all these emotions simultaneously, and she reached out blindly for Wayne's hand. He caught her grip.

Patrice walked around the table, closing the protective gap that Shauna would have rather maintained.

"I'm sorry that I don't remember—"

"Give up this game, Shauna! I am so sick and tired of your using this poor-me routine as an excuse to get your way. I think you remember everything. You owe your father more respect than that."

"I really don't understand—"

"Of course you don't. If throwing you out on your brainless head wouldn't cause Landon a publicity nightmare, I'd never let you come home. It's bad enough that you've been indicted for a felony."

Landon made no move to intervene.

"Patrice," Shauna pleaded, "it was an accident." She hated being reduced to a quaking leaf in front of this cruel woman, while her father acted as if nothing were going on. But she had no reason to expect more from him. Landon was simply being Landon. At her expense.

"I'm not talking about the accident!" Patrice was shouting now, and something in Shauna ignited. "I'm talking about your disregard for all the sacrifices your father has made for you! I'm talking about your disrespect for his career, and your blatant efforts to undermine everything he has accomplished! You are the most conniving, willful brat I have ever met! Don't you dare sit here and play this game with me!"

The accusations hit Shauna like lightning, jolting and deadly. She rose and wiped her hands on her pants. "Landon, none of this is true. Help me. Tell her. You and I have had our share of . . . disagreements, but I've always respected your work."

Without looking at his daughter, the senator turned away from the window and left the room.

His latest abandonment beat the wind out of Shauna. For a moment, she could not breathe.

Patrice leaned in close enough for Shauna to smell stale coffee on her breath. "If you keep this up, I will intervene, and I don't care what it will cost you."

Intervene? "Keep what up?" Shauna said.

"You make a mockery of him at his own functions. You are indiscreet with the company you keep. You tell lies to anyone who will print them. Your reckless driving has cost us thousands of dollars in lawsuits. You are dealing in controlled substances—"

"I am *not*! That is ridiculous."

"I have no reason to believe you, and in fact, I will gladly testify against you when the time comes."

Shauna felt dazed. "What they found . . . it might have been someone else's."

"Someone else's? In *your* car? In *your* loft? Not on your life. You are a stupid, stupid girl!"

"I have no idea—"

"And I, for one, don't believe it *was* an accident. I think you have every intention of bringing your father down, and what better way to stab him in the heart than to take away what matters most to him? You never wanted Rudy to follow his father's lead. Anyone with any perception of reality would see what you're trying to do here."

Shauna tried to slow down her heart. She pulled her hand free of Wayne's grip, and he let her go. Reluctantly, she thought.

"Why would I do—?"

"Shut up. Nothing you say can change who I know you are, Shauna."

"You don't know who I am."

"Get over yourself. I know you better than anyone. And if I were you, I would be looking for the fastest, most certain exit off this earth. You are not worth anything to your father or your brother."

It took only a split second for offense to trump Shauna's reason.

She slapped Patrice.

Shauna didn't even realize she could do such a thing, hadn't even thought about it. And now it was done. A fingernail cut oozed blood at Patrice's temple.

Okay.

Shauna saw the blush rise to Patrice's skin, and saw the drop of blood that rose from the scratch, and saw herself jump onto the wild horse that was her anger, a runaway beast that left her sensible self in the dust.

"You don't have any idea what you're talking about! I love my brother as much as I hate you—you can't even begin to comprehend how much I hate you—"

"Likewise."

"—and I would never hurt him! You, Patrice, you are the reason this family cannot hold itself together! You are the reason my father has turned his back on me—"

Patrice guffawed.

"—and you need to take responsibility for your own mistakes rather than parading mine before the world!"

Patrice pressed her fingers to the cut. In a distant place, a doorbell rang.

Shauna kept going. "You are a liar, and a witch, and have never done anything for anyone that didn't somehow benefit you in the long run!"

"And *you,* child, are the only one on trial for anything at all."

Shauna's wild horse collapsed, all four legs broken in an instant.

"It's all a lie."

"I can't tell you what you want to hear, girl." Patrice picked up the stack of dishes and turned to follow her husband's path out of the room. At the doorway, she paused. "I think it's best you give Rudy some space. Understood?"

Shauna nodded without understanding a thing. She leaned against Wayne. He put an arm around her shoulders.

"I'm so sorry."

"I should have listened to you."

"You know our time's up."

She nodded weakly.

"You know I had to tell the police we were coming here."

Her head dipped once more. She had received her five minutes. That was all he had promised.

"Mr. Spade?"

Wayne shifted toward the voice. Shauna looked too.

An Asian woman stood in the entry. One of the staff maybe. Shauna didn't recognize her but found herself caught by the woman's eyes, which met her gaze though she spoke to Wayne. Two different colors, one dark brown, and one lighter. Hazel maybe.

"There are officers here. They're asking for Ms. McAllister."

5

"Nothing, then?"

"Nothing. When it comes to the last six months, she's as brain-dead as a church mouse in formaldehyde."

"And you're sure she knew nothing before then? So we're clear?"

"As long as her memory of the last few months doesn't return, we're good. But if she does begin to remember, we got us a whole new ball game. Fifty-fifty odds."

He blew out some air. "I still say we do her now."

"We can't. Not yet. We may dodge this bullet yet. If she remembers, we kill her immediately. Until then, we keep an eye on both of them."

"Fine. But this could blow up."

"It's already blown up, remember? She blew it up. We're trying to put the fires out."

Shauna lay on a narrow bench and faced the wall in the concrete detention center. Her nose nearly touched the chipped paint. Though her body was long and slender, she had to balance on the plank to avoid rolling off. Her entire body ached. A sharp pang in her side had knifed her through the night. She focused on the pain. It hurt less than her present situation.

She had been booked the night before and arraigned first thing Thursday morning, thanks to the insistence of Wayne, Uncle Trent, and Trent's influential attorney, Joe Delaney. It seemed the press wasn't yet aware that she'd left the hospital, just as Wayne had hoped. Mr. Delaney set up an appointment to meet with her at his offices October 26, one week from tomorrow, giving her time to attend to her medical needs and get settled in at home again. Her trial date had been set for November 19, more than a month away.

What was she supposed to do in the meantime?

Now she waited for Uncle Trent, who'd insisted on flying in at midnight on a private flight to post her bail. "It's a father's duty," he'd asked Wayne to tell her.

It was. It was.

She closed her eyes, wavering between fading into oblivion or trying to come up with a plan to redeem her latest gross mistakes.

"Let's get out of here, Shauna." Wayne's soft voice roused her, and the sound of a sliding gate jolted her off the bench. He carried a light coat for Shauna.

Uncle Trent entered the cell with an outstretched hand and helped her up into a bear hug. His round face was gently wrinkled and baby soft, and his mouth turned up in a perpetual smile. He wore his trademark turtleneck and blazer on this cool October day, business casual at all times, whether at home or in his executive suite. His short white hair caressed her cheek like velvet.

"Don't you worry about a thing, honey. This is all going to blow over soon enough." She closed her eyes. In the security of his embrace, it was easy to believe him. "You lay low at your dad's place until you're a hundred percent. Wayne here is going to stick around to make sure you have whatever you need."

"I'd rather go home. I mean to my home."

"Honey," Trent said, "your dad terminated the lease on your loft a couple weeks after the accident, had your stuff packed up and moved."

Shauna could not believe what she was hearing.

Yes, she could.

"He really does mean to look after you while you recuperate."

And how would he do that? A man campaigning for president had no time to look after anything but his own interests.

"Landon and Patrice don't want me anywhere near them."

"The place is big enough for everyone to avoid each other. Wayne can help." Wayne nodded. "I can spare the man a vacation, after all. And I didn't have to twist his arm."

Shauna blushed.

"Good then." He dropped a paternal kiss on her forehead. "We want what's best for you."

"Uncle Trent, I'm sorry if I did anything that embarrassed you at the party that night."

"It's entirely forgettable."

She smiled at that. "I guess so."

She and Wayne parted ways with Trent in the main office. Wayne took a deep breath and turned to look at her.

"How are you holding up?"

"Better, now that you're with me again."

Wayne raised his eyebrows and tilted his head slightly. "Missed me already?"

She dropped her gaze, confused by her own confession. She felt at ease with him, as she should with an old friend, and yet she still hardly knew him. Maybe her subconscious was hard at work.

"Is there a back door?" she asked.

"Already arranged," he said. He helped her into the coat. "You'll need this to keep the rain off."

She shoved her hands into the pockets and stayed near the wall, head down, as he took her back toward the middle of the courthouse and then down a marble hallway. She rubbed her fingers against the lining to warm them.

Three sets of stairs took them down to a rear door and out onto a narrow concrete slab between two tall buildings. Last night's drizzle had turned into a light rain and came straight down.

"This way," Wayne said, taking her hand. They started toward the parking lot at the end of the breezeway. Between them and the lot, a blond man in a khaki raincoat leaned against the brick wall, juggling three packs of cigarettes.

Wayne tugged at her to hurry by, but the man moved out in front of Shauna, stepping on her foot and letting the cigarette packs fall to the pavement. She stumbled. The stranger steadied her at the waist.

"Well, I'm no dancer, Ms. McAllister." Shauna looked to Wayne, startled to hear him speak her name. "Sorry about my poor timing."

Wayne pulled her to his side.

"Ms. McAllister, I'd like to ask you a few questions about—"

"Ms. McAllister has no comment," Wayne said, guiding Shauna around the man.

"I won't take any of your time," he insisted, blocking Wayne's route. He was taller than Wayne by at least five inches and broader by the same.

"Step aside, please."

"Off the record."

"No."

"It's about the accident. About the early reports."

"Look, man. Why don't you tell me who you're working for so I can call your boss and file a complaint."

The man picked at one of the cellophane wrappers and looked at Shauna.

"I'd like to know about the other person in your car."

What car?

He seemed to read her mind. "The night of the accident."

Rudy?

Wayne steered Shauna back toward the door they'd exited. "Shauna, don't say anything."

"About Rudy?" she whispered.

"An eyewitness puts a second passenger in the car with you," the man called out.

A second? Rudy was the only one.

Wayne hurried her back to the courthouse door. The cigarette juggler followed, unconcerned. Wayne yanked on the handle. Locked. There was no other way out except through this man. Shauna wiped rain out of her eyebrows. Her hair was getting soaked.

"What's your name?" Wayne asked.

"Smith." He extended a hand. Wayne didn't take it.

"And you work for?"

"I'm freelance."

Wayne scoffed. "How did you know—?"

"I'm a *good* freelancer."

"Well, *Smith,* I was an eyewitness, too, and I didn't see anyone else—"

"Took you a while to come on scene, as I understand it."

"—nor did the truck driver, who was there from the beginning. And if you had done your homework, you would have seen that the accident reports say the same thing. So I'm very sorry to inform you, you've probably paid someone a whole lot of money for a bogus tip."

Smith shoved the packs into the pockets of his raincoat.

"I'm sorry we can't be of more help to you," Wayne said. "Now if you don't mind, Ms. McAllister has had an extremely difficult day."

The man stepped aside and bowed with an arm extended Shakespearean-style.

He pulled a fresh cigarette out and held her eyes as she let Wayne lead her away. With Wayne's back to him, Smith dropped the reporter persona and gave Shauna the slow wave of a sad friend saying good-bye.

6

Shauna was so haunted by the man's wave that she only half paid attention when Wayne took her back to the hospital to meet with Dr. Carver before heading home. He left his keys in the Chevy's ashtray before they went inside.

The brief appointment passed beneath her hazy disinterest and distraction. He gave her five bottles, labeled only with numbers, and explained to her what each pill was, and indicated that she should take them twice a day.

Was there a third person in her car? What if Rudy had a friend, maybe, and the drugs were his? The possibility of a third person could change everything.

No it couldn't—there were still drugs in her loft, not to mention in her blood. And why would so many people not see this unnamed passenger?

"Siders is willing to let you stay at home now, Shauna." Wayne touched her shoulder, snapping her out of her thoughts.

"Good."

"So long as we come back once a week. Dr. Harding wants you in here tomorrow. Check in otherwise as necessary. Sound okay?"

"Fine."

Then they were back in his truck driving toward Landon's and she was back in her thoughts, preoccupied by the events of the past several days. She didn't speak much.

Wayne put the car in park and she lifted her head.

They were in front of the bungalow that was the guesthouse on the McAllister property. With six bedrooms in the main house, few guests ever occupied these more remote lodgings, and the red tiles and stucco that matched the bigger house had fallen into some disrepair. Beautiful towering pecan trees spread their limbs wide and on summer days turned shadows into lace. But this gray October afternoon, the branches merely hovered like tangled clouds.

"Why are we here?"

Wayne looked confused. "You knew we were coming to the estate."

"I mean the bungalow."

"Oh. Your father's idea."

"I see."

"He thought you would have more privacy this way."

"Right. My old room is too close to home."

"Pam's in your room now."

Of course she was.

"There are three bedrooms here, so I'll be close. If you don't mind. The senator has set up a housekeeper for you in the third room. Full-time, at your service. If it's necessary, it will be easier for people to visit you here—doctors, therapists."

"All I see is a place where Landon can keep me under his thumb."

"It'll be good for you here. All that security? No media, no pressure."

Wayne exited the truck, then helped Shauna out, ducking in the rain. She stomped, heavy with the weight of her new life, up the steps to the shelter of the porch.

That dull but precise pain that had irritated her at the courthouse flared in her side again. Appendicitis would be timely and maybe poetic. Ironic even. She could survive being catapulted into an icy river and avoid brain damage and pass through a drug trial with flying colors, then be taken down by an inflamed and useless organ.

But the pain passed.

The screen door squeaked.

A pretty but expressionless woman held it open—the Asian woman Shauna saw in the dining room of the main house last night.

The slight-built woman let the door slap back into its frame. She held a hand out to Shauna. "I'm Luang Khai, your housekeeper."

"I'm sorry?"

"Call me Khai."

"Rhymes with *sky*?"

"Close enough."

"Shauna McAllister. I guess you know Wayne."

Khai nodded, curt. "Mr. McAllister said you might come. The third room is ready for you."

Getting a better look at Khai now, Shauna decided the housekeeper was in her mid- to late thirties. Shauna studied the mismatched eyes for one moment longer than was polite.

"I've lost my contacts," she said, and then she opened the door to invite them in.

Shauna stepped into the main sitting room, which was set up something like an elaborate hotel suite—two bedrooms and a shared bath off one side of the living area, a stand-alone bedroom off the other. A kitchenette and break-fast nook behind a two-way fireplace overlooked the river.

Other than the furniture that had been here for years—the suede camel sofa, a tattered Morris chair that needed refinishing—the room was full of brown boxes stacked three high.

Shauna tried to take it all in. Were these her things?

"These just arrived," Khai said. "When you are rested I'll help you unpack them."

Shauna opened the closest box. Books: accounting law, textbooks, reference books. Stacks of newspapers. A few magazines.

Clothes in the next, thrown in, not folded. Everything would have to be washed and pressed.

More clothes.

Shoes. Linens and towels.

"Maybe you will come eat something first?"

Shauna tipped back the flap of a fourth box.

"I don't know if I can."

"Do you like *tom yam*? Soup?"

"I *love* that soup," Wayne said. "Thai food." He headed into the kitchen.

Shauna lifted trinkets out of this box. Her iPod, a sequined jewelry case, a hand-blown glass vase, a sleek wooden elephant.

This wasn't hers. Or was it something she couldn't remember acquiring? The animal posed with one foot forward and his trunk high, tusks up, as if he was trumpeting. The wood was dark, cedar maybe, and lightly lacquered. A decorative line cut into the wood ran from the elephant's mouth all the way around the shape of his ear, then down his back. She traced it with her forefinger before returning it to the box.

"You eat," Shauna said. "I have something I need to do first."

She snatched up her iPod from the box and dropped it into her coat pocket. Her fingers brushed a piece of paper. She withdrew a small red note folded in fourths. How had she not noticed this earlier? Unfolding it, she saw an address printed in neat letters diagonally across the square. An address in Victoria, Texas.

Did she know someone in Victoria?

Shauna wasn't even sure she knew where Victoria was.

Wayne popped back out of the kitchen, holding a steaming bowl.

"What is it you need to do?" he asked her.

"Rudy." She refolded the paper and dropped it back into her coat pocket. "I need to see Rudy."

Corbin Smith shuffled to the phone on the kitchen counter, lifted the receiver, and hit the speed dial. Number three, after voice mail and the office. He took a chug from a Gatorade bottle and turned to take in the panoramic view of downtown Austin while the phone rang. He'd never get tired of this place. When the time came to give it back to its rightful owner—and he had faith that day would come—he'd have to think twice about handing it off.

Nah, not really. As it was, he was convinced that he'd made the right decision to jump on the place when it went up for rent and keep it ready for her. Even if it did put a dent in his bank account.

His best friend answered the phone. "If you call me again, I'm going to change my number."

"Good to hear your voice, man."

"Have I not explained to you what will happen if—"

"A thousand times. Old story. Got a new one for you today."

"I'll read it in the paper."

"Not this one."

"Just tell me then, so I can get off the line."

"She's up. Walking on her own two feet. Out of the hospital."

That shut him up. Smith heard breathing over the line. He pounced on the silence.

"Didn't I tell you? Didn't I say? You *know* she's a fighter."

"I never said she wasn't."

"I saw her today. Talked to her."

"You stay out of her way! Am I going to have to come up there myself, strangle you with my own two hands? You don't have any idea what you're doing, Corbin."

"Oh, I've got a very clear idea. You, now *you* walked away from this, and I don't understand it, but *you* are the one who doesn't have the clear idea anymore. I'm the bloodhound now, don't you know. I know way more about what's in this stew than you ever did."

That at least earned Corbin a chuckle. "Whatever you say."

"You've gotta come back. Today. Let me bring you up to speed."

"No."

"You've gotta see her. She needs you."

This time his refusal hesitated.

"No."

"If you don't do it, she might come looking for you. I gave her your address."

"Corbin, this is no game."

"I'm not playing with you. You think this situation is forever, and I'm telling you we can turn it around."

"How?"

"I'm working on it. Have a little faith."

"I have faith that seeing me will get her killed, which is a disaster I could not survive. And that about sums everything up."

Corbin reached into his arsenal of persuasion for his biggest gun, the shot that would hurt the most but might set the man in motion. The bloodhound was actually a mule! "She doesn't remember. She didn't know me. She doesn't know a thing."

Corbin took another swig of the cherry-flavored sports drink, hoping for a fight instead of a dead line.

"That's for the best, then."

He inhaled the juice and took ten seconds to cough it up. "Idiot! She needs you now more than she ever did."

"Don't call me again."

Then he got the dead line.

Corbin threw the cordless handset across the kitchen and swore as it skittered into the back of the sofa.

7

It was time to end these games.

Shauna stood, fuming, on a shaded footpath behind her father's house. She had been denied entry to her family's home by three different people on Landon's security detail.

"Mrs. McAllister's orders, ma'am."

Patrice. This was the most insulting, unimaginable position Shauna had ever found herself in.

They had a lot of issues, she and her father's wife, issues that went way back. On Landon's wedding day, Shauna told a reporter who managed to crash the reception that Landon and Patrice were marrying for political ends rather than for love. When the journalist pressed for details, Shauna made up a story about overhearing a conversation between the couple. The gist was how important marriage would be for Landon to advance his career and that Patrice had her own political goals in mind.

Shauna was eleven years old. And she didn't know the guy was a reporter. Mostly she was upset with Patrice for not letting her wear Mama's ruby earrings. Patrice had called them gaudy and said they clashed with Shauna's dress—a frilly Southern belle thing that Shauna hated, hated, hated. They were in Texas, after all, approaching the twenty-*first* century.

She needed someone to understand how unhappy she was, and this man, unlike anyone else at the party, seemed genuinely interested.

The next morning, so was the rest of Texas.

Patrice sold her mother's earrings on eBay years later.

It was the first of many escalations between the women, though Shauna had never caused another so intentionally. She could not say the same for her stepmother.

Shauna faced the east corner of the property and stormed across the scrubby open space. It was time to make her father participate in this mess.

She reached the fitness center in five minutes, winded and weak-kneed. But outrage propelled her through the main double doors and into the sky-lighted weight room at the heart of the building.

A tall man dressed in an unimaginative suit glanced her way. The senator sat on the lat machine.

Landon McAllister's weathered skin endeared him to his constituency, even though he knew next to nothing about ranching. The truth was he hated sunscreen, and the Irish in him wrinkled under the Texas sun. The lined-hide look was convincing, though. His bushy eyebrows and wide mouth suggested competence; his mostly gray hair, wisdom; and the scruffy hairstyle, down-to-earth likability.

She shouted at him while she was still yards away. "What do you think you're doing, locking me out of the house? You invited me here, didn't you?"

Landon did two more reps before bringing the weight stack to rest.

"You locked me out."

Landon sighed from the very bottom of his lungs. "Patrice locked you out. You can't go meddling in her business, Shauna."

"It's *our* business, not hers."

Landon stood and wiped the sweat from his face. "Maybe later, I'll talk to her about it. When Rudy improves. But not now. Not yet."

"What in the world does this have to do with Rudy?"

"You upset him."

"*Patrice* upsets him! Us fighting upsets him!"

"Then why is it that there isn't any fighting except when you're around?"

"I don't want to fight, Landon. I just want to spend time with my brother. Is that a crime?"

"If you break and enter, yes."

Landon moved toward the showers.

"I don't understand why you think shutting me out will be good for Rudy!"

"That's the problem, Shauna. You don't understand much. You go flying through life with one eye closed and then act surprised when you crash into a tree. You are going to take this whole family out, every one of us, one at a time if you don't grow up and get yourself straightened out."

Grow up? Get herself straightened out? Her mind reeled from the verbal battering. No matter what she did, her father would tell her she was wrong. Worthless. Undeserving.

When she failed to retort, Landon McAllister threw the whole weight of his body against the swinging door and separated himself from his daughter once more.

Shauna spun on her heel and screamed her frustration.

It only took a few minutes for her offense to melt into tears. She rushed outside and stepped directly into Wayne, who caught her.

He wrapped his arms around her, the most natural move in the world. The pleasing scent of his shirt, fabric softener mingled with cologne, gave Shauna the fleeting thought that he paid attention to details and might treat her with similar care.

Maybe she would remember something, some place where rejection couldn't touch her, leaning just so against his chest.

"I don't know what to do," she whispered.

He did not let her go. And he did not try to tell her what to do. He simply held her up.

"I don't deserve your support in all this," she said. "What I've done is . . . unforgivable."

"Everybody needs someone."

"Why are you so willing to help me?"

Wayne didn't answer right away. He rocked her gently. "Maybe I need you too."

"For what? I'm a public fool, a criminal nobody, with no past, no job, no friends, nothing worth—"

"Stop."

She stopped.

She tilted her head back to look at him. His eyes frowned at her, not the way her father's always did, condemning. This frown struck her as wounded. *Why would you say those horrible things about yourself?*

"You're going to pull through this," he said.

Where did his faith in her come from?

She wished she could remember the history they shared. It was so unfair to him that she couldn't.

Because he believed in her, she would remember.

She kissed him before deciding that kissing him was the right thing to do.

He took one step back and released her.

"What's wrong?" she asked, not sure whether she felt foolish or amused.

"I didn't . . ."

"Didn't what?" She matched his step and lifted her arms around his shoulders. His muscles relaxed.

"Nothing." He smiled. "You're full of surprises."

Wayne bent his head, tentatively enough that she didn't have to stretch. He pulled her closer and touched his lips to hers softly, lightly, demanding nothing. He tasted like ginger, sweet and spicy.

Shauna felt so safe, so protected, that her simultaneous disappointment came as a shock. Had she been expecting electricity, familiarity? Some sudden restoration of all her lost files?

Even so, all the awful realities of her awakening stood aside for a few seconds as he held her. She would take that gift.

Wayne broke their connection first and pulled her into a slow squeeze. She felt his breath at the nape of her neck.

"Brought you a present," he said, reaching into his jacket and withdrawing a cell phone.

"What's this?"

"A phone."

"You know what I mean, smart aleck."

"New number. The media got hold of your old one. Some guy from the *Statesman* was calling daily after the accident. Scott Norris, I think. And people claiming to know you. Some shrink even. Probably has plans to use you to become the next Dr. Phil. I stopped answering pretty early on."

It was just a phone, but somehow Shauna saw it as a declaration of his faith in her. "That was really nice of you. Thanks."

"Mr. Wilde is going to take care of the bills until you're back on your feet. And I programmed my number already. In case you need anything. Though I plan to stay close. Speed dial number two."

She tried it. His phone rang in another pocket, and she heard it as nothing less than a lifeline.

She kissed him one more time. "You just keep saving me," she said.

The relative peace of Shauna's evening with Wayne did not last into her dreams that night.

Football field: offensive forty-yard line. Shauna leaned forward, ready, waiting for the quarterback's call, less than two yards from a sweating, focused defensive back.

"Blue fifteen! Blue fifteen! Set! Hike!"

She lunged left in a fake before cutting right, then straightened out and slipped past the defender without touching him. Her cleats found purchase in the short turf and she pushed off for the X-post pattern, straight over the middle of the field, strong and fast.

Faster than any other player on the Sun Devils' team. She was, after all, a sprinter first, football player second.

She loved this play. Loved the adrenaline kicked in by the risk of aiming dead center, where getting hit was almost always a given.

She flew, barely touching the grass, propelled by the huffing of that committed defensive back.

One one thousand . . .

"Step it up, step it up! Get a move on, Spade!"

The crowd was on its feet.

Two one thousand . . .

The DB was fast, but not fast enough. Her breathing flowed in sync with her heartbeat. She looked up, right, over the shoulder. The corner of her eye detected the free safety coming at her from ahead. She was the hot read.

This pass would come early.

Three one thousand . . .

She focused on the arcing pigskin and reached out.

The pebble-grained ball connected with her arms like a desert burr.

And the defensive players connected with her, the DB catching her high in the ribs, the free safety hitting low on the back at the hips.

She heard an electric crack and the backs of her eyelids lit up with streaks of falling stars. She heard the crowd wince in unison. Tingling nerves shot out around her waist and began to squeeze her breathless.

Don't drop the ball.

She held tight with both hands as her rubber torso unfolded from its unnatural S shape. Her legs went out from under her, and she hit the turf face first, smelling and tasting damp dirt through the mask. Gravity, velocity, and the great weight of another hulking body crushed her.

The falling stars faded to a clear night, and the roar of the stadium fell to a murmur.

And she heard herself screaming. She had never felt pain like this. Spears plunged the length of her legs and out her heels, plunging and plunging. An invisible iron band constricted around her hip bones. Her pelvis would soon snap.

Someone dropped to the turf beside her.

"It's okay. It's okay."

Oh! It was not okay!

"Shauna! It's okay. I'm right here."

Someone grabbed her wrist and held it to the ground.

She cried out and opened her eyes. She saw stars . . . through a window. A window over . . . the head of a bed. Her bed. Wayne was sitting on her bed, leaning over her, holding her wrists down on the mattress.

Khai rushed in and turned on a lamp on an old oak dresser. The room burst into warm yellow form. Dresser, bed table, overstuffed chair. Three cardboard boxes. Woodblock prints on the walls. A historic map of Austin, Texas. Wayne, in a T-shirt and flannel lounge pants. Khai in a terry robe. She cinched the belt and held it closed at her throat.

Shauna's breathing settled, and Wayne released her arms.

"You okay?" He rubbed his eyes and shifted to the edge of the bed.

She could only nod.

"That must have been a doozy," he said.

She covered her face with her hands. "It was so real. I'm sorry. That's never happened to me before. Not that I remember anyway."

"Want to talk about it?"

How to talk about a nightmare like that? Did it even qualify as a nightmare? Her, playing football? Closer to a comedy.

"I should make tea," Khai said, and she left the room as quickly as she'd come in.

"I wasn't afraid," she started. "In fact, I was playing football for some college team. I don't know a thing about football. How could I have a dream that was so vivid?"

"Tell me what happened."

Shauna told him, as best she could recall. To her surprise, the details of the dream hadn't faded as they often did when she awoke. As she relayed the scene, Wayne did not interrupt her once.

When she finished, he said, "The coach called you *Spade*?"

"Can you explain it?"

"Sounds like a dream I would have had."

Shauna had thought she was dreaming of being Wayne, but dreaming his dreams? That was a knotty idea.

"I used to play football," he said.

"Really?"

He cleared his throat. "A little. Not really built for it. I was fast but got sick of getting nailed. I took a hit in college and called it quits. Not too unlike your dream there." He stood and ran a hand through his hair.

"That's weird." She shivered. "It was one of the most realistic dreams I've ever had. I can't see the appeal of that sport, from the inside I mean. I've never felt pain like that."

Wayne nodded slowly and folded his arms. He looked at the floor. "Good thing it was only a dream."

"Yeah," she murmured. "Good thing." But though her shivering had stopped, her hands were still shaking under the covers, and a quiet, irrational voice at the back of her mind wondered if the whole episode was something far greater than a figment of her imagination.

8

The sounds of heavy Suburban tires grinding down gravel woke Shauna in the predawn hours of Friday morning. Landon's entourage was putting him back on the campaign trail.

At six, unable to go back to sleep, she stumbled out of bed.

The five pill bottles on the nightstand suggested that she should put something in her empty stomach. Shauna tapped out each pill into her hand and, cupping them, went into the kitchen.

Khai was already working, chopping vegetables. Shauna set her medicine on the table, then found a loaf of sourdough bread and dropped a slice in the toaster. Khai's wide ceramic knife *click click clicked* through an eggplant on a plastic mat. When she finished cubing the vegetable, Khai set down the knife and pulled a mug out of the cabinet in front of her. Without asking, she filled it with tea from a pot resting on the back of the stove, then set the cup in front of Shauna on the counter.

"Thank you," Shauna said. She sipped and closed her eyes. Jasmine. Mild and barely sweet.

Khai put the eggplant in a bowl and resumed her work, crushing several garlic cloves with the broad side of her knife.

The toast popped up, and Shauna balanced it on top of her mug as she went to stand by the window. Outside, at the bottom of a long hill, the river rushed toward town. She tried to eat, but the bread formed a hard ball in her throat.

Khai glanced her way a few times.

"That can't taste so good," she said after a minute, scraping the chopped garlic into the bowl with the eggplant. "I had a brother who would eat nothing but dry toast for a time."

Shauna tossed the bread into the trash and came to peek at the contents of Khai's bowl. "With your fancy cooking?"

"Well, I didn't know a thing about cooking then. He was fighting cancer. That toast hurt his throat, but it settled his stomach."

"I'm sorry."

"He's better now. God made a way. We came to the States for treatment."

"How long have you been here?"

"Twelve years or so." She rinsed her knife in the sink and reached for a towel to dry the blade.

"You ever go back?"

Khai shook her head.

"My mother was from Guatemala," Shauna said. "I go down there twice a year. It's one of my favorite places in the world."

"I can understand that," Khai said, smiling. "A strong sense of place keeps us close to our families."

Or alienated from them, Shauna thought. "Did you move right to Texas when you came to the States?"

"No. New York, Florida. We were in Mexico for a while. My brother's still back East."

"Is he your only family?"

Khai's hands, holding the knife and wiping it dry, stopped their motion so briefly that Shauna wasn't sure if they'd truly paused or not. But then Khai nodded, barely. "I'm sorry about your brother," Khai said.

"They won't let me see him."

The conversation lagged behind the women's thoughts about their siblings. Shauna had the fleeting thought that Khai didn't get to see her brother often if he was all the way out in New York. But that thought was eclipsed by her own sadness of being completely cut off from Rudy even while they were on the same property. Shauna returned to the window, scooped up the pills off the nearby table, and swallowed them with her warm tea.

"Do you have any more of that soup?" Shauna asked. "What did you call it? *Tom fam?*"

"*Tom yam.* That Wayne finished it off," Khai said, jerking open a cupboard door. Shauna studied the housekeeper and leaned against the windowsill.

"You don't like him."

"I'm making *namprik num* now. A dipping sauce. You might want some." She withdrew a can of green chilies, set it on the counter, and applied the can opener to it as forcefully as if it were a car tire and she were removing the lug nuts.

"What is it you dislike about Wayne?"

Khai took a deep breath and returned the can opener to its drawer. "He has been very attentive toward you."

"You don't like him because he's nice?"

"I mean that my feelings toward him should have no bearing on yours."

"You have a run-in with him?"

The woman shook her head, picked up her clean knife, and began chopping. She shrugged. "I don't trust him."

"Why?"

"I just don't. I have a sense of people."

"Well, he's been better to me than any of my own family."

Khai chopped until Shauna was sure the chilies had been pulverized.

"How long have you worked here?" Shauna asked.

"Since July."

"Did you know me before I came to the house Thursday?"

Khai shook her head and repeated the process of washing her knife. "No. I saw pictures. Never saw you visit."

"But you knew Wayne."

"He visited once."

"Without me."

"Business with your father. I'm not sure."

"Wayne and I were dating?"

Khai looked at Shauna. "You don't remember?"

"I don't recall much of the last six months or so. I need some answers about . . . what I might have been doing then. All the circumstances surrounding the accident . . . People are saying some things."

Khai didn't ask her to elaborate. She slipped the clean knife back into the block next to the sink.

"What do the other house staff say about me?"

"That you keep to yourself."

She did, in fact, keep to herself, but in her experience, seeking isolation only fueled rumor mills. "I'm sure gossip flies on this property just as freely as it does downtown."

"I don't give much ear to gossip." The housekeeper sealed the bowl of vegetables with plastic wrap and stowed everything in the refrigerator.

"It's that bad, huh?"

"Not what I meant." Khai frowned at her over the open refrigerator door. Those duotone eyes unnerved Shauna. Which one was she supposed to look at? "You kept your distance from this place. From the senator, they say."

"Did you ever hear anything about my trying to undermine Land—the senator's campaign?"

Silence.

"What sort of things does Patrice say about me behind my back?"

"Nothing she hasn't said to your face, I'm sure. That woman doesn't hold her tongue."

Shauna sighed and leaned her forehead against the cool glass of the window. She closed her eyes. Sorting out everyone's reticence involved nothing less than beating her skull against the wall. If she kept hitting her head hard enough, maybe it would crack open and the memories would pour out—

"You're bleeding," Khai said, causing Shauna to flinch. The petite woman was standing right next to Shauna, pointing to the front of Shauna's bright blue shirt.

She looked down. A rosebud of partially dried blood blossomed at her waist. Shauna lifted the cloth and found a larger stain expanding on her layered T-shirt, below her ribs where she'd been hurting. She examined her skin next. A gash looked to have been oozing awhile.

"Oh." She looked around for a paper towel and snatched one off the roll on the kitchen counter.

"Wait," Khai said, heading into her bedroom. She returned with a tote, which she set on the table. Shauna threw away the paper towel and accepted an antiseptic wipe.

"I should do this in the bathroom."

"No need. Let's look at it."

"It's just a cut. I've got dozens of these. From the accident."

"A lot of blood for such a small cut. These should be healed by now."

"I can clean this up."

"Let me help." Khai withdrew a wad of gauze from the bag.

"Do you have gloves or something?"

A pair of latex gloves came out too. "Lots of practice with first aid," Khai said.

She used the gauze to apply pressure to the wound, and Shauna felt a sharp pain. She bit her lower lip.

"That hurts?"

Shauna nodded and Khai withdrew the gauze. A thread of it snagged on something.

"Ow!"

Khai moved her into the morning light coming through the kitchen window, then fumbled around with one hand through her first-aid kit, withdrawing tweezers.

"Hold still."

Khai bent over the cut and in seconds held the bloody tweezers up to the sunlight.

"What's that?" Shauna wrapped her hand around Khai's wrist to see.

The tweezers clasped a thin piece of metal, wet with Shauna's blood, shaped like a boat sail but no larger than a pencil eraser.

Khai shook her head. "Not something that should be in your body."

"Maybe I bumped into something."

"Not if your clothes are any indication."

True. Though her shirts were bloody, they were not torn.

"This is like shrapnel," Khai said, depositing the piece on Shauna's outstretched palm. "This came from inside of you."

"Probably something from the accident."

"You'd think that would have shown up in an X-ray."

Shauna lifted the metal and held it to the light of the window. "You'd think."

Shauna rapped on Wayne's door, three quick hits. It was nearly nine, and she'd been waiting. She needed his help. And his soothing company. She'd gone to the house to see Rudy again, only to be turned away at the door, again. The forced separation from her brother had caused her to pace the bungalow porch for half an hour.

Wayne appeared, one hand on the knob and the other tugging the hem of his T-shirt over the waistband of his jeans. He grinned at her.

"Morning," he said.

"How long will you be able to stay in Austin?" she asked.

Wayne laughed at that and took her hand, pulling her into the room and toward a love seat against the wall. "How long do you want me to stay?"

She dropped onto the seat, and he sat opposite her on the corner of his unmade bed, leaned forward with his elbows on his knees.

"That wasn't what I meant to ask," she clarified. "I was wondering if you have time to show me around."

"Around Austin? You're more familiar with it than I am."

"Around places you and I have been. When we'd go out. If we went out. To places, I mean." She exhaled a balloon's worth of air. "What I'm trying to say is I want to get my bearings again. I feel so shut out of my old life. Literally. I thought maybe if I go somewhere. With you. Someplace we used to go. Maybe that would trigger something. Give me a start."

Wayne nodded his way through her request. Then he straightened and scratched his head.

"You're upset over that reporter, what he said about a third person in your car."

How did he know that? She hadn't even realized that was at the heart of her request, not until he'd said it. She nodded slowly. "Among other things."

"That guy was up to no good, babe," he said. "Reporters like him, they'll cook up anything to get you talking. It's how they get their scoops."

"You think he's lying?"

"I know he's lying. I was at the scene—and so were several other people. No one saw anybody but you and Rudy."

"Maybe you could take me down to the bridge where the accident happened."

Wayne's eyes widened.

"And we could go to my old loft. Any of those things will jog my memory.

Do you have a copy of the accident report? I'd like to read it." It was the first bright idea she'd had.

Wayne held up his hands as if he were police and she were a rush of oncoming traffic. "Whoa whoa whoa. One idea at a time."

She sagged against the love seat. "I know that's all a lot of trouble."

Wayne moved to sit next to her, his body touching hers from shoulder to knee. He tipped her chin up to look at him.

"What is it you want to get back?"

She thought of yesterday's kiss and dropped her eyes. "I want Patrice to be wrong, and I want Rudy to be the way he was. I want my life back. I want Landon to . . . to tolerate me at least." She risked a look at him.

"Remembering won't really get you any of those things, will it?"

Of course not.

"Maybe it's better not to know, so you don't get hung up on things you can't change."

"But I need to remember, Wayne. I don't even know how to talk to Uncle Trent's attorney about all this. How can he help me with the trial if I don't have any information to give him? I might as well plead guilty—I can't defend myself."

Wayne rested his hand on her knee. "He understands what's going on. Give yourself time to pull out of this. Give your body time to recover."

"This is all taking too long. I'd like to remember you sooner than later."

"You will. No hurry. But I think it would be good to get you out of here today."

"Where can we get a copy of the accident report?"

Wayne rubbed his eyes. "I'm sure we can get one from the attorney. How about something more pleasant for starters? I liked your idea of me taking you out, like old times."

"What is it we used to do?"

"Stereotypical stuff, I'm afraid."

"Dinner. Movies."

"Right. You came to Houston a few times—"

"I'm pretty sure I'm not supposed to leave Travis County right now."

"True. So we need to stick to Austin."

"Also, I have an appointment with Dr. Harding today."

Wayne stood and walked to the window, his back to her. "You like to swim in Barton Springs."

His claim surprised her. She had disliked swimming in public since she was a teen. "Really? I haven't gone swimming there since I was a kid."

"Well, this summer we went more than once." Wayne's voice sounded surprised, maybe embarrassed, but he didn't look at her.

Shauna's skin tingled with goose bumps as if she had stuck her feet into cold water. "I don't think I want to swim." She cleared her throat. "The muscles aren't up for it yet."

"Maybe it would be enough to see it."

"Maybe. What else?"

"We went to the indie theater up near the university. Saw *Faded Humor* there in July, and *Eons* in August."

Never heard of them. Surprise, surprise. "I like indies?"

Wayne finally turned around, shoving his hands into his pockets. He avoided her eyes. "I do. I think you mostly just indulged me."

"Or maybe you showed me how to enjoy them."

"I can find out what's playing tonight," he said.

"That'd be great."

A pool. A movie theater. Shauna didn't hold out much hope for those. They didn't sound like her. But at the very least, they'd get her out of this place.

9

Shauna held Wayne's hand as they took the long way into Town Lake Park, toward the three-acre spring-fed pool that was Barton Springs. The October weather was mild enough, and dry today, to lure a few faithful swimmers into naturally warm waters. With an astounding nine hundred feet of pool to swim in, everyone had plenty of elbow room. The green waters were clear, almost clear enough for Shauna to see the natural gravel-and-limestone bottom.

Wayne spread out a blanket under an ancient pecan tree. The hundred-foot lacy-branched shade trees were a common sight in Austin, most older than the city itself.

The view brought back nothing more recent for her than memories of her childhood, doing cannonballs here with Rudy. They'd come in the spring when the towering cottonwood trees were starting to let go of their white fluff, and the tiny clouds would sink through the air and dot the water. She stopped swimming sometime in her teens, self-conscious of the burn scars under her arms.

On the opposite side of the pool, Shauna watched as a sturdy, fit man in a lightweight green jacket, blue ball cap, and sunglasses found a place for himself on the grass, facing them.

Wayne sat down next to her and squeezed her hand. "Anything?" he asked.

She shook her head. "Tell me about you. There's still so much I don't know."

Wayne talked, and she listened to the way the waves of his voice rose and fell in the telling. He reminded her a bit of a news anchor, a bit more mellow than the animated prime-time talking heads. But even her attentive ear couldn't bridge any of the gaps in her mind.

"Born and raised in Tucson. Hardworking blue-collar dad, drunk mom. Track star in high school, high achiever, a military stint after college."

She wished she were a journal keeper. She might have written down what she had first seen in him. That first spark.

The man in the green jacket pulled a large pocketknife out of a sheath on his belt and began using it to pry divots out of the grass. Shauna found the pointless damage to the grounds mildly disturbing.

"Went off to Oregon after I served my four years, got a civilian job in corporate finance, then got called up on reserve duty when the Iraq war started."

Wayne took a breath and stretched out his legs.

"Went on two tours, was honorably discharged after an injury, spent a year abroad in Thailand, and met Mr. Wilde on the flight back to Washington, D.C."

She leaned toward him, grinning, and bumped him with her shoulder. "You should get a job at Cliff's Notes."

"I didn't want to bore you."

"You're not boring! Hobbies?"

"Muay Thai. It's Thailand's national sport, a combination of boxing and martial arts."

"You practice here?"

"It beats the gym."

"I'll have to ask for a demonstration sometime."

"I don't know. You weren't too impressed with the first one."

"You've shown me?"

"Lucky for me you've forgotten it."

She playfully socked him in the arm.

Wayne took notice of the man with the knife. He'd stopped digging and held up the blade to one eye on its flat side. He pointed the tip in their direction. If the weapon were a rifle, he'd be sighting their position.

"He's an odd one," Shauna whispered.

Wayne shifted so that his body blocked her view. He stared at the man long enough to let him know they were aware of his strange behavior. "There's one in every park," he muttered.

"Tell me about your time in Iraq. I mean, if you don't mind."

"Not my favorite subject, but that's okay."

When he didn't start right away, Shauna prompted him, "So in your experience, which story is true: the Iraqis were thrilled we came, or they hated us and wanted us out?"

"Both. And with equal passion."

"I think the war was a terrible idea. So much violence. So much death."

"You're not alone in that opinion."

She put her hand on top of one of his. Hers wasn't much smaller, but her palm and fingers were far more slender. "I can't imagine what you must have seen."

Wayne tugged at a clump of grass with his other hand.

"How were you injured?" She let her fingers trace the ridges of his fingers and tendons.

"Grenade. Took shrapnel to my left hip."

"Ouch."

"In a word."

Her eyes involuntarily went to his hip, and when she caught herself she blushed as if she had been indecent. She looked away, but not before she caught him watching her.

"Were you glad to come home? I know that sounds like a dumb question, but I hear it's hard to leave war buddies behind. The bonding. The shared intensity. Do you think?"

Wayne didn't respond right away. "You hate to let anyone down. But if you're not an asset to the unit any longer . . ."

Not an asset any longer? His implication lingered over the water for a second. Shauna regretted she had raised such a delicate subject.

"Something you'd rather forget?"

He slipped an arm around her shoulders.

"On that point I envy your memory loss."

"You don't," she said.

"I do. Sometimes the truth of your past isn't helpful."

"I've been thinking along those lines myself."

"So"—Wayne leaned in toward her mouth—"let go of the past, whatever it is, and focus on the future."

There was something missing from that plan, something about helping

Rudy and staying out of jail, but with Wayne so close, she couldn't think of what it was. She lifted her face to his.

"Sounds good to me," she said.

The first time Shauna kissed Wayne, still reeling from her father's rejection, she felt nothing. Nothing except perhaps the hope that something might come of it. Eventually.

This time, when his mouth connected with hers, Shauna blacked out.

The sensation of floating in cool water carried her out from under the shade and into a black sky dotted with more stars than she had ever seen from the Austin hillsides. The night was so still, so silent, that the sound of her own breath was a distraction.

It muffled what she was straining to hear: the sound of imminent death.

She noticed her thumb tapping her thigh as she lay on her back. A new nervous tick.

"Marshall!" She flinched at the muffled yell. *Why bother whispering at all if you're going to do it so loudly?* But then she realized what was happening. Another dream in which she was not herself. Her mind evaluated the trick but could not sort it out. She could not step out of this person's perspective of the stars or of the situation. She felt strangely disembodied and grounded at the same time.

"What?" She—Marshall—kept her voice low.

"What are you doing out there, man? Get back in here."

"In a minute."

"You got a death wish?"

"As a matter of fact, *yes.*"

The disembodied voice swore and grabbed her ankle. What? The guy was going to drag her in? She kicked him off.

She heard more swearing, then the sound of someone doing a belly crawl across dirt. She stayed on her back, looking at the stars, as the silhouette of another soldier placed his mouth inches away from her ear.

"You have men in there who are counting on you."

"Plenty of other men to count on besides me."

"Look, I'm sorry about Johnson."

"You know how he died?"

"All of us do."

"Only 'cause Nelson survived to tell."

No answer.

"Waterboarding, of all things. You're not supposed to die from waterboarding." The dissonant sound of Marshall's voice in her own throat spooked Shauna. It sounded identical to Wayne's. What was going on? Some malfunctioning memory bank? Some paranormal groping for a connection with this man?

"That does defeat the purpose. But if the brain thinks the body's gonna die, anything can happen. Heart attack, embolism—"

"I hate it all. Every insane moment. Every stinking body. Every inch of sand. And no one can tell us why we're here!"

"Not our question to ask."

"You get boarded in training?"

"Just once."

"How long you last?"

"Ten seconds."

"I made it eleven."

"You're the man, then. Get your sorry self back inside and do your job."

Marshall grunted and gave up his view of the stars, rolled over on his belly and propped himself on elbows on the sand. "I am so through with this war."

"You and a few million others."

"No, I mean I am over. Outta here."

"You get orders?"

"Don't need 'em."

The silhouette fell as silent as the sky. Then, "And just where are you outta here to?"

"Nowhere I can't go with a few American dollars."

"You'll be dead before you hit the edge of camp."

"You think I didn't spend some time figuring this out?"

"I have never heard a more cockamamy plan in my entire life." The shadow's palm smacked the side of Marshall's head. A thousand needles pricked Shauna's temple. "Put your headgear on. Finish this tour. Go home. Go AWOL later, when you're back on your own turf."

"Either I die tonight or I die tomorrow," he said. "Or the next day. I'll never survive another six months in this Armageddon. I don't *want* to."

The shadow started swearing again and pointed to Marshall's sternum, then opened his hand. "Gimme your tags."

Shauna sat up and lifted her dog tags over her head. "Thanks."

"Thanks, nothing. I don't want to know another detail. I'll find these later next to a poor headless sucker. That's all you get from me." The first barrage of enemy fire hit the abandoned village. The stars disappeared behind the brilliant flash.

"Thanks anyway."

"Well, good luck with the court martial and all. Hope you live to see it." The shadow crawled back into its bunker—an old bombed-out, burned-out house—to deal with the pending mess.

"I love you too," she muttered as she strapped her helmet on tight. She rose to her knees, adjusted her MOLLE vest, and reached for the supply pack at her feet. She slung it onto her back as the second strike hit, much closer. Her heart rate began to climb. Was it her heart or Marshall's?

Marshall checked his handgun. The man's thoughts bounced around in Shauna's mind. No rifle for this run, just the standard-issue 9mm M-9. Had to travel light, and if he couldn't get out of a bind with this, he probably couldn't get out, period. He checked his watch.

Time to go.

Explosions from behind fueled Marshall's momentum as he sprinted out of the village and toward his first contact, faster than a plummeting grenade, dodging the heavy breaths of shellfire and damnation.

Shauna gasped. The assault stopped and was replaced by a breeze that rattled leaves.

She saw Wayne bent over her, haloed by pecan tree branches, eyes wide and worried.

"You okay?"

"What happened?" Shauna said.

"I don't know. You just dropped."

"How long was I out?"

"Four, five seconds. Are you all right? You dizzy? Hurt anywhere?" He took her hand.

The muscles in Shauna's legs were quivering under the surface, the way they did sometimes after an intense workout. She put a hand over her taxed heart and made herself take conscious, slow breaths.

"I can't explain it." A vision of war? Like the football dream, she didn't know enough about Iraq to have concocted such a bizarre scenario. Unlike the football dream, this one made her feel afraid. What was happening to her?

And who was Marshall?

She camouflaged her fear with feigned embarrassment and a giggle. "I've never passed out from a kiss."

Wayne didn't find any humor in that. "It might have been a seizure of some kind. I'll take you to the hospital."

"No—don't. I have an appointment with Dr. Harding already."

"She's not the kind of doctor I had in mind."

"Let's not blow this out of proportion yet." Shauna forced herself to sit up. No spinning head, no tilting earth. She was fine. Really. "I'll tell her what happened." Maybe the therapist could answer Shauna's deeper questions too.

"Dr. Siders needs to know. Dr. Carver too—if this is some side effect—"

"I'll make a note of it, all right?"

Wayne eventually conceded, but he did not seem convinced.

They rose to leave, and as Wayne shook out the blanket and turned to gather up their things, a glint caught Shauna's eye. The stranger with the knife was standing, angling the blade to bounce sunlight in her direction. When he had her attention, he folded the knife and returned it to its case, tipped his fingers to the bill of his ball cap in a gentlemanly salute, and walked away into the trees.

10

Dr. Millie Harding's office for private therapy sessions was a cluttered suite in a corporate complex. The furniture in this space could generously be described as yard-sale: a small wooden desk painted lime green faced two metal folding chairs, and a squat vinyl footstool hunkered down between them.

This office, bright and haphazard, seemed a far closer match to Dr. Harding's inexplicable sense of style. Plum and gold southwestern-patterned rugs over-lapped each other under the crazy furniture. The walls were painted Mexico pink and—today anyway—matched the psychiatrist's blusher. Potted succulents were crammed into the mismatched bookshelves, and books displaced by the plants were stacked on the floor.

Shauna and the psychiatrist sat opposite each other in the folding chairs. She wondered if any of the doctor's patients actually felt calm in this environment.

For her own peace of mind, she focused her attention on the one item in the room that stood apart: a platinum-colored file cabinet, sleek and modern and as out of its element as Shauna at Landon's estate. She homed in on the digital combination pad embedded in the face of the top drawer while she tried to formulate her thoughts about these—*visions*. For lack of a better word.

War? Football? She didn't think she knew enough about either of those topics to give her imagination enough material to fabricate such elaborate stories. Were those Wayne's experiences? It seemed to make a weird kind of sense—he had told her about playing football and being in the military in Iraq. The visions had seemed so real, as if she'd experienced them with Wayne.

How in the world was her mind making these leaps?

She had decided not to say anything to Wayne until she had a clearer idea in her mind what was going on. She was less certain how much she should divulge to Dr. Harding.

So when the therapist growled, in that coarse voice of hers that somehow sounded maternal, "Tell me how you've been sleeping," Shauna was a little surprised not to have any trouble talking about the disconcerting nature of her dreams about Wayne.

"Tell me about what happened before each of the occurrences," Dr. Harding said.

"Um . . . the day of the first one was terrible. The worst twenty-four hours of my life," she explained.

"The dream was that night?"

"Yes."

"And before the second dream?"

"It was more of a vision really. I don't think I slept—it was more like I fainted. Wayne kissed me. That's hardly reason. It wasn't traumatic or stressful anyway."

Dr. Harding crossed her legs. "Well, there are several things going on here, any of which might trigger episodes of dreaming. Stressful episodes, for one, induce the brain to work on problem solving, and sometimes this comes out in the form of dreams, even if they seem unrelated to the inciting event."

Shauna took her eyes off the file cabinet and tried to focus on the therapist. She had such distracting hair, the way it stuck out in a mass of coppery frizz.

"Another factor at work here is that your brain knows it's missing some memories. Then along comes Wayne, who has connections to this blank chapter in your story. On a subconscious level, you figure he can help you fill in the blanks. Your brain might be processing this possibility by generating vicarious scenarios that involve him. Dreaming is really a very personal attempt to construct and reconstruct important memories, but not always rationally."

"Too bad dreams don't distinguish between what's real and unreal."

"Dreaming can be valuable, nonetheless."

"What about the drug trials? Could the pills cause these . . . visions?"

"We'll certainly be looking into that as a side effect. But these drugs aim for the centers of your brain that involve memory storage." She tapped a candy-apple fingernail on her temple. "And because dreaming is about the process of accessing and disassembling memories, it's entirely possible that your dreams are at least partially drug induced."

"Should I stop taking the medicine?"

Dr. Harding's laugh sounded closer to a cough. "I don't think so. We can sit here all day and theorize and not avoid the possibility that the dreams are nothing more than delusional confabulations."

Delusional what?

"You might even consider enjoying them as private entertainment. For now."

The suggestion left Shauna both relieved and dissatisfied. Entertainment?

"Keep a journal if you want. And let me know if the dreams grow more frequent or"—she searched for the right phrase—"change in tone."

"Change tone?"

"Do the dreams frighten you?"

Shauna weighed this. The real sense of pain had frightened her, as had the confusion, the sense that she was someone else.

"On some level."

"I'll want to know if that level goes up. Come see me again Tuesday. Let's see how the weekend goes."

The independent film, a gloomy Scandinavian project that had done well at the Sundance Festival, showed at the Dobie Theater at ten. Wayne and Shauna arrived with enough time to park some distance away and walk down the Guadalupe Street Drag, a street known for its underground bookstores and tattoo parlors and eclectic stores. On this Friday night the Drag was crowded with university students looking for a distraction from their studies and midterms.

The theater was located on the second floor of the Dobie Mall. The movie house was a strange little place that boasted a gourmet concessions stand—Wayne bought a mocha for himself and an herbal tea for Shauna—and four small screens in themed theaters. Their flick was showing in the Gothic Gargoyle room. Shauna couldn't fathom the possibility that she had ever actually enjoyed such a place.

For the sake of her memory, however, she tried. But so far, as at the Barton Springs pool, the location did nothing to tap her past experiences here.

"You're quiet tonight," he said as they took seats on the end of the strange diagonal aisle that cut through the room. There was no stadium seating in this place. Apparently the tall people were expected to be polite and sit in back.

"Just thinking." The grotesque gargoyle murals on the walls distracted her. She sipped her tea, which scalded the cut on her tongue, still tender from her fall at the hospital earlier in the week. "I've been having more weird dreams."

"Daydreams?"

"I wouldn't call them that."

"Tell me: you have some unfulfilled fantasy to play football?"

Dr. Harding's reassurances freed her to get this off her chest. "Yeah, and to fight in Iraq, too, it seems."

He cocked his head. "I haven't heard this one. You take a nap at home?"

"No, when I passed out at the park. And it's a winner too. I was dreaming of being someone else again. I don't think it was you this time—wrong name—but the voice *sounded* like you. You've got to quit getting into my head like this, okay?"

"So you were me. Or maybe not me. In Iraq."

"Yeah. Planning to go AWOL."

He laughed at that, a short, tight-lipped laugh. "A deserter, huh?" Then he took a swig of mocha.

"Some friend of . . . this person's had died, I think. Jones? Johnson? I—oh forget this—they called him Marshall. Marshall was upset about it. I got the impression it was some kind of last straw."

Wayne leaned forward, elbows on knees, cup between both hands, eyes still on her.

"What's waterboarding?" she asked.

Wayne's cheek twitched, and he looked away. "Torture," he murmured. She almost couldn't hear him. "Wouldn't wish it on my worst enemy."

"You've experienced it?"

"Only once, in training. With trainers I trusted. They cover your face, pour water up your nose. It's like drowning on dry land."

"It doesn't sound that awful—I mean, compared to other forms I've heard of."

He opened his mouth and then closed it again, looked at her with the speechlessness of someone who had no adequate words for his experience or her ignorance. Once again, she wished she had thought before she had spoken.

"It's slow-motion suffocation," he finally said. "A controlled execution."

She looked away, mortified, and tried to bring the conversation back to her vision. But there wasn't much else to tell. "Someone tried to talk Marshall out of leaving. But he was committed."

"And that's it?" The theater lights dimmed.

"Pretty much."

Wayne took another drink and leaned back in his chair. "Your mind does take ideas and run with them," she thought she heard him say as the lights went out and the screen lit up.

He downed the rest of his hot mocha like it was a shot of whiskey.

Shauna looked at her watch for the first time thirty minutes into the movie. Her tea had become cool enough to drink, and the story line failed to engage her. Wayne was jiggling his thumb on his thigh, a tapping kind of fidget. But his eyes were glued to the screen.

She tried to tune in to the film, but her ears kept returning to Wayne's vibrating thumb.

A few moments later he leaned toward her ear and whispered, "Be right back," then slipped out. She heard his empty paper cup drop into the wastebasket next to the door as he went by.

When "right back" turned into five minutes, Shauna started to wonder if Wayne was okay. Bad milk in the mocha, maybe? Or maybe he was bored, too, trying to be polite about it without actually having to suffer through any more celluloid. If that was the case, she should say she felt the same way.

No need to waste both money and hours.

She grabbed her purse, her half-empty cup of tea, and went out.

There was no sign of Wayne in the small lobby or near the bathrooms. She checked the tables where several people hung out waiting for the midnight showing of whatever the classic movie of the week was. Not there. She contemplated whether it would be uncouth to wait for him by the bathrooms, but then thought she heard his voice out on the mall.

She poked her head out, saw him standing a few feet off, back to the theater, talking on his cell. She felt slightly guilty for having commanded so much of his time today. Other people needed him. Obviously. His phone was pinched between his right shoulder and his ear while he fished in his pockets for something.

Shauna decided to wait.

The mall stores were closed now, and the night crawlers had moved on to their favorite clubs or whatever it was they did on weekend nights these days. A security guard cruised by. Though Wayne wasn't talking loudly, she had no trouble hearing his voice.

"I can't explain it . . . Of course I haven't. Never. I'm not—no."

He straightened his head and gripped the phone in his right hand, his back still to Shauna.

"So we've got some kind of *Twilight Zone* thing going on here, whatever . . . I can't remember exactly, maybe . . . Who was in charge of cleaning out her loft?"

Her loft?

"Well let's hope they didn't botch it. Either she's been lying through her teeth this entire time or your guys failed to—don't feed me that line!"

He seemed aware that his volume was climbing and dialed it down low. Shauna strained to hear.

"I know what I know. I'm giving it to you straight. I've been with her almost a week. She's not going to be spoon-fed."

A sweat broke out on Shauna's palms.

"It's not too late to make sure she never remembers."

Shauna turned away from Wayne as if she might find some explanation behind her for the fear that hit then.

"Of course you don't like it. But it's less risk."

There was some misunderstanding, some gross misinterpretation of the words that would explain this conversation away.

"No. He hasn't contacted her, but someone's onto her. I'll keep a closer eye on her, see what I can figure out. I've got to get back in. I'll call you . . ."

She did not hear the rest. She bolted back into the theater, under the watchful eyes of gargoyles. She set her cup of tea on the floor by her seat, shaking so badly that she knocked it over. She fumbled through her purse for a tissue to blot up the mess, then bent over and dabbed at the tea. The tissue came apart in her hands.

A shadow blocked the tiny safety lights in the floor.

"Spill?" Wayne whispered.

She stuffed the soggy shreds into the empty cup and nodded, tried to compose herself. "Everything okay?" If she had misunderstood—surely she had misunderstood—he would explain this new fear away.

"Upset stomach," was all he said, and he settled back into the chair to watch the film.

11

Shauna lay awake in her bedroom at the guesthouse, watching the digital clock tick off numbers through two o'clock, then three.

Who had Wayne been talking to? She contemplated trying to get hold of his phone but got only as far as opening her bedroom door onto the silent living room before deciding that was an idiot's idea. She eased her door shut, released the knob, and climbed back into bed.

She pulled the blanket up to her chin.

When Shauna was a kindergartener, her mother taught her a ditty to say in the nights when bad dreams frightened her. How did it go? It had not come to mind for many, many years, so when Shauna found herself saying it aloud, the rhyme surprised her.

God is with me. Jesus is here. The Spirit is greater than my fear.

Tonight, though, the words did not comfort her. Instead, she was pricked with sadness for having forgotten what is was like to have such childlike, simple faith in a good God. Was that something she could ever reclaim for herself?

Her thoughts turned to the blond reporter in the smoky rain jacket.

An eyewitness puts a second passenger in the car with you.

Who was his eyewitness? And who could the passenger be?

She needed to find this Smith. How could a person track down a freelancer named Smith with no more information than that?

Shauna wondered where her laptop was. She needed to do some online investigation.

Newspaper archives search.

Accident report request.

Neither of which might turn up anything that Wayne hadn't already told her.

Was Wayne her protector or a trickster?

She didn't know. She had honestly believed he cared about her.

He did care about her. She was overreacting again. In fact, she was certain there was an explanation for his conversation that would embarrass her gross interpretation.

It's not too late to make sure she never remembers.

Shauna sprang up in her bed like a bear trap, breathless. Her phone was beeping. She looked at the clock. Six thirty-two. She must have dozed.

She grabbed up her phone. New text message. As far as she knew, only Wayne and Uncle Trent had this number. Wayne was in the next room, and Trent didn't see the point of texting when a person could talk. Who then?

From: Unknown
> U R surrounded by liars

Shauna slapped the phone shut.

Was it a threat or a warning?

Either she's been lying through her teeth, or your guys failed.

She put a hand on her night table to balance her rise from the bed. Pill bottle number four fell off and rattled when it hit the floor—her heart jumped at the sound—then rolled to rest under the frame. She recalled a part of her very first conversation with Dr. Carver:

The drugs erase memories?

No, they work by suppressing the intensity of the emotions associated with your memory.

Shauna got down on her hands and knees and groped for the bottle, still clutching the phone in her other hand. How was it, then, that her days had been filled with intense emotions and no clear memories at all? Why was her head filled with visions of delusional . . . whatever Dr. Harding had called them, rather than with reality?

And now fear.

When she had the bottle in hand, Shauna stared at the number four. She didn't even know what this was. She unscrewed the cap and examined the tablet, a little round orange thing that looked as harmless as an ibuprofen.

Was Dr. Carver a liar too?

Shauna took a gamble. She tipped her morning dosage of pills into her hand and flushed them down the toilet.

What was she not supposed to remember?

She flipped her phone back open and tried to reply to the text.

> What do you mean?

Unknown recipient. Undeliverable.

Her hands shook.

Was someone trying to hurt her?

Wayne?

Really, now. If Wayne wanted to hurt her, he'd had no shortage of opportunities.

Was Wayne her bodyguard?

It's not too late to make sure . . .

Nothing was making any sense.

At six forty-five Shauna went into the kitchen, where Khai was preparing tea. Khai, who implied that Wayne was of questionable character. Or was it Khai that Shauna needed to be mindful of?

"Do you know who packed up my loft?" Shauna asked without a greeting.

"Yes."

Shauna had been so certain Khai would deny knowing that it took an extra second for the affirmative to register.

"Why do you want to know?" Khai asked.

The real reason behind her question only revealed itself then—because Wayne wanted to know.

"I can't find my laptop. I need it."

Khai scooped loose-leaf jasmine tea into a ceramic filter and set the core into the center of the teapot. Then she lifted the hot kettle off the stove and poured boiling water over the leaves.

"I'm pretty sure Mrs. McAllister confiscated that."

Confiscated? "Patrice went through my things?"

"I helped her."

"Helped who what?" Wayne stood in the kitchen's door frame, stretching and eyeing the teapot. "That smells great, Khai."

Khai covered the teapot with a cozy and carried it to the table. "Shauna's wondering who packed her things."

"The senator hired a company for that, didn't he?" Wayne said.

Shauna frowned. If he knew already, why had he asked—?

"Two movers did the heavy work," Khai said.

Wayne crossed his arms and sat on one of the wooden chairs. "There you go," he said to Shauna. "Are you looking for something?"

"I was . . . I'm looking . . . my laptop. I want to request a copy of the accident report," she said. "Online."

"I'll call Joe Delaney and get it from him," Wayne said. "That's what attorneys are for."

Shauna turned on her heel and left the room, overwhelmed by a fresh kind of confusion. She didn't know which questions to ask anymore, or whom she could trust for true answers.

"Shauna?" she heard Wayne call. But she couldn't answer.

After an hour waiting for a return phone call from Mr. Delaney, Shauna asked Wayne to please get her out of the house again.

"Let's go to my loft. It might trigger something," she said, pacing the living room.

Wayne sat on the Morris chair before answering, taking care not to lean against the adjustable back, which was missing its cushion and needed its supportive pole repaired. He seemed to be evaluating her agitation, which only made her more nervous. "I'm pretty sure someone else is living there now. We can't just walk in."

"You're right. You're right."

She tinkered with the idea of driving out to the accident site, then dismissed it when the prospect turned her stomach to lead. Soon, she would go. When she was ready.

But today she would try to focus on memory aids that were outside of her own mind. Something concrete, tangible. Something that would perhaps hold out more promise than yesterday's dead ends and terrifying revelations. She needed the accident report, and she didn't want to wait on some busy lawyer to get it to her.

"Let's go to the sheriff's records office," Shauna said.

"I'm sure the attorney will call us back."

"By Monday, maybe. My trial is weeks away. I'm not even on his radar yet."

"You're Landon McAllister's daughter. Of course you're on his radar."

"Then why hasn't he called back?"

Wayne shook his head and stood to get his jacket. "Keys are in the truck."

As she followed him out, she did consider that she might need to find her own transportation now. If Wayne could not be trusted, she might need to be mobile. She would ask Khai to find out where Rudy's car and its keys were. Maybe she could use that for a while, get out on her own if it became necessary.

Wayne drove to the security gate at the front of the property, and a plain-clothed officer stepped out of the shack, signaling Wayne and Shauna to stop. On the opposite side of the little building, Shauna saw an elderly black man sitting in the driver's seat of a shiny blue Lincoln. His pure white hair nearly brushed the top of the interior. His kind face captured her attention. He lifted his fingers off the steering wheel in a courteous wave to her and nodded.

Something about the easy movement of his long fingers made her think about shaking his hand. She imagined it would be warm and gentle, and that he would put her at ease with a crinkle-eyed smile.

Wayne rolled down his window to talk to the guard.

"This here's a Dr. Jeremy Ayers," the man said, referring to a small note-pad. "Says you're a patient of his, Ms. McAllister? Was hoping to see you. We don't have his name in any of our records, though."

She had another doctor?

"Does she have an appointment with him?" Wayne asked, tilting his head for a better view.

"No, sir."

"I don't recognize him," Shauna said, though she wished she did.

"He's not someone you might have seen before the accident?"

Shauna shrugged. "Maybe he could call—"

"Shauna's got a qualified team already," Wayne said to the guard without looking at her. She frowned at the back of his head.

Dr. Ayers had opened the Lincoln's door and placed a foot on the paved drive.

Wayne started rolling up his window. "Get his plate number, would you? In case this becomes a problem?"

The guard nodded, and Wayne pulled through the gates before the doctor fully exited the car.

"Why did you do that? He might have been able to tell me something."

"Look, Shauna, your amnesia isn't exactly classified information. You don't need complete strangers dropping in with lies about how they're your long-lost friends."

"He hardly seemed the type."

"The type is all kinds, Ms. McAllister. Your father might be the United States' president in less than a month."

Shauna sighed and resigned herself—for the time being—to Wayne's over-protective behavior. He did have a point. Later she would see if Dr. Ayers's phone number was listed.

"I'm not sure the report is going to tell you anything new," Wayne had said as they pulled out of West Lake.

"Maybe it won't."

"What are you looking for?"

"I don't know exactly."

"You worried about the drug thing?"

"Of course I am."

Wayne looked at her sideways. "You know, it's entirely possible that the MDMA was Rudy's."

Possible, but highly unlikely. Rudy wouldn't even take a cough suppressant when sick, or aspirin when achy. "I doubt it."

"But you doubt it was yours too."

It went without saying, didn't it? Twelve hours earlier she wouldn't have imagined feeling the need to guard what she said to this man. Now she was suspicious of every word and what it would reveal of her.

"I'm thinking about that third person," she ventured.

"Your phantom passenger?"

The needle of impatience in his tone pricked Shauna.

"And the witness who saw him. Her. Whatever."

"Shauna, just because some mystery reporter—"

"I know, I know. But let me do this, please?" She doubted she'd find a record in the report of another witness, or another passenger, but she wanted to read it with her own eyes.

"Why the sudden urge to turn detective?"

"It's not sudden. I want to stay out of jail."

He turned in to the parking lot. "You're on edge. Everything okay?"

Shauna looked out the window and decided not to answer. Silence might be her most convincing answer. And again, he didn't press her.

They parked and she shucked her jacket as she climbed out of the cab. The day was turning out to be warmer than she had expected.

Inside, Shauna and Wayne found the appropriate clerk behind a Plexiglas partition, paid the fee, and a half hour later held a copy of the report.

Shauna sat down in a lobby chair to read.

"We can take it with us," Wayne said, bending over her.

She waved him off and left him to pace in the dull waiting room, which was dotted with dusty silk plants and cheap prints of modern art.

Over the next fifteen minutes, she perused twenty-five pages of information she already knew. The account Wayne had offered was just as helpful as this verbose document, and far more concise. She had swerved her little Prius into the path of an oncoming truck. Both the truck driver and one witness— the driver of an SUV that she'd nearly clipped—claimed she was driving erratically, lost control of the car, slammed into the truck's grille. Substance abuse was suspected. Rudy was ejected through the side door, which opened on impact, before she went over the guardrail.

No other witnesses.

No other passengers.

Reporting peace officer: Deputy Sheriff Cale Bowden. She would talk to him.

Still reading, Shauna carried the report back to the clerk's window.

"Is Deputy Bowden here today?" she asked over the top of the report.

"The deputies don't work in this office," the petite woman said.

"Of course." Shauna wondered which office was his home base. "I meant—"

"But it happens that he'll be by today around eleven thirty to deliver some paperwork." The clerk grinned. "They say he never brought it in person before I started working here."

What was that supposed to mean? Shauna didn't know and, honestly, didn't really care.

A large, plain-faced clock hung on the wall behind the woman. Ten fifteen. "Do you mind if I wait? I have a quick question about this report."

The woman winked at Shauna. "I'll let him know if you promise not to steal him."

Shauna smiled. She imagined it looked more like a wince.

"Why do you have to talk with the deputy?" Wayne asked when Shauna dropped back into the chair and told him what she was doing.

"I need—if there's any possibility that someone else saw what happened, I want to know."

Wayne placed his hand in hers, and she found the gesture unexpectedly comforting. What was happening to her, that now she couldn't even trust the way she felt about a person? One hour this way, the other hour that. She let the report fall to her lap.

"Listen, babe. Plenty of people saw what happened."

"Two, according to this. Rick Bond, whose truck I hit, and"—she found the right page to make sure—"Frank Danson. I guess I almost hit his SUV too."

"Two's enough. Even if you found three, or four, what will that change?"

It wouldn't change anything. Rudy would still be disabled. Drugs would still have appeared in her loft. Why in the world was she here, after all?

She shook her head clear and withdrew her hand from Wayne's. She was here because Wayne was hiding something from her. Maybe there wasn't someone else in her car that night, but Wayne wasn't telling her everything, which meant she'd have to find out the whole truth on her own. If she were braver she would come out and ask him about the conversation she'd overheard. What did he think she was lying about, and why did he need to keep an eye on her? What was he hiding?

The questions made too little sense in her own mind to imagine what they would sound like if spoken aloud.

He checked his watch in response to her long silence. "Look, I'm going to go down the street and pick up some breakfast while we wait. Hungry?"

No, she wasn't. Not one bit.

"I'll rustle up a breakfast burrito, be back in maybe fifteen minutes, okay?"

"That's fine."

"You want some tea?"

Shauna leaned her head against her propped-up fist.

"If they have any."

He patted her knee. "Back soon."

Shauna tried to think through what she would ask this Deputy Sheriff Bowden when she saw him. *By chance did you leave any critical information out of your report? Did you interview any witnesses who asked to be kept anonymous?* This would take some careful two-stepping.

She read the report one more time.

"How can I help you, young lady?" Shauna flinched out of her hyper-focused state.

"I'm sorry. I wasn't expecting you so soon." She checked her watch. It was only ten thirty.

The appearance of the man standing in front of her did not match her prior experience with Travis County police officers. Instead of the straightforward expression, the professional bearing, the detached tone of voice, Deputy Sheriff Bowden smiled at her as if she were a former girlfriend whom he was happy to run into.

She prepared to stand, but he sat down in the chair next to her, slouched in it so his legs angled toward hers, and set his right ankle on his left knee. He was fit and strong and maybe a little too pleased with himself for that middle-aged accomplishment. He colored his hair with something cheap and dark that clashed with his pale complexion.

Something about the line of his nose, which turned up a smidge at the end, reminded her of someone. Who?

She glanced at the clerk's window and saw the woman who'd helped her get the report staring at them. She did not look happy.

"So what's a pretty thing like you doing in an ugly place like this?"

And with that clichéd line, Shauna was able to make the connection.

"Cale Bowden. Your brother is Clay." Clay used to say stuff like that to her all the time.

The deputy's happiness seemed to increase at this revelation. His dark eyes brightened from sultry to sweet. "That's right. The baby of the family himself. You know him?"

"Went to high school together."

"See there? You and I have something in common already." Deputy Bowden changed his position so that his hand touched Shauna's arm. "Except Clay always did let the good fish slip off his hook."

Shauna failed to anticipate a conversation of this nature. "It wasn't like that, really." She felt herself blush and picked up the accident report off the seat next to her and looked for Wayne. He could only have been gone a couple of minutes.

"I was hoping you could help me."

"Your wish is my com—"

A *thwack* sounded and Bowden ducked. Another officer had entered the room from behind them. He carried a rolled-up newspaper, which he had used to smack Bowden in the back of the head.

"Save it for after hours, Bowden," the man said, not breaking stride.

"Just helping a good citizen," Bowden said to his back, still grinning. To Shauna the deputy said, "That one wears his briefs a size too small, if you know what I mean."

Hit by a bolt of clarity, Shauna knew exactly what Deputy Bowden meant. She lowered her guard, lifted her eyebrows to make her eyes larger, and said, "Maybe we could talk over coffee? When you have the time, I mean? I'm sure you're very busy."

Bowden pushed off the chair and held out his hand to help her up.

"You must have been reading my mind," he said. "I have a half hour coming up, and I know this great place down the street where . . ."

He was still speaking when Shauna slipped her hand into his. She sensed, out of the corner of her eye, the clerk crossing her arms. Shauna couldn't be sure of this, though, because as she stood she was overcome by a much stronger sense, a frightening combination of vertigo, tunnel vision, and collapse. She gripped Bowden's hand tighter to keep from falling.

Another blackout? Please, no.

The room tilted but she worked hard to keep her eyes open. She couldn't pass out now. The walls shifted and began to rotate, but the deputy stayed fixed, so she held on and tried to keep his face front and center.

The space around her spun, picking up speed, a centrifuge. The walls fell outward and the furniture moved out toward the collapsed wall.

Her knees buckled.

A chair flew by her and she grabbed it for balance.

She fell anyway, or thought she fell, out of the vanishing room into the blackness of a starless night filled with the scent of fresh rain. But she wasn't falling, actually, she was still standing on a wet bridge, one hand on a guardrail, dizzy from her shift out of reality.

Another vision?

She was leaning over the side to see what lay below. Gradually, her sense of vertigo settled. There was nothing to see at first except dancing beams of spotlights, though she heard the sound of traveling water. Then one of the lights came to rest on the partial undercarriage of a small car, more than half submerged at the riverbank fifty yards downstream, where it had been snagged by the bank. Two wheels protruded from the shallow river, which was slightly swollen from several days of downpour. Two Travis County sheriff's deputies were approaching the wreckage.

Wayne Spade was in the water, crying out to the officers for help.

"What a mess," she heard herself say. But she was not herself. She stood in someone else's skin. In fact, she was in someone else's uniform. A brown sheriff's getup.

She righted the body she was in and turned back to the sight on the four-lane bridge, illuminated by the spinning lights of emergency vehicles. She made a slow, methodical counterclockwise turn around the site.

Directly in front of her, a cluster of EMTs hovered over a section of the pavement in the eastbound lanes. *Rudy.* Behind the hunched figures, a Chevy pickup idled in the outside lane. She recognized it as Wayne's truck. The driver's side door hung open, as if he'd come upon the limp form, slammed on the brakes, and jumped out.

The dome light lit up the cab.

In the westbound lanes, almost even with the Chevy, a large delivery truck straddled the double yellow center line. She walked around the truck, noting the crushed grille on the front and the damaged guardrail on this side of the bridge.

The car must have gone over here, then taken the current under the bridge to the other side.

A deputy spoke to the delivery driver. The driver's hands shook—nerves, she guessed—and he wiped his cheeks with his palms again and again, trying to rid them of some invisible grime. He was babbling about what happened. It would take the deputy a while to sort out this account. Then the man doubled over and vomited. She jumped out of range, but the spray hit her shoes.

She sighed and decided to talk with that one later.

Ahead of her, about halfway across the bridge, an SUV obstructed the shoulder of the westbound lanes, and a driver, tall and irritable, leaned against the rear bumper, likely having been told to stay put until someone got to him. Clean-cut. Saturday casual. White collar. She assumed he was a witness.

On the east side of the bridge, the sheriff's department had set up a barricade and was turning drivers back into a long and unfortunate detour.

"Got a live one, Bowden!" someone shouted from below. She moved back to the guardrail and looked over again. All spotlights were on the flipped car, and on a figure the officers were lifting out of the water. They stretched out her body on the nearby bank.

One deputy began administering CPR. Behind him, Wayne Spade paced, one hand on his forehead.

She looked again at the victim.

She was seeing herself, lying unconscious on the muddy slope.

12

Shauna opened her eyes. The room had stopped spinning. The walls were upright, the furniture in place. Shauna had dropped to her knees and leaned forward on one hand. Had she passed out? Oh, she hoped she had not passed out that time.

She felt a hand on her back, and Wayne's troubled voice. "What happened?"

"Stood up too quick," she heard the deputy say. "Went down like a boxer but hung on tight. See here?" He chortled at that.

Shauna realized she still had his hand in a grip, her skin welded to his palm by some invisible heat. His fingertips were white. She let them go, too chagrined to meet his eyes, and he rotated and massaged his wrist. Wayne rubbed her back in a circular motion.

"She's been . . . sick," Wayne said. "I should get her home."

"No," she said. Images of the bridge tilted behind her eyes. She tried to think of how to hold on to them without letting go of her reason for coming in the first place. "I need to ask about the report."

"What report would that be?"

Wayne pointed to the chair, and Bowden picked up the paper on its seat. He looked at it, turned a couple pages, then frowned.

"I'm wondering if there were any other witnesses to the accident," Shauna said.

Bowden flipped another page. "Senator McAllister's kids. I remember the aftermath. What a mess."

What a mess.

The deputies had called her Bowden.

Like the coach had called her Spade.

And the soldier had called her Marshall. Who often tapped his thumb on his thigh like Wayne.

What were these images, these scenes? She might have said she was spying into the memories of other people. But that didn't make any sense at all.

Neither did the first thing she thought to say. "You saw them pull me out of the water," she said to Bowden.

"I saw—you're Shauna McAllister?"

The clerk approached with a paper cup, which she handed to Shauna. Shauna nodded before taking a sip of the water. Bowden swore under his breath, then morphed into the Travis County sheriff's deputy she'd expected in the first place.

"I am not supposed to be talking to you before the trial. You send your lawyer in to ask those kinds of questions." He held the report out and shook it, like he expected someone to take if off his hands. Wayne did. "You take the rest you need here and then move on down the road, hear?"

"I need to know what you saw."

"All right there in the report," he said as he turned to go.

"I need to know what's not in the report." The remark did, in fact, sound as stupid as Shauna had thought it would.

"Me seeing you get pulled out of the water is not in the report, for one, so you feel free to make up whatever else you like."

"But you wrote—" And then she could not remember where the lines stood between what she had read in the report and what she had seen in her vision.

"I wrote the facts. And I have no recollection of watching you come out of the water."

"A reporter came to me, said he knows a witness who says there was someone else in my car. Do you know anything about that?"

Bowden stopped, turned, and crossed his arms. "Are you suggesting I falsified my statement?"

"No! No. I'm just wondering if any details presented themselves later. Or some new information after your report was finished. Or—"

"I didn't. Who's the reporter?"

Smith, he'd said. Somehow she couldn't bring herself to say the name. The deputy already thought she was nuts.

Bowden sighed. "Ms. McAllister, I'm sure sorry for whatever you've been through. But I'm going to have to ask you to—"

"The truck driver threw up on your shoes."

Bowden's lips parted. With a sideways glance at Bowden, the clerk blushed and returned to the more sane arena behind her window.

"What are you talking about?" Wayne whispered. He put his hand on the small of Shauna's back.

"No one upchucked on anything." He looked at Wayne. "If you're a friend of hers, I highly recommend she get some coaching before her court date. Talk like this won't help her case at all." Bowden looked at her again. "Sorry I can't help you."

Wayne watched the officer leave. "You need to sit down a minute," he said.

She was already sitting down.

Shauna sat in the soft sofa chair in her bedroom, holding the report on her lap in both hands. Wayne was on a call in his room—some urgent weekend fire to put out at McAllister MediVista's Houston office. Khai had unpacked and put away Shauna's things while she was out with Wayne. Clothes and shoes were arranged in the closet. Books on the case out in the living area. Toiletries in the bathroom. The cedar elephant stood on the dresser.

Shauna read the deputy's account of her coming out of the water twice. *Deputy Andrews administered CPR for approximately fifteen seconds before resuscitating her.* And so on and so forth. In retrospect, she had to admit that nothing in the report could definitively be construed as his personal eyewitness account. He might not have seen anything and relied solely on his deputies for information.

She stared out the window without really seeing. She could not explain what had happened, could not explain how she had seen what she had seen— including herself stretched out on the weed-lined, muddy bank of the river's tiny branch.

Shauna had never experienced what she would call an "out of body" event, so she was uncertain how this latest vision would stand up to the real thing. In her mind's eye she was both herself and not herself; clearly, someone else was looking down over the bridge. Bowden, if she was not deceived.

Even if she believed it, she didn't understand it—not a dream. Not really a vision. A hallucination would explain the spinning lobby, and why she had collapsed, and why she couldn't address the clarity of detail. The whole experience was more like a sharp memory of heightened perceptions.

Like a drug effect.

Was she seeing images of reality, or only imaginations? Bowden denied most of what she'd seen in that vision of the accident site. Could he simply have forgotten? Or had her near drowning affected her mind's ability to reason, to make connections, so that it jumped around at random, trying to create something, anything, to fill the gaps?

Consider them private entertainment, Dr. Harding had said.

Well, watching herself nearly die wasn't Shauna's first choice of diversions.

She heard a knock at the door.

"Yes?"

Khai poked her head into the room. "I'm on my way out for the afternoon. Volunteer work. I thought you might want to borrow my laptop while I'm gone, if you still need one."

"You've got one?" She stood, considering what she would do if she could get online. She followed Khai through the living room to the third bedroom, which was as spotless as the rest of the house. Khai's inexpensive, off-brand computer sat on a secretary desk in front of the window next to a cheap ink-jet printer.

"You have Internet access?" Shauna asked, taking a seat.

"A satellite card." Khai pointed to a device protruding from a slot in the side. "It's not fast, but it works. May I ask what you're looking for?"

"Newspaper accounts of my accident." Shauna launched the browser.

"Well, I will leave you to search."

Shauna went to the home page for the *Austin American-Statesman.* She'd start locally, move outward as she needed to.

Shauna twisted her torso to look at Khai. "You still think Wayne's of questionable character?"

"Does my opinion matter?" The woman was being candid rather than snippy, but her eyes remained guarded. She stood with half her body behind the open door as if to protect herself. From what?

"I wonder if you would help me do something, Khai. I need to find Rudy's car, and the keys. He used to drive an old MG from the sixties."

"The white one? I've seen it in the garage."

"The keys used to hang inside the door. Maybe they're still there?"

"I can look."

"And would you get the remote out of his car so I can open the garage door from outside? He keeps it in the glove box."

"You are planning an outing?"

"An outing for one," Shauna said.

Khai didn't ask what she meant. After Khai left, Shauna clicked on the *Statesman*'s archives' link and pulled up the articles that ran from the day before the accident to five weeks after. Five hits.

All written by staff writer Scott Norris. She knew the name. Wayne had said something about him calling every day.

McAllister Children Gravely Injured

MDMA Suspected in McAllister Tragedy

Will McAllister Withdraw from Presidential Race?

This third piece was a sensational, rumor-filled speculation on how the stoic senator was handling the devastation. The magnitude of his crisis within the critical months before the general election had made him something of a mythological god, a noble father figure who would risk advancing his career for the sake of his suffering children.

A politician could never have too much tragedy in his life, Shauna mused. It was bad taste for critics to take on a man who'd been dealt such a bad hand. Indeed, his popularity was on the rise.

Then,

McAllister Son Gains Partial Recovery

She skipped this article entirely at first. She didn't want to know the details of Rudy's suffering. But when she couldn't focus on another printed word, she went back and printed the piece to read later. She owed it to Rudy to own what she had done.

Bond v. McAllister Lawsuit Settled

Shauna paused at this one. There was a lawsuit? She read. Yes, the driver of the delivery truck she had hit, Rick Bond, had sued the McAllister empire for property damages, physical injury, and emotional distress in the amount of

$3.5 million. Her father's lawyers settled the case out of court for $1.25 million just last week. The attorneys would not comment on the negotiations.

One and a quarter million. Pocket change for McAllister MediVista.

She would need to expand her search to find articles about her own awakening, though she hadn't been approached by a single journalist since her arraignment. And yet she was sure the paper would have all kinds of authoritative "sources" with information about her remarkable recovery.

Who knew what Patrice and Landon had already told them?

No point in searching for those now. As soon as Khai returned with the keys to Rudy's MG, Shauna would drive downtown and pay a visit to Scott Norris.

She typed an address for the *Daily Texan*, the university paper, and instead of hitting the *go* tab, she accidentally struck the URL history menu. Khai apparently spent a lot of time online. Without consciously deciding to, Shauna scanned the list.

www.ijm.org

www.hrw.org

www.incadat.com

No idea what those were. Then,

www.humantrafficking.com

Human trafficking. Shauna briefly wondered at Khai's interest in such a gruesome subject, then returned to her search.

Nothing more on Shauna in the *Daily Texan*. Rudy received quite a bit of attention, as he was a recent alum. She came across several pieces about candlelight vigils on his behalf and rallies to send him well-wishes and that kind of thing. The people who knew him seemed genuinely broken up about what had happened.

Shauna had never invested much time in getting to know his friends, and she regretted it now.

Very little appeared elsewhere about the details of the accident, though there were plenty of allusions to it in the innumerable articles covering her father's campaign. She would need more time to sort through all those.

She Googled Scott Norris and within minutes found a MySpace page that identified him as a staff writer for the *Statesman*. She located a picture. He bore no resemblance at all to the blond and smoky Smith. Scott was about ten years younger, barely out of high school it appeared, with the stocky build of a linebacker, auburn dreads, rectangular-framed glasses, and an obsession with politics.

He even had a link for alums of Arizona State University, from which he'd graduated two years ago.

Arizona.

She opened another tab in the browser and searched for college football teams in Arizona. The Wildcats. The Sun Devils.

That was it—the Sun Devils. The team she'd played for in her dream. The coach who called her Spade.

She located the contact information for the student-athlete center and went back to her room for her cell phone.

She dialed the number. This was a crazy idea, but at the very least it would settle her mind.

Shauna was transferred three times in her search for someone with access to old team rosters. She was one transfer away from giving up the idea when a woman answered the phone, breathless but lively. She sounded as if she'd been born a grandmother, and Shauna visualized a petite seventy-something go-getter wearing a team sweatshirt, polyester slacks, white Keds, and dangling devil-and-pitchfork earrings. She probably gave the players in-your-face pep talks and swats on their rears too.

She might have worked for the team for decades.

Shauna could only hope.

"I'm calling from the *Austin American-Statesman*," she said, wishing she had a better—and truer—excuse. "I'm doing some fact-checking for an article about a former player. Wayne Spade. He played for you"—she did a quick mental calculation—"in the midnineties. Can you confirm that he was on the team?"

"Well, dear, I've been with these kids here for thirty-seven years, and I daresay I still remember the names of every player, and some of their wives and kids too! But Wayne Spade . . . Wayne Spade. That one taxes the gray matter. Except—wait, there was a Wayne Marshall who played here around that time. Let me see what I can drag out here for you."

The clattering of an ancient phone receiver suggested the woman was riffling through a file cabinet, a sound not unlike the clattering going on in Shauna's mind.

Marshall. If Wayne had ever gone by another name, that memory could certainly have been his.

After half a minute of bustle, Shauna said, "I don't mean to put you to too much—"

"There he is. Yes. Nineteen ninety-four. A couple Waynes before and after by a few years, but not in that time frame, dear."

"Do you have any rosters or team photos I could—"

"That Wayne Marshall, now he had a sad story to tell, you know. Played one season as a junior, went down late in the season with a terrible injury, terrible."

"What kind of injury?"

"Hang on here a second, dear," the woman said, and Shauna heard her set the handset on the desk. A loud clap, as of books dropped on a nearby surface, caused Shauna to hold the phone away from her ear. She heard a riffling of pages for nearly a full minute, and then the phone rattled back into the woman's hands.

"You'd think they'd have all these old articles archived on the computer by now. It sure would make my life easier. But they've only gone back so far as 1998. I'll be dead and gone by the time they're all caught up."

Shauna tried to be patient and polite. "I hope not."

"There he is. Handsome young man. Let's see. 'Wide receiver Wayne "the Spade" Marshall'—now see there! I'd forgotten they called him that, the Ace of Spades. Coach used to say, 'He's a card you want in your deck.' Isn't that funny what gets lost over the years? Well, let's see. 'Marshall suffered paralysis of the legs due to a spinal cord concussion after a hit in last night's game against USC.'"

Shauna sank onto the floor, shaking, remembering the electric shock that had catapulted her out of that nightmare. Were Wayne Spade and Wayne Marshall the same person?

"'Physicians suspect the paralysis is temporary but don't expect Marshall to return this season.' That's right. It was temporary, if memory serves, but he never did play for the Devils again. In fact, I think he left the university before he graduated. What's that article you said you're working on? You know what happened to him? Honey? You still there?"

"I'm sorry, no, I don't. Thank you so much for your help." Shauna closed her phone before the sweet woman could ask another question.

She leaned back against the chair and closed her eyes. How to explain this?

She had experienced some connection with Wayne, some—what? Dependence? Intimacy? Maybe she'd been foolish to kiss him, put herself at emotional risk. Maybe her own vulnerability opened her mind up to suggestion or abnormal fantasy. Something that allowed her to tap or re-create some experience from his past.

But how?

With Bowden, she had merely held his hand. And flirted. A little.

This was so far beyond her.

Maybe it was all a fluke, a meaningless coincidence.

Her eyes opened. She needed to know whether Wayne Marshall had ever served in the Marines, and if Wayne Spade was the same man. How could he have enlisted, with a back injury like that in his physical history? Maybe the temporary nature of it didn't matter.

She heard Khai's step on the porch and the rattling of keys.

First, though, Scott Norris.

13

Scott Norris, more giddy than she imagined a dreadlocked man would ever willingly be, returned Shauna's phone call within the hour and agreed to meet her. Four o'clock, at the newspaper office on South Congress Avenue.

For the next several minutes Shauna searched local white and yellow pages online for a Jeremy Ayers, the man she and Wayne had crossed paths with at the security gate, but came up empty even after trying several variations of the spelling. She finally gave up. Maybe the man was nothing more than Wayne had claimed: someone looking for a cheap ticket into public view.

Wayne finished his call at three thirty and came out of his room. "Sorry about that. Some crisis at the office."

"Don't worry about it. Say," Shauna said, not sure he'd buy what she was about to sell, "I scheduled a spa appointment at four." She glanced at her watch.

"I can take you."

"I'll take Rudy's car. It'll be good for me."

The lines in Wayne's forehead deepened.

"You sure you're ready to drive again?"

"I'll be fine," she insisted. "Let's meet for dinner?"

"Where do you want to go?"

"How about the Iguana Grill. It's up on Lake Travis."

"I'll find it."

He seemed appropriately reluctant and yet agreed more readily than Shauna expected. For a man who'd recently promised to shadow her more closely, he'd left her alone most of the day.

He leaned in and dropped a kiss on her forehead. She stiffened and felt her defenses rise, exposed as she was to the transfer of foreign experiences, however it worked. She focused on the tiniest minutia that did not involve Wayne—the breeze from the open window lifting the fine hairs on her forearm. If she focused hard enough, perhaps she could shield herself from whatever made her susceptible to the visions.

Nothing happened.

Nevertheless, Shauna's anxiety about Wayne Spade Marshall hovered at the front of her mind.

But half an hour later, sitting in a chair near the *Statesman's* reception desk, she reconsidered whether she should ask Scott Norris anything at all. Perhaps she should instead see if she could re-create the circumstances that led to her visions in the first place. She needed to understand how this worked.

Did she have to turn on the charm? Get a man to open up?

Shauna laughed aloud and the receptionist looked up from her computer monitor. A door in the side of the room opened and the man with a mane of auburn dreadlocks, the man from MySpace, rushed in, hand extended. With his other hand, he pushed his glasses back to meet his eyes.

"Ms. McAllister, sorry to keep you waiting," he said. She stood and returned his firm shake, half expecting—half hoping for?—another jolting fall into a vivid scene. If she could avoid a dead faint.

His palms were warm and dry. He pumped her arm vigorously.

No connection.

She would have to try a different approach.

"I am so, so happy to meet you," she gushed. "I'm a huge fan. I read everything you write. Everything I can find, that is."

He blinked.

"Uh, thank you." He seemed to recover from her forward personality. "You can't believe how amazing it is to me that you contacted us. I mean, do you have any idea what kind of a fortress your father has up there in West Lake? It's like they've got the phone lines rigged to electrocute anyone who calls. I haven't been able to find out much about you or your brother since you made your break from Hill Country. I'm really sorry about him, by the way."

He led her back through the door and down a narrow hall, walking fast and tilted, as if he were rushing headlong into a strong wind.

"So I take it our little family tragedy has become your beat?" she said with as much excitement as possible, taking long strides to keep up.

"Not exactly. But your dad sorta consumes the headlines. I don't have a lot of competition when it comes to the family stuff."

"Really? That might give you and me all kinds of unexpected opportunities."

He squinted enough to tell Shauna he was not at all following her implications, then plowed on. The hallway opened up on one side to a newsroom that was noticeably quieter than she would have imagined. Keyboards clicked and low voices murmured. A few heads turned to look at her.

Scott reached a conference room on the left and opened the door.

"Even the whole Ecstasy fiasco." He switched on the lights. "You'd be surprised how few people are interested in that."

"Lucky for me." Shauna selected a chair that faced the window and gave her a view of the newsroom.

"They say, 'Shouldn't be surprised that kids of a pharmaceutical giant have free access to the stuff.' It's run-of-the-mill. State of the union. Pretty sorry state if you ask me."

"I guess it would be, if you think your presidential candidates are giving the stuff to their own kids."

"Are they?"

Shauna tilted her neck and shook her head like a scolding mother. Or a teasing mistress. She couldn't believe she was doing this. "Now, I'm pretty sure you're smarter than that, Scott."

"Unfortunately, intelligence is not contagious."

Unfortunately, neither was her sweet-talk. He went to the corner of the room and lifted a half-full coffeepot off a warm burner. Shauna wondered how long it had been sitting there. He poured two cups black and carried them to the table.

"So where'd it come from?" he said.

"What?"

"The Ecstasy."

"I've been wondering the same thing." She wrapped her hands around the cup. "And if you're the journalist I think you are, maybe you could help me find out."

His eyebrows peaked like box flaps over his thin rectangular lenses, and he pursed his lips. "Ooh. Classic garden-variety denial." He took a big gulp of coffee. "But I won't harp on you. You didn't come here to be abused."

This was turning out to be a horrible waste of time. She would have to be more direct.

Did she dare?

"Who would willingly take abuse? I came here to ask a favor of you."

"I can give as well as I take."

"You're going to think I'm a little off."

"Try me."

"Kiss me," she said.

He sputtered. "Pardon me?" He swiped at brown liquid that had sloshed onto the table.

She leaned across it. "Kiss me."

"No."

"Please?"

"Lady, you come from the craziest family I have ever—"

She must have checked her brains at the door to experiment with a journalist. She had just set herself up for the worst kind of exposure. She dropped back into her seat.

"I want to talk about Rick Bond," she said.

He closed his slackjawed mouth, stood, and put his coffee cup in the trash. "The truck driver? You promised me an exclusive interview."

"If you continue to be so stubborn I might have to reconsider."

He wagged a finger like a metronome and moved toward her. "Exclusive."

She glared at him, and he grinned. He leaned down over her and kissed her hard on the mouth before she could react.

She froze, and he laughed. "You got your kiss. I'll get my interview."

Flustered at losing control of the situation, she consented. Anger burned her cheeks, but whether it was from his brazenness, her foolishness, or the fact that the kiss was just a kiss, she couldn't tell. Her vision stayed clear, the room stayed stable.

A complete and utter waste of time.

"Rick Bond," she said.

"Yeah. The guy whose truck you hit. What do you want to know?"

"You interviewed him after he sued my father."

"I did. Tighter lipped than a clamshell until he got his victory. Then the attorneys couldn't make him shut up."

"What did he say that didn't make it into your article?"

"Well now I can't go around quoting everyone from memory. I'll have to look up my notes."

"The gist of things would be fine."

"You after something in particular?"

"I want to know what he said about what happened on the bridge."

"Said he was so upset about hitting you, even though it was your fault, that he lost his dinner all over some deputy's shoes. Ha! *That* didn't make it into the article."

Shauna took a sip of the rancid coffee without taking her eyes off Scott. It was the only way to prevent her from saying something she should never in her life say to a member of the media.

Something more than what she'd already said.

"Critical information," she managed.

Scott was still laughing.

"Who called 9-1-1?"

"Bond radioed in for help. The guy in the SUV—what's his name? Danson?—used his cell phone. You had double coverage."

Well then. She couldn't even credit her mystery passenger with an emergency phone call.

Smith had been full of it, making her think that there had been a third person in her car. What had he meant to accomplish by telling her lies? Was he just a distraction, a pursuit that would take her away from the truth?

She wondered if Scott knew the guy. She tested the water. "There was a reporter that managed to get through that metaphorical fortress you mentioned."

"Yeah? How so?"

Shauna shrugged. "He told me he has a witness who saw another passenger in my car."

"Really? Someone saw this on a dark road on a stormy night? Sounds to me like you found yourself an amateur looking for an angle."

Could be. "An amateur who found his way to me when you couldn't, though. He didn't ask me anything. Except whether there really was someone besides Rudy in the car."

"Was there?"

"I don't remember."

"Convenient."

Shauna grew impatient with Scott's smart mouth. "I'm wondering if this person can answer the Ecstasy riddle."

"Dealers make a profession out of not being found. And of forgetting."

"It wouldn't be a dealer, Mr. Norris. Just someone who remembers."

"You'll have to ask Mr. Journalist to put you in touch with his sources, then."

Shauna sighed.

Scott shook his head and finished his coffee. "He's a phantom too, huh?"

"Did the truck driver say anything about the passengers in my car?"

"Bond saw Rudy fly out through the side door when your little hybrid went airborne. The kid almost came down on his engine."

Shauna found a focal point in the newsroom—a bulletin board next to an exit—and concentrated on the arrangement of the notices tacked to it. Anything to avoid the image of Rudy catapulted into a rainy night sky.

"Can I talk to him?"

"Rick Bond? I wouldn't recommend it."

"Why not?"

The door next to the bulletin board opened.

"I think it's my turn to ask questions now, right?" Scott lifted a small electronic notepad out of his shirt pocket.

A tall, blond man came in through the door into the newsroom.

Smith.

Shauna stood. "Who's that?"

"Who?" Scott looked.

"The blond one. Old army jacket."

"Oh him. That's Smith." Scott studied her face. "Don't expect him to kiss you too." He tapped on the pad with his stylus.

"His name is actually Smith?"

"Corbin Smith. Freelance photographer. Used to be a good one."

"Used to be?" She had her hand on the doorknob now.

"A journalist buddy of his went missing awhile back. Miguel Lopez. Dropped off the face of the earth. Resigned. No notice. Everyone here took it hard, but those two were pretty tight. Brotherly love, you know, nothing weird. Now he's a little off in the head. Conspiracy theories and all that. His pics aren't what they were." He returned his attention to the notepad. "Not sure how much more work the chief is going to give him. You ready for questions?"

"Later," she said, opening the door.

He looked up, and his box-flap eyebrows drew together. "What do you mean, later?"

"You think I'd answer your questions before the trial?" she said, pausing in the doorway. "My lawyer would have my head. But I'll promise you an exclusive afterward."

"You'd better promise to buy me dinner, too, after all that."

She stepped out of the room.

Corbin Smith had paused at a desk, apparently waiting for the man behind it to get off the phone. An unlit cigarette protruded from the corner of his mouth.

Scott called out, "And another kiss!"

At the sound of Scott's voice, Corbin turned toward the conference room, caught sight of Shauna coming his way, and pretended not to notice her.

But she'd made eye contact with him and saw the worry in his downturned mouth.

He withdrew a CD from the pocket of his battered green jacket and dropped it on the desk. "Call me," he said to the man, then he took long steps toward the nearest door that led out of the room.

"Wait," Shauna called after him. "Corbin?" She picked up her pace.

But his legs were longer than hers and moved through the room on autopilot. They carried him through the exit in a few paces.

The door slammed behind him.

She hurried, reached the door, threw it open, and burst through.

A painful grip seized her left arm, and she gasped as the door latched a second time.

"Not here," Corbin said, shoving her in front of him and pushing her down a cinderblock hall toward the rear of the building. She heard the sound of sheetfed presses clattering on the other side of the wall. "I'll talk to you, but not here."

He took the unlit cigarette out of his mouth with his free hand and crammed it into his breast pocket, staring straight ahead at a stairway leading upward at the end of the hall. When they reached it, he shoved Shauna into the shadowed alcove underneath and released her arm. She rubbed the skin where he had gripped her.

"I want to know—" Shauna began.

"Sh."

He fished a piece of paper—it looked like a receipt—out of one pocket and a pen from the other. Put the pen cap in his mouth and started writing.

"Who knows you're here?" he asked around the pen.

"Just Scott. Will you—"

"Don't count on it. Wait here for five minutes after I leave. Then you can go."

"Why do—"

He shoved the piece of paper into her hands and recapped the pen.

"Because we'll both live longer that way," he said. Then he left her alone, and Shauna shrank back into the protection she hoped the shadows would offer her, aware now that she was completely blind to the danger she was really in.

14

She pushed her body into the corner of the shadowed stairwell and tried to take shallow breaths. Though the noise of the running presses would cover most sounds she might make, Corbin Smith had frightened her. She did not respond to Scott's calls when he came lumbering through, leaning into that invisible wind. She pulled her knees to her chest and bowed her forehead onto her kneecaps.

She walked around the bends in her mind without encountering any new ideas until a door slammed.

She looked at her watch. She'd been here almost thirty minutes. Corbin's message was a limp wad in her damp palm. She smoothed it out and read it by the light of her cell phone.

6 am tomorrow—Apt 419

Apartment 419? Of what building? How was she supposed to—?

That was her old loft number.

How did Corbin Smith know where she used to live?

She turned the paper over in her hand. It was a store receipt. Victoria Liquor. One item, $36.72. Maybe a carton of cigarettes.

She guessed her way out to the back of the building, then scrambled around to the little MG in the front. She drove south out of the parking lot through the SoCo District.

A part of her felt foolish for allowing Smith's cloak-and-dagger games to frighten her so much. What if he was only a lunatic conspiracy theorist, as Scott had suggested?

But Corbin Smith had hardly seemed unstable outside the courthouse. Cocky, but not unstable. Truth be told, her foolishness over Scott and the kiss, which had yielded nothing, took away any rights to prejudge the photographer.

It was barely five o'clock. With two hours to kill and no desire to go anywhere alone, not even home, she pointed the car west onto Ben White Boulevard and picked a very long route to the restaurant.

Even so, by the time her car was in the northbound lanes of 71 and she reached the 620 fork at Bee Cave, she didn't turn toward the Iguana Grill. Instead, she stayed on 71 and headed toward the bridge where her car had flipped and Rudy's life was irreversibly changed.

She had time. She needed time.

Her foot came off the accelerator as she approached, and she gripped the steering wheel with both hands.

She couldn't cross.

She pulled Rudy's little MG onto the narrow shoulder near the guardrail, hoping traffic would move around her. A set of tire skids crossed the lanes in front of her.

Her skid marks? She looked, then let her head drift slightly left of the mark, into the oncoming lanes.

A dark stain spread like a malignant cancer on the pavement. After all this time.

She felt lightheaded.

Rudy.

She laid her head on the steering wheel, expecting to be pummeled with vivid and horrifying recall and hoping it would not happen. Dr. Harding was surely right. This could not be an event she wanted to remember. The amnesia was a mercy. The unknown was a deserved but endurable pain.

She should practice putting it out of her mind, moving on.

The pulse of a siren and a loudspeaker jolted her out of her daze.

"Remove your vehicle from the bridge." A gold sheriff's sedan was growing larger in her rearview mirror. She was too far out to back up, not legally anyway. She jerked the car into gear and hoped he would not ticket her. She eased out over the water, focusing on the dashed line, staying in the outside lane. He passed her, and she gripped the steering wheel tight in both hands, opting not to look at him.

There was no other route back into town except to pull a U-turn, probably illegal, and cross the bridge one more time.

She focused on breathing.

It was not until she turned north toward Lakeway that she realized the delivery truck had not left any skid marks in his lanes.

Wayne was already seated when Shauna arrived, distracted and distressed, at the Iguana Grill. The hostess took her to a patio table at the rail overlooking Lake Travis. Wayne stood and greeted Shauna by pulling out her chair.

Not sure what this encounter might hold, she avoided his gaze by facing the lake, which was streaked with the rays of the setting sun.

"I hope you don't mind my sitting down already. The table came open and I jumped on it."

"Glad you did."

"You look great."

"I feel a little frazzled. Maybe I should go freshen up."

"No, I mean it. Your hair is windblown and your cheeks are pink. It's a great look for you. The time out did you good. Enjoy the spa?"

She offered him a noncommittal *mm-hm* and picked up the menu, feeling his eyes studying her face. It had not occurred to her to fabricate the content of her imaginary consultation before now.

She set the menu down and leaned in toward Wayne. "Actually, I should tell you what happened."

He took her hand and kissed her palm.

A knifing pain behind her eyes and a bright light cut through her vision. She saw behind the light a crowd of people running toward her, hundreds of people, a stampede in a swath so wide she expected to be trampled. She turned around—maybe she could outrun them—and realized that she was encircled. They rushed toward her, the center, in an implosion of arms and legs.

Shauna braced herself to be crushed. She tried to focus on faces. Someone who would help her, sweep her up into the crowd so that she didn't get sucked down under it. But they came too fast. She held up her arms and felt her knuckles hit limbs. Bodies jostled hers. She fell. She closed her eyes, started grabbing for someone stronger than she was.

She seized a muscular forearm and held on tight.

The crowd vanished.

All except for one man. A brown-skinned Latino, handsome, in an attractive blue guayabera shirt. But his dark brown eyes were nearly black and popping with fury. She let go of his arm, and he frowned, distorting his sleek and symmetrical anchor beard.

He was pointing a gun at her.

She gasped, surprised but simultaneously aware that she might not be the target.

Was this Wayne's memory?

Had this man threatened Wayne?

Then the image vanished.

All in less than a second.

Wayne flinched.

"What happened?" he asked.

She dropped her hand and blinked. Caught her breath. Decided to meet this mess she was in head-on.

"I need to talk to you about something."

Worry lines creased his brow. "Anything."

"I don't think your name is Wayne Spade."

Relief filled his laugh. "Is that all? You about made my heart stop. My name is Wayne Spade, legally anyway. I changed it a while back. Unfortunate family issue. Used to be Wayne Marshall. What kind of digging have you been doing?" His tone was good-natured.

"I was actually trying to figure out . . ." Something entirely different, for sure. *I was trying to figure out whether my dreams belong to you.* Not an explanation that would roll off her tongue. As it was, he'd just reduced her mountain to a molehill. Maybe he could obliterate it completely.

"Last night at the theater," she said, "I overheard a part of your phone conversation."

He dropped his shoulders and leaned back into the chair. He blew out a sigh. "You did? Well, this is awkward."

A woman approached the table and offered Shauna a drink. She asked for water, and Wayne asked for more time to look at the menu.

When the server was out of earshot, Shauna said, "Can you help me understand?"

Wayne looked out at the lake.

"Are you protecting me from something? Something I can't remember?"

"When you and Rudy collided with that truck—your uncle Trent went ballistic. He cried foul long before anyone suggested MDMA might be part of the case. Said someone was sabotaging your father's run for office by harming you both."

"Patrice suggested something similar. Only she blames me."

"Trent never thought the accident was . . . an accident."

"Why didn't he tell me this? Why haven't *you* told me?"

"For your dad's sake. I know you and your father have issues. But I wish you could have seen his reaction to what happened that night. He flew in from New Hampshire on a private jet. I honestly thought that the blow might kill him, both of you at once. If he thought the accident was an attack on his family . . ."

Confusion turned up the heat in Shauna's face. "So instead of figuring out if it was, you two thought it would be better for Landon if the world blamed me? Let me take the fall so my father can take the White House? Is that what I'm not supposed to figure out?"

Wayne took her hands in his again, and his expression pleaded with her to understand. "We didn't plan that, Shauna. But we can't prove any alternative theory. Everybody tells the same story. Everyone's accounts line up. The sheriff's investigation doesn't contradict anything—not the reports, not the eyewitness testimonies, not the forensics, nothing."

"But why keep this from me?"

"You would rather go around believing someone tried to kill you? Might try again?"

"I don't like either option."

"Trent will be really upset when he finds out I'm telling you all this."

"He doesn't have to know."

"I offered to stay with you. Wanted to. Trent thought—" Wayne ran a hand through his hair.

"He thought what?"

"He thought that if he's right about the staging, if anyone still has a mind to hurt you, you would need an ally close by."

A breeze came in off the lake, and Shauna looked around at the other diners on the open-air patio with them. Was anyone here a threat?

"Is Rudy in danger?"

"I doubt it. The McAllister property is a fortress, especially with the elections so close. And we had Pam Riley checked out. She's square. I'm thinking we're lucky, that whoever is responsible for this is satisfied with the damage he's already caused."

"What about Smith's film noir behavior?"

"You know what I think of that."

"The guy with the knife at Barton Springs?"

"Nothing but a nutcase."

Wayne took a sip of water.

"My freaky visions?"

Wayne paused. "You having more?"

"A couple."

"Did Dr. Harding help with that at all?"

"Not in a way that makes me feel in control. I feel disembodied. Like—have you ever had anyone pull a gun on you?"

"I'm an ex-Marine, of course I have."

"Not in a combat situation."

"Noncombat? Once or twice."

"Once or twice? Wayne! That's crazy! What happened?"

"In Thailand . . . look, it's nothing worth recounting. We're talking about you. Are you saying the visions make you feel threatened?"

"Not exactly. I'm really fumbling with this." Was looking down the barrel of a pistol so inconsequential to him? Shauna didn't know what to make of it.

"You sound stressed. Did the spa help at all?"

"I didn't go to a spa today."

He winked at her and stroked the back of her hand. "I know."

He did? "Then why are you asking me leading questions?"

"It's hard to know what's best, Shauna. I'm sorry if that was wrong. But I didn't want you to feel imprisoned, or babysat."

"I'm sorry for lying."

He picked up his butter knife and tipped it onto its point, turning the handle under his forefinger. "Well, you've exposed a few lies of my own that I should apologize for too."

For several seconds, they focused on the knife he was playing with. "Well, it's good to have all that out in the open," she said.

Wayne sighed. "I do agree. No more secrets?"

"No more." Relief washed over her. All her suspicions about Wayne had finally been put to rest.

"So what was so urgent at the *Statesman*?" Wayne said.

"The staff writer who's been following our story. I thought he could connect me to Rick Bond."

"Who's that?"

"The truck driver who sued Landon after the accident."

"Right. Why do you want to talk to him?"

"I'm looking for someone who knows what really happened."

"Still looking for your ghost."

"I'm looking for someone who remembers."

"Let's ask the attorney—"

"Why? He wasn't there. He knows less than I do about what happened."

Wayne sighed. "You might be looking in the wrong place. If your accident was planned, a killer wouldn't have put himself—or herself—in the car with you."

Shauna nodded. "It was a dead end anyway."

"How about your venture to the bridge?"

"I'm sorry you had to see that."

"I didn't, since we're being honest. I only followed you to Bee Cave. Thought you'd want to see the bridge by yourself."

"There isn't much to say about that. Except . . . did you know the delivery truck didn't leave any skid marks?"

Wayne nodded. "The driver told deputies he didn't even have time to hit the brakes. Wasn't that in the report?"

"Maybe. That sort of move is kind of reflexive, isn't it? Even after the impact?"

"That would be my guess. But I don't know much about that kind of thing."

"There's probably some obvious explanation. So far I've been making federal cases out of nothing."

"Cut yourself some slack. Anyone in your shoes would feel the way you do."

"Oh—you'll never guess. I ran into Smith at the *Statesman*."

Wayne laid down the knife he was playing with.

"The reporter? His name is really Smith?"

"Yes, and he's a photographer."

"What did he say?"

"He was very private eye, kind of paranoid. Scott Norris says he has some kind of emotional issues."

"Did he recognize you?"

"Yes. He wouldn't speak to me at the office. But he asked me to meet him tomorrow morning. Early. At my old place."

"The loft downtown?"

"If I understand his cryptic note correctly."

"You shouldn't go alone. In fact, maybe you shouldn't go at all."

The waitress returned, and Shauna picked up her menu and scanned it quickly. "I'm hoping you'll come with me," she said.

"You couldn't keep me away."

15

Shauna made another attempt to get into the house to see her brother. With any luck, she might slip under the radar of some night-shift agent who hadn't gotten the memo on her lockout. Or some softhearted fellow willing to bend the rules while Landon was gone.

An empty hope. The burly agent on duty didn't even speak to her, just shook his head when she approached.

Back at the bungalow Shauna dressed for bed with a heavy heart, tossed out another dose of pills, and turned back the sheets when Khai knocked on the door that led into their shared bathroom.

"You weren't already asleep?" she asked when Shauna called her in. Khai was carrying an oversized manila envelope that was bulky and open at the top.

"Not yet."

"Wayne says you won't need breakfast tomorrow."

"That's right. We've got a meeting early."

"Did you find what you were looking for today at the newspaper office?"

"Not exactly. But it was informative."

Khai approached the bed and held out the envelope. "Maybe this will be of help."

"What is it?"

"I don't really know."

Shauna took the package and looked inside. A haphazard collection of newspaper clippings, a CD in a green jewel case, and white sheets of copy paper tested the seams.

"It's from your loft."

"Where did you find this?"

"I found it the day we packed."

Shauna tipped the contents out onto the bed. "So far, Khai, I haven't understood anything you've said."

Khai sat down, her slight form barely depressing the mattress.

"Mrs. McAllister and I went to your home the day before the movers arrived. She assigned me to the bathroom and kitchen. I was to pack up as much as I could that wasn't breakable. She wanted to do your bedroom and living room. In particular she was interested in your desk."

"She wanted my computer."

"Yes. But I think she wanted more than that."

"Like what?"

"She didn't tell me what she was looking for, but she was aggravated not to find it. Information of some kind. The woman put her nose into everything, even the microwave, the tank of the toilet. Then she decided to sweep all the contents of your desk into a box. She did the same with each drawer in the house that did not contain clothing. Three large boxes. These she set aside before she left, and when I came back the next morning to let the movers in, they were gone."

"Where did they go?"

"I have not seen them since."

"And what is the connection to this?" Shauna spread the papers out.

"I found it above the cabinets. I was dusting."

"You think this is what Patrice was looking for?"

"I don't know what Patrice was looking for. But this looked like something you wanted to stay hidden. Of course, I didn't anticipate that you wouldn't remember what it is."

"Why didn't you give it to Patrice?"

Khai held Shauna's eyes with her own, the brown and the hazel, for a few intense seconds before she settled on saying, "I understand how it would feel to have my personal secrets invaded."

"You have secrets?" Shauna smiled at her.

"As we all do."

Shauna glanced at the headlines of the newspaper clippings. They seemed to focus on her father's campaign, dating mostly within the current year. The white papers were photocopies of similar articles, with a few e-mails from someone whose handle was *Sabueso*. Short and cryptic one-liners. Like:

The problem is in the profit-sharing structure. And,

Subsidiary on page 72 has no public record—can you research?

The CD was not labeled.

"May I use your computer again?" Shauna asked. "Tomorrow sometime?"

"Yes. Any time you need. I will be out again for much of the day." She watched Shauna scan a few more sheets of paper. "I was able to see your brother today. Ms. Riley says he is well, that we should all hope for his improvement."

Shauna looked up and found herself tempted to simply agree with the nurse's optimistic sentiment. Instead, when she opened her mouth she heard herself say, "I don't think he'll ever recover."

Khai folded her hands around her knee and nodded, somber.

"You understand this," Shauna said. It was not a question. "I don't think anyone else in my family does. Certainly not Landon."

"Some fathers hope in the impossible," Khai said. "Sometimes it makes them better fathers."

"Not always."

Khai shook her head. "No. Not always. But my brother is a father, and he does this."

"Is he a good dad?"

"Yes." Khai took a deep breath. "His cancer is back. It has metastasized to his brain."

"Oh, Khai. I'm sorry."

She reached across the blue and brown pinwheel-pattern bedspread to touch Khai's arm. Later she would remember the sensation of static that rose off Khai's skin, the fine hairs lifting themselves to stand tall as if magnetically drawn to Shauna's fingers. In her dreams she would believe she heard a snapping and hissing, a sizzle of energy arcing through some invisible space.

But then, she only heard the electric crack, felt the sting of a simple shock, and saw Khai jump up off the bed.

It was happening again.

The room disappeared and she sensed that she was collapsing on the ground, crying hysterically, screaming and yelling, screaming and yelling, at the side of an empty bassinet—little more than a basket—in a tiny room lit by gray morning light. Her raw throat hurt. She had been crying for hours.

She clutched at a blanket hanging off the side, a striped cotton cloth, green and yellow, that smelled like a baby. Her baby.

Shauna opened her eyes and realized she was doubled over on the bed, clutching her stomach, groaning.

She raised her head and saw Khai, several steps away from the bed now, staring at her, eyes wide.

"Darn, that's embarrassing," Shauna said, planting her face in the bedspread. One joint at a time, she unfolded her body, which behaved as if it had been contorted for hours. Every stiff limb cried out.

"Can I help you?"

"No."

Khai did not move.

"You lost a baby," Shauna said.

Khai covered her mouth with one hand.

"I'm so sorry," Shauna said, trying to recover her composure, not sure if she was apologizing about the child or her behavior. "Please, can I ask you what happened? I need to understand this thing that is affecting me." She immediately regretted what she'd said. How could she dare take advantage of someone else's tragedy in the name of solving her own mystery?

She tried to take back her request. "No, no. I shouldn't have—"

"My daughter," Khai said. "I lost my daughter. She was three months old. How did you know?"

Shauna spread out her arms over the top of the paper-strewn bed. "I'm seeing visions." That was the only explanation she could come up with. "I saw you . . . I *was* you, screaming and crying by her bassinet. You were in a small room, gray, furnished with a bed and a dresser and an empty bassinet. A yellow and green blanket."

Khai shook her head. "I don't remember that."

She didn't remember? How could someone not remember that kind of event?

Well, how could Shauna not remember her own crisis?

Khai's voice dropped to a whisper. "I don't understand this. All I remember is pain. I feel like I have had a dream and forgotten it on waking."

Shauna's head was still spinning. This encounter challenged everything Shauna had processed so far. These dreams and visions weren't only from men, not only triggered by a kiss or a flirtation. Something else was at the center of these encounters—

"You describe our room. And her blanket. I still have it."

"How did she die?"

"Not dead," Khai whispered. Tears collecting in her eyes reflected the light from the nightstand lamp. "Taken."

"Kidnapped?"

"Sold. On the black market."

Shauna thought that if it had been her baby, death might have been the lesser evil. "How? Who?"

"By her father. He fixated on the impossible, and it turned him into a monster."

16

In spite of the emotional extremes of her day, Shauna experienced a merciful, dreamless sleep and woke Sunday morning one minute before her alarm was supposed to go off at five thirty.

October 21. One week since her awakening. It seemed like a year.

Her phone was beeping again.

She flipped it open. Three text messages from the same number. A local number that she didn't recognize.

3:25 > red room in the morning, Shauna take warning
3:27 > Tis better to 4get and b happy
3:40 > R U happy?

Hands shaking, Shauna punched in a reply.

> Who are you?

She waited. No answer. Had she expected one? She dropped the phone into her purse and rushed to clean up the papers and CDs that were still spread across the mattress. She pushed them into the back of her bottom dresser drawer, under her clothes. If she had wanted them hidden before, chances were she should keep them hidden now. Until she knew what they were.

Until she knew whom she was hiding them from.

She threw on a pair of jeans and a black turtleneck, ran her fingers through her hair, and decided to do without makeup. She didn't have a steady hand to apply it.

In Wayne's car, Shauna's put the messages behind her. Her head was a jumble of anticipation for the meeting with Smith, reflection on her conversation with Khai the night before, and confusion over the mystery of how these visions were working. She didn't talk much, which seemed okay with Wayne, preoccupied with his own thoughts as he pointed the truck toward the dawn.

As best Shauna could tell, she was tapping other people's memories. Most of them seemed to involve physical pain or some kind of misery, tragedy. Maybe people were sharing them with her? Reaching out subconsciously to alleviate the hurt?

"Do you remember getting a spinal cord concussion during a football game?" she asked.

Wayne blinked as if his mind had been whiplashed out of wherever it was.

"How did you know about that?"

"I dreamed it, remember? You told me at the time you had a similar injury."

"Yeah, I did, didn't I? I guess I didn't think . . . I mean, it seems really coincidental."

"Maybe it is only coincidence. I don't mean to make more of it than it is. I was curious if you remember what happened."

"I don't, actually. I remember parts of that night—the first half of the game, the hospital stay afterward. But not the actual hit. Not even the play, now that I think about it."

He didn't even remember the play.

Her dream *was* the play.

She wasn't sharing memories, she was taking them somehow.

Stealing memories.

How? What was happening to her to make this possible?

She took a deep breath and a risk.

"How could you have joined the Marines with an injury like that?"

"When you're young and determined, there are ways."

"Like changing your name?"

"No. That came later. I thought I explained that last night." He seemed slightly annoyed.

"All that trouble, just to go AWOL?" she asked.

He laughed, but the tone set Shauna on edge. He waved a finger in her direction. "All what trouble? Like I said before, the desertion thing is a total fiction."

"You don't remember?"

"How can I remember what never happened?"

Maybe so. He might remember going AWOL and be ashamed to admit it. He might not remember the night he left.

It might never have happened, though she felt pretty sure it did.

She would try to find out. How could one find out that sort of thing?

For the duration of the drive into downtown Austin, Shauna pondered this strange ability she had acquired and wondered if there was a way for her to control it. What were the circumstances that allowed her to access the memories of others? Could she create them at will? How did she get this bizarre skill? And when? Could other people do the same thing?

Then, *if* she could determine how the memory stealing—what an unattractive label, but she couldn't think of anything else—if the memory stealing worked, could she influence which memories she had access to?

Could she use other people's memories to help reconstruct her own past?

With access to the right people, could she find the answers to her questions about what happened that fall night, about who was trying to hurt her, about what she was really guilty of?

Did her thieving hurt people? Was she causing invisible injury in an attempt to save herself?

Wayne followed the Colorado River down to Barton Springs Road and then took South Congress Avenue across Town Lake. Shauna involuntarily closed her eyes and held her breath across the bridge, though this one was wider than the bridge on 71, with sidewalks and substantial guardrails. The capitol and downtown high-rises—the stair-stepped Chessboard Palace, the multifaceted Frost Bank Building—framed their drive toward her former home on Ninth Street.

The loft was undeniably a perk of being a senator's daughter. She couldn't have afforded it without Landon's generous allowance, one of the few and easy gestures of paternal obligation the businessman allowed himself. Keeping up appearances, she always said. She had never protested too loudly, hoping that one day he might be motivated by genuine affection to provide for her.

At this time of the morning, they found a metered parking spot not too far away from the address.

Wayne restarted the conversation as they entered the complex and took the stairs to the fourth level. "I still think this guy is looking for an angle on you, some exclusive story."

"He's a photographer—what would he be writing about?"

Wayne shrugged. "Sometimes I think photographers are worse than reporters. Paparazzi. You sure this isn't a setup?"

We'll both live longer that way, Corbin had said before he left her yesterday. Shauna wondered if she was endangering Wayne's life by bringing him here with her.

"No, I'm not. But if it is, you know his name and where he works."

"But he wasn't willing at all to talk with you on his own turf, it sounds like."

"He sounded scared."

"He wasn't scared when he cornered you outside the courthouse."

"We didn't know who he was then."

At the fourth floor, Shauna led Wayne down a hardwood hall with only four doors leading off it. Her former home was at the east end, a corner loft with a panoramic view of downtown. A small but coveted piece of real estate.

"Six on the nose," Wayne said, looking at his watch.

Shauna knocked on the door.

They waited.

After half a minute, she knocked again but heard nothing moving inside.

Wayne reached out and tried the knob.

Unlocked.

Shauna did not think twice about going in. Being here was like coming home. Sort of.

There were no lights on inside, though the morning sun brightened up the place. The reflective screens that protected against the glare were drawn only halfway down the surface of the panes.

No television sounds, no radio, no rustling newspaper. No scent of coffee or breakfast. Only cigarette smoke. And the sound of dripping water.

He had forgotten the meeting?

Or had she misunderstood his note?

"Corbin?" Shauna called into the main room. A permanent partition separated the open living space—a combined kitchen, dining room, and sitting area—from a bedroom and bathroom. The area had changed dramatically since she occupied the space. Her shabby chic had become bachelor bum. Bare brown walls, dull brown leather couches, and dirty dishes piled in the sink would have been more fitting up at one of the university frat houses. Stacks of newspapers covered almost every flat surface in the room.

Shauna stepped across the threshold onto a throw rug. "Corbin?" Wayne followed her in.

As if to confirm that the scent of smoke indeed belonged to the photographer, Shauna spotted his battered army jacket dangling from the back of a dining room chair.

"That's his," she said. Shauna shivered.

How could a freelance photographer afford such a place? More than that, how could she possibly be so intimately connected to a man she did not know, a man who followed her moves without being seen, who wouldn't speak to her except on his terms, who believed both their lives were at stake?

Who was Corbin Smith?

"No one's here," Wayne said. "We should go."

"Wait a minute," Shauna said. She scanned the apartment for something, anything, that would give her the information she was hoping for.

"Why?"

"I want to know what this guy is about."

"Looks to me like he's about cigarettes and Gatorade." Wayne toed a plastic bottle standing empty by a wrinkled and sunken leather recliner. Shauna counted four other bottles in the room, and several quarts of the stuff on the kitchen counter.

She moved to the coffee table: ashtrays, newspapers, TV remote, dirty socks. Music, under the television—hundreds of CDs lined up on their sides, organized as if someone cared more about them than the real estate. A tripod stood in the corner of the room without its camera. Maybe he had rushed out to cover some breaking story.

On the kitchen counter: a cordless phone, a scrap of paper bearing a hastily scrawled address, unopened mail, the remains of a microwave dinner. Everything was so ordinary, so expected.

So disconnected from her. No note explaining his absence. She checked the answering machine. No messages.

What was she doing here? She couldn't decide if she felt disappointed or angry.

She turned in a slow circle and caught sight of the bed behind the partitioned area. And feet, protruding from the untucked blankets at the end of the bed.

"Corbin?" She moved toward the bedroom.

The shock of what she saw as she rounded the doorway forced her backward. She doubled over. Wayne was right behind her. He caught her around the waist.

The feet were attached to a body that lay on blood-soaked sheets. A clean horizontal cut across Corbin Smith's windpipe was partially covered by his bloody hand, raised there as if stunned to wake and find he couldn't breathe. His wide eyes took their last photograph of the wood-beamed ceiling.

He hadn't even had time to get up.

Shauna heard Wayne talking as he pulled her away from the scene, but she wasn't sure what he said. She caught only, ". . . here while I call the police."

Then she found herself standing in the outer hall, back to the wall opposite the door, sliding down to squat on her heels while Wayne talked calmly into his cell phone.

A bulky detective named Beeson took Shauna aside and spoke to her in a silky bass voice. Large enough to be mistaken for Emmit Smith, he nevertheless moved like he was on a dance floor, guiding Shauna by the elbow away from the apartment. Her body obeyed his direction.

She answered Beeson's questions like an automaton. Corbin asked me to meet him here. He gave me a note; here it is. Yes, I used to live here. No, we've met only twice.

And on and on. Her mind numbed to the questions. I walked through the rooms, over there, and over there. I touched the answering machine.

Another detective questioned Wayne separately. Protocol, Beeson said. The detective's round cheeks and pudgy hands prevented Shauna from prejudging him as sharp edged. His tone promised not to judge her, and Shauna thought that even if she were guilty of Corbin's death, Detective Beeson might be as patient with her. She guessed him to be a rookie, not on the force long enough to have become jaded.

Maybe she didn't believe in the basic kindness of human beings anymore.

Shauna hoped she was thinking clearly enough to be giving the same true story as Wayne.

No, she didn't know what Corbin wanted to discuss. No, he wasn't connected—so far as she knew—to her pending case. See, she had this memory gap. Yes, amnesia of a kind. Her doctor was Siders, at Hill Country Medical Center.

Shauna's despair grew as each long minute finally passed. After a half hour of questioning and another half hour of paperwork, Beeson left her alone, and Shauna felt the full weight of this murder settling on her. Corbin's promise to connect her to her past had been broken, and the jagged edges of the break tore open the cage of her worst fears.

She would never remember.

Within the next five minutes, Shauna decided she never wanted to remember.

From the corner of her eye, she noted an investigator talking to Detective Beeson, bodies leaning unnaturally close together, the way parents consult when they don't want their children to hear. The investigator handed something to the detective. A slip of paper the size of a fortune from a cookie, sealed in a plastic bag.

Beeson brought it to Shauna, reading as he came.

"Does this mean anything to you?" he asked, holding the bag out to her so she could read its contents.

The paper appeared to have been taken from a book; she could see through the page to the printing on the back. It was thin paper, the onion-skin sort of literary anthologies. She'd had one as a text once. Two lines of a poem had been neatly cut from such a book. The slip of paper was spotted by something damp.

She didn't want to read the words.

Better by far you should forget and smile
Than that you should remember and be sad.

"We found this in the victim's mouth. It's possible the killer left this as a message for someone—do you have any idea who?"

For the first time in her interrogation, Shauna lied.

She turned away from the lines. "No," she said. "It could be anyone."

17

Wayne drove Shauna back to the guesthouse, where she climbed into bed and did not emerge from her room for the remainder of the day. The lamp in front of the window became a shadowy sundial, casting its form across the room.

Better by far you should forget.

At this point, she thought she should.

She had told Wayne on the way home about the poetry fragment.

"The text message—this mess . . . I'm worried about your safety," he had said. "Maybe it would be best to give up this quest you're on. Please. I don't want you to get hurt."

Things were what they were. Corbin Smith had understood that her life was in danger but offered a different kind of advice: you must find it within yourself to remember, he seemed to say in their brief encounters.

But the killer left her a clear message: Leave the past behind you. Don't look back. Forget, and smile.

And live. Avoid Corbin's fate.

What would it cost her to forget, really? Shauna thought of her father, her stepmother, her brother. How did she fit into this life of theirs anymore? They were no family to her.

She had few friends, casualties of her own withdrawal into the anonymous life she preferred but could not get as a McAllister. She had no job.

She had no past to explain her present condition.

Did she have a future?

She could pack up, slip away, and start a new life. How hard would it be to change her name? She might even leave Texas, go somewhere with less heat and more water. Oregon maybe, or Washington State.

She could forget all this if it didn't mean becoming a fugitive.

A noise at the door startled Shauna. She rolled over on the bed and saw Khai coming into the room with a tray of tea. Early evening light spilled across her smooth face.

"Wayne asked me to speak with you," she said, setting the tray on the dresser. "He thinks a woman's view might be more persuasive than his. He wants you to drop this searching you're doing." Her eyebrows went up, and her chin dipped as if she thought the idea was foolish and wondered if Shauna felt the same way. Shauna gave no indication of her feelings.

"He wants you to let your memory recover in its own time," Khai said. "Wayne thinks you will be better off this way."

"I might be."

Khai shook her head and handed a hot cup of tea to Shauna, then took a seat at the window. "My daughter turns fifteen today, if she is still alive," Khai said. "Sometimes I wonder if I would know her if I saw her. I wonder who she looks like, and what her voice sounds like. I wonder if she remembers any impressions of me."

Shauna closed her eyes. She was not in the frame of mind to engage Khai on such an intense topic.

"In a way," Khai said, "she and I don't know each other at all. But there is a part of me that senses we have never stopped knowing each other, that we have never forgotten each other." She nodded, contemplative. "Yes, I'm pretty sure I would know her."

"That's nice."

"Can I tell you a story?"

Shauna let her eyes say yes even though her mind said no.

"When my husband, Chuan, took our daughter away, people told me to forget her. I must get on with my life, they said, there was nothing I could do. Chuan returned to our little home with his dirty money and said we would have more children. He more than anyone wanted me to forget. Forget, forget!

"For a while I considered this. The pain was so deep and so raw. There were days I would have died just to forget. The problem was, I couldn't figure out how to get her out of my mind. How do you kill that kind of pain?"

"If you're going to tell me that my amnesia is a mercy—"

Khai held up her hand. "No. Wait. I had heard of a missionary in our village who was said to help people forget the darkness of their past. Some said he was a miracle worker who knew how to cover up everything terrible that followed you like a shadow. His God could cut it off and replace it with hope. I went to this man thinking he could help me to separate from my shadow."

"Peter Pan magic," Shauna observed.

"Didn't you ever wonder why that boy always wanted his shadow reattached?"

This conversation was baffling Shauna.

"But the missionary was no magician," Khai said. "When I told him and his wife what I wanted, they should have laughed at me, but they didn't. Instead they told me that my past was not something God wanted to amputate. He wanted to cast a new light on it so that my life could have new meaning. He wanted to restore it so that it would become useful to him and to others. If I tried to deny that shadow in my life, the truth of it would be useful to no one."

"I'm thinking some truths are best forgotten—suffering, for example."

"Have you ever read the Old Testament, Shauna?"

The old sadness over having lost her mother, lost her mother's faith, washed over Shauna's heart. "Parts of it. A very long time ago."

"When God's people were rescued from great suffering, he commanded them to remember it. He asked them to make altars and feast days and memorials so that they would not forget—not only their rescue, but what they were rescued from. And who rescued them."

"I take it you swallowed this man's philosophy, then?" She didn't mean to sound cruel, but this kind of God-talk had not served her own life so well as an adult.

"It is so much more than philosophy, Shauna. I will try to explain more to you at the right time. But I took a completely new point of view. I prayed to God that I would never forget my baby, never. I prayed that the pain of remembering would make me a better mother."

"And did God answer your prayers?" Shauna could not avoid the cynicism.

"Yes."

"You don't have more children."

"True, but listen: I never forgot my daughter. I am, in fact, more than a little upset that you seem to have stripped me of a memory concerning her."

Khai's accusation shocked Shauna. She looked into Khai's eyes and saw the pain of her theft there. It was a fair enough claim, but Shauna had not anticipated that Khai would so quickly pinpoint Shauna's own suspicions—she was stealing memories.

"I'm so sorry if I hurt you in any way."

Khai's eyes glistened. "I forgive you." The memory in question presented itself to Shauna in full color, surprising her with deep, personal agony as if the memory were her own.

She supposed it was her own, now.

"You can't possibly miss that kind of pain."

"Even our worst memories are valuable."

"I would need to be convinced."

"The month after Chuan sold our daughter for two hundred fifty dollars, he died of the liquor he bought with it," Khai said. "Two months later the missionary introduced me to a human-rights organization that was affiliated with his church. Their goal is to recover trafficked children, especially babies sold into the black market. I went to work for them, and we recovered and returned twenty in the next three years. For these babies, I was able to be the mother I have not yet been able to be to my daughter—the mother who will go to the ends of the earth to find her and bring her home."

"You don't really hope to find her?"

"That is not for me to decide. But Areya will be my daughter even if I never find her."

"Areya is a pretty name."

Khai nodded. "I speak it out loud every day. I came to Texas because Mexico is among the top suppliers of children to North America. The organization helped me to get a work visa. I had to learn English, earn money to live on. I waited and earned my citizenship. It has taken me twelve years, and I will keep doing what I can."

"Why here? Americans don't traffic in babies."

"They do. More than five thousand babies a year. People pay *thousands* of dollars for each child—twenty, thirty, forty. More if their intentions are dishonorable."

"You said your husband got two fifty for your daughter."

"The money paid for these children does not go to the biological parents, you can be sure."

"Why have you told me all this?" she asked.

"Because Wayne wants you to forget your pain. *You* want to forget your pain. I mean to tell you that doing that will only cause you more hurt."

"I don't want to forget my pain, Khai. I want to *live*. Something happened to me that someone else doesn't want me to remember."

"Of course they don't! Listen to me. The only things worth forgetting are the offenses others have caused us. Those will distract you from living. But if someone tells you to forget your own history, you can expect he has his own agenda in mind. His own selfishness or his own intolerance for pain. Or something far more harmful."

"I haven't forgotten anything *willingly*."

"Then you will have to work harder than the average person to hold on to what is true. If you forget, Shauna, your suffering will rule you instead of free you."

She resented Khai's telling her what to do. The housekeeper couldn't understand what Shauna had been through, the pain of being responsible for her brother's condition and another man's death, the fear of being hunted, the loneliness of facing it without confidence in anyone or anything, not even herself.

"I am sorry about your friend Corbin," Khai said after Shauna's silence.

"I didn't even know him," Shauna said.

"He cared about you."

Shauna set her teacup on the night table.

"You *knew* him?" Shauna said, surprised.

"I don't think our encounters went that deep."

"What exactly were your 'encounters,' then?"

"Back in September, about a week after your accident, I helped a writer at the *Statesman* with a story on human trafficking over the Mexico border. We were put in touch by the organization that sponsors me. I participated in a group interview about a sting operation we had organized."

"This is before you came to work for my father."

"The sting was before, but I had been working for your family about two months when the interview happened. The writer brought a photographer with him, and he heard me mention that I worked for the McAllisters."

"Corbin Smith."

Khai nodded. "Our director wouldn't allow him to take any photos, but he stayed through the discussion and drew me aside afterward. He said he was a friend of yours and that he was afraid for your life."

"You trusted him?"

"I didn't have any reason not to. He offered to help me with some . . . research I am doing, if I would call him when you were released from the hospital."

"Research about your daughter."

"Indirectly."

"So when you found those documents at my house, you kept them aside for me because you understood that they were connected to Corbin in some way."

"I kept them because they were hidden. I did see his name on the credit lines, but I never told him I had them. The way Patrice behaved! If she found out . . . then again, I'm not sure they were what she was looking for. Do you know?"

Shauna shook her head.

"Well, I thought if Corbin was right, and you were in some kind of trouble, and Patrice was also connected—"

"I doubt she's connected to anything except her own interests."

"She is not a compassionate woman."

Shauna sighed and flopped back down onto her pillow. "This is a lot to process."

"But you must figure it out."

"Why?"

"Because all the pain of your history, all the things you can't explain right now—all that contains the power to save lives. Including your own."

"Just because yours did doesn't mean everyone else's can."

"You have to believe it first."

"I don't know if I do. Who wants to hold on to their regrets, or their failures, or their disappointments? Why would I want to remember what might kill me?"

"Not hold on to them; be changed by them. Changed for the better. There is a significant difference, and it always leads to life. Remembering Areya saved my life."

"That's ridiculous, Khai! I'm talking literally here, and you're getting all philosophical on me."

"Do what you want then." Khai stood and put her still-full cup back on the tray. "Forget. Turn your back on what you are. Make a little life for yourself that looks safe to you. I promise you: it will be poor and entirely unmemorable."

For an hour Shauna stewed, experiencing irritation and epiphany and apathy in various combinations. Wayne intruded to ask if she wanted some dinner; he would go out for something if she was interested. She asked for a bowl of soup.

Shauna understood that Khai believed what she said. And she knew it was another reasonable argument that she would have to weigh in making her decision about whether to follow Wayne's advice or Khai's.

Even her own desires competed with each other. She really did want to live, and she feared for her life. And yet if someone would kill her for trying to uncover the truth, the truth must be compelling, valuable. She really did want to know what happened, ideally to acquit herself of the guilt she felt over her brother's condition, and maybe even to keep herself out of jail, though there were no guarantees that the truth would do either of those things.

In the end, she took the coward's way out by landing on what was less a decision than an ultimatum.

She had the files Khai had brought to her the night before. She would read them thoroughly, once, and see if they contained anything to spur her forward. If she finished and still nothing made sense, she would abandon everything and let the future lead where it may.

Shauna rolled off her bed and went to the dresser where she had stashed the articles and e-mails. She separated them into three stacks—articles, e-mails, a lone CD—according to date. The material spanned February to August of that year, beginning with Landon's victory in the national primaries and ending roughly one week before the accident.

She read the first two articles, which focused, respectively, on Landon's victory and the landmark health care reform bill he proposed that was so popular among the middle class. She turned to the third article and paused at the photo, a flattering shot of Landon and Rudy on the campaign trail. They sat shoulder to shoulder at an RV's dinette, leaning over a single sheet of paper, intimate and focused while the other bodies in the background were a blur of motion.

The photo accentuated similarities between father and son that Shauna had never before noticed. Rudy and Landon had always looked alike, but the depth of resemblance in this image unnerved her. Their body posture, the tilt of their necks, the way in which their fingers clutched their pens—how could two men so dissimilar in personality be such twins?

"Senator Landon McAllister (D-TX) and son Rudy McAllister, deputy campaign manager, review changes to his stump speech en route to Massachusetts."

Shauna looked for the credit line.

Corbin Smith.

She held her breath. Riffled through to find other photos. Many of them were by Corbin.

She looked at the article bylines, starting with the two she'd already read. Miguel Lopez. Miguel Lopez.

Every article in the stack was written by Miguel Lopez.

She reached for her cell phone, found her list of calls made, and scrolled down to Scott Norris's number. She selected it. Would he be in on a Sunday evening? If he had caller ID, she trusted he might answer.

"Shauna! You call to set up dinner?"

"Did you hear about Corbin Smith?"

"Hours ago. You just hear?"

"Scott, I need to talk to Miguel Lopez. Can you tell me how to reach him?"

"Migu—You are all over the map! I told you yesterday that the guy vanished, disappeared, doesn't come around here anymore."

Shauna's hopes took a dive off their high board into an empty pool. *Miguel Lopez.* Scott had mentioned him.

"Yeah, you were only half paying attention then."

"When?"

"Yesterday."

"I mean when did he disappear?"

"Oh, I dunno. A month, two months ago. Yeah. It was the beginning of September. Chief figured he'd skipped town to work for some bigger fish. Lopez had been hard on the political beat, tagging along with your father now and then . . ."

Shauna didn't hear the rest of what he said. Her accident happened September 1. Corbin knew her. Miguel knew Corbin. Miguel and Shauna were connected by this window in time that contained more mystery than reality so far.

Maybe Miguel was Corbin's witness.

Maybe Miguel was long dead.

Her mind vaulted a dozen other possibilities.

". . . sent a formal letter of resignation, no explanation. We all thought it was out of character, but you never really know, do you?"

Shauna jumped in when Scott took a breath.

"Where did the letter come from?"

"You mean was it from Lopez?"

"Really, Scott. I mean what city?"

"How am I supposed to know that?"

"Could you find out?"

"Why would I?"

"Because you're naturally curious."

"Well HR is closed right now. It's Sunday, so it will—"

"What better time to take a look than when no one is there?"

"You heard of breaking and entering?"

"You're a brilliant man, Scott Norris. I'm sure you can find a loophole."

"And risk my career for a source who won't even talk to me? I don't—"

"Think of me as a source with connections that might advance your career."

His half-second hesitation cracked his resolve. "I want an exclusive about the scene at Smith's."

"How did you know I was there?"

"I've got connections too, you know."

"Done. But all that comes later. Call me back?"

"Maybe."

Shauna closed the phone and leaned back against the foot of the bed. If Lopez's resignation letter took her to a dead end, where would she look next?

18

Shauna's phone rang in the bedroom an hour later, while she and Wayne were finishing their soup in the kitchen. Khai had gone out for the night. Shauna excused herself to answer it. Scott Norris's number showed on the ID.

"Yes?"

"Old home address on the letter, on the return envelope. Not helpful. But you might be interested in this: a Victoria postmark?"

Could mean anything. Dropped in a post office box en route to anywhere. Mexico, for example.

Looking for a particular Miguel Lopez in Mexico would be like looking for a one-cent error in Microsoft's books. Impossible to find.

She sighed.

"Thanks anyway."

"I still get my exclusives."

"Sure. But later."

"Don't be a stranger."

Shauna stood facing the wall next to her bed for a full minute, closed phone in her hands, before her mind remembered what her eyes had registered on two other occasions. Corbin's receipt, the one he had scrawled his message on, was from a liquor store. Victoria Liquor. In Victoria? Or was that just a name? She had given that note to Detective Beeson this morning. If she racked her brain hard enough, she might remember.

Nope.

What was the other? *Victoria, Victoria.*

The address on the paper that appeared in her coat pocket the day she arrived at the guesthouse.

The day Corbin had confronted her outside the courthouse.

She recalled his awkward toe-stomping. Had he dropped the address into her jacket then? She hurried into her closet to find it.

"Everything okay?"

She whirled. Wayne leaned against the door frame. "Yeah."

"Who called so late?"

Why did she feel relief that she'd stowed away the newspaper articles before he returned with the meal?

"Wrong number."

Wayne didn't challenge her, but his eyes didn't believe her either. Instead he said, "I called Trent today to explain why I spilled the beans last night."

"And?"

"He's worried about you."

"I guess that's better than being angry at you."

"I'll say. You should give him a call tomorrow. Put his mind at ease." He gestured toward the living room sofa. "Up for some TV? Get your mind off things? We can avoid the news channels."

She straightened a blouse on its hanger. "I'm sorry. I'm so tired—I've been lying in bed all day and I'm exhausted." She tried a halfhearted laugh. "How does that work? You go ahead though. Maybe tomorrow we can do something?"

"I understand. A good night's sleep does wonders for the perspective. Sleep well then."

"Thanks."

Wayne closed the door and Shauna continued to search for the jacket, remembering a minute later that she had left it in Wayne's truck. Without a good reason to tell him she needed it, she would have to wait to fetch the address. In the meantime, she would assume Victoria. Yes, she was pretty sure the address was somewhere in Victoria. Her memory of the past few days seemed unexpectedly sharp, sharper than the first few days in the hospital.

Almost anything could explain that. Natural recovery or pharmaceutical help. Shauna considered the pill bottles, still by her bed. Or perhaps her decision to avoid those medications had allowed a fog to lift. Somehow, there was a connection between her memory and those drugs. In her anticipation of meeting Corbin, she had forgotten the morning dose. Tonight, then, she would dispose of twice as much. See what happened.

Shauna picked up one of the bottles. Had she been given these same drugs while she was in the coma, or something different? It hadn't occurred to her to ask Dr. Carver.

She returned the pills to the nightstand, stepped into the bathroom, flushed the toilet, turned on the shower. Then she opened the door adjoining Khai's room, and by the light of the bathroom, booted up the laptop.

Khai had said anytime.

She brushed her teeth, then returned to Khai's computer.

She popped the unlabeled CD into the drive. It contained a single PDF file labeled *MMV Annual.* McAllister MediVista's latest annual report, easily downloaded from the Web. Why would she have set this aside? She knew two of the firm's three top executives—Wayne and Uncle Trent—not to mention her father's role as president. She tabbed through the first fifty pages. MMV had experienced a year of record-breaking profit margins, and the report oozed with self-satisfaction.

Nothing else remarkable. She ejected the disk.

Shauna MapQuested Victoria, though she did not have the address. The town was just over two hours away, in what she guessed was a residential neighborhood.

Then she Googled Miguel Lopez. More than half a million hits. She tried "Miguel Lopez American Statesman" and found hundreds of links, all in the newspaper's archives.

In the first ten pages she found three articles that were about a Miguel Lopez rather than written by a Miguel Lopez.

The first was about a driver apprehended for driving under the influence during the holidays last year.

The second was the obituary of a beloved local farmer who donated pumpkins to schoolchildren every October.

The third featured a journalist who received an award for his coverage of a flash flood in Austin that destroyed an entire neighborhood and killed five people. The article was accompanied by a picture of him holding the plaque and shaking hands with a man identified in the caption as the publisher.

Even in profile, his face was instantly recognizable to Shauna. Square hairline, trim beard, full lips. Modestly happy here, furious the only other time she had seen him:

In her vision at the Iguana Grill, pointing a gun at her.

Shauna bolted awake in the predawn darkness of Monday morning as alert as if she'd injected espresso into her heart.

She had a decision. She would drive to Victoria with the picture of Miguel that she had printed off last night, go to the address Corbin had given her, find out if Miguel Lopez lived there. Or if the person who lived there knew of him.

Of course, it was possible that the address had nothing to do with Miguel Lopez.

But if Corbin had gone to such trouble to sneak it to her without Wayne knowing, it must have some connection to her situation.

The thread of possibility was so slender that Shauna realized she had stopped breathing, as if the breeziest wind from her own lungs might snap it in two. She stared at the shadows of her surroundings, aware of many reasons why she shouldn't go, the first being her slim chance of actually finding Miguel Lopez.

Then there were the terms of her bail. She was not supposed to leave Travis County.

Which was what Wayne would say to try to talk her out of going. And if he did, what would she have then? A name. A collection of articles and e-mails. A picture with no other facts to frame it.

She sat up in bed and swung her feet over the edge. She felt the solid support of the looped berber carpet underneath her toes. She looked at the clock: 4:22. She could take Rudy's car and get there well before any resident left the house, be back late morning.

Sooner if this was yet another dead end.

How hard would it be to leave without being noticed? She would have to hurry.

She dressed in the dark and gathered up the articles she had stashed in the dresser drawer. She found her purse, which still held Rudy's keys, and her cell phone.

She wrote a note for Wayne by the light of the phone's LED display and left it for him to find on her nightstand. *Please don't worry. I'll be back by noon.* She would have to think through a reasonable explanation for her absence by then. She waffled, then decided to leave the phone with the note. Wayne would think it had been a mistake, and might be less worried than if she ignored his calls.

Shauna eased open her bedroom door. The silence of the little house generated a hum in her ears and she hesitated. Visions of Corbin bleeding in his own bed challenged her decision not to tell Wayne what she was doing. Did Corbin's murderer have eyes on her too? Was he waiting for her to be alone?

Wayne would most definitely stop her.

A killer would stop her permanently.

But she had to know about Miguel Lopez.

She passed through the dim living room, exited the house without incident, descended the porch stairs, and approached Wayne's truck. The cab was unlocked. She eased open the door and slipped her left arm behind the passenger seat to reach her jacket. With any luck the address would still be in the pocket. Her fingers closed around the collar, and she pulled.

The coat snagged, and she gave it a yank. It flew out the door, tossing two silver objects onto the ground, clattering like stones.

She grimaced at the noise, then looked to the house, expecting a light to flicker on.

All stayed dark.

She exhaled and bent to fetch the items, but when she saw them, she hesitated to pick them up. Moonlight glinted off the cool shell of a cell phone that had popped open when it hit the ground. And a camera.

The phone was not Wayne's. She looked at the backlit display.

C. Smith.

Corbin Smith?

She reached out to pick up the camera, then stopped at the sight of a laminated tag attached to the camera strap by a plastic toggle.

It was a press badge. Corbin's photo ID smiled up at her from the ground.

All lingering doubts she had allowed herself to entertain regarding the intentions of Wayne Spade solidified into certainty.

The fear that rushed her now was new and unfamiliar. Blood rushed out of Shauna's head, causing her to drop to her knees for balance. She shivered.

It occurred to her that Wayne's decision to hide these here made no reasonable sense. Did he mean to point the finger at her?

She had the presence of mind not to touch Corbin's things with her bare hands. Holding her jacket in front of her, she slipped her arms into the sleeves and swaddled the camera, then the phone, and held the bundle close to her chest.

When her lightheadedness eased, she closed the door of the truck with only a click—loud in her ears—and moved as quickly and smoothly as possible to Rudy's little two-seater.

Inside, she locked the doors right away. She was parked at the front of the guesthouse and knew that firing the engine would awaken someone. So she slipped the car into neutral and allowed it to roll backward down the sloping drive that led up to the guesthouse. She backed it into the area near the garages of the main house, then turned the key in the ignition and drove off the property.

No doubt one of those security agents had caught sight of her. They didn't worry her, though, not like Wayne worried her.

Within minutes she was on the 183 headed south out of Austin.

As she passed through Lockhart, she spotted a Wal-Mart, took the next exit, and doubled back to buy a box of latex gloves. When she couldn't find these, she settled for a pair of rubber cleaning gloves. They were bulky, but at least she was still able to handle the phone and camera.

Parked under a lot light, Shauna pulled Corbin's things out of her jacket, then fished for the slip of paper she hoped was still there. It was. She opened it up and stuck it on the display panel in front of her speedometer.

Then she flipped Corbin's phone open. She scrolled through the contacts list but didn't recognize any of the first few names. She quickly scanned the list of calls made and found, at the very top, all three of the troubling text riddles sent to her phone the morning of Corbin's murder. There was her reply as well: *Who are you?*

Corbin had sent these? Why?

These riddles taunted. *Shauna take warning . . . 4get and b happy.* Her two encounters with Corbin were full of mystery but not threat. These messages were closer to the poetry, the fragment the killer had left for her to read. *Better by far to forget and smile . . .*

She checked the times. Nearly half past three in the morning. Had Corbin's killer sent these, wanting her to make the connection? Why? To frighten her into giving up this pursuit?

Was Wayne the killer?

He had known Corbin wanted to see her in the morning.

He could have left the bungalow that night without her detecting it.

She hadn't mentioned these text messages and wondered now what he made of her keeping the information from him. She returned to the contacts list and searched for Miguel Lopez. She found him, listed with just one number, an Austin area code. Without thinking of the time, she sent the call and hoped for—

What on earth was she hoping for?

A message told her the number had been disconnected or was no longer in service. Of course. He wasn't in Austin anymore. Only then did she realize how foolish she had been to use the missing cell phone of a murdered man.

Even so, she forced herself to check every other entry, just in case. Near the bottom, she stopped. *Sabueso*. The handle on the e-mails from Khai's envelope. The phone number was attached to a 312 area code. Corpus Christi?

Was *Sabueso* Miguel Lopez? The hidden Lopez? She had no idea, only a Latino name and a Spanish word . . . maybe.

Should she use the phone at all? She'd already made one call. A second couldn't make anything worse than it already was. She pressed *send*. It was not even a quarter after five.

The phone rang and rang, without a voice mail service to pick it up.

Discouraged, she tossed the phone into the plastic shopping bag on the floor of her car and picked up Corbin's camera, a high-end digital Nikon. D3, the face said. She didn't know much about cameras but imagined a professional photographer would have invested generously in something like this. Shauna hoped she hadn't damaged the mechanisms in dropping it.

It took a few minutes of fumbling, but Shauna figured out how to power up the LCD monitor and scroll through the stored images.

First were photos of an accident scene. Auto versus motorcycle. Dated Saturday. Then what appeared to be a board meeting of some sort. Perhaps a school—angry young people and their (she guessed) parents. Dated Friday. A few other images.

Shauna caught her breath. Digital time stamps for Friday and Thursday ran at the bottom of dozens of photos of her. Standing in line at the Dobie Theater with Wayne. Entering her appointment with Dr. Harding. Wayne kissing her at Barton Springs. Arriving at the guesthouse on her father's estate! How had he gotten onto the property? Outside the courthouse. Outside the courtroom. Her making a plea at the arraignment.

Corbin Smith had documented her every move in the days following her arrival home. Had she known, she might have been more frightened of him than she had ever felt toward Wayne.

Scrolling past Thursday, into the earlier part of the week, Corbin seemed to have been entirely focused on work.

Shauna viewed the stories in images all the way back to the previous Saturday and was prepared to shut the camera down when she spotted a familiar face.

Wayne, in conversation with two other men at a location she couldn't identify. A dozen photos of the same gathering gave her only slightly more context; they were in an industrial complex of some kind. A shipyard, maybe.

The battery in the camera died. For now at least, there was no way for her to recharge it. Taking caution, she shut off Corbin's phone too.

What was Corbin's interest in Wayne? Surely these photos were taken on the sly. Wayne had not recognized Corbin outside the courthouse. Either that or Wayne had lied. Again. Everything Wayne had ever said to her was open to question now.

Shauna sighed, knowing nothing more than she had a half hour ago. She looked at the clock on Rudy's dashboard. Nearly five twenty-five. She retraced her path and headed back toward Victoria.

At six thirty, she borrowed a local map from a gas station attendant, and by six forty-five, as the morning sun was casting a glare on the dirty windshield, she drove past a modest park in a middle-class neighborhood. She made two left turns and found the home she was looking for, a small brick bungalow with a neglected front yard buried in brown leaves.

Shauna sat behind the steering wheel, disbelieving that she had come on such a harebrained adventure. Certainly she didn't expect to knock on a door at this hour of the morning and find a man with the answers to all her questions.

Yes, that was exactly what she expected. Anything else would fail her. She got out of the car, passed through a chain-link gate, crushed leaves underfoot on her way up the walk, and lifted her fist to the peeling blue door.

19

If her entire morning hadn't already been saturated in self-doubt, Shauna might have been more certain of what she saw behind Miguel Lopez's tired eyes in the heartbeat it took him to scan her face.

She had seen the fleeting expression one other time, when her mother's doctor exited the surgery room to bring her father life-changing news. Shauna did not understand what the doctor said, and she kept her face turned up to read her father's expression. His eyes told her that their lives were irreversibly changed.

In the moment Miguel Lopez registered Shauna's features, she saw hope and anticipation, devastation and disappointment, accidentally colliding at such top speeds that it was hard to describe what had happened, or if they had in fact existed at all. Because on impact they vanished, nothing more than a magician's illusion, leaving her feeling stunned and slightly manipulated.

He murmured a Spanish word that she could not make out.

She blinked, and Miguel Lopez's eyes were only emotionless black asphalt.

She stuck out her right hand.

"I'm Shauna McAllister. I'm hoping you can talk to me for a few—"

"No." He moved to close the door.

"Please! Your friend Corbin Smith is dead!" she yelled at the closing door. The door stilled. "Murdered. Please let me talk to you."

She kept her eyes on the two-inch crack in the door. It widened.

"He called me here not more than an hour ago."

"You're *Sabueso?*"

Miguel neither confirmed nor denied it.

"That was me. I called, looking for . . . I have his phone." She swiveled to face the car. "I can show you the call logs."

The man hesitated but did not speak.

"Why didn't you answer the phone?" she asked, turning back to him. He refused to answer that as well.

Shauna held up the folder of e-mails and articles that she clutched in her left hand. "We've corresponded. About the presidential campaign." She shoved the folder toward him. "Please," she said again.

Miguel Lopez reopened the door and took the folder from her hands. His eyes glistened as if rain had fallen on their dark surface.

Facing her, he flipped open the folder and dropped his attention to the top page. An article he had written and a photograph Corbin had taken. She read the headline from her upside-down vantage point. He turned to the next page. An e-mail printout. From *Sabueso* to ShaunaM.

HealthWay profits up 30%, production up only 6.3%. Retail steady. Let's find out where it's coming from.

He stepped back from the door as if making room for her to come in but now seemed to avoid looking at her at all. "You drop in on everyone at this hour?"

"I can come back later."

"You're here now." He left her standing in the entryway and stalked off.

Drawn curtains darkened the little house, which smelled damp but clean. She closed the door behind her, unsure whether to follow or wait.

"When did it happen?" he asked from another room.

Shauna knew without needing clarification that he was speaking of Corbin. "Yesterday." She stepped into an eat-in kitchen that held a glass table flanked by two chrome chairs. He flipped the light on over the sink and stood with his back to her, still reading—or pretending to read. He stopped turning pages, didn't say anything for a while.

Then, "How?"

"In his sleep. They cut his throat."

Miguel's shoulders slouched. The hair at the back of his head was matted. She'd dragged him out of bed for the awful news.

"I'm sorry," she whispered. "From what I hear he was a very good friend of yours."

Miguel turned around and frowned at her, tilting his head slightly as if perplexed by what she said. Or maybe he was studying her intentions.

He finally said, "Corbin was like my brother. He always said that . . ." Miguel sighed and shook his head. "How did you find me?"

"Corbin gave me your address. In a way. He didn't tell me what it was, but I found it, and it was a gamble, but I thought maybe . . ."

As she spoke, Miguel closed the folder and crossed the floor as if to give the documents back to her. Instead he held them close to his chest with one hand and stepped into her personal space so that their toes were inches apart. He held her eyes with his, asking an unspoken question that she couldn't decipher.

She could see how smooth his skin was, and each hair at the edge of his beard. A long cut over his right eyebrow was in the last stages of healing. Tiny laugh lines framed the corners of his eyes, though he wasn't smiling now. She imagined he was at his worst at this hour, tired, rumpled, dragged out of bed by a crazy woman pounding the door. And yet she found him attractive.

She took an involuntary step backward.

He matched it, closing the gap. His cotton T-shirt smelled like laundry soap. Someone she knew used that kind of detergent.

His gaze was persistent, but she didn't understand. She dropped her eyes to his olive skin and splayed hand pressing the folder to his chest. She could hear him breathing and felt her own lungs quicken, which confused her. She held her breath to bring it under control.

This did not feel like fear, but like a high school crush about to be devastated. Was he angry that she had come? Was her intrusion offensive? What was he going to do?

She knew in a second: he was going to refuse to help her.

The image of him raising a pistol to her face sent her backward one more step. Her heel hit a wall.

This time he did not move except to hold the papers out to her.

"Mr. Lopez . . ." she said.

The light laugh that escaped his lips at this formality was more a burst of sound, a single short note that could have suggested either mirth or pain. Shauna reached out with her left hand to take the papers and he grabbed hold of her palm, flipped it over, rubbed his thumb across the back of her fingers once in a quick gesture at once intimate and impersonal, then let go.

He finally broke eye contact. "Thank you for telling me," he said. And then he left the kitchen as if to see her out.

She caught her breath, then followed. "There's something else."

He continued to the front door, opened it, and kept his hand on the knob.

"Corbin was helping me to reme—to investigate some things."

Miguel stayed where he was.

"I was in an accident. My brother . . . almost died. I was driving."

Miguel looked at the tile floor. Shauna approached him but stayed at a distance.

"The story they're telling me about what happened doesn't make sense. Maybe it's that I don't want to believe it, but really, I can't. I couldn't have done what they say I did."

"How is it that you don't know what you did?"

"I can't remember it."

"You can't remember?"

Shauna swallowed, hearing aloud how improbable that sounded.

"I was in a coma. A drug trial. My head—look at me, please."

Miguel would not.

"I've lost months. I need to get them back."

"I'm a journalist, not a brain surgeon."

"Corbin says—said—he was in contact with a witness. Someone who has a different version of the story to tell. I need to find this person. Do you know—did Corbin ever tell you?"

Miguel released the doorknob. Crossed his arms. "Did he say he told me?"

"No."

"Then he didn't. I can't help you. You really ought to go."

Two observations kept Shauna rooted to her spot. The first was that the weight of disappointment simply would not allow her to move. It pressed down on her shoulders and wrapped around her hips and screwed her heels into the carpet. Miguel Lopez didn't know anything. Her last resort was a dead end. All the other questions she might have asked him had this not been the case fled her mind and exited the open door.

But the second realization turned her eyes back to Miguel's mouth, which had formed the words *you really ought to go* but got the tone all wrong. The shape of the words was regretful rather than adamant, self-contradicting in fact, and seemed to say instead, *I really hope you won't.*

She heard what she wished for, and the disappointment released her. Shauna kicked off her shoes to make her refusal clear, turned into the adjacent living room, and took a seat on one end of the sofa.

She began counting, hoping the numbers would lead her to the right thing to say, the right questions to begin with. She had reached number eleven when she heard the front door gently close. Miguel came into the living room.

"I really can't help you," he said. She believed he wished he could.

"Can I have a cup of tea?"

"Tea?"

"Do you have any?"

Miguel took a deep breath, looked up at the ceiling as if tea might be hanging there from a string, then returned to the kitchen.

Shauna stayed put and listened to him fill a kettle with water, riffle through a cupboard, set a cup on the counter, free a tea bag from its paper envelope. He did not speak while he waited for the water to boil and did not come out of the kitchen while the bag steeped.

Nine minutes later, Miguel returned.

"I'll take a little milk and—"

"Take it or leave it." He held out the cup filled with tea the color of caramel. There was already milk in it. She sniffed the steam. And sugar. She tasted it. Raw sugar. The way she preferred it. As if she had made it herself.

Miguel watched her.

Her hands turned clammy against the warm mug. "You know me," she said.

"We've corresponded."

"About how I take my tea?"

He sat on the other side of the coffee table in a chair and asked, "Why are you still here?"

"Because you haven't thrown me out yet."

"Yet. I mean it. I can't help you."

Maybe she had only imagined his prior wishful tone. She sipped.

"How did we know each other?" she asked.

"I covered your father's campaign for a while."

"I cut the campaign a wide berth."

"I'm a journalist. I see people who don't want to be seen."

"And when did you become one of us?"

"Who is *us*?"

"People who don't want to be seen."

Miguel shrugged. "I really don't know what you mean."

"You left the *Statesman* within days of my accident."

"I imagine a lot of people you don't know did a lot of things within days of your accident."

This was a veritable tea party with the Mad Hatter.

"Why did you leave the political beat?"

"I didn't. I just left the *Statesman*."

"Why?"

"Greener grass."

"In Victoria?"

"It's a wireless age." He gestured to his laptop on the coffee table. "Green grass grows almost anywhere."

"You're obtuse and annoying."

He leaned back in his chair. "You're a danger to yourself."

Shauna drank her tea to give her time to fathom what he meant.

"A danger?"

"Because you don't know what you are doing."

"There it is: so tell me what I am doing."

"I am not the one to tell you."

"Then who is?"

Miguel crossed his hands over his stomach. He nodded to her drink. "You almost done with that?"

"It's rude to run off a guest."

"It's rude to wear out your welcome."

Shauna scooted to the edge of the sofa cushion and set down her half-full mug on the coffee table, struck by an idea. She stood and walked around the coffee table, then sat on its opposite edge so that she was knee to knee with Miguel, shins almost touching.

He shifted to put some distance between them.

"You don't want me to go," she said.

"You're self-absorbed too."

His eyes seemed pained.

She leaned forward and rested one hand on his knee, hoping for a connection, an image, a memory.

Did she have any control over this . . . this *thing*, this ability at all? Miguel studied her hand but made no move to withdraw further or remove it from his knee.

"Why would anyone want to kill Corbin?" she asked.

He seemed not to have heard her.

"Corbin seemed to think I was mixed up in something. He acted"—Shauna weighed her words—"secretive. Protective."

The staccato sounds seemed to snap Miguel out of his reverie. He met the challenge in Shauna's gaze and matched her body posture, leaning in toward her face.

"Do you want to be protected?"

"What on earth am I in danger of?"

In one swift move he took her chin in his hand, not the gesture of a lover, but of a scolding parent who wanted his child's full attention. When he squeezed her jaw between his fingers, she winced. His frown deepened and his eyes turned glassy.

"You are in danger of everything that you do not think is dangerous," he said.

"Are you dangerous?"

"Yes."

For a shocking moment, Shauna thought he was going to kiss her. Or hit her. She tugged against his grip and, when she found herself immobile, she closed her eyes and held her breath, waiting for whatever came next.

Though she had been hoping for it moments earlier, she was not prepared for the flash of light when it came—the bright promise of an insight, the expectation of a coveted piece of information that Miguel would not give up on his own.

Nor did she expect it to be followed in an instant by blackness, immediate and total and chilling. She'd come away with *nothing*.

Her mind reeled as if it had been kicked across a field. She opened her eyes and spread out her arms, palms down, dizzy.

Miguel was on his feet, standing back from her, his chair toppled as if he had jumped up and knocked it over. He was staring at her, one hand bracing the crown of his head, the gesture of a desperate man.

He leaned over and gripped her by the arm, yanked her upright off the table.

"You really ought to go." This time, there was no discrepancy between the words' meaning and their delivery. He marched her out of the room.

On the way past the sofa, he bent over to scoop her folder off the seat, slapped the manila against her chest so that she was forced to take it, then, still gripping her arm, dragged her to the door.

"There are things you need to forget," he said, throwing the door open with his free hand.

What had happened? How had this gone sideways so quickly?

"You sound like Wayne," she complained, sinking under the burden of disappointment again.

"Like who?" Miguel's grip tightened and her fingers began to go numb.

"Wayne Spade. A . . . colleague." The image of Miguel leveling that gun would not leave her mind. "You know him, I think. Don't like him, I'd guess."

"And why would you guess that?"

"How many journalists you know walk around threatening to kill people?"

"Is that what he told you?"

"Not in so many words."

"Does Wayne know you're here?" Miguel asked.

Shauna shook her head. Miguel released her and she let herself sink against the wall, hopeless. Nothing about this man or his place in her past life—real or imagined—made any sense at all to her. He dragged a hand down over his neat beard, considering her frustration. She slid down the wall into a squat and tipped her head back.

"Shauna." When she looked at him again, he was kneeling in front of her. The sound of his voice, now soft, speaking her name, was hope resurrected.

"I am helping you in ways you can't understand right now. Whatever this looks like to you, I need you to believe that it is protective. It is for your best."

She shook her head.

"Shauna."

"I need more than that."

"I can't give you more."

"You mean you won't."

"I mean *I can't.*"

"Why not?"

Miguel sighed and reached for her shoes, which she had kicked off just a few feet away. He cradled her right foot in his hand and slipped on her shoe in one smooth motion, a gentle act that caused her mind to drop every other crushing reality except one: this little bungalow in Victoria, Texas, might be the only safe place for her in the universe.

He did the same with her left foot, and then helped her to stand.

"I will tell you one thing that you ought to know."

"*Please.*"

"Wayne Spade is not your friend."

"How about something I don't already know?"

Miguel stared at her. He dropped her hand and took a step back. All tenderness abandoned, he laid a hand on her shoulder and directed her out the door.

"You will not come back here," he said.

She turned around and he set the door between them. She heard the deadbolt turn.

20

Shauna did not see much of her surroundings as she pointed her car north and set it on the highway back toward Austin, where Wayne and the legal system expected her to be. She needed to process this. She needed a plan.

Going to Victoria had been a ludicrous idea. On the other hand, it was no more ludicrous than her other method of fact-finding, to be sure—stealing people's memories. And Miguel Lopez in the flesh was at the very least confirmation that the memories she took were real. Her faith in her ability was on the way up.

She had become a memory stealer without having the foggiest idea where this skill had come from. But she understood so little these days, and she had other more important questions to sort out.

How could she get more memories? And how could she get the ones she needed most—the memories that she could use to reconstruct her own story? She needed to try harder than she had so far, hoping with haphazard wishes for something to happen.

Shauna tried to boil down her experiences to the bare minimum factors that were present each time she'd experienced a dream or a vision. By the time she reached the little rural town of Gonzales, she had narrowed the field to two:

Physical touch.

Emotional vulnerability.

The first was easy; the second much harder to create. She could only invite that kind of openness in a person. She couldn't demand it. And still unknown was whether she could fish for particular memories. If she was at the mercy of neurons that fired through history at random, unearthing the truth would take too long.

And the cost to her pride might be more than she was willing to pay. The whole fiasco with Scott Norris could very well show up in print someday.

Nevertheless, by the time she entered the southern city limits of Austin, she had formulated a thin plan to gather as much of the truth as possible from Wayne.

No more secrets, he had said. She would hold him to it.

Shauna considered rebooting Corbin's phone but thought better of it— what if Wayne recognized the number?—and pulled off to use a gas station's pay phone instead. She called Wayne. He picked up before the first ring had sounded through.

"Shauna?"

"Way—who is this?"

"Shauna, where are you? We've been worried sick!"

"Uncle Trent?"

"I came in this morning to see you, honey. Wayne told me you know everything."

"Not quite everything, I'm sure." She wondered how many lies Wayne had told her father's best friend to keep up his charade, how many plates of deception Wayne could spin at the same time. She would need to take care with what she said or risk endangering Trent Wilde's life as well.

"I'm sorry for the secrets, Shauna. I wanted to talk with you about it myself when the time was right. That came sooner than expected. I hope you understand why we felt it was necessary."

"Of course." Although this particular piece of knowledge left many other questions unanswered. "Where's Wayne?"

"Gone crazy with worry."

"I left him a note."

"Not always enough, sweetheart. He's wrapping up a shower."

"Tell him I'm on my way in."

"Better: meet us at Town Lake in half an hour. The picnic area off the south parking lot. We'll pick up some breakfast."

"I'd really rather—"

"Landon is back in town, Shauna. Let's talk first before you see him again."

"If I'm lucky I won't see him again."

"Town Lake it is, then."

"Uncle Trent? How's Rudy?"

"Missing you, honey. But otherwise fine. Pam Riley knows her stuff."

"Can you talk to Patrice for me? About lifting her lockdown? Letting me back in the house to see Rudy?"

"Well, I can talk, but as to whether she'll listen . . ."

"Landon won't even try to convince her."

"I'll do what I can, sweetheart."

"Thanks."

"See you soon."

She waited in the grass along the side of the bike path, watching the water flow downstream and contemplating whether her idea would work or fail spectacularly. If the latter, she would probably face consequences that she could not foresee. Maybe she should abandon this angle, dream up something more reasonable.

As if anything about her situation fell into the category of reasonable.

She heard a shout—her name—and turned to see Wayne waving at her and walking ahead of Trent Wilde. Wayne outpaced his boss in just a few strides and reached Shauna quickly, pulling her to him.

"You're okay! Where did you go? Why didn't you tell anyone?" She had not expected the worry in his voice, and it set her on edge, deception after deception.

She could play along.

"I left you a note—didn't you see it?"

"I did, but after Smith's murder I couldn't imagine . . . you should have woken me up, or Khai. *Someone.* Where have you been?"

"I . . . the murder rattled me too. I needed some time to think."

"Think *here* next time, okay? With me? I can give you space and stay close at the same time."

He was so dangerously convincing.

"I will. I promise."

"Where did you go?"

"I just . . . drove. To clear my head."

Shauna turned to greet Uncle Trent, but Wayne kept an arm around her waist. She leaned into him willingly even as Trent placed an affectionate kiss on her forehead.

"You look good, honey," Trent said, smoothing the front of his wool blazer. Black turtleneck today, contrasting with that fuzzy white hair.

"Feeling better."

"Glad to hear it." His permanent smile widened. The man was downright optimistic at all times and never failed to warm her heart.

"Does Landon know about the murder?" she asked Trent.

"The news stayed local as far as I know. If he heard, I doubt he knows you're connected in any way," he said.

"I'm not exactly connected."

"I doubt Landon and Patrice would see it any other way," Wayne said.

"Well, so far the press is in the dark, fortunately," said Trent.

The dreadlocked Scott Norris flashed across her mind. She would have to promise him yet another favor to keep him quiet on that point.

Instead of explaining, she said, "And so we're going to treat this news just as we've treated the accident."

"There's no need to *treat* it any way so long as Landon remains unaware," said Trent. "What he doesn't know won't hurt him, right?" He winked at Shauna.

"That's not really up to me, is it?"

"What do you mean?" said Wayne.

"Detective Beeson comes around asking more questions and Landon will figure it out soon enough. Nothing I can do about that."

"You were an unfortunate witness," Wayne said. "He has your story, no need to keep poking around in it. And Landon is almost never around these days."

He spoke so easily for a man with a dead man's camera and phone in his possession. She kept her voice level. "The detective has no reason to think my story's true. I don't even understand all of it myself."

Wayne squeezed Shauna. "What you know is true. You're still too wrapped up in everything you think you don't know, Shauna. Have a little faith."

Oh, she did have plenty of faith in the truth she had unearthed thus far.

"And we'll make Beeson go through the attorney, honey," Trent said. "This will be over soon."

"That would be nice. I'm ready to move on, put the past behind me."

Wayne's eyes caught hers and brightened.

"I've talked to Delaney," Trent said. "You meet with him Thursday?" Shauna nodded. "He says this whole thing can be handled in a simple plea agreement. You won't even have to serve any time. We'll keep your record clean, get you moving on with your life."

"That sounds nice. I need to start looking ahead."

"You let us help with that, okay?" Wayne said.

"That's right, honey. You let us help. I've got a place for you at MMV if you want it. You come with us to Houston, and I'll make sure my girl is taken care of. But you take the time you need, hear?"

Shauna smiled and hoped it looked genuine. "That is really more than I deserve. Thank you."

"Not at all. Now, Wayne, my man"—Trent handed over to Wayne a white paper sack that he'd been holding—"you two fill your bellies while I go pay my respects to the senator. Gotta be on the afternoon puddle jumper to catch a meeting tonight."

"Thanks for coming all the way out, Uncle Trent."

"Happy to do it, sweetheart."

He shook hands with Wayne, and Shauna watched him leave.

Wayne released her waist and took her by the hand, then led her down the path to a picnic table in view.

"I can't tell you what a relief it is to me to see you move on."

She breathed more evenly, buoyed by the possibility that he believed her claims. "I never meant to worry you about it."

"No no no. It's not like that." Their steps hit the ground in sync. "But I do care about you."

"You've been wonderful. I'm sure I haven't made it easy."

"Well, that's not your fault now, is it?" He set the bag on the table and turned to take Shauna's other hand, so that he held them both as she faced him. She couldn't have choreographed this more to her favor. "But your choosing to leave the past behind does make things easier. There's only so much I can do to help with that, and the rest of the time I have to stand on the sidelines and worry about your getting hurt. This way you'll get—we'll get—a clean slate. Come with me to Houston."

Wayne's request was so full of anticipation that it invited her to take a step closer, closing the gap between them. She looked her first real intentional opportunity in the face.

He half leaned, half sat against the short end of the table.

"I have to wait for the trial."

"Maybe not so long, if we can strike a plea agreement."

"You don't care about the Ecstasy charges?"

"I don't believe there's anything to them. And I know what I believe about you."

She dropped her eyes and her voice. "Which is?"

"That you are stunning and wise and incapable of hurting anyone."

Wayne was taking this act to greater distances than Shauna had anticipated. She tried to match his stride.

"And you have been more kind than I deserve."

He smiled at her.

"How about the drug trial, my therapy?"

"Nothing that can't be done in Houston."

"And what about Rudy?"

"What about him?"

"I can't leave him."

"Houston isn't that far away. You're making excuses now?"

She laughed. "No, I'm just trying to think through everything. Think in a new direction." She made sure to look directly into his eyes. "You seem to know how to get me where I need to go."

She slipped her arms up onto his shoulders, half wishing she could have the security he offered instead of the hit-or-miss answers her pretense might be able to get from him. She allowed her fingertips to brush the fine hairs at the base of his neck.

On the other hand, did it really matter if there was no clear-cut line between what he willingly offered her and what she wanted to take? Maybe not. She had to know what she was capable of learning.

He pulled her closer to him and she went willingly. "I don't know what I would do without you," she whispered.

"No need to find out," he said, so close to her that she felt rather than saw his lips move.

This time, she waited for him to kiss her. She closed her eyes and in the breath it took him to meet her lips, she set her mind firmly on the night of the accident—on Cale Bowden's accident report, on the skid marks she'd seen on the bridge, on Wayne wading into the water to save her—hoping that Wayne's mind might give up what it had stored away.

The lake threw off a breeze that caught the back of Shauna's neck. She shivered and felt her knees give way, and then it seemed the ground opened. She started to drop and instinctively closed her eyes, but when she continued to fall, she found the will to open them.

She fell through a vertical black tunnel lined with images, three-dimensional, nearly holographic. Random images, hundreds of images, of schools, sports, clubs, office spaces, people. She tried to focus on one or two and found the rate of her descent decrease. She reached out to touch one of the pictures and got an electric shock.

Foreign locations—a desert, a forest—were in some of the pictures. She saw her family. She saw herself. She saw a hospital. Water.

She saw her car and reached out for the image as if she could grab it and stop her fall completely. Her hands burned when she plunged them into the grainy image. She kept falling, and then the bottom of the tunnel opened like the platform of a dunk tank and dropped her into a well of freezing water. Her breath caught in her throat and her body went numb.

The cold rose to her waist.

She opened her eyes and saw herself coughing in the water of a black river, slapping the surface as if it might hold her up. Was this her own memory? She had come close enough to dying then, perhaps.

No, it was the memory of someone watching her.

Wayne. He had pulled her out.

She saw herself call his name between gasps of frozen breath, and he reached for her. Gripped her shoulder with his left hand.

Shoved her under the water.

Held her down.

Held her. Under.

Shauna could not be sure if the fear that penetrated her then was cast off of the memory or resident in the moment, in the truth of what she saw. Wayne Spade had tried to drown her.

He had, in fact, tried to knife her. On his right hand, she saw his blue class ring; and in his right palm, a short knife with a pearl handle.

He dropped the knife into the water behind him as if it were a scoop on a water wheel, and brought it up against the drag until it hit flesh. Her flesh.

He withdrew the blade and drove it in again.

In some other world, Shauna felt a pointed ache in her ribs.

The third time, he lifted the weapon out of the water, and the moonlight bounced off a broken tip.

Sirens sounded, bouncing off the bank of the river.

He swore, crammed the knife into his pocket, and bent over her, scooping her up under her armpits. She appeared to be unconscious. The water fell off her skin as he dragged her in, her heels scraping over rocks and grit onto a shore covered in dry winter scrub.

He rolled her onto her back and began to administer CPR.

When he covered her mouth with his, she lifted her palms to his chest and pushed him off.

Opened her eyes onto the blues and greens of Town Lake.

Wayne released her waist immediately and she realized they were both shaking. They were two steps away from the picnic table, and the breeze had become a whipping wind. She wrapped her arms around herself. Wayne's hands quivered and he tried to find something to do with them. He covered his mouth with his right hand, and the blue ring caught the light. His eyes were as cold as the water had been.

"I'm sorry," she said. "I didn't mean—"

He dropped his hand. "No. It's my fault. That was . . ."

When he groped for the word she said, "Pretty intense."

He laughed. It was forced. "I hope I didn't come on too strong."

"No! No. Not at all. I wasn't expecting . . ."

He didn't try to fill in her blank, though he studied Shauna for several long seconds. What had he sensed of that encounter, above and beyond the immediate reality? She had never thought to ask whether her gift opened information highways that ran in both directions. How much had they shared, if anything?

She rubbed her own arms to hide the shaking. Though no longer cold, she was filled with fresh terror.

Better by far you should forget and smile
Than that you should remember and be sad.

Oh, how she understood now.

She attempted to lay a hand on his arm in a gesture that she hoped would ease the awkwardness. Protect her from his probing gaze. He turned out of her reach quickly, pretending, she thought, not to have seen her move. He shoved both hands into his pockets and looked at the food sack.

"You hungry?"

21

For the rest of that day and into the next, Wayne seemed intent on both avoiding Shauna's touch and not leaving her side, breaking this code only once, when he gave her an overstated peck on the back of her hand before they parted ways for the night in the living room of the guesthouse.

She awoke in the night to sounds of him moving about in the living room. Keeping watch to make sure she didn't run off again? Planning to come in, smother her while she slept?

Shauna did not go back to sleep.

How could she get out from under his murderous eye?

He had not wanted her to remember that he had tried to kill her. He had insinuated himself into her life as her lover in order to hold the memory at bay.

If she hadn't developed this bizarre ability of hers, Shauna had no doubt it would have worked. She would be planning now to leave this miserable home behind and make a new one in Houston with her worst enemy.

Would he kill her there? Stage another tragedy? Another accident?

Had her accident been staged? If it had, she wasn't responsible for Rudy's condition. Someone else was. Wayne Spade. If she could prove it, she could have peace of mind and Rudy could have justice, if not his old life.

Assuming Wayne hadn't simply made an opportunity out of an unfortunate event.

Why had Wayne wanted her dead in the first place?

Maybe Corbin had known the answer to that question.

If that was the case, why didn't Corbin tell her that day at the *Statesman?* Why bring her, and his death, to his home? What was more dangerous about telling her then and there?

Okay. So maybe Corbin didn't know, but his witness did.

That didn't make sense. Why wouldn't Wayne kill the witness? Because he didn't know who the witness was? Did he kill Corbin to warn the witness? To draw the witness out?

A headache took root in the back of Shauna's head and snaked around over her ears.

Maybe there was no witness. Just a straw man Corbin created to protect himself, though that had done little good. If, however, he knew of a witness who might divulge what he—she?—had seen, why withhold this information until Shauna snapped out of her coma? Why not go right to the police on day one? What would be the point of telling her and not the law?

Simply to keep her out of Wayne's reach?

That didn't make sense either. Corbin could have said so without all the dramatic mumbo jumbo.

If Miguel Lopez were the witness who wanted to keep her alive, he would have said, "Wayne Spade wants to kill you." Not, "Wayne Spade is not your friend."

Not your friend. Understatement of the eon.

At this point Shauna believed she understood more about this situation than Miguel and Corbin ever did. When the first beam of light rose off the floor of her room, she had more questions and only a few certainties:

She was not safe with Wayne.

She was probably not safe anywhere until she knew why Wayne had wanted her dead. Maybe still wanted her dead, though this was not clear. She couldn't exactly ask.

A nice conundrum. She could pretend to "forget," go with the flow, go to Houston, and perhaps end up dead anyway. Or she could keep along her present path, find all her answers, and probably die in the process.

What decided her course was the possibility that she could redeem her reputation and her relationship with her father. If he believed she did not harm her brother, he might forgive her. He might allow her back into that very small family circle that she had been expected to leave. He might. She needed to escape Wayne, and until she figured out how, she would do all the pretending she was capable of.

Something had happened to Wayne during that kiss, and as he drove her to her therapy appointment that morning with Dr. Harding, she spent the mostly silent commute speculating about what it was, what he thought it was, and whether he believed she had engineered the event.

"I appreciate your driving me," she attempted at one point.

He smiled at her, the same kind smile he had offered her several times every day since she had first seen him at the hospital. But today he smiled to disguise something. Or perhaps he always had.

"No problem."

"I thought I'd ask her what she thinks of our Houston idea."

Wayne nodded and kept his eyes on the road.

"Well, if she thinks it's a bad one, we'll go to Houston and find you a second opinion." He chuckled at his own joke. She laughed along.

They had become the proverbial cat and mouse.

Maybe they always were, and she had been the mouse. Now she would make herself the cat.

He reached across the gear shift and squeezed her knee, then released it. A test. She smiled at him, confident that nothing would put his memories at risk with his guard up so high. Maybe he would eventually find false security in that. For now, she needed to find other ways to test the measure of her ability.

She needed to know if she could duplicate yesterday's success.

She needed a person who would open up to her, a person whose memories she had not already snagged.

And she needed to know if she was truly snagging them, not merely sharing them.

She needed a guinea pig. She needed Dr. Millie Harding.

Wayne had promised to wait in the car while Shauna had her appointment.

"An hour's a long time to wait," she protested.

"I've got the laptop with me." He retrieved his phone from the console. "And I can make a couple calls to the office."

"You're supposed to be on vacation."

"If it's more vacation than work, it's still vacation."

She had considered calling Uncle Trent, maybe talk him into luring Wayne back from vacation prematurely. She would have to head off Trent's worries about her safety without telling him that the real danger was practically hold-ing her hand. If she jeopardized her only "uncle," she would tie one more stone around her neck before casting herself into the Colorado River. She'd have to come up with a plan to reassure Trent that she was perfectly fine and would be even better if Wayne were gone. Getting Wayne to do what his boss wanted would be more tricky. No, getting Wayne to leave her would be virtually impossible, once she thought it through. Maybe she would have to wait out this season and hope Wayne didn't knife her before it was over.

An unfathomably stupid idea.

Now, forty-five minutes into the conversation, Shauna still pondered how she could steal a memory from Dr. Harding and then verify that it was stolen. This was an opportunity she could not waste, but in fifteen minutes there would be nothing left of it to retrieve.

While she considered this, her mind barely engaged in the session, she convinced Dr. Harding that visions they'd previously discussed had become a nonissue, that she didn't know any more about the six months of her vacant memory than she had at their last meeting, and that her relationship with Wayne, while pleasant, had not done anything to illuminate Shauna's history.

"So Wayne has been supportive," Dr. Harding observed.

Shauna did her best to gush. "More than that: *attentive*. I could not have survived this without him."

"He does have a sensitive side, doesn't he?"

The observation begged Shauna to take note of it. The words themselves were benign enough, but something maternal in the tone caused Shauna to say, "You know him? Personally, I mean?"

The psychiatrist's cheeks twitched. "I was only basing my remark on what you've told me."

Shauna nodded, smiled to restore the ease in the room. Was Wayne a patient of hers? A colleague?

A boss?

Dr. Harding cleared her smoky throat. "You seem far more relaxed today than you did on our first meeting." She picked her cup of tea off the small tray that balanced on the vinyl stool.

"I suppose I've had time to grow accustomed to the idea of having a gap in my life."

"Has it caused you any unexpected hardship?"

Woefully unexpected hardship.

"Surprisingly, no." Shauna tried on a light laugh and let her eyes flit around the room. They landed on that glistening file cabinet at the same moment that her opportunity presented itself. If the wild-haired psychiatrist knew Wayne Spade, perhaps Shauna could find evidence to that effect in the file. A memo, an e-mail, a whole file.

That, and the cabinet was locked by a digital combination. Could Shauna fetch this information from the doctor's mind?

She would try. At the very least, Shauna believed she could find a detailed set of notes and evaluations about herself. That was worth something.

"It's little things," Shauna said. "I have outfits in my closet I don't remember buying. Pictures from a party I don't remember attending. I can't remember why I quit my job or where I put my latest résumé—it didn't help that the family moved all my stuff around! Sometimes I mix up phone numbers. Yesterday I forgot the PIN number for my ATM card."

Shauna did not feel the smallest pinch of guilt over any of these fibs. Her life was surrounded by lies and liars, it had turned out, and if she had to tell a few herself to see her way through them, so be it.

Dr. Harding nodded and set down her pen. "Well if it's any comfort, I forget numbers like that all the time."

Shauna sipped from her own cup, moved in. "There's so many to remember!"

"True. Today the average person's memory is taxed by so much information, it's a wonder we can function at all."

"How do you do it?"

"Do what? Function?"

"No, remember all the details. Online passwords, your bank account numbers"—she noted a wedding band on Dr. Harding's left hand—"your husband's social security number?"

"Oh goodness. I don't remember all of it. Memory is accidental sometimes.

We remember something only because we use it over and over again. I tend to remember that sort of thing."

Of course. Repetition. Shauna's eyes went to the high-tech file cabinet for a fleeting second. *Think. Think. Think.*

Shauna leaned forward and picked up the teapot to warm the psychologist's cup. "More?"

"Thank you." Shauna allowed herself a heavy sigh as she focused on pouring the tea.

"I would like to remember what that feels like," she said. "Everything seems so . . . jumbled."

"Give yourself time, Shauna. It will happen." Dr. Harding removed her narrow reading glasses and folded them on her notepad. Shauna moved the teapot over her own cup. "I have a son your age."

Shauna held her breath and set down the pot.

"You remind me of him somewhat. He's impatient too." Dr. Harding smiled as Shauna lifted a cup and passed it to her. Now was the time to try. She grasped the handle so that she nearly covered it with her fingers, and wrapped the other side of the cup snuggly in her other hand. She appeared to be a wind-chilled adventurer looking for warmth, and maybe she was.

The grip forced Dr. Harding to touch her to take the cup.

Shauna closed her eyes and held the image of that file cabinet front and center in her mental screen. She held it there, willing it not to be knocked over by an explosion of other memories.

There was no explosion, but Shauna was hit with an unexpected rush of data like heat from an oven. First a list of names, random and senseless but short: Jacobsen, Brown, Paulito, Vu, Allejandra. Then equally random labels: Active, Committed, Closed, Pending. Then *Harding 4273464.*

Dr. Harding let out a shout of surprise, and Shauna snapped her eyes open. She had sloshed the tea in the psychologist's lap.

"Oh no. Oh no. I can't believe I—"

"Are you okay?" Dr. Harding said. She was rubbing her left temple with two fingers.

"I am such a klutz."

"Not at all." The doctor's detached persona resurrected itself, politeness not quite covering up her thoughts.

"Are *you* okay?" Shauna stammered, disbelieving how little control she'd had over what had happened. "Are you burned?"

"Just wet. That had cooled off a bit."

"What can I do?"

"Stay put a minute while I go dab up. I'll bring back some towels."

She moved off past the desk to a bathroom and kitchenette at the back of the office. Shauna grabbed her purse to find tissues.

4273464.

She looked at the file cabinet, then, prompted into action by a ticking clock that she could sense but not hear, she strode across the office in four long steps and punched the number into the digital panel.

Enter.

The top file drawer popped open.

She hadn't expected it to.

Shauna was so surprised that she took several seconds to register the manila folders lined up in front of her in the drawer, an unremarkable row of both thin and bulky files labeled with surnames and initials. Nothing worthy at first glance of being in a high-security drawer.

Shauna heard water running in the bathroom. She moved quickly. She looked for Wayne's name.

The drawer ended in the *Ks.*

She opened the one beneath it, reaching for the back. *Spade, W.* Not there.

No! She needed something. She rushed in search of her own file. Then she would try the other drawers.

McAllister, S.

There she was. She snatched the folder, a skinny little thing, out of the drawer. Should she take it with her? She looked at her chair, her tote bag. There was room in there.

No. That was idiocy. All she needed to know was that she was beginning to manipulate this gift of hers more precisely. She had no business adding real stealing to the mix.

But her life was in this folder. Would it truly be stealing to take it? Shauna lay the thin file on Dr. Harding's desk and flipped through it, scanning the woman's notes on their meetings so far. No surprises jumped out at her.

She took the notes anyway, leaving a few other documents behind, then rushed the empty file folder back to its drawer.

She flipped back through the names to put it away.

Madigan. Matthews. Marshall.

Marshall, W.

Wayne? She set her own folder on the adjacent counter and, holding the spot with one hand, withdrew his file too. She opened it. One page.

At the top: *Wayne Marshall, aka Wayne Spade.*

The bathroom door opened.

Shauna snatched out the paper, married it to her own notes, dropped the folder back into place, and eased the drawer shut, hoping for silence. The gliders didn't make a noise until she heard the slick click that explained how expensive this four-drawer cabinet was. She raced back to her seat, crammed the pilfered documents into her tote bag, and straightened up holding a tissue packet at the same time Dr. Harding emerged with a dish towel.

"I can't say how sorry I am," Shauna blurted. "I'll leave the hospitality to you from now on."

"No harm done." The psychologist's bright blue broomstick skirt was wet black across the lap. Shauna hoped the woman kept a change of clothes handy.

Shauna blotted at the damp chair, and her tissues disintegrated in seconds. "I hope this won't stain."

"I'll add it to your bill." Shauna straightened, her back to the desk and the file folder, and saw that Dr. Harding was smiling at her. She held out her hand to Shauna. "Let me toss those for you."

Shauna deposited the tissues in her palm and took the dish towel. "If you have to have it cleaned, please send me the tab." She bent over the chair again.

Dr. Harding didn't answer, and when Shauna looked, she saw the red-haired woman bend over the counter to toss the wad in the trash can, then straightening, eyeing the folder on the surface.

She hadn't. Oh, she had. She'd forgotten her own file.

"I must have left this out," the woman murmured. Shauna pretended not to hear. She folded the damp cloth and placed it on the tea tray, then sat down and returned the tissue packet to her purse while she watched from the corner of her eye.

Dr. Harding walked to the cabinet and positioned herself between Shauna and the digital panel. She lifted her hand to punch in the security code and then paused without touching the keypad. Shauna held her breath.

"That's ironic," the therapist said, glancing over at Shauna. "Weren't we just talking about how easy it is to forget things?"

Shauna had her answer. The memories collecting in her mind were not merely borrowed; they were stolen, lifted, filched, as absent from the victims' minds as experiences that had never happened.

Back in the car with Wayne, Shauna found her phone on the passenger seat.

"Detective Beeson called while you were in," Wayne said. "Wants you to come see some photos."

"Now?"

"I told him we could come when you finished."

"Let's go, then."

What would Shauna have done if Dr. Harding's memory had included only patient names and unattached diagnoses? Was it sheer luck that she'd landed on the combination, or information Shauna had successfully targeted? Shauna really didn't have a handle on this at all yet. What if Dr. Harding had unwittingly divulged her bank account information? Her PIN number? How would Shauna have verified the truth of that?

Would Shauna go so far with her need to know that she would commit a crime?

There was confidential data on Wayne stuffed into the side pocket of her purse. So she had already done something illegal. But besides that, how would the law classify her stealing of memories? Most likely she'd be laughed out of her handcuffs at any police station. But assaulting a person with intent to harm—now, that was no laughing matter, was it?

Intent to harm. Sheesh. She wasn't harming anyone.

Was she? She of all people understood the pain and consequences of lost memories.

An image of her mother frowning at her with arms crossed flashed through Shauna's mind.

This wasn't the same.

No. It was not even close to being the same. She was in pursuit of truth. Someone had tried to kill her. She looked at Wayne. She needed to hone this gift just to survive him.

She needed to do this one more time. As was quickly becoming clear to her, she'd likely not have too many opportunities to put her hands on the memories of any one person. Her thievery left impressions.

So what next? What could she reasonably hope to find out with Wayne all but dancing on her toes? She didn't want to fish for life stories and pin numbers.

And who could tell her about her own past? Patrice? That woman wouldn't open up to her any time in the next millennium. Landon? Shauna, frankly, didn't have the guts. Rudy? Too much of a gamble, even if she had access to him. Who could say what might or might not be intact in her little brother's mind? He couldn't afford to have her take any of it.

Her mind moved out of the house. Scott Norris? The reporter was among her failed attempts. Too big a risk to revisit that.

Who, who?

"What did she say?" Wayne asked out of the blue.

"Hmm?"

"What did she say about Houston?"

"Oh that!" Shauna had completely forgotten it. "She said it's a great idea. She said you've been really instrumental in my progress, and she thinks it'd be good for me to stick with you."

He smiled at her. "I'd like that."

"Me too," she murmured. His words were so easy to believe. She had to match them.

"Look, I'll call the attorney today, try to move up your appointment with him. See how quickly we can get this behind us."

Quickly, quickly. Yes. She needed to move fast. Faster than Wayne could move, if she wanted to avoid another Detective Beeson–type processing her murder as well as Corbin Smith's. Faster than might be possible.

22

"Those are pictures of me," Shauna said from the doorway, not sure what she had expected. Murder scene images, maybe. Not this.

They sat in front of a computer monitor in one of Detective Beeson's labs, scrolling through a brief slide show of images. Five images of her, duplicates of the images she had seen on Corbin's camera, but only five. There she was in the courtroom with Wayne, and dining with Wayne, and driving with Wayne, and moviegoing with Wayne. She winced at the photo of her kissing Wayne.

"These were found on the laptop we took from Corbin Smith's apartment," Beeson explained in his baritone voice. Her apartment.

"How many did he take?" she asked.

Beeson uncrossed his arms and shook his head. "Impossible to say without the camera. It seems like these are a select few of many, though. An edited few."

Shauna looked at Wayne. She could not read his expression.

"Why do you think that?" she asked.

"Each of these was e-mailed to the same account at six-hour intervals across Friday and Saturday."

"What account?" Wayne asked. "You have an address?"

Beeson produced a printout of one of the e-mails, which showed the header and the attachment. The message read only, "Snap out of it!"

Shauna looked at the recipient's handle. *Sabueso.* She felt sick. Wayne studied the sheet, swore under his breath.

"You know the recipient?" Beeson asked him.

Wayne shook his head. "Which is only more infuriating," he said.

"Was Mr. Smith stalking you?" Beeson asked Shauna.

She had expected him to ask her about the e-mail address, and so she could not have anticipated the actual question if she'd had an hour to imagine it.

"Stal—*no*. No! He was a member of the media, for goodness' sake."

"That day at the courthouse he all but sneaked up on you," Wayne said.

"Like any paparazzi would." At the same time, Shauna recalled Scott's claim that her story was not generating much public interest.

"Tell me about that," Beeson said.

"I was trying to get her out through the back," Wayne said. "The man was there waiting, practically jumped her."

"He didn't *jump* me."

"But he anticipated where you would be?"

"Obviously," Shauna said. This revelation irritated her.

"Did you ever receive any suspicious phone calls?" Beeson asked. "Anything off-color, maybe any you thought were pranks?"

"No! Not since going home. He didn't even know my phone number!"

"You sure? Because phone records show evidence of three text messages sent to your cell phone from his the night of his death. And a reply from you."

Shauna looked at him and shook her head. Her nerves were zinging, cuing her to flee the room as fast as she could. With all her strength, she kept her feet in place. "What did they say?"

"Don't know. Can't find the phone. Just the records. Care to offer me your phone?" Detective Beeson had moved around the table and now leaned over the back of the monitor.

"Not without a warrant," Wayne muttered. He was writing down *Sabueso's* e-mail address.

His intervention on this point stunned Shauna. She looked at him, still finding it likely that he had sent the messages from Corbin's phone after killing the poor man. So why wouldn't he want Beeson to see the phone? Why was he still compelled to keep up his love-and-protect act?

She'd expected Wayne to hand her over to the authorities, along with Corbin's camera and cell phone, which she had hidden in the closet of her bedroom.

"I'll have one after lunch," Beeson said. "In the meantime, let me get a clear picture here, Ms. McAllister: Mr. Smith was photographing you since the day you left the hospital, but he was not stalking you."

"My father is a media darling. Corbin was a journalist—"

"A photographer," Wayne said.

"He moved into an apartment you used to inhabit, but he was not obsessed with you."

Shauna gripped the back of a chair. She had yet to sit down.

"Tell me again the nature of your scheduled meeting with him?"

"He claimed to have information about the accident I was involved in."

"You said he wasn't connected to your case."

"He *wasn't.*"

"Was the information incriminating?"

"I don't *know* what the information was! And if it was incriminating, why in the world do you think he would give it to me?"

"Because he was obsessed with you. Because he wanted to extort money from you." She dropped her head into her hands. "It would explain how he paid for the place."

Beeson straightened and crossed his arms again. "Let me tell you what I think happened: Daughter of a wealthy politician is in a high-profile accident, accused of pretty serious charges. Most of the evidence county sheriffs are able to collect is circumstantial. Did you know there were no fingerprints lifted from the bottle of MDMA purportedly found in your car?"

Both Shauna and Wayne snapped their eyes to Beeson's. "I haven't met with my attorney yet," Shauna said through tight lips.

Beeson's mouth turned downward, musing. "Maybe the water destroyed the evidence, but from what I can tell the thing was wiped clean."

"I thought that case was in the sheriff's jurisdiction," Wayne said.

"We're not so territorial as you might think," Beeson said. "But I haven't finished my theory yet: local reporter-photographer, whatever he is, realizes he is in possession of incriminating evidence—"

"What evidence?"

Beeson's eyebrows rose. "—and rather than deliver it to authorities, he decides to take over your old life, stalk you, blackmail you."

Shauna sank into a chair and Wayne put a steadying hand on her shoulder.

She shrugged it off. Word by word, Detective Beeson shredded her first impression of him as a softhearted rookie.

"You are furious. You want off this legal hook. You set up a meeting with him to buy his silence."

"I didn't."

"And because he would overpower you in a fight, you let yourself into his home—for reasons I cannot guess, he has not changed the locks—"

"The door was open."

"And kill him in his sleep."

She shook her head.

"You can't prove any of this," Wayne said.

"Ms. McAllister, where is Corbin Smith's camera?"

Shauna balked. She could not let Wayne know she had it. "It was gone when I arrived that morning."

"When you arrived with Mr. Spade it was gone. Where did you take it the night before?"

"I didn't," she whispered. "I wasn't there."

"Shauna, babe, he's fishing." Wayne placed his hand under Shauna's arm and directed her to the door. Her stomach seized, smothered in this room with a man who wanted to kill her and a detective who wanted to convict her. "Is she under arrest?"

Of course, if Shauna could get Beeson to arrest her, she might stand a chance of bending his ear without Wayne around to listen. But an arrest would also further complicate everything.

"Not yet."

"Then she is not going to sit here and take this abuse from you."

So much pretending.

"I'll be in touch after lunch, Ms. McAllister. Stay in the area."

The afternoon glare cut through the colonnade of river birch that lined each side of the McAllisters' private drive. The trees hadn't yet started to bud, and the naked branches cast shadows in lines alternating with harsh noontime sun.

Shauna closed her eyes against the strobe effect. Exhaustion from her sleepless night and circumstances pounced on her.

"What should I do?" It was the third question Shauna had asked that Wayne did not answer. He gripped the wheel of his truck and frowned as he drove, apparently undecided about his own course of action.

Shauna hadn't wanted him to answer any of the questions so much as buy into her act of dependence on him. She was even less certain than before, however, that he bought anything from her at all.

"Did you really get three calls from Smith's number?" he said after a full minute of silence, as if she hadn't spoken a word.

"Text messages," she said. "I didn't know who sent them. I could delete—"

"Why didn't you tell me?"

Shauna thought hard on her answer. This question did not contain the usual warm concern. And what to do with her belief that he had sent the messages?

"You were so worried about the other stuff already. I didn't want you to stop me from going to see—"

"What did they say?"

"I don't—I can't remember exactly." She pulled her phone out of her purse, trembling. "I'll show you." She flipped the cell open and found the first message, handed it off to Wayne. He scrolled through, only half his attention on the road now. He spent more time studying them than it could have taken to read them. What was he looking for?

She feared his next question would be about Corbin's camera. It was impossible that he hadn't realized it was gone from his truck.

"Will Beeson really get a warrant?" Shauna asked.

"Yes. Did you reply to any of these?" She showed him. "Don't erase anything. I don't see how this incriminates you. If anything, it could help."

"Shouldn't we ask the attorney?"

"No." He gave the phone back to her. "You should have told me about these."

"And what would you have done if I had?" Shauna hadn't meant to sound annoyed, but there it was. Wayne looked at her sideways and frowned.

He measured his words. "I would have prevented you from getting involved."

She tested the waters. "Involved in what?"

"What do you think?"

"I don't know what to think, Wayne. How could you have known that the texts were connected to Corbin?"

"What exactly are you suggesting?"

"I'm suggesting that you"—she barely caught her recklessness before it ran away—"would have known. Corbin's number. Would have known that he was in trouble of some kind."

"And just how would I know that?" Wayne pulled into the drive and threw the gearshift into park, turned, and drilled her with his frustration. His eyes were hard.

She reached out to him to defuse the situation. She had gone too far.

In one swift motion, though, he snatched her wrist and yanked her arm toward him. She gasped, surprised both by his force and his anger. Why did Beeson's accusations of her have him so rattled?

"Don't try to smooth this over, Shauna." Her name was a hiss between his teeth. "I have done my best to earn your trust, but if you're going to go sneaking around because you think I'm the bad guy here, there won't be anything I can do to help you."

Shauna tugged on her arm but he held it fast. His breath was hot on her face.

"*Tell me* what you think my involvement with Corbin was."

She could not come up with any lies. Only a half-truth. What would he do to her if she told? If she didn't?

"I found Corbin's phone in your truck."

Shock replaced the anger in Wayne's eyes. Shauna knew she was not as good a judge of character as Khai might be, but she believed fully that the news had stunned Wayne. His lips parted and he dropped her wrist. He straightened and stared out the windshield for a moment, and when he looked back at Shauna, all hostility had left him.

If he knew she was not telling the full truth, he would ask her what else she had found.

"Where was it?" he asked.

"Wrapped in my jacket."

Wayne grabbed his laptop out of the back, then put his hand on the door and opened it. "Where is it now?"

"It's in my room."

"And what a perfect place for it. Why don't you set it out on the table for Beeson to find?"

His condescension stung. She stared at him.

"Go get it," he said. Then he stormed into the house.

Shauna stumbled up the steps after him, thinking through how to retrieve the phone without also showing him the camera.

What was she going to do with the camera?

Wayne took his laptop into his room first, giving Shauna just enough time to grab a tissue and get the phone out of the WalMart bag that she'd hidden on the floor in the back of her closet. She rushed out her bedroom door, right into Wayne's chest.

She held the phone out to him, wrapped in the tissue. He evaluated this, then took it from her while looking her in the eye.

"You're smarter than a lot of folks give you credit for, Shauna."

She was too afraid to be insulted.

He leaned in to her and placed a cold kiss on her forehead.

"Don't go anywhere. I'll make some calls."

He returned to his room and closed the door.

Shauna moved immediately. She had only minutes, if not seconds. She rushed to her closet, collected the camera, and burst into Khai's room through their shared bathroom without knocking.

"Khai, I need your help."

Khai was putting clean linens on the bed. Shauna shoved Corbin's bundled camera into the woman's hands.

"This camera belonged to Corbin Smith. I need you to take it to a detective at the police department for me."

"How did you—"

"I found it in Wayne's truck. I don't have time to explain, but I need you to take this down now. Do not tell Wayne."

Khai lifted her eyebrows but didn't ask.

"The detective is Beeson. Tell him that I found this in Wayne's truck. Tell him what you told me about how Corbin was helping you, that the pictures on it might connect some dots—" And in that split second, some dots connected in Shauna's own mind. "What was Corbin helping you to investigate?"

"I volunteered him to help the organization document a suspected human trafficking ring in Houston. He was working with police up there."

"Human trafficking?" Shauna murmured. "What had he found out?"

"I never knew. It's only been a couple weeks. We didn't talk much."

A dozen new possibilities opened to Shauna regarding those pictures of Wayne at the shipyard, but there was no time to process them. She would have to do that on the road. She had to leave. Now.

"Just tell Beeson that Corbin's pictures might shed some light on his murder."

"Why can't you?" Khai followed Shauna back into her room. She grabbed her purse, her cell phone, the keys to Rudy's car.

"Because he thinks I did it. And because I won't be able to find out the truth if I'm in jail."

23

For the second time in two days, Shauna pointed the little MG south toward Victoria, wondering how long it would be before Wayne figured out that she was no longer home. That she'd driven away without his noticing was remarkable.

She needed to call Uncle Trent.

"Shauna, sweetheart! To what do I owe this unexpected phone call?"

"Uncle Trent, they're looking at me for Corbin Smith's murder."

For several long seconds, Trent didn't reply.

"Uncle Trent?"

"I don't understand."

"I didn't do it."

"Of course you didn't."

"I will explain everything, but first I need your help."

"Anything. Tell me what you need."

"Wayne doesn't know I'm gone yet. When he figures it out, I expect he'll call you. He knows you're the first person I would go to."

"As you should. Come here to River Oaks, Shauna. I can take care of you here."

"Houston is the first place he'd look for me if he wanted to find me."

"And why will Wayne want to find you?"

"He thinks I know . . . more than I do."

"You are going to have to fill me in, sweetheart."

"I think *he* was behind my accident."

"Behind it?"

"I think he might have staged it."

Trent whistled. "Now that's going to take some explanation, and some pondering, honey. But if it's true, I'll be the first to—"

"I can't prove it. Yet."

"Where are you going, if not Houston?"

"I'm headed . . ." That would take too long to explain. "Can you meet me in Corpus Christi tonight?"

"Absolutely. Where do you want me to come?"

"I'll let you know when I get there."

"Do you want me to call your father?"

"No. No. I don't see the point of involving him now."

"Whatever you say. I'll be on the next flight to Corpus Christi. You let me know when you get there."

"Love you."

"Love you too, honey."

She shut off her phone and turned her mind toward Miguel Lopez. If the man didn't care about helping her, he might at least still have a heart for his best friend, and for bringing the man who killed him to justice.

That would be good enough for her.

⸻

Shauna turned onto Miguel's street in time to see him, on foot, turn left at the next cross street. Should she wait at the house for him to return?

She chose to follow him instead, and he led her into a park less than four blocks away. Miguel turned left onto the gravel pathway that ran the perimeter of the open space. Shauna parked and evaluated the setting.

The path was, by Shauna's very rough estimation, maybe half a mile around the park, but it was not entirely visible to her from the parking lot. Opposite where she stood was a modest grove of trees on the downward slope. She cut across the grass toward it in hopes of crossing Miguel's path rather than chasing it.

Her feet hit the concrete on the other side and she turned in the direction she expected Miguel to come. The path took a sharp downturn into the trees and then followed a winding route through the shade. She went about fifty yards and stepped off into the lower branches of an especially leafy tree. She felt some uncertainty regarding how he would respond to seeing her here, having been quite clear what he expected her to do—or not do, rather—just yesterday.

She waited for several minutes, hoping she hadn't misjudged his route.

"I asked you not to come back."

She spun. A branch whipped her cheek and scraped her soft skin. Miguel Lopez stood ten feet behind her. How had he come up on her so quietly? How had he seen her, known she would be here?

She placed her hand over her heart.

"You scared me."

"You should be terrified to be here. What are you doing?"

"Helping someone."

"That would be Wayne?"

She matched his biting tone. "Corbin."

"And what do you think you can do for a dead man?"

"Why are you so cold toward me? What did I ever do to you?"

She watched him wish his remark back into his mouth, considered the way his eyes dropped to the dirt. He shoved his hands into the pockets of his light jacket.

Miguel had cleaned up in comparison to his fresh-out-of-bed appearance yesterday. His beard was trimmed, his hair in order, his clothes clean and pressed. He looked naturally good.

She stepped toward him and let the loose branch snap back behind her.

"Did Corbin talk to you about the projects he was working on?"

Miguel's manner softened. "There was a time. But not recently."

"Did he ever mention a human trafficking story he was working on?"

Miguel shook his head. "He probably was partnered with another journalist."

"What about Wayne Spade?"

"What about him?"

"Any connection to something like human trafficking?"

Miguel's eyes narrowed. "Wayne Spade is connected to your father's multibillion-dollar corporation. If he's also connected to trafficking, that would be bad for you."

"Me? What does he have to do with me?"

Miguel sighed. "I was referring to your family in general."

"And yet Wayne seems to have taken a personal interest in me. Do you have any idea why?" Miguel set his mouth in a line. "Let me rephrase that," Shauna said. "Tell me why Wayne is so angry at me."

"Angry at you? You think he is *angry*?"

"Then what is he?"

"If I did know, what good would it do you? Isn't it enough for you to stay out of his way?"

"Is it enough? Because I don't know, Miguel. Will he chase me down? Do I need to change my name? Will I be able to lead a normal life?"

"I, I, I. Listen to yourself. What is going on is so much bigger than you, Shauna. When did you become so self-centered?"

"*I* came here to connect Wayne to Corbin's murder, Miguel. Maybe my motives are selfish. But if you care an ounce about Corbin, you could at least stop trying to push me away."

Miguel averted his eyes.

"What is 'so much bigger'?" she asked.

Miguel shook his head. "I never thought I'd be pushing you away."

The remark derailed Shauna onto an unexpected trail of thoughts. What did he think he would be doing? But the idea of *them* took her mind back to the e-mails they had exchanged before her accident.

"What does *Sabueso* mean?"

"Bloodhound."

"What were we sniffing out, bloodhound?"

He shrugged. "Nothing that matters now."

"What matters now? What do you write about?" She came close enough to touch him if she reached out her hand, and he didn't back away.

"I haven't written in more than a month."

"So that is what matters, then: you are a journalist who has given up writing. For 'greener pastures,' you said. What do you do with your days now?"

"I think."

Shauna blinked. She lost track of where this conversation was headed. Did he think of her, of the work they had done together, of something that once mattered? She shifted her weight.

"*Sabueso* has become a philosopher then. What do you think about?"

When his silence filled long seconds, Shauna caught his eye.

"I believe you think about the past," she said.

He was looking at her, and his eyes were not as silent as his lips. He seemed to read her face like a poem, tenderly. Her boldness turned to dust.

He finally asked, "Did he hurt you?"

"Who?"

"Wayne."

"Do you mean since the accident?"

Miguel took her hand in his. "I'm so sorry."

"For what?"

"For not being able to stop what happened."

"But you can tell me what happened." She felt more hopeful than she had in days.

He shook his head.

"I realize how serious this is. I've been spending all my energy trying to remember. I've thought, if I can remember, I can make everything right somehow. I can get back to where I was. I can find what I lost. You are my last connection to truth, Miguel. I was really hoping that you . . . is there anything that you could tell me"—she was grasping now—"anything that would make sense to me?"

Miguel studied her hand. "There's very little that makes sense to me, either. I'm sorry, but I can't risk—"

Angry now, she moved her fingers to release his hand, but he held on. He pulled her as close to him as they had stood in his kitchen, and she had the fleeting thought that her attraction to Miguel Lopez was far stronger than anything she had ever felt toward Wayne.

"Today, I can't," he said. "Maybe even tomorrow I won't be able to. But I will make you a promise. I will promise to start turning my thinking into a plan that will end this. Your coming here yesterday made me think that maybe I can find a way. And then I can tell you everything."

She shook her head. She needed answers today, not tomorrow or in the next century. What good were promises to her, to Uncle Trent, to Detective Beeson, to Corbin?

"I can't wait."

"It's a small favor."

"I can't." She tightened her grip on his fingers and took hold of his other hand as well. "I'm sorry for this, but I can't." She closed her eyes and put her mind squarely on his nickname, *Sabueso,* and on the first e-mail message from him to her that popped into her mind.

The problem is in the profit-sharing structure.

She centered her mind. She blocked out all images except the expression Miguel wore when he opened his front door and saw her for the first time yesterday. The one expression that conveyed half a dozen conflicting emotions. The expression that would tell her the most.

And this time, Miguel's memory unfolded for her more vividly, more completely than any she'd had so far. It swallowed her whole.

24

Shauna chose the space in Miguel's mind that grew brighter in pulsating bursts of light. The light of this memory expanded rhythmically until it became the fluorescent lighting of a predictable corporate-office hall.

Gray industrial carpeting butted up against artless gray walls, stubby gray cubicles, and towering picture windows at one end. Silence filled the empty after-hours space. Beyond the windows, city lights poked holes in the darkness.

This was the view from the top floor of McAllister MediVista, a small perk afforded to the senior-level administrators who served the executive suite. Shauna had been here many times over the course of her life, first as an impressionable child and later as a cynical adult visiting her father and her favorite uncle.

There was no such association in Miguel's memory, however, only seething hatred propelled by fury and grief.

Grief for Shauna.

The unexpected power of the emotion nearly snapped Shauna out of the moment. She had never experienced grief of this nature, grief driven by severed passion, not even when her mother died or when she discovered her culpability in Rudy's present condition. There was no guilt in this grief, no sense of being abandoned, no fear of being lost. Only a yawning, earsplitting pain, the scream of pressure valves blown wide open.

Grief for her.

Love. For her.

Outside her mind, confusion tipped Shauna sideways. How could someone who had felt this way toward her be so cold now? Had she hurt him somehow? She gripped his hand harder and tried to hold on to her focus.

Miguel strode down the hall to the windows, steps heavy and quick, then turned into a long corridor. Industrial gray fluorescence gave way to cherry-wood and warm recessed lighting. In one sweaty fist he gripped a slick object the size of a domino. A flash drive.

The corridor opened onto a round room, at the center of which was a receptionist's desk. Living plants and trees lined the cherry walls on the entry side, growing long toward the atrium skylight. The carpet was the color and scent of glazed almonds.

On the opposite side of the room, behind the receptionist's desk, a glass wall exposed three offices designed more for form than function, and through the floor-to-ceiling windows behind the offices, a spectacular panorama of Houston, its office buildings twinkling in the rising sun, looking up at McAllister MediVista like needy serfs.

Etchings in each of four glass doors in the glass wall identified the occupants: To the far right, Chief Operating Officer Leon Chalise. Next to that, President Landon McAllister. To the far left, Chief Financial Officer Wayne Spade. And back toward the center, sharing a wall with her father, CEO Trent Wilde.

Inside Leon's office, just beyond the reach of the light, the COO's shadowy form, an obese Hitchcock silhouette, moved against the cityscape. Miguel blazed a trail into the man's office. The heavy door sprang inward under the weight of his body.

"You are dogs," Miguel bellowed, moving around the desk in the dark. Leon registered Miguel's presence without the slightest surprise, even when the journalist shoved him toward the window.

Leon's body smacked the thick glass. He barked out a laugh as if it had been forced by the impact.

"Think twice, bloodhound," he said.

Miguel punched him in the stomach with the fist surrounding the flash drive. The man doubled over, but not because he was injured. Miguel's fist had made no impact at all.

Miguel's knee came up into Leon's chin, and his teeth cracked together. Miguel dropped his fist between the soft shoulder blades, and Leon drove forward, lifting the wider, more athletic Miguel at the hips onto the desk and shoving him over, clearing the surface. A clock of crystal and engraved brass plunged to the floor and cracked in two. Miguel's body hit the clients' chairs on the other side of the desk and then flopped onto the carpet.

Not at all disoriented, Miguel grabbed one half of the clock, sleek and broken like a split rock, grappled with the chairs, then stood, facing Leon, the desk between them. The skin beneath Leon's lip had split open, and he dabbed at it with his fingers, smiling, as if still in possession of the upper hand.

Miguel held up the clock in one fist and threw the flash drive at him with his other hand.

"Take it."

The drive bounced off Leon's chest. He didn't even look at it.

"A week ago, that might have helped your cause," Leon said, not even winded. "But now . . ."

Miguel threw the clock piece at Leon's head. This time the businessman ducked, and the crystal hit the window with the sound of a gunshot.

In the precise moment that the crystal and tempered glass met, a rocket of pain exploded through Miguel's thigh, dropping him to the floor. His arms failed to break his fall, and he crashed into one of the nearby chairs, breaking a finger, he thought, as he landed on top of his right arm. Fire licked at every muscle, consumed his blood like fuel, kissed every skin cell.

He groaned but couldn't move, then started to hyperventilate as if oxygen were anesthesia.

He had been shot? No. Something else. The fingers of his left hand brushed against a wire protruding from his pants leg. Tasered. The almond carpet scraped Miguel's face, and he pressed his cheek against it, seeking some kind of counterbalance to the agony, which faded quickly but left him immobile.

In the time it took him to reorient his mind, Leon had come around the desk and squatted next to him, elbows on knees, fingers linked.

"You tried to kill her," Miguel managed.

Leon shrugged. "She isn't dead yet."

The words dialed back the confusion in Miguel's mind a few degrees. He tried to stay calm. Focused.

"You're going to kill her anyway."

"Yes, we are."

Miguel cried out.

"I'm very sorry about it, to tell the truth. The point is not to be in the killing business. I personally would like to see as many people as possible survive this fiasco you've created. Especially someone as sweet and smart as Shauna."

"She was an innocent bystander."

"If anyone is innocent here, it would be Rudy. Shauna, on the other hand, is as guilty as you. No. More guilty."

"Of what?"

"You are only guilty of greed, bloodhound. But no more greedy than anyone. You just want a good story, and believe me, I'd love to be the one to give it to you. But Shauna McAllister is guilty of betrayal. Shauna McAllister is a traitor."

Miguel dared not move. Even breathing stabbed his nerves.

"After all," Leon said, rubbing his chin, "she's in critical condition. And we're not miracle workers."

"You can't," Miguel whispered. Blood pumped through his abdomen like acid.

Leon stood, yanking the Taser prongs from Miguel's legs and gathering the expended wires. He sniffed and muttered something Miguel couldn't make out. The sound of scraping footsteps traveled along the surface of the carpet into the hollows of Miguel's ear, pressed over it like a suction cup. The scent of expensive leather planted itself in front of Miguel's nose, and a new voice said, "Oh, we can."

Miguel refocused and found it within him to smile. "But you won't," he said.

His eyes took in the smooth leather, the creased slacks. He turned his head upward, traversing a tailored jacket, climbing the mountain ridges of hands that had seen a few decades. This man wore a blood red sweater and held a Taser, which he set on the desk behind him.

"Tell me why not," said Trent Wilde.

Shauna disengaged involuntarily. Some disbelief, some inability to accept the possibility—let alone the reality—of this image, terminated the link. The scene blinked out though she still gripped Miguel's hand, and though her brain disengaged, her body could not let go.

He let go for her, snatched his hand away as if it had been shocked.

"What are you doing?" He squinted, confused. "What was that?"

Having no answer to disconnect her tongue from the image smack and square in front of her mind, she said, "Trent Wilde shot you with a Taser. Uncle Trent shot you."

Verbalizing what she had seen did not make it any more real to her. In fact, the sound of her words was even more ludicrous than the vision. Wayne with the Taser would have made more sense.

Perhaps these visions were becoming like dreams, full of random and mixed-up details rooted in reality but horribly skewed. Perhaps they were less reliable than she had talked herself into believing.

"Did Trent shoot you?" she asked.

Surprise escaped him in a short burst of noise. "I'm not sure. Yes. I'm not— it's not a hundred percent clear." Miguel folded his arms over his chest. "Explain this to me."

"Why would he shoot you?"

Miguel refused to answer.

"This would be so much easier if you would—"

"We've been over this." He turned to go.

"I can't just keep guessing."

"Well you're doing a good job of it so far."

"Miguel. Please. I need your help."

"Then tell me why you think he did it."

Confronted for the first time by a direct question about her strange new ability, Shauna stalled, then mimicked Khai. "I have a good sense of people."

"You have more than that."

"I can't explain it."

Miguel uncrossed his arms and examined his hand, the one she had seized. He held it out to her and she looked away.

"Look," he said. She refused.

"Look," he said again, and this time he held his palm beneath her nose. "How can you not explain this?"

Miguel's beautiful brown skin blazed as if he had laid it on a stove. A small white depression marked the middle of his palm. Shauna was pretty sure that was where she had placed her thumb when she gripped his hand.

"I hurt you," she said.

He shook his head. "Not my hand. It doesn't hurt at all."

"I'm sorry."

"How did you—"

"I have no idea."

Really, she didn't. How could she explain this to him when she didn't even get it herself? Worse, how could she *do* this to someone like Miguel, who had wanted nothing more than to find a way to keep her alive?

And here she was, living and breathing and stopping the gaps in her past by stealing the memories of others. What price had Miguel Lopez paid so she could do that?

In that moment, this man standing in front of her became someone entirely different from Cale Bowden, or Wayne Spade, or Luang Khai, or Scott Norris, or Millie Harding. She would not steal his memories, no matter how hot her cause burned in her own mind. She'd apparently already stolen a great deal from him.

His career, for example. Certainty smacked her across the face. Miguel Lopez's departure from the *Statesman* had something to do with her.

After all, the murder of his close friend Corbin had something to do with her.

Shauna was convinced she was thinking unselfishly for the first time since she regained her broken awareness at the Hill Country Medical Center. Shauna processed all this in a matter of seconds, while Miguel studied her as if he had an eternity.

She wished her decision back. She wished she had never come here, that she had never taken anything from him. She wished she could give it all back and hated that she didn't know how.

Couldn't anything be undone?

"I'm sorry," she said again.

Miguel shrugged at his palm. "It's nothing."

"I mean for everything else."

He seemed to weigh what *everything* might mean. "You remember?"

"No. But I see some things. And I'm so sorry."

He reached out to put his burned hand on her shoulder and she stepped away from it, unwilling to risk his touch.

She searched her jacket pockets for something to write with, but came up empty. "Do you have your phone?"

He fished it out and handed it to her, not asking what she wanted. She flipped it open and entered her cell number into his contacts list.

"I won't bother you anymore," she said. "You have already . . . done so much. But if anything changes, call me. If your . . . thinking . . . leads you to some solution. If you uncover some way of figuring all this out."

Miguel let his hand fall to his side.

"What happened to you?" he asked. She gazed at him, unable to answer.

Trent Wilde would be the one to tell her. Or show her.

25

An hour and a half of driving sharpened Shauna's mind to just how bad the situation really was.

Trent and Miguel had forced each other's hands, or rather, each other's silence. Silence that was somehow related to Shauna's life.

She had told Trent she believed Wayne had tried to kill her.

And according to Miguel's recollection of things, Trent was a part of the attempt.

Impossible.

Entirely possible.

But why?

Shauna pulled to the shoulder of the highway, threw her door open, and vomited outside the car. The two men she had trusted more than any others—Wayne and Trent—her worst enemies. If only hoping for some alternate reality could have made it true.

She wiped her mouth with a tissue from her console, a tissue that quivered in her shaking hands. *Think. Think. Breathe.*

God is with me. Jesus is near. The Spirit is greater than my fear.

The rhyme came to her unbidden, along with a strong, irrational sense that the words were true. What had triggered that?

And how could she believe the words? She wanted to, as much as she wanted her mother's arms around her, telling her that this terrifying moment would pass.

She envisioned her mother leaning over her, protecting her with the strength and softness of her love. *Nothing can separate you from the love of God, Shauna.*

Her mother had said that to her so often. When had she forgotten it?

The terror passed.

Her hands stopped quaking and her breathing evened out. Her mind refocused.

What on earth did Wayne and Trent not want her to know? And how, not knowing it, was she of any real concern to anyone? Of course, her pursuit—reckless now, in retrospect—in unearthing what happened the night of September 1 must have unnerved them.

She envisioned Wayne on his way to Corpus Christi, alerted to her whereabouts by her uncle.

No matter how she arranged this half-pieced puzzle, she saw only one picture forming: she was merely running from one unknown to another, one form of danger to another. She needed a way to convince Wayne, or Trent—both of them—that she wasn't worth an ounce of their worry.

Could she do that and unearth the truth at the same time?

She leaned her clammy forehead against the steering wheel. Not even the truth could be worth this agony. She considered what it would take to disappear.

Then she considered Corbin Smith. She owed it to him not to run away.

She considered Miguel Lopez. For a man unwilling to lift a finger to help her, she shouldn't worry too much. And yet . . . The excuse rang flat within her when she remembered the sting of the Taser's shot. He had helped her in some way she could never repay. How does one repay a lifesaver? Her mind took a lightning-flash detour to the grief his memory had encompassed. Grief for her. And pain. So much physical and emotional pain.

He had loved her.

Maybe he still did.

In spite of the discrepancy between the possibility and his reticent behavior, the idea did not repulse her.

She lingered on it for a moment.

Just a moment.

A degree of warmth returned to her skin.

And then there was Rudy. To leave him now might mean never to see him again. Or worse, to put him in harm's way. She still owed him a debt. Abandoning him now would be criminal. No, worse than criminal.

Not to mention the other pestering factors of her looming trial, how she would explain herself to Trent—or, if she didn't, the consequences to her father's campaign and her own legal standing. Would she be a fugitive or a missing person? Probably both.

Details.

Still undecided, Shauna pulled back into traffic and gnawed on her unidentified options until the 181 met the 37 in the heart of Corpus Christi. She began to look for a gas station, where she planned to fill up Rudy's little car, purchase breath mints if not a toothbrush and a few other necessities, and further postpone a decision about what to do. Where could she go now? She would need to call Trent soon. It was nearly three o'clock.

She spotted a Stripes station and pulled in.

Wayne's wine-red Chevy truck sat beside a pump. Her palms turned slick on the wheel and her breath caught in her throat. Wayne himself was not anywhere near it.

Shauna swung the car around the back of the store like a lacrosse ball, then shot back out onto the street. In her rearview mirror, she saw him exit the convenience store.

There it was, possibility made reality: Wayne could not have known she was here unless Trent told him.

What now?

Shauna had enough cash with her to buy a night at a motel without leaving an electronic trail. It would, at the very least, also pay for some time to think.

Within the hour she had settled into a La Quinta, parked behind the Denny's next door, and sat on the end of the bed to read the sheet she had stolen from Dr. Harding's file.

It was dated seven years earlier and appeared to be some kind of pre-employment psych evaluation. Or maybe just the summary. Handwritten. Perhaps the notes that preceded the report.

Dr. Harding, in cryptic psych lingo, identified Wayne Spade as a young business professional with experience in international markets, primarily in Asia. There was no mention of a family history, just a glowing statement of his mental and emotional health.

Shauna read the document a second time, more carefully, and paused at this: "Detected some residual resentment re: indebtedness to TW, i.e., effacement of military record."

TW. Trent Wilde?

Effacement of the records—the AWOL business? Trent had done Wayne some favor to cover that up, and now Wayne owed him?

She'd have to ponder that one.

At the bottom, Dr. Harding had written in red pen: *Approved for clearance.* Whatever that meant.

Shauna fell back onto the bed, lost in her indecision. Every trustworthy option but one had been stripped away.

And was Landon McAllister trustworthy? Or was he just another man who'd stooped below the most base moral standards to achieve high levels of power?

There was a time in her life when he would have intervened to save her from predicaments she'd dropped herself into. There was the time a classmate in high school stole a paper Shauna had written on *The Scarlet Letter*, then accused Shauna of plagiarizing her. The injustice of the accusation tilted Shauna into an uncharacteristic fit of violence—though she was no demure Hester Prynne, either—and she punched the girl in the arm hard enough to leave a mark.

She received an F on her paper and a week-long suspension. Landon had to pay a personal visit to the principal to prevent her from being expelled.

But he had believed her side of the story.

Shauna wondered what he would believe of this.

When had he stopped intervening? When would he have stopped Patrice from making her outrageous, slashing accusations and defended his own daughter?

Shauna couldn't recall ever having felt so isolated.

And afraid.

She examined the disconnected puzzle pieces spread out on the table of her mind.

A botched murder attempt.

A dead photographer.

An estranged journalist.

A hovering killer.

A collection of cryptic e-mails.

An annual report.

She took a mental walk around the table and looked at the pieces from all angles. She sat at the table. She stood and leaned over it. She turned the pieces around.

Until there it was: the beginnings of plausible sense. Miguel Lopez had cracked a story that Wayne and Trent did not want the world to read. A story that could topple MMV? It had to be big. Corbin knew the story and had planned to tell her. Remind her. Against Miguel's wishes? Miguel's silence was making more and more sense.

Miguel understood what was at stake. The options were truth and death, or life in the shadows. And yet he'd chosen to hide within two hours of his old life. Why would he stay so close to danger?

And more questions, so obvious she wondered why she hadn't asked them first: What was her involvement in all this? Why did Corbin need to tell her the story? Why did Wayne need to watch her so closely?

Because she already knew the secret. Somewhere, lost in the labyrinth of her mind, she knew.

The expanding light shone on several empty spaces in the puzzle. She knew which pieces fit here.

An argument with her father.

A violated trust on the part of her uncle.

An election year.

A record-breaking profit margin.

Shauna pinched the bridge of her nose and knew.

McAllister MediVista was funding her father's campaign.

Perhaps not legally.

Somewhere in the pages of the annual report—*the problem is in the profit-sharing structure . . . the subsidiary on page 72 has no public record*—

The hotel phone rang, and Shauna gasped. Seven o'clock. She stared at the phone.

Who would call?

Wayne couldn't have found her here.

She checked her cell phone. It was still turned off.

The phone rang a fourth time and Shauna moved to the blackout drapes, drawn across the window. She looked out, half expecting to see Wayne's leering face on the other side of the glass.

She saw only parked cars. No wine-red truck.

The phone was still ringing. Nine? Ten? She'd lost count.

It was possible the last occupant had requested a wakeup call that hadn't been disconnected yet.

It was . . . possible. At seven in the evening on a Tuesday.

Ridiculous.

Angered by her runaway fear, Shauna marched around the bed and snatched the phone off the base. She pressed the receiver to her ear but didn't speak.

"This is the last time I let you out of my sight, babe."

Wayne. Shauna dropped the handset and snatched up her purse. In two steps she'd reached the door. She couldn't get it open. The dead bolt. She fumbled, threw it, and raced down the hall for the exit onto the rear lot. If Wayne had talked the concierge into ringing him through, he would be in the lobby.

How had he found her? Her car? She would have to find another way out of Corpus Christi.

Shauna hit the door running and burst through. From the corner of her eye she saw a form lunge, then a body hit hers. Arms seized her around the waist and lifted her off the ground. Her momentum caused them both to spin. She saw a black cell phone hit the sidewalk and skitter across the concrete.

She smelled Wayne, breathing hard in her ear. He chuckled, holding her an inch off the earth while she kicked out.

"Good to see you, Shauna."

26

Trent greeted Shauna by opening the door wide for her at a hotel suite several miles away. "I'm glad you could make it, sweetheart."

Wayne shoved her into the room. A seating arrangement of sofa, love seat, coffee table, and chair filled the center of the room. A poker table took up one corner, and a wet bar, one wall. In a second she registered overstated décor: three chandeliers, South Pacific blue carpet, filigreed picture frames, and heavy draperies.

Wayne crossed his arms and said, "It would help us to know exactly how much you've learned, Shauna."

"I don't understand," she pleaded with Trent. They wouldn't know yet that she knew about him.

"Considering that you're not shocked to see me here, I'd say you do."

She was an idiot! "You two haven't exactly been telling me the truth yourselves."

Wayne said, "Very little of anything I said to you was a lie. I tried to protect you—"

"You tried to kill me!"

Wayne's eyebrows shot up. "Spoken like a woman whose mind has been playing tricks on her. I tried to *save* you. But you wouldn't let me. You should have let me. You should have done what I said. Things would be so much more painless if you would take our advice."

"And I told you she wouldn't," Trent said. "So now that you both have done things your way and made this situation far worse than it ever needed to be, we're going to do it my way."

"Uncle Trent—"

"Shauna." He held up a hand in front of her face. "You know I love you like a daughter. But some values in this world stand higher than family."

"Values like political power? Money? Greed?"

"Values like putting health within reach of the world."

"At what expense? How dirty is the money that's making this possible?"

"Shauna, sweetheart, calling it *dirty* is looking at the ethics from an upside-down perspective. Your world is so much more black-and-white than the one the rest of us live in. Maybe I can help you see things from a fresh point of view. Now, you know I would give my life for you. But I expect you to be willing to do the same when duty calls."

"What are you saying?"

"I'm saying that Wayne and I expected more cooperation from you, after all our efforts, but we have been disappointed."

"What is it you want me to do?"

"Accept what is, sweetheart. Don't try to change it. Don't try to reconstruct it or remember it." He lifted his hand and stroked her hair. "We've gone to so much trouble for you."

His touch chilled her.

"All I wanted was to believe I wasn't the one who hurt Rudy."

"What does it matter who did it?" Trent asked. "That's what I mean, Shauna. Things are what they are. Knowing how it happened doesn't change anything."

"It would change what Landon thinks of me."

Trent chuckled. "I doubt anything would change what your father thinks of you, my dear."

"You have nothing to fear from me," she whispered. "I honestly don't remember anything, and what I've learned doesn't make sense."

"You've made plenty of sense to both of us over the last few days," Trent said. "But maybe we've misunderstood. Why don't you explain?"

She could not think of anything to say but the truth, and yet the truth was utterly unconvincing. She might say, *A journalist I knew dug up a story about*

MMV, and you wanted it buried. But then they would want to know how she learned about the journalist, if she didn't remember him; how she figured out that there was a story. Anything she could explain would bring harm to Miguel. Even to Khai.

"First tell me why I don't remember."

Trent smiled. "MMV is a pharmaceutical research company come of age in an era where people are begging to forget their lives. They want to leave their pain behind them, Shauna, and they have been self-medicating with addictions that don't really help. Now we have the real technology to make it possible. Considering what is available to you, I myself am stunned to see you running headlong into a past you could abandon."

"I noticed you left your meds back at the house," Wayne said.

"I didn't have time to pack," she spat. Would they force her to continue taking the pills? Would they continue to wipe out her recall?

"We gave you a clean slate," Wayne said. "We gave you the opportunity to re-create the truth of your life. To believe whatever you wanted to. Do you know how many people *want* this and can't have it yet? You could be a little more grateful."

"You stole from me," she said. But the accusation was weak and impotent.

"There you go again," Trent said. He turned to Wayne. "We give and give and give, and she stands there and accuses us of stealing."

"You stole from me, and from Rudy," she said. "From Corbin, and from Miguel. And from who knows how many other people."

"What I'm curious to know—for the sake of the drug trial reports, of course—is how you know about Miguel Lopez, seeing as you claim not to remember him."

Heat flared in Shauna, not for having been cornered now, but for all she'd lost, and for all everyone else had lost at the hands of this god-sized ego that she'd once trusted.

"I can steal too," she said.

"As can anyone," said Trent.

"But I steal memories. Wayne's memories told me about Miguel Lopez." The men exchanged glances. She leaned toward Trent's face. "But Wayne won't remember what they told me. Put that in your report."

Using plastic ties, Wayne cuffed her to the pipe under the vanity sink.

"Is this really necessary?" she asked.

"Being nice to you didn't work."

"You didn't mind getting a few kisses out of it though, did you?"

Wayne cinched the ties tighter than necessary to prevent her hands from slipping out. If she moved the wrong way, they might cut her skin.

He left, and she heard the low tones of Trent's voice in the living area.

She imagined they pondered their most current dilemma. Certainly their lives would be simpler if she were dead, and yet neither man had spoken of killing her, and deep within her, she believed it was because they couldn't—that something worse would befall them than the possible exposure of what she had pieced together so far.

Something that Miguel had engineered.

After all, her stolen memories weren't exactly eyewitness testimony, and she couldn't imagine how they would hold up in a court of law.

Also working in her favor was her claim about stealing memories. Wayne seemed easy enough to persuade, as if her explanation, wild though it was, struck right at the heart of his own questions about what was going on. Trent was the skeptic, and her suggestion was outrageous. Even so, she was pretty sure Trent saw her, at the very least, as a valuable test rat.

More frightening than the possibility of her death, however, was the likelihood of a fresh drug regimen. A stronger dose. How did this stuff work? Could she believe anything the bushy Dr. Carver had told her? After all, he was on Trent Wilde's payroll. Was it possible for them to administer the drugs at any time, or only after a trauma? Did she have to be in a coma for it to work?

Or—and her mind darkened at this possibility—was it possible that her coma was drug induced in the first place?

Could they create a new trauma? A new coma? Was the memory wipeout contingent on dosage? On mental distress? Could they determine to wipe out six months, eight months, a year? How far could they go without actually killing her?

This, not murder, was what terrified Shauna.

Her wrists and tailbone had gone numb, so she adjusted her position, cracking her head against the bottom of the vanity counter.

The blow stung and brought tears to her eyes. She leaned her cheek against the cool pipe until the pain faded.

A half hour passed before Wayne came back in. He cut off her plastic cuffs and let her stretch out. He went to the sliding door that led out onto a third-floor balcony, raised the curtain, and looked outside.

"I could use something to eat," she said, sitting on the queen-sized bed.

"You'll stay here tonight, then tomorrow you'll go with Trent up to Houston."

"Why tomorrow?"

"Because he's having a few things brought down for you."

"Like?"

He dropped the curtain.

"As I said before, it would help us to know exactly how much you remember. Or don't."

"You wouldn't believe anything I told you."

"That depends."

"Help me out here."

"Trent is both unwilling to travel with you in your current headstrong state and unwilling to administer another round of narcotics—"

"*Narcotics?*"

"There are several different ways to get us all back to square one. That's the easiest option."

Shauna couldn't speak.

"But that's also risky. If it's true you can take memories from people—"

"I have plenty of yours."

"And I wouldn't know it, would I?"

"I think you *do* know it. You know without a doubt that I know things I couldn't otherwise, and that I've asked questions about you that no one else would think to ask."

Wayne dropped onto the bed next to hers and faced her. "This is what I hate about the human brain. It's so hard to quantify. But as I was saying, *if* it's true, Trent doesn't want to lose any data about this . . . bizarre side effect."

"Then all he has to do is keep me drug free."

"You understand why that's not reasonable for us."

"Why don't you kill me then?" she whispered.

"Many reasons. One being that you are valuable research now."

"Most lab rats die sooner than later."

"And if I can prevent that from happening, I will."

"Don't insult me."

"I only kill when it's absolutely necessary. I never wanted to kill you."

"Oh? So then why did you try?"

Wayne stood, looked around as if he would find the appropriate words somewhere, then managed to say, "I am considerably in debt to your uncle."

"He's not my uncle! And yes you are in his debt. He paid your way out of a court-martial and now you've got less control over your own life than you ever did in the military."

The light in his eyes went flat, and Shauna realized that her words had struck their mark.

Wayne sighed, loud, dramatic, and leaned over to open the drawer of the nightstand between the two beds. He withdrew a syringe and a vial. Shauna recoiled.

"Please don't."

"Nothing in here but a sleep aid," he said, pricking the vial with the needle and vacuuming the suspension into the plastic tube. "Just something to keep you from getting all upset over nothing."

"I don't need it."

"You'll have it anyway."

She jumped up for the door, but he was more agile and lithe than she. He secured her before she even left the bed. Her reflexive scream was cut off by his arm, which he threw down across her throat at the same time that he pinned both her legs down with his shin.

"Believe me"—his words slapped her face—"if it were strategically wise to kill you, I would have done it awhile ago."

He plunged the needle into her thigh and she groaned at the burn.

"Correction," he said. "I do *really* want to kill you. So don't give me any more excuses." He released her, and she rolled over to face the wall.

After a half minute of silence, Wayne left the room.

At the click of the door, Shauna tumbled off the bed and onto her feet.

How much time did she have before the stuff kicked in? She reached the closed door and opened it wide, ready to face Wayne and Trent with nothing but her wits and luck and dare them to try to keep her here.

The door screeched on its hinges.

They were not there. The door to the bedroom on the opposite side of the suite was closing. Wayne? Maybe.

She felt her muscles begin to sag.

A man rose from the love seat, a pistol holstered under his left armpit.

She recognized this man but could not come up with a name for his face, nor a context in which she might have known him. She didn't spend much time on that, however, recognizing in his body language a clear message: *I am your babysitter.* This man was the reason Wayne was free to leave her uncuffed in the bedroom.

He crossed his arms and looked down at her. He was easily over six feet. She was tall herself but less than half his weight, she estimated. His white shirt and tie, black slacks, and glistening shoes suggested FBI, but the scotch glass on the coffee table, more than half-full, contradicted this image of on-duty, law-abiding, law-enforcement officer.

Shauna looked at the door that exited onto the hall and mentally calculated whether she could reach it before he did, if she chose that option.

The man bent over, picked up his drink, and took a swig of the alcohol, withdrew a knife from his belt with his other hand, and threw it at the door. It embedded itself in the frame at what would have been the height of her ears, were she standing there.

The knife had a pearl handle.

Where had she seen that pearl—?

"You were stalking me at the park," she blurted.

The man snickered. "Not you, my boss."

His boss?

"Wayne owes me some money."

"Wayne? Why?"

He looked at her as if she didn't really expect him to answer.

"You're working for him now anyway?" she asked. What kind of business relationship did these two men have? Her head felt thick. She put her fingers to her temple.

"You ask too many questions." He sat back down and put his feet up on the table.

"What? He promise to pay you later? Wayne's a liar, y'know." She sensed the room begin to tilt.

"Yeah. We're surrounded by liars, aren't we? Get back in your room now, before I have to take you in."

Shauna closed the door before she fell back into the bedroom, not even able to reach the bed.

We're surrounded by liars. Where had she heard that before?

27

Someone kicked her out of her stupor, tripped over her body, and grunted his surprise. She had been dreaming of football, of all things, of backyard scrimmages and scuffles, of bodies hitting each other without the protection of bulky gear.

At the physical sensation of being tackled, new images swept the athletics aside. Drugs and needles and scowling men in lab coats accelerated her pulse and warmed her bloodstream. She rolled onto her back and stared the black room in the heart, so dark in her own mind that she couldn't make out shadows.

She heard herself breathing hard, scared.

"Wayne?" she said.

A male voice whispered something but she could not distinguish the words. She was so frightened, but not clearheaded enough to think her fear through. She noticed tears on her face, running into her ears.

Firm hands gripped her arms and hauled her up into a sitting position. Her equilibrium lost its footing, and had she not been held up, she would have fallen right over. She felt her neck tilt backward and snap back up, barely hinged.

The voice spoke again. More whispering.

She heard herself mumbling. "IdunnoIdunnoIdunno . . ."

He laid her down gently and left her, then reappeared in the form of chilling water, splashed all over her face and neck. She gasped and opened her eyes wide, still seeing nothing in the black room.

"You need to wake up." Low, barely audible.

Shauna couldn't will her body to move. Her tears started flowing, but she didn't know why.

A hand clamped down over her mouth.

"Sh. You'll wake him up."

Who? Who would wake up?

"Get up."

The demands twisted her fear into fury. She was aggravated, disoriented. She was wet and cold.

"No," she managed. She thought she sounded drunk.

He left her alone again—seconds or minutes, she wasn't sure—and found it within her brain to wonder if she would be doused again. She didn't care.

He returned and gripped the front of her blouse, pulling her upright by the collar. When she was vertical, he emptied a bucket of ice down the front of her shirt.

Her breath left her, and she went rigid. The ice pooled in her lap and seeped into her slacks. She shouted her protest. The hand clamped down on her lips again until she quieted.

The dropped bucket bounced silently off her leg and onto the carpet. She sensed smooth palms grasp her wrists. The man tugged on her arms until they threatened to leave the sockets, and her body raised off the ground.

"Stand up or I'll have to drag you out of here by one arm, lovely." The words reached into Shauna's consciousness clearly this time, and she allowed herself to believe that he did not mean to harm her. *Lovely?* She tried to remember what the word meant. She focused on her knees. Bend. Lift. Straighten.

Sway.

She leaned in to a sturdy body and sagged.

"Wayne?" she said again. She knew it wasn't him, but she couldn't think of any other names.

"Not on your life," he said.

"I need more water," she muttered.

Together they wobbled a few steps, to the vanity, she thought, and she heard water running. This time when he threw it in her face, she was sure he got himself wet as well.

She found this unreasonably funny.

And also, underneath her giggles, which she tried so hard to stifle, illuminating.

Shauna took a deep breath and tried to focus her eyes. Still too dark for her to make out his face.

"What next?" she said.

"We leave."

"Race you."

"I'd like to see that."

"I'm fast."

"I need you to shut up now."

She nodded, but then thought he couldn't see her. So she said, "Okay," and kept an arm around his waist as he half guided, half dragged her toward the door.

He opened it onto equal blackness. The creaking hinge was all the prompting her mind needed to fill in the details of the room. Chandeliers. Scotch. Knife. She wondered where FBI-not-FBI was.

"Where are—?" There was the hand over her mouth again. So annoying.

Her head was taking way too long to clear out. Right then and there, she decided she really wanted to go back to sleep.

Water dripped from her hair onto her shoulders.

Her body was moving toward the door, then a sharp object clipped her in the thigh. Hard enough to bruise.

"Ow!" She hadn't meant to shout, but there it was.

Her companion swore and dropped his own efforts at silence. He shoved her into the wall, using it to help hold her up while he fumbled for the doorknob.

"You don't have to be—" Shauna began.

He threw the door open and whipped her out into the hallway, spraining her elbow in the process. She whacked her wrist on the door frame as her limbs slipped through, still not fully connected to her brain.

There was the pain, and then, in rapid succession, three other observations that struck her like hailstones and finally awakened her from her bleary state.

The first was a blond watchman crumpled in the hall outside the door.

The second was the face of her cohort, one frowning Miguel Lopez.

And the third was the sound of an opening door inside the room, accompanied by a shout.

"Show me how fast you can run," Miguel said, yanking her away from the elevator and toward a red exit sign.

Run down stairs?

Her legs somehow remembered what to do, though Miguel would not let go of her wrist and would have pulled her along regardless, she thought. Either that or he would have amputated her hand with his tourniquet grip and run off into the night.

They both fell into the crash bar of the exit at the same time Wayne Spade threw the hotel room door open and spotted them at the end of the hall. He lifted a gun in their direction, but didn't fire before they fell through.

"Idiot," Miguel said, pushing Shauna down the stairs ahead of him. "Doesn't he know not to leave his valuables in a hotel room?"

Shauna made it down two flights before the heel of her shoe snagged on a step, as instantly disabling as gravel under a turning motorcycle. Her limbs locked up and her mind missed the beat, and the fog of her sleepiness crowded in on her again as she took seven stairs face-first, watching the handrail rush up to meet her eyes.

Wayne stood over Frank Danson with a gun, spinning a silencer onto the end of his barrel. The man was collapsed in a chair, only just starting to arouse from his electrified stupor.

"You know why I asked you to come here," Wayne said. It was not a question. "I was thinking it's time for a little one-on-one about that cell phone you dropped into my truck."

Frank couldn't move any more than his eyes. He grunted.

"And I don't mean a conversation."

Without looking, he shot one round into Frank's chest, the impact flipping both man and chair over backward. Then Wayne left the hotel.

This time, he would let someone else clean up the mess.

"What a disaster, a complete disaster," Miguel was murmuring over her, holding her hand and stroking her knuckles with his thumb, when she came to in a small examination room of a medical clinic. Oddly enough, her mind was far more clear now after the fall than when he'd tried to rouse her.

"I look that bad, huh?"

Miguel smiled for the first time since she'd met him. A full smile that lit up his face and deepened all the creases around his eyes. Beautiful.

"That would be impossible," he said. "And I wasn't talking about you anyway, lovely." The endearment took the chill out of the room.

"And yet we are in the biggest, stinking mess of my entire life."

"Could be."

"I feel a bit swollen." She touched the ice pack that covered most of the right side of her face.

"Hairline fracture in your cheekbone." Miguel traced his own face with his finger to indicate where her bone had cracked. "It could have been much worse."

"My nose, for example."

He laughed with the relief of a man who had escaped a burning building. "Something like that. You might get a black eye yet."

"That's why they call me *lovely*. Is it time to go yet?" Her face throbbed, but otherwise she felt quite herself and thought—hoped—the effects of her injection were nearly worn off.

"They want to keep you under observation. You were out for a few minutes."

"Just a few minutes."

"Total. You faded in and out on me on the way here."

"I'm sure it was the drugs."

"That's what I'm hoping. Do you know what they gave you?"

She shook her head.

He looked at his watch. "I'm not sure how much time we have, but you are priority one right now. You need some time."

"I'm fine. We should go."

She tried to sit up, and Miguel gently held her shoulder down. The muscles beneath her shoulder blades shot a warning across her back and down her arms. The ice slipped.

"In a minute."

She adjusted the ice pack. "Tell me what happened after I fell."

"Adrenaline happened. That's the only way I can explain it. I scooped you up without even thinking you might have hurt your neck—"

His eyes went to the jacket draped across the back of his chair. "I haven't always made the best judgment calls where you're concerned."

"I promise not to hold anything against you. Does Wayne know where we are? Speaking of which—where are we?"

He drew a hand down his trim anchor beard. The rest of his face needed a shave.

"After-hours emergency care center. I figured he'd check the ER rooms first, thought this place would buy us some time."

"So my name's on file here?"

"I got you in as a Jane Doe, said I'd found you in a stairwell."

"They bought it?"

He shrugged. "It's a problem that I drove you here myself instead of calling 9-1-1. I can only imagine what they think."

"One more reason to be on our way."

"When you're ready."

She closed her eyes and tried to relax. No easy feat, as her mind went directly to Wayne, searching hospitals with a gun and his hired help.

"What happened to the guys on watch?"

"They'll be fine. I'm a journalist, not an assassin. And they love their scotch. That helped."

She laughed. "I would like to have seen it."

"I never should have let go of you," he said.

"Don't beat yourself up. I would have taken you down with me if you'd been holding on, and then where would we be?"

"No. I mean, I never should have let go of you. I should have found another way, not let them decide our future for us."

Our future. Shauna tried to recall the last time she had been included in an *our* of any type.

"Maybe we'll have time to remember it together," he said. He stroked the inside of her forearm.

Shauna had once thought that reconstructing the past she supposedly shared with Wayne would help her to get back on her feet, find her way through the black holes in her mind. Was she about to sing the same song in a different key? Should she guard against Miguel too?

The thought seemed ludicrous. She most definitely wanted to remember the bonds she might have had with this man. She understood more clearly now what had pulled them apart. Maybe she could also re-create what had first pulled them—

A light flashed behind her mind, and she jerked her arm out from under his fingers.

Nothing else happened.

She exhaled. She needed his stabilizing touch, but more, she needed to respect him. Respect him enough not to steal from him. He clasped his hands together as if her retraction was to be expected. But he could not hide his disappointment.

"How did you know where to find me?"

"One can do many things with a girl's cell phone number."

She didn't understand.

"It has GPS."

"Ah. So that's how Wayne found me. Please tell me you ditched that thing."

"Wish I could take the credit for that, but you left it behind. I moved too slowly to get to you before he did."

"I'm incredibly lucky that you got to me when you did."

"Well, not being a subscriber to luck, I look at this disaster a bit differently."

"How do you look at it, then?"

"Like a clear sign that I shouldn't leave you alone any longer. You have always been so tenacious. After you came the second time, I understood that hadn't changed."

"And you saw me running headlong into stupidity."

"The only thing worse than running headlong into stupidity is running headlong into it without your memory."

She laughed at that and, strength renewed by the presence of Miguel Lopez, she pulled herself upright and set the ice on the mattress beside her.

"Well, *Sabueso*," she said. "I have a lot of questions for you and very little energy to endure the kinds of questions I'll get from the doctors. And since you understand exactly how tenacious I am, maybe you could show me the way out before I attempt to find it myself."

"You're sure?"

"So sure I want you to cut this ID bracelet off my wrist so we can leave it here."

Miguel looked around the room for something to cut it, then remembered something in his own jacket. He withdrew a pocketknife. A pearl-handled pocketknife.

"This is overkill maybe, but it oughtta—what's wrong?" Miguel said.

"Where'd you get that?"

He grinned. "It was sticking out of the door frame when I snuck into the hotel room. Banged my head on it. The tip is broken off, but other than that it's in good shape."

He sliced through the band.

"Would you believe me if I tell you I have the tip? Back in Austin?"

"I'm sure I'd believe anything about now."

She swung her feet off the bed and rose slowly.

"This might require a little more stealth than our last breakout," he said.

"No problem."

He threw two one-hundred dollar bills onto the bed, then held out his hand to her. She didn't take it. She didn't dare.

28

Miguel Lopez drove an old beater Jeep that Shauna thought might be older than she was.

"Nineteen seventy-four," Miguel confirmed when she asked.

They drove back toward Austin as the sun broke Wednesday's horizon, all the scenery in her mind rather than on the road. The highway of her brain was littered with questions, and she didn't know which to ask first.

What was the huge secret Miguel had tried to expose?

Where should they go?

What should they do next?

Miguel started the conversation for her by answering a question that she had abandoned eons ago. "I was in the car with you that night."

Her breath caught in her throat and she turned to him.

"That was what Corbin was trying to tell me."

"I don't know what Corbin was going to tell you. He did a lot of things without caring whether I wanted him to. He found me a couple weeks after the accident—I'm still not quite sure how. He was a better bloodhound than I, truth be known. What happened to him . . ."

Dashed white lines reflected the Jeep's headlights rhythmically.

"Shouldn't have happened to anyone," Shauna whispered.

"He did what I couldn't. He kept a close eye on you."

"Through Khai," Shauna thought aloud.

"The housekeeper? Yes, she might have helped. He thought that I shouldn't take Wilde seriously, that once you were well again and safe, we could go pick up the story again, see it through, go public with the whole nine yards."

He fell silent for a quarter mile.

"But you doubted that."

"It was what I didn't doubt, Shauna. I had no doubt Spade would kill you if he had to."

"You ever threaten Wayne with a gun?"

"He tell you that?"

Shauna was noncommittal.

"I did. I went back home once before going to Victoria, to get a few things I needed. He was there, ransacking the place. I sent him on his way."

"And that was it?"

"Until now. Other than disappearing, I didn't know how to guarantee your safety. Really"—for a split second he lifted both hands off the steering wheel in a shrug—"I still don't."

He rubbed his beard again and looked out the window. His silence was loaded with far more than regrets over an abandoned exposé.

"It's drugs. The reason I can't remember. Experimental drugs." She fiddled with the armrest on the door.

She guessed Miguel also pondered the ramifications of that over the next mile that lapsed in silence.

"I'm a clean slate now," she finally said.

He half smiled.

"Wayne didn't recognize Corbin when he confronted me outside the courthouse."

"I doubt their paths crossed before then. I don't think Wayne was ever on the campaign trail."

"How important was the story we had?" she asked.

"Not as important as you. I couldn't have predicted what would happen . . ." Miguel shifted lanes to pass a slow car.

"What was the story, exactly? I'm guessing it has something to do with my father's campaign. Dirty money? Finance law violations? Illegally bundled contributions?"

"Almost. Money laundering. MMV was moving funds into your father's campaign without a clear paper trail."

"How much?"

"Nearly forty million, last count."

"Forty!" Shauna angled her body toward Miguel, trying to piece together what information she could drag up from the distant past. "That's how much he's contributed from his own pockets."

"Exactly."

"You think it's not his money?"

"*We* thought it was not his money. Not technically."

"Why? Landon's worth more than ten times that much."

"His worth is wrapped up in assets, not cash."

"Well, MMV had a record-breaking year last year."

"They've broken records for seven consecutive years, in fact."

"There you go then."

"What could explain that besides good luck, considering the state of the economy and the public records of other corporations like MMV? Not one in the field has had similar growth in the same time frame. Like I said, I don't subscribe to luck."

Shauna sighed and ran a hand through her tousled hair. She probably looked terrible.

"So you started covering Landon's campaign—when?"

"Two years ago."

"And you got suspicious? Did some number crunching?"

"*You* did the number crunching. Forty million made a lot of people suspicious. It's over-the-top. Most candidates aren't even able to raise that much. Jeffrey Billings is worth more than three hundred, and even he only contributed four and half million to his own campaign."

"Was the story scheduled to run?"

"No! We hadn't gotten that far—for all we knew the money was legit."

"But you don't believe that now."

"I didn't ever believe it. But we never proved it, either."

She faced the dashboard and leaned back into her seat.

"Okay. Let's back up a little bit. How did we meet?"

Miguel cleared his throat. "How much do you want to know?"

"You'll have to start with the bones. I'm already on information overload. These past twenty-four hours have been . . ." She didn't have words.

"Campaign stop in Houston. May this year. McAllister brought the family out for a public appearance. Not something you typically did. But Rudy really wanted you there. Talked you into it."

"I'd do anything for him."

"He didn't deserve what happened to him either."

Tears sprang to Shauna's eyes. She swallowed. Miguel noticed and squeezed her shoulder. Shauna put her defenses up quickly, to prevent herself from opening a channel to his memories.

She said, "So we met, and . . . ?" She moved out from under his touch.

"And you were captivated by my wit and charm, and I was captivated by the fact that you worked for the CPA who audited MMV's books."

She chuckled. "I never would have disclosed that to you, Prince Charming."

"You didn't. I knew the firm. You only told me you worked there. I talked you into the rest."

"No you didn't. Landon and I have our issues, but I wouldn't have betrayed him like that."

"You did it to prove me wrong, Shauna." She looked at him. Well. Yeah. She might have done that. "You love the truth, you know."

The first rays of light broke the horizon on Shauna's side of the car. "So, what convinced me that you were right?"

"The facts convinced you: A profit-sharing structure that shifted the quarter immediately preceding MMV's first profit spike. Exponential profits in certain MMV subsidiaries—eight, to be precise—rather than across all nineteen. International subsidiaries that looked more like shell companies than legitimate businesses."

Shauna blew her mussed-up bangs off her forehead. "That's all?"

"The shift in profit-sharing reduced employees' takes to a stunted rate that was much slower than the actual growth. In theory, the executive officers took the balance, but in reality, the sum total was tipped into McAllister's coffers. And not one of them objected."

"That kind of thing is hard to hide."

"Not when everyone is in on it. They're being compensated some other way."

"What did we learn about the subsidiaries?"

"That they're nearly phantoms. We got far enough in investigating one of them to find a residential address. That's it."

Shauna let these details sink in before she said, "Wayne found out. I tipped him off somehow."

"He's not stupid. And you asked a lot of questions. I still have some things to teach you about subtlety in investigating."

"Guilty, and sentenced to time already served?" She apologized with a smile.

"I'm not blaming you, lovely."

Shauna returned to the trail of her thoughts. "Money laundering isn't something most people commit murder to hide."

"No. It's not. Although it's also true that people murder for far less."

"But we're family," she murmured.

"You are."

"And Rudy. No one loves Rudy like Landon and Uncle Trent do. What happened to him nearly dashed Landon's will to run. Why would anyone hurt Rudy?" Shauna let her question hang for several seconds. "Maybe I have this all wrong. Maybe the accident was a freak coincidence? Wayne jumped on the opportunity? I was upset that night—"

"That's not what happened."

She turned toward him again. The morning sun revealed the strong lines of his face, his certain jaw.

"Rudy wasn't supposed to be in the car. He insisted on riding back with you after you argued with McAllister."

"Landon and I fought about the money?"

"You challenged him on where it came from. He kept reciting the party line."

"Of course he would." She sighed. "You were with me—you let Rudy come?"

"Rudy was so good for you, Shauna. He was always cool when you were hot. I zipped my lips and let him work his calm on you. Where I went wrong was letting him talk me into taking the backseat. If he—"

"No ifs. None of those. It's all I can do to handle the facts. So Rudy wasn't supposed to be there."

"If the argument hadn't taken place, it would have been just you and me in the car. Someone had a plan in place. A plan that they couldn't retract."

"Not Landon. Not even Trent. I can't believe it. They would have called it off." Wayne, of course, could think up something that heinous.

"You came down onto the bridge. An SUV swerved into the oncoming lanes."

"A black SUV." She saw it in the memory she had taken from Deputy Cale Bowden. The witness leaning impatiently against the rear fender. She gasped.

"That's where I saw him."

"Saw who?"

"The guy drinking scotch in the hotel. He was driving the SUV. And I saw him one other time—at the park. Barton Springs. He had a knife. The knife you picked up."

"You sure? How could you have IDed him? He flicked on his high beams and blinded all of us. He straddled the lane lines so you couldn't veer right. You went left."

"Directly into the truck behind him." She still didn't remember any of it though she knew the scenario by heart.

"I swear, he didn't try to dodge you."

"No. I don't think he did. He works for Wayne—" Several possibilities clicked together in Shauna's mind. "He told me Wayne owes him money. Do you think it's because I didn't die in that accident?"

"It's possible. No pay for an incomplete job. If it's true, you can bet the man didn't get paid for keeping an eye on you at the hotel, either."

"I'm not going to lose any sleep over that. How did you avoid being hurt, Miguel? When we went off that bridge."

"The back window popped out. I can't explain how I was thrown. I was in the water—that part is not clear to me. By the time I made it back to the car, they had you in the ambulance. If only I'd—"

"No ifs."

Miguel took a deep breath.

Shauna said, "Tell me about the deal you made with Trent Wilde."

"How did you know about that?"

"I . . . am putting things together in my mind." If she was right, he would remember this part—the details of their agreement hadn't appeared in the memory she'd taken from him. "You disappeared to protect me, you said."

"I promised to drop the story, stop pursuing it to the end."

"Not enough for the man, I'm sure."

"I also promised to disappear, sever all ties to you. Your family."

"In exchange for my life."

Miguel nodded.

"And if I died?"

"I told them I had hidden the information I'd collected so far, and that if either one of us died, the person who held it for me would release it."

"Corbin?"

Sadness crossed Miguel's features. "No. But they probably thought so."

"Who had it?"

"It was a bluff, really. You had it."

She had it. Of course she did. Her mind went to the papers Khai had rescued for her. Shauna leaned forward. "So what's to prevent us from reopening the story now?" she asked.

His mouth fell open. "Uh, the fact that it nearly killed you the first time? The fact that I don't give a rip anymore about where the money comes from? They can keep it."

"But I still have the information."

He ran a hand through his hair.

She shot her question to him with her eyes.

"If they had killed you . . ." he said. The possibility thickened the air. "If they had killed you, that story would have been the last thing in the world I cared about. I only need them to believe someone has it."

"I have it. Khai brought me some papers—"

"No, Shauna."

"Listen, *Sabueso*. I would have—"

"I mean no, it's not in those files."

"Then where is it?"

"Shauna, don't. We can leave this all behind us."

"And never know the truth. And never feel safe. Don't tell me you don't care about that. I wouldn't believe you."

He hit the steering wheel with the flat of his hand.

She put her hand on his shoulder, ready to pull it away if she had to. "Don't you see? This isn't about money laundering. It can't be. Murder doesn't make sense otherwise. This is about something much bigger, about a father who's trying to kill his children, and a criminal who's sitting in the White House."

"*That* is well outside the scope of anything we can prove, and you know it. In fact, I'm pretty sure it's beyond what you even want to believe, Shauna."

"Call me lovely. Please."

His shoulders dropped a quarter inch, and Shauna sensed him soften.

"Tell me where I hid it. Because if everything you're telling me is true, I'm certain I would have told you."

29

From a warm coffee house in the SoCo District of Austin, around the corner from the *Statesman,* Miguel and Shauna nursed hot drinks and waited for Khai, who was coming into town by the metro bus.

Miguel's foot tapped against the rail beneath their stools at the window front, out of sync with the music.

Though Miguel had not yet bought into Shauna's plan to follow the money laundering story to its full revelation, he had convinced her of the fool-ishness of returning to the McAllister estate to retrieve the data. So, during the long wait for Khai, Shauna found herself sitting gingerly on the twin blades of impatience and caffeine. This morning she drank the bitter coffee that she normally avoided, thinking she could hold off the lingering effects of her forced sleep. It had been a long time since her mind felt sharp.

Khai finally appeared at the door, toting a small paper shopping bag with twine handles, which she set on the counter between them. Miguel got off his stool and held out his hand to greet Khai.

Instead of taking his hand, Khai stood on her toes to wrap him in a warm hug. "I'm so sorry about Corbin," she said, stepping back to see Miguel's face. "He kept your secret for you."

"Thank you for keeping ours now," he said.

Khai nodded and gestured to the bag. "That's it, yes?"

Shauna reached in and withdrew the cedar elephant, trumpeting as if happy to finally be remembered.

Miguel nodded. "That's it. May I get you something to drink?"

Khai held up her hand. "I'll get it. You take care of this." She gestured to the wooden creature.

As Khai went to the counter, Miguel and Shauna moved to a booth away from the window. Miguel waited for Shauna to sit, then slipped in on the opposite side.

Shauna examined the elephant, which was about the size of a small cantaloupe, but didn't see how it was a container as Miguel had claimed. "You'll have to show me how this works," she said, holding it out to him.

He took the carving from her. "Guatemalan puzzle box," he said. "A gift from me to you. Two weeks before the accident."

"What was the occasion?"

"An anniversary. Of sorts."

"My mother was Guatemalan," Shauna said.

Miguel grinned. "As was mine." He caught the expression on her face and said, "You were surprised the first time too. Now watch."

Miguel carefully pried the elephant's tusks off its face. They came away as pins that held the trunk and head together. One piece at a time, in conscientious order, Miguel dismembered the animal until it looked neither like an elephant nor a box. Shauna counted eight pieces on the table, plus the container that Miguel still held. It would have been the bulky abdomen, formed in two parts and now separated from the legs.

He parted the halves and revealed a small bundle of black fleece in the center that prevented the contents from rattling.

Shauna lifted it out of the wood and set it on the table to unwrap it. The bundle wasn't tidy; maybe she had wrapped it in a hurry.

No doubt.

The flash drive hidden by the fleece was almost identical to the one she had seen in Miguel's memory.

"This looks familiar," she said, handing it to him to examine.

"That's a good sign, right?"

Shauna wondered when—and how—it would be appropriate for her to tell him why it was familiar. She rolled the question around in her mind, fingering the fabric absentmindedly. Her fingers came upon a hard round object in its folds.

"There's something else," she said, pulling back the material.

Tucked into one corner that had been carefully folded into a pocket shape was a ring. A solitaire princess diamond set on a wide platinum band, the brilliant-cut square flanked by two baguette diamonds. Stunned, she looked at Miguel for an explanation.

He looked as stunned as she. But only for a moment.

"Well. Yeah." He coughed and took a sip of his coffee. "It hadn't occurred to me you'd hide that here, but it makes sense."

Shauna couldn't manage to form the right question. She picked up the ring and slipped it onto her left ring finger. A perfect fit. She took it off right away and laid it back on top of the fleece. She was certain she blushed.

"You didn't say anything about this."

Miguel fingered the paper napkin on the table between them, his eyes averted. "You told me you only wanted the bones."

"But this—this is like a whole skeleton."

She hadn't meant to come off so negatively. To soften the mood, she asked, "Why would I hide it?"

Good-natured humor flickered across the surface of Miguel's distress. "You can't think of a single reason why you wouldn't want your family or your bosses to know you are—were—engaged to me?"

Well. When he put it like that. Obviously, she'd been stunned once again out of reasoned thinking.

"*Were*? Did I break it off?"

He hesitated. "No."

"No, but . . . ?"

"But I won't hold you to a promise you can't remember making," he murmured.

Shauna stared at the ring. It was beautiful, the design and cut she would have picked for herself if she'd had the choice. Maybe she had.

"When were you going to tell me?"

"I don't know. I hadn't figured that out. If I should have said something sooner—"

"It's okay. Really."

She picked up the jewelry and laid it in her palm, sensing all of Miguel's emotions—yearning, fear, love, regret—focused on her. She did not have to look to know his gaze rested on her rather than on the ring. Embarrassment and giddiness tangoed in her stomach.

"That first time I went to see you," she said. "In the kitchen."

"I didn't believe you couldn't remember," he said. "Corbin had told me, but . . ."

Now more than ever, she hated that she didn't remember. She hated that a good man was in the position she'd put Miguel in, the position of knowing that the woman he loved didn't at all feel the way she once had, and through no fault of his own. She tried to imagine how she would feel to have lost something, someone, like that.

She thought of Rudy. Not even close, she knew, but as close as she herself could get.

She wished she could tell Miguel she loved him, but she couldn't. Not honestly. Not yet. She barely knew him.

He held out his hand, palm up. "This is more awkward than I could have predicted. I can hold on to that for you if you want. For now."

Something about the idea of his taking the ring back triggered terrible reluctance in the deepest part of Shauna's heart. She didn't want to give it back, and she couldn't explain why. Keeping it would be unfair to him, though. Irrational.

But some part of her—she could not tell if it was merely wishful or something real, cloaked in a cloud of forgetfulness—believed she could love him easily and soon. How could she not, she reasoned, after the kind of love he had demonstrated toward her? How could she take all that in and not eventually find herself exploding with love that begged to be returned?

Acting on faith, she closed her fingers around the ring to prevent him from taking it, then slipped it onto the ring finger of her right hand. "If it's okay with you, I think I'll keep it," she said. "For now."

He nodded and began to pick up the elephant puzzle without looking at her, fit two pieces back together. "You should keep it. No matter what happens."

Thirty minutes later Shauna and Miguel had their first fight.

They sat in the old Jeep, Khai tucked in the back, and were headed back through Austin to West Lake. Shauna had stashed the thumb drive in her jeans pocket and entrusted the elephant to Khai. They would drop her within walking distance of the house but, beyond that, couldn't agree on a plan.

"We should take what we have to that detective. What's his name—Beeson?" Miguel said. "He can offer you protection."

"I can't."

"Why not?"

"Several reasons, first being that he suspects me of killing Corbin." Miguel's eyes widened. "And he knows Corbin's camera was in my possession."

"How—?"

"I have no idea if the images on the camera have turned Beeson's attention away from me. And then there's the fact that I skipped town even though I'm not supposed to. I'll go to jail for that alone."

Miguel shook his head. "We'll call him then."

"What for?"

"To tell him what we know. Would you compromise on that for me?"

Shauna considered this. Giving Beeson Corbin's camera hadn't resulted in any disastrous outcomes. Yet. What worse could happen if they called the detective?

"Okay. But we should find my father first," Shauna finally said.

"Don't you think Wayne would expect you to seek him out?"

"No. Landon and I have not been on speaking terms lately."

"But all things considered—"

"Wayne knows you're with me, Miguel. From his point of view I have no reason to seek out my father. Where would you take me if I were not so stubborn and obstinate? Where would Wayne think you would take me?"

"Japan."

"Seriously."

"I don't know."

"The point I'm trying to make is, he won't expect you to take me to my father."

"That's because I won't."

"Miguel! I need to know how deep Landon is in this. He might not be involved at all. The election is less than two weeks away. I can't go shooting from the hip—"

"And look at what happened the last time we tried that! What makes you think he'll treat you any differently this time? He doesn't care about you, Shauna. He doesn't care that you're his daughter. Why is protecting him important to you?"

"I'm not protecting him. I'm talking about getting to the bottom of the truth first before I do something that could kill his reputation. If he's responsible for any of this, I'll be the first to stand aside."

"You're not going to kill his reputation, because you're not going to do anything at all!"

Shauna crossed her arms and met Miguel's eyes, frowning. "I dare you to walk away from the truth."

"Already did once. It's not so hard."

"But if you'd kept walking I wouldn't be here. It's an ugly choice, I know that. But what's happened isn't about you and me. Don't you see it?"

"He'll deny everything, as he did the night of the accident. We don't have anything new to talk about."

"We have Rudy. Do you know what Landon will do when he figures out that Wayne hurt him intentionally? That Wilde is behind it? You were right, I don't believe it. He can't possibly know. He would never have let the two of them set foot in his house if he knew."

"The two of them have found a way to successfully and illegally finance his campaign. Rudy was an unforeseen casualty of our great political system. Why do you think your dad blames you for the accident, Shauna? The man wants to stand as far away from the truth as possible. He can't possibly confront it. He has too much to lose."

"He only thinks I did it because Wayne set everything up to support that idea. Before now, nobody could support any other option."

"Nobody but you, you mean. You've been shouting innocent, and the senator can't hear a thing you say."

"But now I have evidence." She pointed at Miguel.

"I am hardly the evidence that will convince him. I sure wasn't persuasive last time."

"We have data."

"Half-fleshed data. Data that wasn't even sound enough for me to run with before the accident. I hadn't even put it in front of my editor yet. Besides, for all we know the senator is not ignorant of what has been happening. He might even be the mastermind behind it all."

Shauna glared at him. "I don't believe it. I can't."

"Why not? The man has to keep up appearances. You don't think he'd hire Wilde and Spade to keep his own hands lily-white?"

"He would have killed them himself to protect Rudy."

"Well, I wouldn't go basing your actions on your gut right now. Not unless you want to get yourself killed. Because I guarantee you McAllister doesn't feel the same way about you."

The fact stabbed Shauna deep. Even though his words were true, they were cruel. She made her hands into fists and pressed her knuckles against her eyelids and took a long breath.

"Mr. Spade called me this morning," Khai said. Shauna startled. She'd forgotten Khai was in the Jeep with them.

Miguel twisted to look over his shoulder. "That would have been nice to know."

"He was upset, worried. Said he'd gone to meet you in Corpus Christi and found your car, your phone, some clothes. He asked me to call him if I heard from you."

"This was before or after we called you about the elephant?"

"Before."

Shauna held her breath.

"I called him back after we spoke and told him you were with someone, I didn't know who. That Wayne Spade, he is dangerous. I said you told me you needed to get away, that you were going to Guatemala and asked me to have some money wired to you. I remembered you telling me that you went there often."

Shauna's relief expressed itself in a light laugh. "Brilliance happens," she said. "Thank you."

"Why would he believe Khai?" Miguel said.

Khai said, "I gave him the name of a bank there. I found it online."

"You made up account numbers too?"

"He wouldn't have asked me for those, even if he doubted me."

"That doesn't mean he'd go there," Miguel said.

"But it could mean he won't waste his time coming back here," Shauna said.

"The truth is, we can't possibly know where he is," Miguel said.

Khai said, "I offered to collect the things he'd left at the house, have them ready for him. He said he wouldn't be coming by and instructed me to ship them to Houston."

"He's going back with Wilde," Miguel said.

"Or just as easily on his way to Guatemala," Shauna countered.

"The point is, he's not here."

"But the senator is," Khai said.

Now Shauna twisted in her seat. "What else do you have up your sleeve?"

"He leaves again tomorrow morning," Khai said. "His car came up the drive as I was leaving."

Shauna decided. She needed to talk to Landon, needed to seize this opportunity.

"This is an in-your-face chance, Miguel. We should take it."

Miguel shook his head. "Your father knows me. If he's in on this, if he sees me with you . . ."

"You're right. We can't let him see you until we know," she said to Miguel. "I'm going in with Khai. Wait where you drop us, and I'll be back out as quick as I can."

Miguel set his jaw, and she braced for a list of reasons why he would not let her out of the car.

Instead, when he parked a short distance from the house, he studied the windshield and said, "Watch out for Spade."

30

Shauna was slightly surprised when the security detail allowed her to enter the house through the kitchen. Perhaps Patrice was not here. Or Trent had kept his promise to talk with Patrice about ending the lockout—before their falling-out.

The women parted ways in the red-tiled hall. Khai squeezed Shauna's hand. "Don't be afraid," she said. "God is with you."

The sentiment caught Shauna off guard. "My mother used to say that to me. Is that from the Bible?"

Khai nodded. "For those who believe him."

"She also used to say, 'Nothing can separate you from the love of God, Shauna.' Is that in the Bible too? Or is it just a nice idea?"

Khai's mouth broke into a wide smile. "It's from the book of Romans. 'Neither death nor life, neither angels nor demons, neither the present nor the future—'"

Shauna hardly heard the rest. *Neither the present nor the future.*

"'—will be able to separate us from the love of God.'"

Goose bumps trickled over Shauna's arms.

"If Wayne finds us, you will not be safe," Shauna said, worried for the woman who had so selflessly helped her so many times.

"I'm not afraid. I'm taking leave this afternoon to visit my brother."

"I hope this is a . . . memorable time for both of you," Shauna said.

"It couldn't be otherwise." Khai left her with a hug.

Shauna watched her go, wondering if it was possible that God's love, like her mother's, had never abandoned her, whether she had merely stopped looking for it in her life.

A noise in the kitchen snapped Shauna out of her reverie. She considered where Landon might spend the afternoon, if an hour or two was the only time he had. The fitness center, maybe. Her father's study was on the other side of the house, the large patio between them. She stepped to the nearest window.

No one at the pool. It was October 24 and unseasonably cool, too cool today to be out, even in Texas. Taking the full-circle hallway to the back wing, then past the bedrooms, she kept an eye out for Rudy, whom she wanted to hug, and Patrice, whom she planned to avoid. She saw neither.

Coming into the wing containing the offices, she turned right and stopped to listen before she would come into anyone's view. She heard voices. Patrice, on the phone in her office, door open. And Landon, having a one-sided conversation with someone in his office, probably also on the phone. She caught mention of a poll. She eased herself into a position where she could, she hoped, see into his office without being seen.

The tone of Landon's voice pulled her closer. This was a voice she had not heard since—since she couldn't say, easy and unaffected by a public expectation. This was a voice she had heard more often as a child, well before her mother's death, and if she'd been asked a moment sooner, she would have said she couldn't remember it. But there it was. Patient, smooth like pumpkin pie, and warm like the sun on a winter's day.

This was not the strained voice of a man days away from a national presidential election. Whom was he speaking to? She dared to look.

The curtains of Landon's office were drawn against the noon glare, and bulky bookcases lit by dome lights provided the main lighting. Landon sat at his desk with his back to the door, tipped back in the leather seat as far as it would go, stocking feet on the ink blotter, big toe looking green under the emerald glass shade of a banker's lamp. He cupped a tumbler full of melting ice in both hands and laughed at his own joke.

In his own mechanical chair on the opposite side of the desk sat Rudy.

Shauna moved into the door frame and leaned against it, smiling at her brother. The horrible bruises around his eyes had faded. Or maybe it was the lighting. He looked good. Better anyway.

Landon must have noticed Rudy's eyes shift, for as his chuckles tapered off, he put down his feet and shifted forward in the chair to see who stood at the door. She had the presence of mind to turn the ring on her right hand so that the diamonds faced her palm.

He lifted his empty glass her way, a meaningless toast offered with a shrug.

"Shauna. Rudy and I were just catching up."

The tension of their last encounter still reverberated.

"Hi, Landon." She took a tentative step into the room, then rounded the desk and stooped to place a kiss on Rudy's forehead. "Hey, Rude. Didn't mean to interrupt."

She took the seat next to her brother. Landon looked at her, silent, as if she couldn't have hoped to enter the conversation he was having with Rudy and so wouldn't continue it.

"That's quite a shiner you've got," he said, tipping up his glass though there was nothing left in it to drink. Shauna glanced toward the bar at the back of the room.

"Can I get you some more?" she said.

He waved her off. "Day's young. The gray cells have a long way to go yet. Rudy and I were celebrating the passage of a little bill of mine today."

Shauna noticed for the first time that an identical tumbler one-third full of dark creamy liquor over ice sat in front of Rudy.

"Congratulations."

"A bit prone to accidents these days, are we?" His gaze fell on her swollen cheekbone again.

"Apparently so." She looked at Rudy, grateful for his presence. "Landon, I need to talk with you about a . . . sensitive matter. Do you have a few minutes?"

"Campaign's going fine, thanks for asking. Ahead in the polls by 15 percent and growing, so long as I don't slow down and Anderson doesn't make any more royal mistakes in front of the press."

Landon referred to the deputy campaign manager who had replaced Rudy and couldn't resist a camera.

She knew she would have to wait, let him stay in control of the conversation. "I'm sorry he's been such a headache."

"Well, I can tolerate a dull pain so long as it gets me where I need to be. Rudy here, though, he gets the credit for the grunt work. Anderson didn't have to do a thing but keep Rudy's strategy in motion. You did a fantastic job, son."

Shauna felt a fresh grief for what she had lost in Rudy. Grief, it turned out, was all that connected her to her father anymore. The loss of her mother and the loss of Rudy fell heavily on them both, but from different angles. She wondered if grief would eventually be what severed their thin ties.

Perhaps. If Landon continued to blame her for the wreck.

"Will Rudy go to the White House with you?" she asked.

"Maybe. Like to have him there. But his therapy is here. We might have to wait and see, give him time." His mouth moved around these words like someone else had fed them to him. Patrice, no doubt. The practicality couldn't hide the underlying passion. If it were up to Landon, these two would never be apart.

Shauna took a risk. "I would like to help with Rudy. Here. As long as he needs it. If you trust me with that."

"Pam's doing a fine job."

"I didn't mean—"

"What was so important that you crashed our little meeting here?"

Faced with the opportunity she had insisted was so critical, she realized she didn't know where the front door was. How to enter this conversation? There was the direct: *What part are you playing in the laundering scheme that's funding your campaign?* There was the oblique: *Would you tell me about the profit-sharing structure at MMV, why it was changed a few years ago?* There was the reluctant: *I heard this rumor, and I can't possibly believe it's true.* And there was the desperate, bottom line: *Wayne tried to kill me, and I need to know you're not a criminal about to take the White House; I need to know you weren't behind it; I need to know you love me too much for that.*

In one second she shut the door on each of these options, seeing intuitively how far south they would go, and how fast. These questions would fail to get her closer to both her father and the truth. Was there even a way for her to have both—intimacy and honesty? Or were they mutually exclusive where Landon was concerned?

When her father rose from his seat as if to end the conversation, she threw off the burden of her hesitation and spoke the next words on her lips without thinking them through.

"You and I fought right before the accident."

"I'm not sure an apology is worth much at this point."

"I wasn't—that's not what I meant to do."

"Of course you didn't."

Shauna took a deep breath.

Landon said, "Rudy would not have gone back with you if you weren't so hot under the collar."

"Tell me what we fought about."

Landon dropped back into his seat. "Now isn't that ironic? You can't even remember."

"Tell me."

"You got some crazy notion into your head that my out-of-pocket donation to the campaign was dirty. That's ridiculous, Shauna. I can't believe you would think I would—"

"It wasn't just my notion." Wrong thing to say!

"No, I don't doubt that *Statesman* reporter was feeding you ideas, taking advantage of your employment at Harper & Stone. And who knows what else."

The insult made her flush. She had to keep this conversation on target. "I think the mistake I made was in assuming you were aware of how MMV's profits had skyrocketed. I assumed you engineered it."

She hoped he hadn't engineered it. Oh, how she hoped!

"And how would I do that? I haven't been involved in their strategies for years. Wilde took that over when I entered politics and has never screwed it up. He's had great success, 'Wilde Success,' we call it, in the international markets. Indonesia, Thailand, even Cambodia. What's shocking about that? I'll tell you again, Shauna, and I said this that night—you can check my tax returns, you can audit me, you can hold a magnifying glass over every penny I've ever earned. I would not jeopardize my career or my office by doing something so inordinately stupid."

Shauna put her hand on Rudy's knee and dropped the tone of her voice to a low, even level. "Landon, I'm pretty sure that my hunches were correct—not about you, but about the money. And I'm even more sure that the accident was no accident at all. Someone set that up."

Landon shook his head and wagged a finger at his daughter. "Shirk your responsibility all you want, Shauna. It's still pinned on you, no matter what outrageous ideas you'll cook up."

"Wayne and Trent and Leon are in a position to rig MMV's policies in any way that's beneficial to them."

Landon snatched his glass off the desk and marched back to the bar. "This sounds like some half-baked theory that reporter would feed you. What was his name? Lopez?"

Shauna was glad her father wasn't looking at her. She didn't want to bring Miguel into this yet.

"I tipped my hand, asked Wayne the wrong kinds of questions. He figured me out."

"He would have gone to Wilde, and then Wilde would have come to me, and my issues with you would be a whole lot more complicated than they are now." Landon uncapped the bottle of liqueur and poured it over his watery ice.

Shauna rose and crossed the room to stand next to her father. She needed to keep him calm—for Rudy's sake—and hoped he would open up to her, for the sake of truth. For the sake of their crumbling relationship.

"He went to Wilde, but the two of them didn't go to you. Wouldn't it make sense for them to keep you in the dark? You get legitimate deniability. The less you know, the less you're guilty of."

He spun to face her. "I'm not guilty of anything but tolerating your pitiful need for attention."

She pleaded with her eyes for him to remember that Rudy was still in the room with them. Landon took a drink.

"Of course you're not." She laid a hand on his arm. "But Wayne . . . Landon, I have evidence that he tried to kill me." She pointed at Rudy. "Wayne did this. Uncle Trent did this. Not me."

"I don't believe you."

He was closed to her touch. She wasn't getting anything.

"Rudy wasn't supposed to be in the car."

"Wilde would have stopped it."

"But Wayne had put the machine in motion. *Dad.* Can't you see what's going on?"

Landon exploded with just enough self-control to protect his son. His voice and emotions were restrained, but his face was bright red in the dim room. He set his drink on the counter and leaned in close to Shauna.

"*If* Wilde and Spade were involved in anything so illegal, and *if* they thought you were going to expose them, they would have found a dozen other ways to keep you quiet. They would have sought my advice. They live and breathe on my authority. And *if* I knew about it, and *if* I was such a devil that I needed to cover it up, I would have taken out that loco Lopez, not my own children."

"Wayne tried to kill him too."

Landon closed his eyes, exasperated.

"Miguel Lopez was in the car with me."

"You were at the party together? What do you think that says about your motivation, Shauna? And why wasn't he on scene? Why isn't he in the accident reports? Are you the only one who saw him? I suppose Wayne planted drugs in your car too?"

Shauna looked at Rudy, unable to bring the conversation around.

"And who else has our dear Wayne Spade tried to take out?"

She knew better than to bring up Corbin Smith at this point.

"People don't *murder* over money laundering, girl. They don't kill over a plain vanilla, white-collar crime."

"No, they don't. They kill to gain the presidency, Landon. Listen to me. There is something so much bigger than we realize going on here. I don't know what it is yet, but I promise you—if it's big enough to kill for, it's big enough to destroy everything you've ever worked for."

She cupped his face in her hands as if he were the child. "Dad. I'm only here because I couldn't bear to see that happen."

As she spoke the words, she was not at all surprised to understand that they were true. She sensed the gap between them close by a hairline, as if he was dropping his defenses against her. Would he give her access to his own mind? Was that what she wanted?

She wanted to be close to her father. She didn't want to steal from him.

She was close enough to see the horizon of his mind, crowded with a city-scape of memories. She saw the street forged by Landon's fraternity with Trent. It cut through the peaks and valleys that she recognized as McAllister MediVista's booming growth. She saw in the background, barely perceptible, the smaller world of his childhood. In the foreground were buildings crowded with people: colleagues he trusted, political opponents he had grown to hate. She spotted her mother in a mansion at the calm center and was tempted to linger there, but unwilling to take something so precious from her father. She saw Patrice, her arm linked in Landon's at a fund-raiser held at Columbia University, where she was a tenured professor of economics. Shauna saw herself. She saw Rudy.

Rudy, in fact, was everywhere.

He had enough of Rudy to spare.

But that was as close as she would get.

The cityscape vanished. Landon had withdrawn from Shauna's touch. She caught her breath.

"It's not possible," her father was saying, moving away from her into the dim office space. "Trent Wilde would never put us at risk. I trust him with my life."

She found her bearings again. "But I don't. If you knew what I have been through . . ."

Landon scowled. Wrong approach.

"Look," Shauna said. "I haven't asked you for anything in years. I need your help now. I know you're mad at me. I know you don't believe me. But will you help me?"

"If it will keep you clear of me until November 13, sure."

"I need a place to stay. I need time to sort out the truth in my own mind."

"And isn't that a laudable pursuit." Patrice leaned in the door frame. Shauna did not know how much of the conversation she had heard. "What's all the drama about?"

Shauna stayed silent.

"It seems my daughter has fixated on a particular problem that doesn't exist. She's planning some vacation time to clear her head." He opened a safe in the wall and withdrew a set of boat keys. "You can stay on the Bayliner. I took it out last time I was here. Nothing for you to do to get it ready."

She hesitated to take this gift horse. The senator's cabin cruiser wasn't exactly a safe house. But maybe it would buy Miguel and her an hour or two to sort things out. She made one more attempt to keep the encounter with her father from unraveling further.

"I can't tell you what a relief it is to know you're not . . . that you weren't . . ." Shauna tried to explain.

Landon's expression softened from granite to sandstone. He dropped the keys into her palm but didn't speak.

"Thank you. You won't . . . if Wayne or Trent ask you . . ."

He guffawed. "I'd have to be drunk to tell them what you've just told me. I can't afford to look like a half-wit this close to election day."

31

Shauna stayed only long enough to dash to the guesthouse for a fresh set of clothes. And the medication—maybe she could have someone analyze the pills. And Deputy Bowden's accident report—she wanted Miguel to read it. And a little bit of cash tucked away in a roll of clean socks.

She left before she decided she needed a suitcase.

Miguel looked relieved enough to hug Shauna when she dropped into the passenger seat of his Jeep carrying her load. In fact, he did hug her, leaning across the gearshift sideways and surrounding her with his strong arms.

Shauna felt her back stiffen before she pulled away.

"I shouldn't have done that." He held up two hands. "I'm just really glad to see you."

"I can't have been gone more than twenty minutes."

"The twenty longest minutes of my life. With one exception."

"Well, I was fine. But it was good you weren't there. Your name came up."

"He thinks I've filled your empty head with ideas."

"Something like that."

"That was pretty clear the night we argued with him."

"Before my head was even empty."

He laughed. "So, was he more receptive in the privacy of his own home?"

"Receptive, no. Not at all. He thinks I'm crazy. Still, I'm pretty sure that what's going on is happening behind Landon's back."

Miguel did not say anything to that.

"You still think he's involved," Shauna said.

"I don't see how he couldn't be. In his position, with money coming out of his own pocket? It's too much of a stretch to think he's blind."

Shauna understood that this latest confrontation didn't prove anything, not even to her. For now, however, there was no way to explain this to Miguel. She held up the keys to the cabin cruiser.

"I know where we can go until we decide what to do next."

"What we need to do next is take out Wayne Spade and company before they take us out."

"Can't do it without a nap. When did you last sleep?"

Miguel had to stop and think. "An hour here and there, since you showed up Monday."

"You and I both are going on nearly three days then. Landon has a boat at Yacht Harbor Marina."

Miguel shook his head. "That's like taking a nap on a bull's-eye."

"If we sat in the slip, maybe. But out on the water . . ."

"I'd rather find a hotel for you."

"And pay to stay for two hours? What will people think!"

Miguel was in no humor to joke about that. "Can you put a price on safety?"

"Really, Miguel, what can happen in two hours on a lake when no one outside my own home knows where we are?"

Miguel turned the key over in the ignition, willing neither to go along with her nor to fight. He surrendered by changing the subject.

"Give me the thumb drive," he said.

She fished it out of her pocket and handed it to him. "What are you going to do?"

"If you won't go see Beeson in person, we'll overnight it to him. I'm not going to walk around with this thing."

"I had some time to think while you were in talking with your father," he said as he drove away from the FedEx office and toward the marina where Landon kept his boat.

"And what did you think about?"

"I was thinking about how you recognized the driver of the SUV as being the same man who was in the hotel suite. Or more to the point, how you remembered the driver at all."

When she didn't answer right away, he said, "We haven't really talked about what this memory loss has been like for you. Is it something you can explain to me?"

"I'm not sure I have explained it to myself yet," Shauna said.

He waited.

"The experimental drugs I mentioned—I was told they were designed to counteract the effects of trauma on the brain. But I'm pretty sure now, based on what Trent told me yesterday, that that was all . . . a fabrication. I think maybe even the coma was medically induced."

"Why?"

"I didn't have any brain damage." She laughed wryly. "Although—that might remain to be seen."

Miguel looked at her sideways. "I mean, why would they put you in a medically induced coma if your injuries weren't to your head?"

"To give Trent time to devise a story my father would believe? To give the medications time to work the way they were supposed to? I'm not sure."

"So you're pretty sure medications wiped out your memories."

Shauna nodded. "It's not so far-fetched. They've known how to wipe out certain memories in lab rats for quite some time. It's an ideal plan: You vanish. I forget. Trent Wilde and company rake in millions and put their man in the White House. Trent takes a cushy job in the cabinet."

"I wonder if it can be reversed."

"The money scheme?"

"Your memory loss."

"Probably not. But our minds are pretty sci-fi, you know? There's so much we don't know about how they work. Did you know Pam said there's a small chance that Rudy can recover?"

"Really? That's something."

"It has to do with the kind of injury he's got. I don't pretend to understand it. As for my own mind—it's like it's trying to rebuild what got lost."

"I don't get it."

She laughed, nervous for the first time in Miguel's company. She turned his ring around on her finger. "It's crazy."

"Say it anyway."

"I can take memories from other people," she said before she could think herself out of it. She wouldn't look at him. "I can pick which memory I want to have. I can use them to re-create the context of my own story. Such as it is."

Miguel's silence was loud in the car.

"I got the image of our SUV driver from a sheriff's deputy who was on the scene. It was one of my first. I didn't even know what I was doing then. It just happened, dropped me to the floor. But it's my memory now."

She heard the feathery sound of Miguel's hand drawing down over his smooth cheeks, his pointed beard.

"I'm a thief," she said. "I steal from people. I don't have my own memories, so I take what belongs to others. It's the only way I can figure out this mess I'm in right now. It's like I don't have—"

"I believe you," he said.

"You do?"

"Tell me how it works."

As if it were a computer program. She stole a hesitant look at him. His expression was unreadable. "I need . . . I have to be able to touch a person."

"You take memories from anyone you touch?"

"No. It's not so haphazard. A person has to be willing to let me into his mind."

"So how does that work? You just ask them?"

"Hardly! They have to trust me. Let their guard down somehow." She shivered. "I try to make them want to connect with me. Maybe make them hope I have something to give them. Or maybe even want something I can give them."

"So you need an emotional connection as well as a physical one."

She nodded. "In that sense it's mutual. I can't take anything from anyone who shuts me out."

"This is a new . . . ability? Something that's happened since the accident."

"I'm sure it is."

He still hadn't looked at her. She wasn't sure how to interpret the underlying stiffness of his voice. Was it caution? Repulsion?

"How did you learn to do it?"

"Learn? Hardly. It just happened. I can't explain it. My best guess—this is some freak side-effect of that drug experiment. Those were designer pharmaceuticals. They were formulated based on my genetic code. How many variables could they possibly have foreseen? And how I can actually *take* a memory is even more inexplicable. These people I steal from haven't had any drugs."

"Is this something you can control? From your end anyway?"

She hesitated. "I'm getting better at it."

"Do they know what you're doing? I mean, the people you take memories from."

"Did you?"

He snapped his head to look at her.

"When?" he asked. His tone was softer now.

"In the park."

"My hand—" He turned up his palm. The skin was still white where she had squeezed it.

"I can't explain that. That particular effect hasn't happened to anyone else."

"What did I give you?" he asked.

"You mean what did I take?"

"No. I mean what did I give you?" He smiled. "Because you know you can have anything you want. You can wipe me clean."

Shauna stumbled over her reply. She had not expected his belief in her, let alone this extreme, inexplicable trust.

"I saw your memory of confronting Uncle Trent after the accident. In his office at MMV."

"Ah." Miguel nodded as if their bizarre conversation in Victoria now made sense, but his eyebrows drew together and he looked back at his hand.

"What was it like?" she asked.

"You holding my hand after everything that had happened?" he teased. She allowed the corner of her mouth to rise.

"No, goofball. Losing a memory."

"It was like knowing you've been to a certain city but not remembering the reason for your visit. Or going in to work every day but not being able to remember each hour in detail. Everything is familiar, but incomplete. I can remember that I bargained with Trent, but I can't remember what happened in the moments before."

"What did you feel when I did it?"

"I felt like I'd stuck my hand into a pool of water charged with a low current of electricity. At the time, though, I believed that sensation was something else entirely."

"Do you remember being in Leon's office?"

"I remember laying out how I wanted this to work. I don't remember how I got there."

"So you don't remember Trent attacking you?"

Miguel shook his head. "Just the deal. And Leon hauled me out after that."

"If I had it to do over again—"

"Think of that memory as something I entrusted to you." He reached for her hand. "You can tell me about it when I need to know. Though it doesn't sound like a bedtime story I'll want repeated on a regular basis. But if you and me stick together, we won't have lost a thing."

His touch sent an electric jolt up her fingers. She snatched her hand away, set up a barrier in her mind. What he was saying was all wrong. She had no right to rob him for her selfish gain, to make herself complete. She wouldn't. She didn't want to.

He didn't try to insist. He only said, now understanding, "That's why you won't let me touch you."

She could barely nod. "I don't trust myself."

"Would you trust me?" Miguel asked.

On this point? They weren't exactly talking about financial investments here, or political outcomes or journalistic sources.

Shauna didn't know the answer.

The thirty-two-foot cruiser, tall and as shiny new as the first day Landon bought it, sat in one of the largest covered slips in the Yacht Harbor Marina, and it took the two of them and a deckhand working together only a matter of minutes to get the canvas off and the boat backed out into the lane. They left the bimini top in the locker—wouldn't need it today.

Shauna was familiar with the controls and gave Miguel a quick 101 before stepping down into the cabin to shower and change into fresh clothes.

By the time she returned to the deck, Miguel had turned the engine off to float on the open water. He was stretched out on one of the deck's wraparound lounges. A phone book from the galley lay on the deck beside him. He sat up right away.

"I thought I'd have to go wake you up in a couple hours," she said.

"You will, but first we should call the detective."

Shauna nodded.

"My phone's in the cockpit." He fetched it and returned to the seat, then held on to the phone when she tried to take it. "Before you call . . ."

"You've been thinking again."

"Yes. He'll want you to come in."

"I expect he'll want both of us."

"I want you to consider going."

"I have already told you all the reasons why I won't."

"I get that, but honestly, jail might be the safest place for you right now."

"Right. No one ever got killed in jail."

"Shauna. Please."

"I'm sorry. I don't want to fight." She sighed and put her hands on her hips. "If I go, what will you do?"

"I can stay on the outside, help in ways you won't have the chance to."

"I think the police are perfectly capable of doing their jobs without you."

"I wasn't talking about the police. Some of us can get a little farther faster when we don't have to worry about procedural red tape."

"Now you're talking like a journalist."

"That's right."

"What did you have in mind?"

She caught hold of his idea at the same time he uttered it. "Scott Norris," they both said aloud together.

"What can he help you discover that Detective Beeson couldn't?" Shauna asked.

"You said you think Wayne deserted the Marines?"

"It was a memory of his. He denied it, but something about it showed up in his psych file. When I accused Trent of paying Wayne's way out of a court-martial, that seemed to hit a nerve."

"You wouldn't happen to know Scott Norris's daddy, would you?"

"I'm afraid Scott wasn't interested in taking me home to meet the family."

"Mr. Scott Norris, Sr. works for the CIA, Office of Inspector General."

"I can't imagine he gives Scott—"

"No no no. Senior is a devout American," Miguel said. "He wouldn't necessarily tell us anything, but he might be interested in Wayne Marshall. And anyone who helped him out of the military. Especially if that person might be connected to the White House."

"We're looking at Trent for this, not my father."

"Whoever. I'm thinking if we can connect Wayne and Trent to some military subversion, we might be able to come at the money laundering issue through the back door."

She cracked open the phone book to look up the police department's switchboard number.

"Well, I already owe Scott Junior dinner," Shauna said.

"I have a hunch we'll owe him more than that by the time we're through." He handed Shauna his phone.

"Don't go promising our first child to him or anything like that, okay?"

32

The problem with falling asleep on a rocking boat in the middle of a lake was that Shauna might as well have fallen asleep in a womb, with only the pain of contractions for an alarm clock.

For Shauna, these came in the form of a ringing cell phone. She awoke with a jerk that tapped her injured cheek into the pillow. She winced, and her hand rose up to cover the swollen skin. How had she rolled onto that side without waking? The cabin was dark. She shifted in the bed, not in the mood to get up yet.

Miguel's voice, as groggy as her mind, drifted into the lower level from the cockpit. He talked for a minute, maybe two, but she couldn't make out the words. How long had they been sleeping? Not long enough, that was sure.

"Shauna?"

"I'm up." Very slowly, she righted herself, then tried to find her shoes, which she'd yanked off and dumped before collapsing on the bed.

"I never meant to doze off for so long," Miguel said. "My fault."

"Guess we needed the rest." Her groping hand bumped into her boots. She fumbled to pull the left one on first.

"That was Beeson. We missed your meeting time." Before crashing, she had finally agreed to have Miguel drop her off at the station at seven before he looked up Scott Norris.

"Beeson think I took off again?"

"I assured him you hadn't."

"What time is it?"

"Nearly ten."

"Ugh—how is that possible?"

She pulled on the other shoe, then ran her fingers through her hair. It looked mussed when she styled it and downright horrifying after a sleep. She could only imagine how it would scare small children now, having slept on it after a shower, and paired with her pretty black eye.

Miguel extended a hand from above as she made her way to the stairs and onto the deck. Shauna lifted her arms into a cat stretch. Miguel was grinning at her shagginess.

"You could use a shave or two yourself, *Sabueso.*" She tweaked his beard quickly.

"Beeson said your friend Khai told him that Corbin was helping her human-rights-watch organization document some suspicious activities."

"Right. Human trafficking activities," she said.

"Those photos of Wayne are of him in Houston, making transactions with two other men."

"Beeson know who they are?"

"Not yet. But they made a close match with one of them to someone in the Interpol database who was wanted on allegations of trafficking. Black-market babies." Shauna's stomach turned. "Beeson sent scans to the Department of Justice for verification."

"This just gets more and more awful."

"Come be my copilot. I'm going to need your help guiding this girl back in."

Shauna activated the navigation lights and stayed close to Miguel in the cockpit during the fifteen-minute ride back into the marina. Their easy silence joined hands with the restfulness of her sleep and created a calming effect. It was possible that she hadn't felt so secure, so hopeful that she would reach the bottom of the truth, since she came around.

She broke the silence. "I'm not sure how I feel about you going off to talk to Scott Norris without me."

"You think I don't know how to chase a story?" He didn't sound offended. Maybe he was even glad that she didn't want him to be away from her.

"You know that's not what I mean." But she couldn't put what she really meant into words. Verbalizing what she felt would make her appear childish and vulnerable, insecure. Surely she could handle being on her own for a few hours after being on her own in every meaningful way for these past critical days.

So she was grateful when Miguel did not demand she explain and that he seemed intuitively to understand. After all, he did know her better than she knew him.

She thought she'd like to level that playing field when this was over.

"After we're done with this tonight, we should let Beeson and Norris and whoever the relevant authorities are handle the rest of this mess," she said, lacking the imagination to envision where they could go that was out of Wayne's reach, or how they would get there, or how they would stay safe once they arrived, or how—

"I think you have great ideas," Miguel said.

"Too bad the world doesn't make much room for them." Shauna sighed. They would have to sit tight under Beeson's watchful eye until her trial was decided. And what then, if Wayne proved too slippery an eel for the charges against her to stick to him?

The lights of the marina's docks began to take a recognizable shape.

As Miguel directed the bow into the covered space that was her father's, Shauna caught sight of the phone book they'd left out on the deck. She picked it up and returned to the cabin to stow it in its drawer as Miguel cut the engine and let the vessel glide. Below, she heard him jump out onto the dock to secure the moorings.

Within seconds, she heard his feet hit the deck again. Tying off in that speed would have made him a veritable seafaring cowboy. He landed heavily, a lumbering jump that she would not have expected of him.

"You all right?"

His response did not come from the deck, however, but from the dock, and in the form of a warning shout.

"Stay down!"

Ignoring his command, Shauna took the cabin stairs in two long steps up. Her head broke the plane of the deck at the same moment that an arm came around her neck and pinched it in the nook of an elbow. She smelled days-old sweat on the muscled skin, and when she scratched at the arm with her nails, they scraped over hair.

She cried out as the man dragged her off the steps. His arm was a vise.

She saw his free fist swing in to meet her temple, and her dim vision lit up with summer sparklers. She sagged but did not go out. She called for Miguel, but the pressure on her voice box stifled the sound.

Without being fully aware of her reasons for doing so, she collapsed face-first onto the deck, dead weight. Her captor's elbow, still folded in front of her jaw, cracked on the surface of the flooring. Judging by the screaming in her ear, it might have even fractured.

Shauna struggled. Behind her assailant's cries was more distant shouting. Miguel's voice, mixed with another. She twisted, saw Miguel jump back onto the boat and throw himself on top of the body tangle she was in, pummeling the guy above her. The vibrations of each hit reverberated through her kidneys.

Then the body rolled off of hers, and Miguel's hands were under her armpits, yanking her upward.

"Go go go go go!" Her legs were tied in too many knots to get them up under her. Miguel heaved, lifted her.

Another man dropped onto the Bayliner's deck, which resounded like a timpani. *Boom.* The vessel rocked, and Shauna would have fallen if Miguel had not been balancing her with the absorbent shocks of his own two legs.

Somehow, she found herself stable enough to follow Miguel's lead. He rushed her toward the seating at the back of the open boat. The man who'd attacked her rolled on the deck, gripping his elbow and groaning. The other lunged for Shauna's ankles, catching her by the boot as Miguel lifted her onto the vinyl cushions.

She kicked out and Miguel balanced for both of them. Her thrashing foot caught the man in the nose before the boot slipped off her foot completely.

Shauna heard her own loud breathing, and then Miguel's voice in the moment it took for the two attacking shadows to find their feet.

"Let go," his lungs punched out.

She had to do what made no sense, she had to trust what she didn't understand. If she didn't, the time it would take her to unravel the meaning of those two words would kill them both. *Let go.*

She let go of Miguel, and he picked her up with the strength of a Samson about to die. One of his hands slipped under her armpit and the other gripped her opposing knee. She tucked her free leg close to her body.

He launched her off the back of the boat. Just one swing. Back. Out. And she was airborne.

Shauna held her breath, her awareness of what Miguel had done sharpened by anxiety. Why hadn't he jumped with her? Didn't he understand that these men would kill him? They would haul him off the senator's boat and kill him far away from any political spotlight—in some Texas desert—and no one would even miss him, no one would ever know to look for him because no one even knew he was no longer in his own lonely universe of self-imposed hiding—

The cold water that smacked her back might as well have been an ice rink. She hit hard, lost her breath, saw her own mind lock up, fixated on the last time she'd taken a plunge into icy black water.

Black water and ice and automotive metal and the smothering mask of air bags, holding her down. She knew, though she could not see, that she was alone and would die if she didn't find her bearings. Her lungs would open up any second and take on water. She flailed, kicking and swimming, forcing her body up and out. She thought it was up and out. She hoped.

Her hands hit something solid and she grabbed hold of it, a sharp and broken surface that drew blood off her palms. A barnacle-riddled pile. She followed it upward, keeping her body close, the blades shredding her blouse and scraping the skin on her stomach.

An image of a shattered window cutting into her belly flashed through her mind. The first memory of her own.

She needed air. Shauna could not understand how the blackness of her surroundings became blacker, only that they did. If she didn't breathe now—

Shauna's survival reflexes took over against the will of her mind and opened her mouth, opened her lungs.

And filled them with air.

She breathed thick, sweet air, clinging to the support beam of a deck adjacent to her father's slip. She breathed and breathed, trying not to gasp like a snagged fish, trying not to announce her location.

A crash opened her eyes and turned them toward the source. A drama in silhouette, backlit by the yellow lights of the main dock: Miguel's body was doubled over the deckside galley, punched into position by one of the men. The other was standing over the stern, staring into the water and holding his bloody nose, shouting, "I need a light."

The shadow with Miguel was too busy to get the man a light. He forced Miguel into an upright position with one arm and landed a heavy fist to his rib cage. Miguel collapsed, his chin meeting his opponent's knee. His head snapped backward, and he spit. The one-armed bully swung his knuckles across Miguel's face.

The hulk who demanded a light jumped off the seating and, with an easy kick to Miguel's shoulder, dropped him out of Shauna's view. Together the pair had no trouble subduing him.

Shauna's whole body was shaking, but she was not aware of the cold.

One of the men withdrew a cloth and snapped it open. A gag? In only moments she saw Miguel lifted off the deck, hands tied behind his back. It took them both to lift his limp form. A black sack hooded Miguel's head. Shauna's heart collapsed.

"Now get your light," said the one.

Shauna held her breath and shifted behind the narrow pile as if it would prevent her shaking body from dispersing telltale ripples. She looked around for a way out from under the deck. Without light of her own, she might well strangle in the mess of support beams and cables down here. How to climb up, run away? The nearest service ladder was several slips down. Even if she could reach it, she wouldn't be able to get past them unnoticed.

Could she swim to the bank?

She couldn't even see the bank.

Her toes and fingers were numb. Her cheekbone ached. *Miguel.*

A high beam reached out across the water behind her father's boat and moved toward her deck. She held her breath and slipped beneath the surface without a splash, though of course the water would not hold still for her.

Above her head, the pile cut the beam of light in two. It hovered over the water for three seconds that felt like three minutes. Her lungs would burst.

The light moved on. She came back up, no louder than a puff of wind.

"No way to find her in this without creating a scene," the light holder said, clicking it off.

"The one'll have to do, then."

"You be the one to tell Spade."

"Spade doesn't like what we do, he can do it himself."

"This one's as good as two anyway. We can use him to bring the girl in."

Their backs turned to her, and Shauna could not hear the rest of their conversation. They wrapped Miguel in a tarp, leaving his head protruding, then methodically returned the senator's boat to its resting condition, canvas snapped down as if the boat hadn't even gone out. She stayed in the water, limbs turning to immobile lead in the cold. She leaned her head against the pile and cried without a sound.

A new silence aroused Shauna out of a frozen stupor. The lights above the deck were off, except for the dim safety lighting at the end. The men were gone.

Miguel was gone.

Shauna listened for hidden danger. Nothing. She moved her arm to push off the pile, and the water snapped around her like a firecracker.

As best she could tell, no one had heard.

The safety lights were made brighter by the fresh darkness of the boat slips, and Shauna followed them down to the access ladder that she hoped was not merely a false memory. One slip. Two slips. How far down was it?

How far down would this story take her?

How much would her search for truth cost her in the end?

Landon was the only person who knew where she and Miguel were—who else could have ordered the hit? And what kind of father would want his children dead? Because if Landon McAllister had not betrayed her and Miguel to Wayne's hired thugs, she would have to believe that Wayne was not human at all, but some kind of sinister, supersensory minion who could intuit her whereabouts.

Shauna's fingertips brushed the metal rung of an access ladder, and her short-term memory opened wide onto a new reality.

Patrice knew Miguel and Shauna would be here. Patrice McAllister. Macbeth's very wife, a mastermind of murder and power, standing in the doorway of her father's home office with bloody daggers in her hands.

33

Please, God. Please keep Miguel alive. Prove that you love me and keep him alive.

A cold wind picked up off the lake. Shauna lay prone on the dock, her toes still touching the top rungs of the ladder, as she tried to recover from the chill of the water. She pressed her body into the planks, shivering and fearful that someone had stayed behind in wait for her. What next? She needed to get to Beeson before Wayne got to her. She had to move.

But was that the best thing? Would the detective be able to do anything for Miguel? Would he believe her story? Would he care?

It must be ten thirty by now. She wondered where the keys to Miguel's Jeep had gone. She wondered what had happened to his phone. Maybe they were still on the boat.

She needed dry clothes. She needed to get warm. Shauna pushed herself up onto her knees and crouched down to return to the boat. Her feet squished and slapped on the dock, one soggy sock to one limping boot, back down to the slip.

The air stung her sliced palms. Her fingers shook so badly from the cold that she nearly couldn't pry the snaps off the canvas cover. Pain pierced her fingertips. If she wasn't more careful she would tear them to bits before she was through. But she undid enough to roll into the boat, landing on a stiff object that poked her in the ribs. Her missing shoe. She gripped it and held it out in front of her to ward off the blackness.

Move, move, move. If she moved, she didn't have to think. She stumbled into the cabin and found the light in the bathroom. Her breathing leveled out in the verifiably empty space. In minutes she had stripped and towel dried and donned her stale but dry clothes. Only the one boot that had gone overboard with her remained waterlogged.

Shauna was buttoning her blouse—she had needed to wait until her hands stopped quaking—when the phone rang.

Miguel's phone.

They hadn't thought to take it with them. Above. It was up on deck. She stumbled up, couldn't see. The sound was coming from the cockpit, she thought. She crouched to get into it under the cover.

Two rings.

Her hands skimmed the surfaces and found everything but the cell.

Three rings. The noise bounced around under the canvas.

She cracked her shin on the swiveling helm seat. Blast!

Four rings. No, no, no.

The phone silenced.

She leaned over, holding herself up with two hands braced on the arms of the chair. Where was the phone? If she were Miguel, where would she have put it? Where would he have it close? Where would he not worry about it getting wet?

The dry box. She spread her fingers wide and reached out for the locker behind the seat. Fumbled the latch, flipped it open. "There!" She said the word aloud as her fingers closed around the beat-up black cell.

Her hand knocked something next to the phone, and she heard it slide off the stack of chamois cloths they rested on. Clattering into the bottom of the box, she knew. Keys. Miguel had emptied his pockets to sit more comfortably. Then dozed off.

She pressed a button on the side panel and used the LED as a flashlight to find the keys. They'd fallen down past a spare set of wetsuit booties, a laminated navigational map, and a braided line into the bottom of the box. Shifting the items around, she finally closed her fingers around the small ring and pulled it out.

And there was his wallet, with his driver's license smiling at her through a plastic view pocket in the side. Man, that was a bad picture of him. But in the moment it was the most beautiful thing she had ever seen.

She studied his squinty smile, hoping again that he was still—

The phone trilled in her hand, and she dropped it. Accidentally disconnected the call. Turned off the light.

Find the phone. Find it find it find it.

The phone rang again and lit up. She snatched it out. Private number. She pressed the talk button.

"Yes?" She was breathless. How could she be winded?

"I was starting to think you didn't want to talk to me."

Wayne. Her head filled with hate and fear in equal amounts.

"How did you get this number?"

"Oh, he gave it up easily enough. We just weren't sure whether you were still in the area."

Oh no. No no no. She had to get out.

"Don't worry, babe. I pulled my guys off your detail. I need their energies elsewhere right now."

She pushed her wet hair off her forehead and stumbled out of the cockpit, gripping his keys and wallet in her other hand. She tried to pinpoint the place she had entered and breathed heavily into the phone. It was so dark in here.

"Where's Miguel?"

"On his way to spend some time with me." She found the opening in the unsnapped canvas. "I like your taste, thought I'd try to figure out what it is you see in him."

"I asked *where* he is."

"Somewhere between you and Houston."

"Is he alive?"

"You're asking dumb questions, Shauna. Hasn't the journalist taught you better?"

"What are you going to do to him?"

"We're a little short on lab rats these days, so we thought we'd put him to work in that capacity. See if we can duplicate what we've created in you. On any level. The rest depends on you."

"What do you mean?"

"Really, am I going to have to spell this out for you? The next question should be, *What do you want me to do?* You're going to have to be a quicker study than that if you want Miguel to stay alive."

"What do you want me to do, you sick—?"

"I want you to come to Houston with us. Without any police." Wayne's voice smiled. As if he were inviting her on vacation. "It'll be fun."

Shauna rolled back out onto the deck and took a splinter in her thigh. She would deal with it later. She had to get out. Up on her knees, then her feet. She started to jog.

"Good idea. You hurry on down here now, fast as you can get here."

She really should be less obvious. She turned her breathlessness into a moan. "I'm *hurt*, Wayne. You dog. I can't even walk."

Wayne sucked his tongue against the roof of his mouth.

"I should send someone over to help you then."

"You have the most demented concept of the word *help*."

Shauna reached the security gate and pinched the phone between her ear and shoulder to open it up.

"Look, I'm not going to eat up minutes on our dear friend's plan," Wayne said. "I'll cut to the chase. You be in Houston in four hours, all by your tall beautiful self, or Lopez won't live through the night."

Shauna's stomach morphed into a brick. "Not possible," she said. "I'm injured. I don't have a car. And it's three hours there without any of that going on."

"Then I'll arrange a ride for you in an ambulance."

"I'd call for my father's motorcade before I'd get in any ambulance you sent."

"Bright girl! If anyone could find a way out of your predicament, I knew it would be you."

"Five hours."

"You're not in a position to negotiate, Shauna, though I'm a good-natured fellow. Four hours is all I can offer."

"I need a guarantee you won't kill him when I get there."

"The only guarantee you'll get from me is that we'll kill him if you don't."

Shauna stumbled into the parking lot.

"I'll be in touch," he said, and she started shouting.

"Where? Where should I go, you animal?"

But Wayne had disconnected the call. She punched through the call log to find his number and call him back. Private number. She dialed *69 and got a recording. Shauna groaned at the sky.

She checked the phone's digital clock. Ten fifty-six.

Shauna slid into Miguel's Jeep, locked the doors, slipped the key into the ignition, and cranked the heat. Wayne's phone call had undone her plans to go to Beeson. Wayne would kill Miguel if she went to the police. Even if he didn't find out about her ratting him out, if she didn't show up in Houston in four hours . . .

She would go after Miguel herself. Most likely, Wayne would wait until the last possible moment to let her know where to go. She had to outthink him. She had to unravel how he worked, stay a step ahead.

She needed help, the help of someone who knew Wayne better than she did. Knew his methods. Maybe even knew where he operated outside of MMV.

Someone who hadn't been so easily duped as she. She was so angry at herself.

Trent Wilde. Leon Chalise. Not options.

Millie Harding. No idea where to find the good doctor at this time of night.

Wayne's hired hand. The man she'd seen on so many occasions—the SUV, the park, the hotel. No idea where to find him either. Didn't even have a name. Didn't know if she could trust him.

Unless . . .

The man who drove the SUV was a witness listed in the accident report. It was still here on the floor of the car with the medications she had meant to take to Beeson. She held the report up to the dashboard under the lot light and flipped through the pages until she found his name.

Frank Danson.

And Frank Danson's address.

Shauna rushed to open Miguel's glove box, hoping he kept a street map in it. In fact, she found several, lined up like a stack of pillows under the pearl-handled knife Frank Danson had thrown into the hotel's door frame.

She withdrew the Austin map, found the street, twenty minutes away. She looked at the dash clock. Eleven oh one.

What was the greater risk here? Going to Houston at Wayne's mercy, blind, or going to Danson's home with no guarantee that he would be there, or, if he was, that he wouldn't kill her and haul her body off to Wayne to get this money that Wayne owed him? It wouldn't be hard for him to do.

Miguel would have told her she was crazy. He would have told her to go directly to Beeson, and in lieu of that, to stay clear of *anyone* associated with Wayne.

She fingered his ring. Miguel would be of no help in this decision.

How had Wayne reacted to Frank's failure to kill her that night in September? Add to that his failure to prevent her escape from the hotel . . .

They couldn't possibly be on good terms. How much of a risk would she be taking to assume that Frank and Wayne were unhappy enough with each other that she could turn Frank against him?

A few moments later, Shauna decided to take the risk. Frank could possibly tell her how and where Wayne operated in Houston. He might even know what had happened to Miguel.

She could only hope that Frank Danson was still alive, and that he would talk to her.

Strike that last part. Shauna didn't really need him to talk to her, not if his memory of working for Wayne Spade was still fully intact. She could use him if he never said a word. If she was careful.

Eleven oh four. She pulled Miguel's truck out of the lot and sped toward the south side of town, one of the last places on earth she wanted to be.

34

Frank Danson kept a middle-class town house in a neighborhood that was slipping into lower-class disrepair. His was number 503, at the end of a row. Shauna pounded the door without letting up until she heard footsteps.

The door flew open. "What?" he complained. Then he saw Shauna and slammed the door on a stream of expletives.

Shauna pounded again. "Frank! You don't want me to make a scene!"

Shauna shouted as loudly as she could. "You want to talk with me, Frank! You want to talk with me about why I shouldn't call the police—" Stupid girl! If he was with Wayne on the abduction of Miguel, he would call her bluff. She winced, unable to turn back. "Why shouldn't I tell them how you're hooked up with Wayne, how you engineered the wreck—you and Wayne and Bond—what you did to me in Corpus Christi! You involved in the trafficking too?"

He yanked the door open again, then dragged her inside. "What the— *trafficking*? Drugs are *not* my area, so don't you start."

Frank shut the door behind her, gripping her upper arm.

"And I didn't do *anything* to you in Corpus. How did you find this place?"

"Accident report. You didn't use an alias?"

He turned the locks and then moved around the lower level of the townhome to close the window coverings, hauling her behind him. "I shouldn't have had any reason to use one," he muttered. "Wouldn't have, if the job had been done right in the first place. That was Bond's fault."

He dragged her back into the living room. She had been crazy, coming here by herself. Crazy. The man was twice her size and would crush her. She pictured Miguel on the floor of Leon's office, writhing. For her sake. She could do at least that much for him.

Frank was wearing a flannel shirt, unbuttoned, and on his chest was the largest, most ghastly bruise she had ever seen, a purple and green explosion across his ribs.

"What happened?"

Frank released her so roughly that she staggered. He buttoned his shirt to cover the bruise.

"Your sweetheart shot me."

"Wayne?" This news encouraged her efforts.

"Who else?"

"You wore a vest?"

"What do you think?"

"I think you two have issues."

"No, we understand each other. I understand I should always wear a vest in his company. Might get shot in the back."

"Or the heart, I see. It's a wonder he didn't go for your head."

"Looks like he went for yours." Frank gestured to the bruise on Shauna's cheekbone.

"That's right."

She raised her eyes to the side of his neck. Twin burn marks scored his skin like a snakebite.

"Wayne do that too?" She lifted her fingers to touch it. He slapped her hand away.

"Your boyfriend gets credit for that one."

So that was how Miguel got into her hotel room.

"Bad day, all around," she said gently.

"You here to make it worse?"

She shook her head and lowered the pitch of her voice, hoping it would lower both his defenses and her worries about what this encounter might hold. "You think Wayne would break up my face and then send me here after you all by myself?"

"I don't bother trying to second-guess that man anymore."

"I need you to try to second-guess him for me just one more time. As a favor."

"Why would I do that? What kind of favor could I possibly owe you?"

"This could work for both of us, Frank, if you're open to a deal."

Frank moved to the old brown sofa and lowered himself onto it. He reached for the sweating glass of scotch on the end table.

"This oughtta be good."

"I know what you're thinking," she said. She sat on the cushion next to him, crowding his personal space a little. "You're thinking, 'Frank, this girl is your worst nightmare. This girl keeps showing up on your watch, and you did *not* sign up for so much trouble.' Am I close?"

"You're a mind reader then."

She put her hand on his knee. She couldn't get it to stop shaking. "You could say that."

He picked up her quivering hand and moved it to her own knee. "Then go read Wayne's mind."

"I'm on my way. But first, like I said, I need a favor."

"You're the one who hasn't named it yet."

"I need to know where Wayne works in Houston. Where he would go if things got hot."

"And if I knew that, why would I tell you?"

"Let's try an easier question then. Why does Wayne want to kill me?"

Frank chuckled. "Is it so hard to guess how you could drive a man to kill you?"

Shauna painted her face with an expression of taxed patience. "You need to know that I am not the problem here, Frank. Wayne is about to present you with a much bigger problem than me."

"I don't know what—"

"Yes you do. That's your instinct talking, but you can speak freely with me. Because you and I both know Wayne for the wolf that he is. Now am I right or am I wrong that you are just plain tired of getting yanked around?"

"No one yanks me around."

Shauna hoped to be an exception to his rule. But this would not work if she could not keep her nerves under control. She focused her mind and began to spin a fiction, a story she had concocted on the drive to Frank's home, hoping it would lead her to truth. "Wayne has tipped the police off to you, Frank."

Frank guffawed. "Wayne thinks I'm dead."

Yes, well, that bit of news would force her to think on her feet.

"Austin PD thinks you're very much alive. Wayne set this in motion before he got fed up with you. Cops found your prints in Corbin Smith's apartment."

Shauna still believed that Wayne was responsible for Corbin's death. But if she could get Frank to believe Wayne had framed him, she was sure she could swing Frank to her side.

The claim wiped the smirk off Frank's face. His cheek twitched, but he said, "Who's Corbin Smith?"

"A very dead photographer. But aren't you more concerned about why Wayne would have planted your prints at his home?"

"Actually, I'm wondering how you would know this."

"Friends with the lead detective." She hoped he wouldn't ask her to prove it. "It's only a matter of time before they bring you in, Frank."

"Cock-and-bull story."

"About me, or about you?"

"Get to the point quickly now."

"That knife you left in the hotel's pretty door frame? I took it with me. They're looking at it as the murder weapon."

Frank's laugh was strained. But he swiped his palms across the legs of his jeans, darkening the fabric with sweat.

"That's Wayne's knife," he said.

"I know. Wayne used it to try to kill me."

"You're babbling now. I don't know what you're saying."

"Where'd you get the knife, Frank?"

Frank swore again.

She took a deep breath and hoped she wasn't transparent. "I know this is upsetting, but if you don't get yourself jackhammered into the ceiling, I think we can help each other."

"I don't need your help."

"Oh you don't now? Why do you think you haven't been arrested yet? Why do you believe no murder or kidnapping charges have been filed against you?"

Frank took a swig from the glass, then leaned toward her to breathe scotch on her face. She managed to keep her eyes open.

"You tell me."

His stench nauseated her, but she lifted her finger to the bottom of his chin, a test of her ability, and a request that he look at her. Her touch did not generate a thing.

She didn't have time to finesse this plan. She stood and leaned over him, pressing his shoulders against the back of the couch. She put her face much closer to his. The shaking in her hands had moved down to her knees. She silently berated herself.

"I don't have to tell you what you already know, Frank. Because I am not police. I am not here because I care about what happens to you, or because I'm looking to start a new career. I am here because I think Wayne Spade needs to come back down to earth with the rest of us humans, and because I think you feel the same way. And if you do not, you should. Because after that escapade at the hotel—and I'm so sorry to have ditched you like that—I'm sure you are among the least of his favorite people." Her fingers alit on his chest where the bruise was. The slightest pressure of her fingertips would keep him from moving. "Two botched jobs in as many months. That can't be good for you, Frank."

She thought she could hold his stare longer than he could hers, but in the end she dropped her gaze to his lips. Two seconds more and he would have surely called her bluff.

He finally said, "What do you propose?"

She squatted in front of him, resting her hands on his knees. "Help me, Frank. Help me bring him in and there's a reward for you in it. Chief among them, I won't press charges for your part in trying to kill me."

"I never tried to kill you." He moved to stand, but she pressed her palm into his bruise and he gave up the effort. She took his hands in hers, halfway surprised when he didn't snatch them away.

"No, you set me up. But unfortunately, to the police it's pretty much the same thing. It was that rat Rick Bond who actually rammed me with the truck, wasn't it? You made me swerve, sure, but he was the one who pushed me over."

Shauna placed Frank's left hand against the side of her cheek and held it there. His palm and fingers nearly covered the side of her head. He didn't move. Her heart was about to thrash its way out of her ribs.

She whispered, "So tell me, Frank, how is it that Rick got paid so hand-somely? Did you ever see any of that settlement money? Did Wayne ever keep any of his promises to you when I didn't roll over and die?"

Frank did not move, and Shauna hoped her knife had gone in deep enough. Slowly, cautiously, she kissed his hand. "We can help each other, Frank."

His fingers stiffened and slipped over the back of her head. He squeezed the back of her neck, tipping her head back.

"Or I could kill you now."

Dear God, don't let me die.

She made eye contact with him, keeping her voice even and low. "You could, but you won't. You wouldn't give Wayne the satisfaction."

That, and he wouldn't risk getting his own hands dirty.

He believed her, and she knew it. She knew it because in that moment he decided that he hated Wayne more than he feared Shauna, because in that moment she was in, with his grip still firm on the top of her spine. His mind opened, memories sprawled beneath her this time like candy from an upended trick-or-treater's sack, and she had her pick.

Her pick, and only a matter of seconds to decide before he disconnected from her. She rolled her mental hand over the top of those candy memories, trying to reduce the mountainous heap to a single layer, spreading them out for a bird's-eye view.

There were just so many.

She needed to find Wayne. She needed to find Miguel. She needed to know anything that would help her get inside Wayne's mind, tell her why he wanted her dead—anything at all that she could use to save Miguel's life.

If she was lucky, she would pick a memory that Frank wouldn't miss. A memory that, when brought to light like a confession, could be re-created for the rest of the world by evidence.

If she was lucky.

35

Landon McAllister had grown accustomed to sleepless nights in the two decades since his first run for political office. Since he'd announced his candidacy for president, though, he rarely slept more than five hours a night and had come to thrive on this way of life. Uninterrupted hours of reflecting and strategizing while the rest of the world slept gave him his edge.

Tonight, he could have packed in seven hours, a luxury he occasionally indulged in. Instead, at midnight he sat awake at home, by Rudy's bedside, only half-aware that he couldn't have slept if he'd wanted to.

Rudy slept trouble-free.

The house was silent, empty except for the security detail that Landon found ways to ignore. Patrice had left after dinner, gone to Houston for a public appearance at a pediatric hospital first thing in the morning.

She had kissed him good-bye at the garages.

"You seem distracted tonight," she observed.

"I was thinking about some of the things Shauna said."

Patrice set a small overnight bag in the trunk of her car, then returned to Landon, who held her purse and coat. "Don't you know by now how to prevent that girl from keeping you up at night?"

"Yes. In fact I've become quite good at it." He helped her into the jacket. "Maybe unfortunately good."

Patrice faced him. "Well, try to get some sleep tonight."

"You do the same. We'll need it in the next couple of weeks."

She smiled and ran a light hand down his arm. "I'm not planning on sleeping much at all in the next four years."

He kissed her on the nose. "Then I'll spend my waking hours tonight planning to make insomnia a reality for you."

She wiggled her eyebrows at the double entendre and kissed him once more before heading out.

Instead of devoting his mind to the elections, though, Landon's thoughts turned to his daughter.

His daughter, who was so much like her mother—beautiful and passionate and stubborn—that at times Landon found it painful to look at her. Shauna reminded him of a life he'd lost long ago, a loss he'd had to turn his back on, just to survive it. The distractions of politics and the selflessness of his sharp-witted wife, Patrice, who had done all she could to help with Shauna's upbringing, had made it possible in some ways. Rudy, however, was the heartbeat of the new life Landon created for himself.

Shauna, on the other hand, behaved like some gangrenous limb that wanted to be amputated.

Her continued insistence about that campaign money disturbed him. Hadn't her doctors said she'd lost half a year's worth of memories? Those kinds of details got buried under more pressing matters. Even so, how had she recalled their argument, and why was she so fixated on this thing? She had never shown an interest in his business or political affairs. She'd separated herself from them years ago.

He'd always thought Shauna's spats with Patrice and her vocal aversion to the political world was a means of seeking attention.

If he were honest, though, he would have to admit that Shauna had no more propensity to lie than her mother. *Xamina* . . . Landon sighed. Xamina, the Guatemalan beauty with a name as exotic as expensive perfume, had never failed to tell him the truth with take-it-or-leave-it frankness. Shauna, as a child anyway, had behaved much the same.

Pressed to think it through, he could think of no time she had stopped being as direct and hopeful as her mother.

If it's big enough to kill for, it's big enough to destroy everything you've ever worked for.

Was it possible that Trent Wilde had misappropriated MMV's funds for the purposes of this election? The idea turned Landon's stomach to acid. He had entrusted the business to Trent for so long that he couldn't recall the last time he'd studied an annual report. He'd been briefed by Trent at every board and shareholders' meeting, which he sometimes attended by proxy. MMV had always been a healthy company. But recent years were especially fruitful. They'd set profit records every year since—

Dear God. Every year since Trent had insisted he could take the presidency. They'd started talking about that during his second senatorial term. Seven years ago.

If the money was dirty . . .

Could it be that the car accident was not Shauna's fault? That she had been targeted for her questions about the funds? That Rudy was just a bystander in all this?

His *children!* Why would Trent harm them? He loved them—Landon had never second-guessed that truth.

No, if something criminal was going on, someone other then Trent must be the instigator. Leon Chalise, for example.

Landon patted the blankets spread out over Rudy's outstretched legs and stood. He needed to go find a few reports. Look back through his e-mails to see if Shauna had ever sent him anything that he might read in a different light now. She communicated so little, it wouldn't take long to review.

He would study what he could find, then call Trent when he got on the road tomorrow morning. Put all this to rest. Begin an investigation into Leon if they had to. Get a jump start on damage control.

Turning into the hall outside of Rudy's room, Landon stepped past the plastic sheeting that protected the rest of the house from his remodeling project. Pam wasn't exaggerating when she said that Landon hadn't spared any expense to take care of Rudy. The wall between two bedrooms on this wing had been knocked out, creating one large therapy room, filled with cutting-edge, high-tech contraptions related to Rudy's rehabilitation therapies. The work was scheduled to be completed before the elections.

Just in time to leave his son behind.

Landon sighed and turned down the hall that led to his office. He could get a lot done in the next few hours. He looked at his watch. Eleven fifteen. The night was young.

Shauna needed so much from this one moment. She needed to know where Miguel was, where Wayne had gone with him, what they were doing to him. If Frank even knew. She needed something that would make Frank her ally. She needed so many things, and she looked for them all.

All she saw was chaos. A jumble of apparently unrelated people and possessions, places, a history in a pile of pieces. The memories were so disorganized that she had trouble focusing on any one of them. She looked for Miguel, for Wayne, for any recognizable face, and when that began to hurt her head she started looking for her accident site, where she knew Frank had been, and then, desperate now, anything from Austin. Anything ever-so-slightly familiar.

The sound of a ticking bomb clacked loud in her head.

Was this the mind of a distracted, rootless man? Were no memories of his any more important than another, none more vivid than another so as to stand out? Was he so detached from his own life that he gave his own recall no priority?

Shauna sensed Frank pulling away from her.

Wait! Corbin.

There. She saw Corbin's face. She grabbed for it. Her arm barely reached it as the candy pile began to drop away from her.

She touched the memory, gripped it in a fist, and hoped she had something worth anything.

And she did.

Oh, she did.

She watched, and her hope grew, as not one memory, but an entire string of connected images flew away from the pile intact, one long candy rope of sweet success.

She opened her eyes, breathless and happy.

Happy? No. This was not happiness, only relief. The size and weight of this memory string was more than she first understood, a burden heavier than any other she'd lifted so far.

And that was her burden—wasn't it?—to carry these memories she had stolen? It occurred to her that she hadn't tossed any of them off, that not one of them had faded from her brain since she started this mind-robbing business.

This accumulating weight, maybe more than the loss of her own memory, was the real punishment for all she had done.

Shauna opened her eyes, the memory sequence vivid.

"You really did kill Corbin Smith," she said before she could stop herself.

Frank rolled his eyes. "You keep beating that drum."

Of course. Wayne had hired him. The shock of realizing that her fabricated story had in fact been the truth, all but Wayne's planting of the evidence, stunned her.

"You took the job because you needed the money, but you were still ticked about not getting paid for my accident."

Frank pushed Shauna away from him. "You're nuts. I don't have any idea what you're talking about."

She stood, understanding that Frank might have just slipped through her fingers. "You rented a truck that looked like Wayne's, drove it to Corbin's. Snuck in and . . ." This, here, was the grotesque truth: She would have to live with this memory as if it were her very own. She felt lightheaded. She backed toward the door. "You slit his throat with Wayne's knife. How did you get Wayne's knife, Frank?"

Frank laughed, nervous now. He stood and took a step toward Shauna. Her back hit the doorknob, and she reached behind her to grip it.

"You can't possibly—"

"You waited for Wayne and me to arrive the next morning, and you put Corbin's camera and phone in the back of Wayne's truck then. You thought the police would find them before we did."

"Quit messing with my head!" Frank yelled. "You're talking like *you're* the one who did this. Are you? Are you with Wayne, sticking this to me?"

"The reason why you can't remember killing Corbin Smith is because you can't remember *anything* about your life last Sunday night, can you?"

Frank's face confirmed her words.

Shauna was shaking and mad now, mad with disappointment over the fact that she'd uncovered nothing to help her find Miguel, nothing to give her an edge against Wayne. She was furious over having brought this horror of an incident into her mind and heart, furious that these last two weeks of confusion had forced her hand.

She started shouting, less concerned about what he might do to her than needing to fight against the injustice of her situation. "I know exactly what it's like to have a gap in your mind that's black and empty, and how desperate you feel to fill it up so that this crazy world makes an ounce of sense! I know exactly what that kind of insanity is, and how pointless is *this*, this futile effort of mine to pull together some sort of meaning out of other people's memories. How do you like it, Frank? How do you like knowing that I have pulled a thread and unraveled a full six hours of your existence and left you with nothing of it?"

Shauna took a step forward and screamed in his face. "How did you get Wayne's knife?"

Frank reached out and shoved Shauna into the wall. She twisted, smacking her ear against the Sheetrock. "He dumped it on me after the accident. At the bridge. Didn't want to risk anyone finding it on *him*."

Shauna finally understood: That was why Frank had planted evidence on Wayne after Corbin's death. That was why Wayne was so truly surprised over her discovery of the cell phone. He hadn't counted on Frank weaseling a little retribution into that job.

Frank placed his fingers around Shauna's throat, and Shauna regretted her lack of self-control.

Miguel, I'm sorry.

She saw a way out, though, an escape a fraction of an inch wide. She leaped for it. The only thing she had going for her at this point was the fact that Frank had actually forgotten this murder. His original false denials, before her kiss, had now become genuine claims.

If she went about this the right way, he might believe he hadn't killed anyone.

She started laughing like a crazy fool and said, "I can't believe you bought all that. You know that Wayne killed Corbin—he's really messed with you, hasn't he?"

Frank slapped her. Oh that burned! Her breath snagged and took too long to finally fill her lungs. She snapped back from it and raised her eyes to his. She said, "But you see what kind of claims Wayne can make, don't you?"

"It's a lie."

"It's not a lie that Wayne tried to hire you to kill Corbin."

Frank released her neck. "He did. Called me. I told him I'd do it, but . . ."

Shauna waited, driving her fingernails into the palms of her hands. Frank studied her, as if he was momentarily confused. He frowned and pressed his fingertips to his temples, then finally said, "But I didn't go through with it. Wayne did it himself. I'm sure of it."

"Of course he did," she crooned, hoping her own lies were more believable. "But you know he's a liar. You told me that yourself, didn't you? *You're surrounded by liars.* Wasn't that message from you?"

She interpreted his silence as a yes.

"The two of you are a bad match, Frank. You bring out the . . . stupidity in each other. Wayne has cooked up such a convincing story about you."

He opened his mouth, but Shauna interrupted, "I have a proposal."

"I can't think of any reason to—"

"That's because you need to think a little less of yourself, Frank. You are Wayne Spade's hired hand." One of them, at least. She massaged her throat. "People who hire others to do their dirty work are usually pretty high on the food chain."

"I don't know what you think I'm involved in."

"I'll testify on your behalf if you help me bring down a bigger fish. I won't press charges for anything you've done to me. I'll talk my friends at the police department into cutting you some slack for cooperating."

"How big is the fish?"

"How does 'presidential' sound?"

Frank's eyes widened.

"And we'll take care of Wayne in the process. Wrap up all his stories with a nice, tidy ending."

"That's more interesting to me."

"You bail on me, you're on your own."

"Fair enough."

"What time is it?"

Frank's eyes went over her shoulder to a clock on the wall. "Eleven forty-six."

"Let's go to Houston. I'm driving."

"First you tell me your plan."

"First we get on the road. Then we'll talk."

The fact was, she didn't have a plan. Not yet. But she had muscle now in the form of Frank. A necessary asset. She'd figure out the rest on the way.

"What's in this for you?" Frank asked as he followed her to the door. "Sweet revenge? A piece of Wayne's big pie?"

Shauna didn't answer right away. The question was too personal.

"Ah," Frank breathed. "The boyfriend. True love."

At first glance, Shauna supposed, that was it. But also something larger.

"My past," she said, fishing the keys out of her pocket. "And my future."

"You have high expectations. I'd settle for a paycheck." His stomach growled. "And a burrito."

36

Shauna drove across midnight into Thursday morning five miles over the speed limit, understanding that few things could be worse at this moment than getting pulled over by highway patrol. A breakdown might fall into that category. A flat tire. An empty gas tank.

No point in worrying about those. She had to stick to what she could control.

"You know how to reach Wayne?" she asked Frank just after midnight. He sat in the passenger seat, having refused to strap the seat belt across his bruised chest.

"You think he's taking calls from dead men?"

"I thought we'd send a text."

"Not from my phone."

Shauna handed Miguel's phone across the seat to him. "Use this."

"Don't you know his number?" Frank griped.

"Never memorized it. And I don't have the phone it was programmed into. And I'm driving."

"What'll it say?" Frank started punching buttons.

"'Where am I supposed to go?'" Frank typed it, sent it.

They did not speak until the phone vibrated that a reply had come in.

"'Touched that you remembered my number, babe,'" Frank read.

"Wait it out," Shauna said.

A minute later the phone vibrated again.

"'Where are you?'" Frank read.

"Tell him 71 and 10."

"We're not that far yet."

"Doesn't matter. If he doesn't know where we are, I'll wager that phone doesn't have a GPS unit in it."

"Heck no. This thing's a dinosaur. Surprised it can text."

"Tell him."

Frank typed, then later chuckled. "He says, 'Go east on 10.'"

Shauna fumed. "Smart aleck."

"I could call him worse if you're too timid."

She stuck her hand out to get Miguel's phone back, then dropped it in her lap. "We won't be hearing from him for a while."

Frank tipped his head back against the headrest and closed his eyes. "MMV has a warehouse in the Houston Ship Channel."

Shauna snapped her head right, almost pulled a muscle in her neck. "That would have been nice to know."

"No time lost."

"Yet. You know where it is?"

"Never been there."

"What's the address?"

"Sorry."

"Then shut up until you have something helpful to say." She felt badly for behaving more raw around the edges than usual.

Frank dozed off, smiling.

What to do when they got to Houston? So much of that depended on Wayne.

So much of that depended on her.

She would need to make some assumptions, some plans.

Assumption number one: Miguel was not dead. She acknowledged that might be wishful thinking rather than an informed guess, and yet she would hold on to it. If she could not assume he lived, nothing else mattered.

Nothing else. With the thumb of her right hand, Shauna turned his ring on her finger. Once. Twice. Again.

Assumption number two: Wayne would kill Miguel as soon as she showed up. If she stayed out of Wayne's reach, could she keep Miguel alive longer? She wasn't sure about that.

What did Wayne want her to do? Or, more accurately, what did Wayne want to do to her? She didn't think he would kill her. That was too risky a move for him in light of all that had happened, all the suspicions that had been raised surrounding the circumstances of her accident.

Murdering Miguel, on the other hand, would cost Wayne nothing. She continued to turn the ring, then fisted her right hand, impressing the diamond into her palm.

The reason behind Wayne's attempt on her own life was to protect discovery and information. And so she believed she could reasonably make assumption number three: Wayne and Trent would follow through with their threats to wipe out her memory again. And this time, she should expect more extreme measures. They could not risk her knowing anything, or remembering anything that she once knew.

She caught her breath and came to her final assumption: They would hide Miguel from her. They really couldn't risk that she knew where he was, ever, at any given point in time.

Wayne would never tell her.

She might never see Miguel again.

The likelihood of this sent new fear vibrating through Shauna's bloodstream. She needed to find out where Miguel was. She needed Wayne to tell her.

She needed to force Wayne to tell her.

How?

Shauna slipped the platinum engagement ring off her right ring finger. Holding it with two hands balanced on top of the steering wheel, she tried to angle the diamond to catch moonlight. Too dark. The rock blinked halfheartedly under the dash lights.

Miguel Lopez had saved her life—how many times? Twice that she remembered already, and once that she had forgotten. He'd saved her life and set aside his own.

That was love. Without a doubt, she recognized it as the deepest possible kind of love.

And yes, she loved him like that too. She would show him. If she could find him.

How could she find him?

Shauna slipped the ring onto her left hand.

Her clever little memory-stealing trick, her freak-show ability, was worth nothing on Wayne anymore. He knew what she could do, even if he didn't understand it. For crying out loud, she had *told* him what she could do, handed the information to him on a silver platter! At the time she thought it would keep her alive. Now it seemed to her things might have gone better, for Miguel at least, if she'd kept her mouth shut.

Wayne wouldn't come within arm's reach of her if he could help it.

What were her options? She stole a glance at Frank. His brawn could help her. That was her initial idea in bringing him along anyway. She could maybe have him knock Wayne out, and she could kiss the man—she shivered— while he was unconscious.

Assuming Wayne wasn't flanked by a thousand sycophants there to do his bidding. Assuming she and Frank weren't bound and gagged the moment Wayne spotted them. Would Trent be at Wayne's side? Maybe he would be with Miguel while Wayne attended to Shauna. No way to be sure. No way to plan for every contingency.

Too many unknowns. To many "have tos" that could go wrong.

Her mind returned to its image of Wayne, knocked unconscious on the pavement of some back alley. Even if she and Frank could get that far, she didn't know if she could take anything from an unconscious person. She needed contact—easy enough—and she needed access. Vulnerability. Openness. A free will that said yes to her probing.

Not sure she could get that from someone whose mind wasn't fully engaged with his surroundings.

She tossed that option away.

She could drug him.

The same problems reared their heads, plus the fact that she didn't have access to any kind of narcotic that would do what she needed, namely, to keep him both conscious and sedate.

She punched Frank in the arm. He stirred.

"Frank, you got any drug connections?"

He scowled at her and closed his eyes again. "Told you that's not my territory."

"Do you know anyone whose territory it is?"

"No. Now let me sleep until you figure this out."

"Thanks for the help."

She could pretend a one-eighty, a complete conversion to every piece of advice he'd ever offered. Frank would be her proof, evidence that she was on their side now, that if they cut her in to their schemes, however complex or illegal, she would forget *everything*. She would speak his language. Break down the wariness that held up his defenses. Seduce him with a touch, a lover's kiss. Make him believe that his own playacting at concern for her was authentic.

Shauna's stomach flipped over. Impossible. She couldn't convince him under such circumstances. He would never believe her. Even thinking about it caused her hands to quiver. What she had done with Frank marked the outer limits of her abilities.

Besides, Frank was supposed to be dead.

She could weaken Wayne somehow. Physically. Stab him like he'd stabbed her. She mocked the flimsiness of her own mind. As if she could even touch an ex-Marine if he didn't want her to. An ex-Marine trained in some form of martial arts she'd never heard of. Frank could, maybe, but Shauna couldn't risk that Frank might kill him.

Wayne needed to stay alive. There would be no other way for her to find Miguel.

She could see no way to find out from Wayne where Miguel might be. In that case, she would throw out assumption number four. She could hope Wayne might lead her to Miguel and stay in the shadows.

And then what? He'd kill them both?

Shauna felt her despair slide off her shoulders and give way to a fresh fury. She hated Wayne Spade, hated that he had stolen from her again and again and would most certainly do it once more. What he had done to her was nothing less than a rape of her mind, a plundering of her most valuable personal belonging—her memory, her history, her journey, her identity.

He had stolen her brother. He had muzzled the man who loved her. He had turned her own father harder against her. He had skewed truth. He had betrayed her with an imposter friendship and a false sense of security. He propped her up on a scaffold of lies that claimed lives when it began to collapse.

He had even tried to kill her. Drown her—

An idea came to Shauna with all the surprise of a bucket of ice thrown in her face.

That she was capable of even thinking it made her shudder. Was she capable of such a thing? She studied Frank's hands, his thick palms and long fingers. Was she capable of talking someone else into such a thing?

Yes, she was.

For the sake of Miguel's life, she was. For the sake of truth, and justice, and making wrong right, she most definitely was.

She caught Frank awake, looking at her. She held his gaze longer than was safe, until he turned back to watch the road on her behalf.

He'd help her.

If he didn't get them both killed in the process.

"Let me tell you what I'm thinking," she said.

37

By a quarter to one, Landon's usually tidy office was strewn with papers and glossy blue and yellow booklets bearing MMV's logo.

Annual reports, prospectuses, executive memos, magazine articles about MMV's golden era, hard copies of electronic presentations made at board meetings. He had also pulled out campaign documents: finance reports, accounting summaries, donor records, anything he had at his office pertaining to the monies flowing through his coffers. These were less helpful; the most detailed files were at campaign headquarters, not here.

Even so, Landon found nothing amiss, nothing at a glance to support Shauna's fears. He rubbed his eyes and sighed. Maybe he'd been right, that Shauna's behavior was only a pathetic cry for attention.

But the timing of MMV's dramatic profitability spike would not stop needling his mind. Trent had been so confident that Landon would have the funds he needed to take on a race for the White House, and at the time, Landon had read nothing into that but the unflagging faith of a dear friend.

Trent had approached Landon about this at Easter of that year. The following January, MMV posted their fourth-quarter results to much trumpeting and fanfare.

Where was that quarterly report?

Landon riffled through the stacks but couldn't put his hands on it. He found all the files for the following year, but not that one. Irritated that it wasn't there, he got up from his desk and went to Patrice's office to see if it was in her files. He didn't really believe that the document would shed any further light on his questions, but the fact that it was missing from his own files bothered him. He needed to find whatever would set his mind at ease.

He flipped on the overhead light, which sent a glare across the green paint and floral draperies. This place had always reminded him of an English tearoom.

He crossed the room to the oak file cabinet in the corner and opened the drawer where he knew she kept her copies of MMV paperwork. The contents were a mess: she didn't even use hanging file folders for this stuff.

Patiently, he went through the pile. Nothing. Fine. Time to give this up.

He closed the drawer.

It wouldn't shut.

A closer examination of the problem revealed a small wooden box in the drawer beneath, standing on end next to a similar pile of unfiled paperwork. The box was the size of a large hardback book and appeared to have slid off the top of the papers, perhaps when Landon opened the drawer above it.

Landon reached behind the open drawer to pull the box out of the way. This was an awkward feat, because the open space was barely large enough for his arm to slip through. But he managed to grip the container and lift it out of the lower compartment. When he pulled it through the top, however, the hinged lid snagged on the back of the drawer and flew open, spilling its contents.

Landon swore under his breath, set the box on top of the file cabinet, and began to collect the dumped papers.

They were letters, it appeared, most on simple stationery. He paused at a glimpse of the handwriting. Trent Wilde's handwriting.

My dearest Patrice . . .

In the past few years, Landon had taken more beatings by pundits and political opponents than he could count. But not one blow had struck his heart so dead center as those three words.

He collected the papers and read love letters that sickened him. He read them anyway, picking up each note before he'd finished reading the previous one.

His fingers landed on a glossy sheet of paper. He looked at it, registered with a vague disconnection the blue and yellow MMV logo.

It was that first quarterly report he'd been searching for.

He dropped the other letters and opened the report. There, on the page that pronounced the bottom line, the impressive figure had been highlighted and circled with a red Sharpie. Scrawled across the page in the same bloody ink, in the same blasted handwriting, was a note that sent a blade through Landon.

> *To My Future First Lady, My Only Love,*
> *Keep your eyes on the prize.*
> > *Always,*
> > *Your Wilde Man*

Landon put his fist and the report through the wall next to the file cabinet, then yanked both out again, raining drywall over the rosebud-covered carpet.

The physical pain in his knuckles kicked his mind into gear. He turned his body toward the door and plotted a change in his itinerary. He was not the fool Trent and Patrice had played him to be.

Nor was his daughter.

~∂~

The three-hour wait did nothing to settle Wayne Spade's nerves. It was approaching two o'clock, and Lopez should be on-site any minute. Wayne was still pacing the rear office of the warehouse, a room temporarily converted into a jerry-rigged medical room.

"I can't promise this will work." Will Carver, the pharmacologist who had overseen Shauna's memory wipe, shoved his hands into his pockets, took them out again. At two in the morning, he looked more harebrained than usual.

"Why can't we expect the same results we got with Shauna?"

"Different circumstances."

"Nothing different. We traumatized them, knocked them out. Shot them up with anesthesia. When he gets here, we'll give him the same cocktail."

"There are variables. Like the simple matters of gender. And more complicated issues. Her cocktail was tailored to her DNA. We had more time to evaluate the details."

Wayne kicked the closed door. "What's that got to do with anything?"

"And Siders administered MDMA to her when she got to the ER."

"I can get more if you need it."

"I'm just saying this isn't exactly a controlled environment. I can't guarantee the outcome."

Wayne swore. "It seems none of us can."

"Are you prepared to keep him under for the full six weeks? Follow the regimen?"

"That depends." On Shauna. On how much damage control was needed before this blew over. He could always kill the journalist if he had to. In fact, he might do it anyway, because the Mexican was such a troublemaker. Once Shauna arrived, Miguel Lopez's life would diminish in value considerably.

"What do you make of the memory stealing?" Wayne asked.

"I can't even begin to theorize. Can she prove it?"

Prove it? Doubtful. He wasn't sure if she'd actually taken memories from him or if he'd simply forgotten a few details, the way most memories fade over time. And yet he could dream up no other explanation for her discovery of so many secrets. How had she dreamed of his football injury, and why couldn't he remember the actual event? When had she discovered he'd gone AWOL, and why couldn't he recall anyone trying to talk him out of it?

Any half-good scientist could come up with an experiment to test it, he mused. Provided they could ensure Shauna's cooperation.

Wayne studied Carver. "Maybe I'll hook her up with you and we'll find out."

A door slammed outside the building. Lopez was here.

"Leave me what I need," Wayne said.

He strode out and followed the aisles created by crude-oil barrels and cargo containers stacked two high. The outer door swung open before he reached it. Two men entered, dragging a limp form between them. They dropped the figure on the floor in front of Wayne. He crouched over the face of one unconscious Miguel Lopez.

"You're alive as long as it takes Shauna to get here," Wayne said. "After that, we'll see what you're worth."

"Take him to Carver," he said to the men. "Then get him out of here. Stay mobile until you hear from me."

He tossed his phone from one hand to the other and back again while they dragged Lopez back out of the room. In less than an hour, he'd summon Shauna.

"It won't work," Frank said around a mouthful of burrito.

They sat outside a filling station near the 10 and the 610, anticipating that Wayne might direct them south toward the Ship Channel.

Shauna had filled the tank with gas, then bought a map and two large bottles of water. She'd become increasingly distressed that Wayne hadn't yet contacted them. It was two forty-five. She was not exactly in the mood to discuss the merits of her precarious plan with Frank.

"I mean"—Frank swallowed—"you won't be able to trust anything he says. He'll be talking fear, not sense."

"I don't care what he says," Shauna snapped.

"It's one of the most ineffective means—"

"All I need is for him to *think*, okay? If he's scared, that will work in my favor."

Frank shrugged. "What you're planning is illegal. Banned internationally. You might want to think twice."

"Look, Frank, why are you here?"

"Because you hate Wayne Spade more than I do."

"Do you want this to work or not?"

"Well sure."

"Then put a little effort into it."

Frank shrugged. "It's your gig. You want sunshine and rainbows, I'll lighten up." He took another huge bite.

Shauna inhaled a calming breath.

"There's so much riding on this. Be my muscles for five minutes—less than that if everything goes well. I'll be finished and you can do what you want with him."

"Five minutes, then I get my turn."

She nodded.

He grinned and sang, "You are my sunshine, my only sunshine . . ."

She glared at him until he continued eating.

Miguel's phone buzzed. Shauna flinched.

She placed the phone against her ear. "Where's Miguel?" she said.

"It's a text message, Shauna," Frank said.

Shauna lowered the phone and checked the display. An address. She showed it to Frank, who crammed the remainder of his meal into his mouth and opened the map.

Where's Miguel? she typed.

Wayne answered in seconds.

> On the road

She asked,

> Is he with you?

> I'm no dating service

> Prove he's alive. I need to know

> You don't need to know. You'll come anyway

It was true. It was true, and they both knew it. Shauna's eyes burned.

"Found it," Frank said. "Near Brady Island. Minutes away."

> When will I get to see him?

> I'm waiting

Shauna tossed the phone onto the floor between the seats and pulled out of the gas station, allowing Frank to navigate. They headed south on 610, got off on the south side of the channel, and moved into the industrial complex just east of the small, commercial island.

The thick shadows of the surrounding oil refineries looked to Shauna like an alien ghost town. The moon had shifted and dimmed. A couple hundred yards from the location Wayne had given her, she pulled off the road. Frank got out of the car.

"Promise you won't lose me," she said. He responded by tipping his fingers to his forehead in salute, then walking off.

It was important that she show up alone.

Shauna picked up the phone. She located the address Wayne had sent, then found the phone number Detective Beeson had given to Miguel earlier in the evening.

She was stupid, no doubt, to dive headfirst into this shallow pool called Wayne Spade, but she wouldn't be a complete fool about it. And Frank Danson didn't count. She composed a brief message for Beeson in front of the address:

> You want Wayne Spade for Corbin Smith's murder, for my accident, for much more. I have murder weapon. Laundering data possibly connected to White House will reach you today. We're here

She hit *send* and shut the phone off.

She guessed Beeson could be there in an hour, if he was even awake and had access to a police helicopter. Or she might only have ten minutes if he notified Houston PD to get a move on ahead of him. Or he might not get the message for hours.

She only needed five minutes. If Frank followed through.

38

The small warehouse sat fifty feet off the nearest dock. The narrow Houston Ship channel divided here, one branch cutting under Brady Island and the other heading north and west toward the heart of Houston. Shauna pulled the Jeep in at the back and grabbed her bottles of water before getting out. A mild onshore breeze ruffled the collar of Shauna's blouse and gave her a chill.

Walking around the building, she passed an exterior metal staircase that ran up the east-facing side to what she presumed were offices. Beneath the steps, she found an open door. A light over the top spilled out into the unpaved alley between this warehouse and the next.

She set the water down against the steel siding before stepping in. The door closed behind her and created an echo that bounced off oil barrels and shipping containers. The air smelled burnt and dusty.

"Back here, babe." Wayne's voice bounced around too, but even if she had known where it came from, she wouldn't have followed it. She needed him to step outside with her.

"I've come as far as I'll go," she said. "Where's Miguel?"

"I don't know. Come back here and maybe I'll tell you."

"You'll never tell me."

"Getting smarter, are we?" She heard another door shut, and the sound of his hard-soled shoes on concrete. She pressed her back against the crash bar, not sure from where he would appear. "You know why I won't tell you?"

She didn't answer.

"Because I really don't have the information." He emerged from the right, popping out of shadows at the end of a row of containers. He wore dress shoes and a lightweight jacket.

"I don't believe you. You've never spoken a word of truth to me. Maybe not to anyone."

He nodded, shrugged. "I guess that would make the truth all the more confusing when it's finally spoken."

She didn't believe him. The whole point of this maneuver was to manipulate her—he knew exactly where Miguel was. Wayne took a step toward Shauna, and she shoved the door open with her backside. She spun and ran toward the Jeep.

She had taken six long strides down the alley toward the rear of the building when Wayne took her down from behind, tackling her at the shoulders and driving her into the gravel. The grit grated her chest. The wind left her, and her vision clouded at the edges.

Her spirit sagged. This was not what she had intended. She meant to get closer to the Jeep.

Wayne flipped her onto her back, then straddled her waist on the ground, trapping her hands with his knees. She felt her throat gape, willing to take air in but drawing nothing. The muscles in her own chest would suffocate her if they didn't relax.

She finally took in a gasp. Wayne patted her cheek.

"That's it, Shauna. You stay calm now." She gulped air, and he withdrew an object from his jacket pocket. Two objects. A roll of tape, and a paper packet that fluttered to the ground. He tore off a long piece of the tape, then used his knees and his free hand to set her on her side. She fought him, but he outmuscled her easily.

"You could make this so much easier if you'd let me take care of you," he muttered.

Wayne bound her wrists, then turned her back over so that her hands were like a rock under her spine.

His hands found the paper packet. It was a sterile packet of some kind, like the kind that held gauze. Only she feared this one held something less benign.

He peeled the wrapper away and withdrew a patch that looked like an extra-large bandage. Then he opened the top two buttons of her blouse and slapped the patch right over her heart. He shoved the wrapper back in his pocket. Shauna's breath quickened. Where was Frank?

"That won't take long," he said. "Not as fast-acting as a needle to the bloodstream, but safer for me with all the thrashing you do."

"What are you doing?"

"Taking you back to the beginning."

The skin under the patch burned.

"I need you to tell me where Miguel is."

"Like I said, I don't know. I think I've figured out how this little mind trick you've developed works, and the sad thing is, I don't think it's very effective against your enemies. Which puts me at a nice advantage in a case like this. The problem, of course, is that it doesn't make the drug very appealing on the foreign markets. So we need to work out that little kink. You and Miguel can help us with that."

"Don't you have enough of a foreign industry going to keep you busy?" If Frank had ditched her . . .

Wayne seemed surprised at that. "You found out about our little operation? Well, we'll have to take care of that particular memory. Maybe there's a way to target specific—"

"Human rights violations? Trafficking in children? There are thousands of ways to break the law, Wayne. Why would you pick that one?"

"Nice paycheck. Cushy lifestyle." He leaned over and exhaled directly over her mouth and nose. "Pretty women." Wayne hovered for a threatening second. "And the loyalty of the most powerful man in the world." He shifted as if to stand.

"If you think he'll stay loyal when he finds out—"

Wayne laughed. "You always were naive, Shauna. That's what I like about—"

A cannon that was Frank shot Wayne off of Shauna's body and hurtled him sideways. The men wrestled and she heard Wayne shout. Shauna rolled to her knees and eventually found her feet. Frank, who was probably thirty pounds heavier than Wayne, found the top of the pile and lifted a fist.

"Don't knock him out!" she yelled. She rushed over.

Frank swore and cuffed Wayne in the shoulder instead of the face.

"My hands, my hands. Frank, help me get loose!" She needed to peel this thing off her chest. She needed to stay alert. Her blood was zooming through her veins now, carrying Wayne's drugs to her brain.

"Kinda busy here," Frank grunted. He'd pinned Wayne beneath him but had yet to secure the man's thrashing arms and legs.

"Tape in his pocket," she said, rushing to the stairwell. She checked the metal railing. It was so hard to see! She leaned her shoulder into the rail and dragged it over the surface, found an edge sharp enough to snag her shirt. She lifted her wrists to it and began to saw. She hoped she still had enough time.

Shauna's vision tunneled for a second, then cleared. She had to hurry before the full dose of whatever sedative was in that patch reached her head.

She felt the tape giving way by the time Frank hauled Wayne to the stairs with wrists, knees, and ankles bound. She rushed Frank.

"Help me!"

He had her wrists undone in seconds, and she clawed at the patch, peeling it away and tossing it into the gravel. She raced for the water bottles, stumbled halfway there, then kept going. She could not mess this up.

By the time she returned, Frank had Wayne inclined on the stairway, head on the bottom step, feet pointing toward the top. Frank held him by the ankles. Wayne's shirt was bloody, and from the awkward position of his body, Shauna thought one of his legs might have been broken.

"Was that really necessary?" She knelt on the ground at Wayne's head, felt her equilibrium tilt, then level out.

"You said I could do what I want."

"When I'm done." Shauna unscrewed a bottle. Between the two, she had about a liter.

Frank held his watch up to the faint moonlight.

"I give you three more minutes."

"Let me have your shirt."

"What?"

"Take off your shirt."

He peeled it off and tossed it to her. She wrapped it over Wayne's face. He rolled his head around, but she secured the cloth by tying the arms behind his head.

Wayne was groaning, from pain, she thought. She tipped the bottle so that water ran into his nose through the cloth. He choked and sputtered.

"Remember when you tried to drown me, Wayne?" He thrashed as she let another dump rush into his mouth. She gripped the hair at the back of his head to keep it steady. "Maybe you don't, because your memory of that moment is mostly mine now. Your memory of stabbing me in the ribs. So I thought I'd re-create the moment for you."

She held the bottle up so that the water came out in a steady stream. She'd get a few seconds' worth out of this, and that might be enough.

Wayne thrashed violently, but she held on. "I need you to tell me where Miguel is, Wayne."

"Dunno," he managed.

"You do, and I need you to tell me now, because the whole world is about to descend on this place and haul your sorry self out of here."

The water continued to flow, and Wayne's back went rigid.

"He's not gonna say a thing," Frank said.

Shauna lifted the bottle and stopped the flow.

"Where?" she said.

"Wilde," Wayne said. "With Wilde."

She emptied the bottle on his face.

"Not true," Frank said. "Don't believe it."

Shauna leaned in to Wayne's ear as her first bottle ran out. She reached for the second bottle.

Wayne gulped air.

"I only need one word, Wayne. You know what that is?" She unscrewed the cap. "It's *please*. You say please. You tell me you don't want to drown. You beg me to save your life. Because otherwise, I will keep you under."

Wayne cried out. She tipped the next bottle over his face. "Just say please, *babe*."

This time, Shauna let the water flow, slow and even, enough to keep the sensation strong. Honestly, she didn't care if he said please. She really didn't need him to say anything. She only needed him to need her. When he acknowledged that she had the power to keep him alive, he would need her more than ever.

He started convulsing.

This would take all of a few seconds. She could find Miguel hiding out in Wayne's mind in maybe ten more. Surely a trained marine could hold his breath for that long.

Of course, from Wayne's point of view, that wasn't how this particular form of suffering worked.

He was hysterical now, choking on his own need to stay alive.

She was almost out of water.

"P-p-pless," he sputtered. "Plsss."

She had another two inches of liquid. Five, four, three, two—

Shauna threw away the bottle and removed the shirt from his head. Pinching his nose, she covered his mouth with hers. She pressed hard, felt his teeth against her lips, jerking with the spasms of his body.

No more barriers stood between them. No more walls, no more pretending. He needed her now. Oh, did he need her.

She started looking for Miguel.

Though Shauna had accessed Wayne's memories on three other occasions, she had never seen them from this wide-angle view. Her theft of the first two memories had been almost accidental opportunities, like finding a twenty-dollar bill dropped along the street.

She had advanced her skill since then, though, and had much more control now, which might account for this new sight.

Shauna saw water again, but this time the liquid was an ocean, and Wayne's memories were grains of wet sand, sticking together, a sand castle half-finished.

She saw an image of herself in the uppermost turret, next to Wayne's most recent memories. Her on the ground, him slapping that patch onto her chest. And there: the warehouse where they now battled for control. And Dr. Carver? And a medical office, a bed, racks of medicine vials and syringes. Cell phone calls.

Shauna saw each grain as if the images they contained were life-sized, though she could scoop up a handful of them in her palm. She examined the memories, pinched them and spread them out with her thumbs across the pads of her fingertips, looking: a ride in Wayne's truck through the middle of the night. A stop for gas and CornNuts.

There: the man with the nose she had broken. And Miguel! At the man's feet. At Wayne's feet. Unconscious. Where had he gone? She looked closer, listened.

You're alive as long as it takes Shauna to get here. After that, we'll see what you're worth. Take him to Carver. Then get him out of here. Stay mobile until you hear from me.

Stay mobile.

A sob escaped Shauna's lungs and broke her contact with Wayne. Wayne sucked air. He'd intentionally prevented himself from knowing where Miguel had gone.

"You monster!" She smacked him full across the face. He seemed barely conscious. "What's their number? Where's your phone?" Somewhere at the bottom of her brain she felt herself slipping out of full awareness, making room for whatever drugs her skin had absorbed. No, not drugs this time. This was despair in its purest form.

She thought his ragged exhale sounded like a laugh, a mockery. His breath on her face fanned her inner fire.

Shauna stopped thinking about what she was doing. She could not accept that she had gotten all the way here and was still so far away from her goal, that Miguel was so far out of her reach, maybe even dead. She could not believe that one man had knocked down every brick of her life, every soul that had shared it with her—and for what? Why? Because she loved the truth?

Because Miguel loved the truth?

She gripped the hair behind his ears with both hands and cried aloud into Wayne's mouth. She saw his mind in her own, saw the stupid, childish sand castle, the foolish and fragile life he had built for himself, and she started kicking it down, started crying and screaming and wading across moats and kicking down turrets. Her eyes filled with grit, and the grains packed themselves under her fingernails, tangled in her hair. She pounded down bridges and courtyards and walls and the keep. The sand caked her lips and chafed her skin under her clothes and stuck to the pads of her feet.

Grief collapsed her while she was only half-finished with her vandalism. Grief and the burden of these sticky, heavy memories. She doubled over, breathless, and felt strong hands on her shoulders.

Someone yanking her, tugging her up. Off.

Off of Wayne.

She breathed.

Frank had her from behind, and she heard herself gasping for air. She staggered under her own weight and pressed her fists against her temples. What had she done?

What had she taken on? What would she have to live with? The magnitude of her theft had exceeded her intentions and accomplished nothing. Not anywhere in all those stolen images—those dark, nefarious, smug images—was anything that told her where Miguel was. And there was no going back.

Her pulse throbbed in her ears, a drumbeat that coursed under the misery of this other life, this dirge of unfortunate choices and lost opportunities. Shauna had taken ten, maybe fifteen years. She dropped onto her hands and knees and started to wail. Frank dragged her to the wall and set her up against it.

"Get a grip, Shauna."

She couldn't. She just couldn't.

Wayne lay at the foot of the stairs, blinking inside the circle of light. He lifted a limp arm a couple inches off the ground, then dropped it. He was hyperventilating.

Shauna's stomach cramped and she sagged to one side. She sensed Frank next to her and reached for him. For support. He withdrew clear of her touch.

"Don't you lay a hand on me," he warned. He raked a hand through his hair and glanced around as though he was looking for someone. "I don't understand a thing I've seen here."

39

The pain of gravel under the heels of her hands sharpened Shauna's awareness. She was on all fours at the base of the warehouse's exterior staircase, staring at the ground through swollen eyelids. Salt from tears had dried on her cheeks.

The area was quiet. The single light over the warehouse door that had illuminated the area earlier was out, the dirt alley lit now only by the low moon. An even coat of blackness spanned the sky.

She strained her eyes to see into the alley. She made out the form of Wayne, laid out ten yards from her, unconscious or sleeping or dead—she couldn't tell.

Frank had vanished.

She didn't care.

Shauna unfolded her body one joint at a time, managing to stand then walk to Wayne. She saw his chest rise and fall.

She timed her breathing to match his, a calmer pace.

Wayne had bested her tonight. In some ways.

She, on the other hand, had destroyed him. The rest of Wayne's life would be a punishment for years of choices he couldn't remember making, for being a person he couldn't remember becoming. He would have no chance for redemption, no ability to pull meaning out of his past for the sake of forging his future. He would be forever young, forever stunted, forever confused. Because of her.

What had she become?

She vowed then, looking at Wayne's expressionless, passive face, never to forget what she had done here. She would allow herself to be haunted by the shock of it. The memory would warn her away from the dangerous cliff of her ability. Tonight, she had stood at the edge.

She felt deep, agonizing pain. For what she had stolen from Wayne would topple the entire McAllister empire. She thought she had already lost everything. But not compared to what was about to happen.

And all those feelings paled next to her sorrow over having failed Miguel.

The grinding sound of a vehicle moving slowly over dirt turned her eyes to the road. Frank?

A police cruiser moved past the building, a high-powered flashlight beam sweeping into the alley. Shauna didn't even care if they spotted her. And yet she and Wayne were beyond the light's reach.

The car moved out of sight past the end of the warehouse, but she heard it turning around. They'd come back for a closer look if Beeson had sent them.

A phone rang.

Wayne's phone.

Behind her. It lay in the dirt at the opposite end of the building, where Frank had ambushed him, its flashing LED light a tiny square of blue in the darkness. She rushed to get it. She had to shut off the noise.

A car door slammed as Shauna reached the phone. She squeezed the button on the side to silence the ringer. No name was attached to the number. Did she dare answer it?

Stay mobile until you hear from me.

What if the caller had Miguel? Someone awaiting orders from Wayne? She couldn't answer, couldn't risk that her voice, spoken in lieu of Wayne's, would tip her hand.

She would communicate by text as soon as she was clear of this place.

She ran on light feet back to the end of the building, intending to slip into the safety of Miguel's Jeep and pull out.

She rounded the corner. It was gone.

Frank! Gone with Wayne's knife, with her meds, with his address on the accident report. Miguel's phone and wallet were in there too, and Beeson's phone number. She could only hope Frank didn't know the total of what he had.

She stewed over Frank, simultaneously aware that the officers were headed around the other side of the building. The phone in her hands rang again. Same number. She ended the call before it sounded a full ring, then sent a text.

> NO AUDIO. TEXT ONLY.

New hope that Miguel might not be out of her reach pushed her anxiety to the background. She wondered where Wayne had stashed his truck. He wouldn't have come here without his own transportation.

> Wher th hck ARE u?

Someone was waiting for Wayne. Where? Wayne was handling so many snakes that Shauna couldn't be sure which one this was. She had to think like him.

Think like Wayne. That wouldn't be hard now, would it? Her cluttered mind snapped into sharp, organized focus. The intensity of events had distracted her from the solution so easily within her grasp:

Wayne's memories told her exactly which of his snakes she had to charm. These men were waiting for Wayne to tell them where to take Miguel. Wayne intended to tell them after he had secured Shauna. She replied.

> The ? is, where are U?

Shauna closed her eyes and tapped more of Wayne's recall: she saw his truck parked two blocks south, away from the channel.

> Duz it mattr? Tell us where 2 go.

Where to go with Miguel.

Where should she send them?

> Is he alive?

Footsteps were moving in her direction. Shauna had not been paying attention. She dropped behind a barrel, understanding in a second that she did not have enough cover to stay hidden.

Two men in uniforms came around the end of the building, their flashlights sweeping over the top of her hiding place. Only the barrel separated her from them. Shauna closed her eyes as if that would help hide her, the display of the phone pressed into her clammy hands. If Wayne's guys texted before—

They stepped past the barrel, so close that Shauna could smell cologne. All they had to do was look to the right.

"Body," one of the officers said. Their eyes locked onto Wayne, and they jogged toward him.

She watched them, moved when the sounds of their footfalls gave her enough noise cover. And then she ran in time with them but in the opposite direction, toward the shipyard building on the other side of the alley.

> Technically alive

She would take that as good news for now. When she was sure she was out of the officers' range of hearing, she stopped to punch in an address in River Oaks, on the other side of Houston. It was the only address in Houston that she knew. She thought she might be twenty, twenty-five minutes away.

> Reply with your ETA

They would have to map it, make an estimate.

She picked up her pace again in the direction of Wayne's truck, careful to keep an eye out for the officers on scene.

She found the Chevy without any trouble, as if she had parked it herself. Shauna climbed into the cab and went immediately to the ashtray. There were the keys, as usual. The phone vibrated in her palm.

> Thirty minutes

She could beat them there.

> Go

There was only one way to get Miguel out of this disaster, and that was to give herself over to Trent Wilde. She would ensure Miguel's safety by surrendering her head and body to science.

At least one of them would live. Because if she couldn't save Miguel, she would die anyway.

40

To Landon's great annoyance, it took more than ten minutes to explain to his security detail that he had added a leg to his travel plans, then wait for them to approve his route and destination.

Ridiculous, he said.

Imperative, they said, this close to Election Day.

After some wrangling they agreed to take him to the west side of Houston—one car, two agents, period. It wasn't like he was driving to Argentina.

He spent the three-hour trip contemplating how he had failed his second wife and how Trent Wilde had not. It was never only about one event, he supposed. In his case, living fifteen years in a plot not of his making must have played a role.

And it all began when Wilde had introduced him to Patrice. How fateful that little detail seemed now.

The car passed through the 610 Loop and turned onto River Oaks Boulevard at four twenty-five, then wove itself into the affluent neighborhood. Landon instructed the driver to pull over a block away from Wilde's home, a monstrosity for the wealthy divorcé, who lived alone.

"Wait here," Landon said.

"Sir—"

"Enough. I'm dropping in to visit a friend."

He exited the black Lincoln and slammed the door, unwilling to enter any more arguments.

One car pulling out of a neighbor's gated drive was the only stirring at this sleepy hour. A chill kept even the birds quiet.

Trent didn't bother with gates, but an impressive circular driveway surrounded a garden, and a broad flight of brick steps rose to the double-wide entrance. In a matter of seconds Landon found himself, surprisingly composed, eye to eye with an engraved brass knocker.

He opted for the doorbell and rang it three times before Trent appeared, cinching the belt of a housecoat around his waist. His left cheek bore an imprint from bedsheets.

Trent's eyes registered Landon, then darted to the stairs to the left of the entry. "Well, this is an unexpected surprise. What brings you here? Where's your detail?"

Landon pushed past him into the foyer, then stood at the base of the stairs, looking up. Trent closed the door slowly, lingering in shadow.

"Where's my wife?"

Trent shoved a hand into one pocket of his jacket and raised an eyebrow. "Apparently you think she's here."

"Patrice!" Landon shouted, directing his booming voice to the upper level. He turned back to the man he had called *friend* for so many years. "What's wrong with you that you can't keep your hands off her?"

"Oh, I think it was the other way around."

"Do not underestimate me!"

Trent raised both hands and took a step back, the gesture of mock surrender taunting Landon.

He brought his fist up into Trent's jaw with such speed that the man's fuzzy head snapped back and cracked the glass of the door's sidelight. He blinked and leaned heavily against the door frame, dazed.

"Now, now." Patrice appeared at the top of the stairs in a blue silk robe. "That kind of behavior is not very fitting of a future president."

"Really? Let's talk about *fitting* behavior."

She began to descend the steps.

"You have used me for your own gain from day one," Landon said to Patrice. "You've manipulated and lied. You've even destroyed my relationships with my own children, and for what? A lying backstabber like him?" He glared at Trent.

Patrice joined the men on the tiled floor, eyes locked on Landon.

"What do you think this does for us?" he continued. "A sexual scandal before I even set foot in the White House? What happens if the story breaks before the election?"

Trent had righted himself and now rubbed the back of his head. "It's gone on under your nose for eight years, Landon. What makes you think anyone will find out about it now, unless you're the one who tells them?"

Landon was unwilling to bear the depth of this humiliation alone. He threw his hands up. "All of us will pay!"

"No, we won't," Trent said. "Isn't that why you came here by yourself, at this hour? So no one would know? So we can still finish what we started out to do, no matter what?"

Landon shook his head and started to pace. The clicking of his heels on the tile echoed off the atrium ceiling. "What have you done?"

"Ask me that in two weeks and I'll say, 'I put Landon McAllister in the White House.'"

Landon stared at Trent. "What is my nomination built on?" he asked.

"Money." He shrugged. "Aren't they all?"

"Not principles, idealism? Hope? Workable solutions? *Morals*?"

"The American dream? You always were the romantic, McAllister. It's why people like you get elected. Otherwise I would have run for office myself and convinced Patrice to divorce you. But it's good for a presidential candidate to be married."

Landon grunted, disgusted. "Is the money dirty?"

Patrice laughed low and moved to stand between Landon and Trent. "If I didn't know better, I'd say your daughter has gotten under your skin with her ideas."

"I have a brain of my own, woman."

"Landon," said Trent, "there's nothing illegal going on. Just great business in an economically friendly time for the medical industry. I swear to you, every dime is legit."

"Why should I believe anything you say to me, Trent? My employees took a cut in their profit-sharing benefits to put me here. Is that legit?"

"It's certainly not a crime."

"*Convince me!* Convince me that if I go on, I won't be tainted forever.

Convince me that I can trust you, because I'm sure you can see that I have every reason in the world not to."

Patrice answered for Trent. "Shauna is the only one who doesn't trust us."

He sneered at her, tempted to make her feel the same pain he felt at her betrayal. Instead he managed to grind out his anger through clenched teeth.

"Not anymore."

Trent took a step toward the kitchen, eyes on Landon. "Come sit for a minute. Have a cup of coffee. I'll answer all your questions, but really, they're all going to boil down to one, Landon. Will you withdraw from the race or not? I'm pretty sure you'll see that you're all worked up over nothing more than an open relationship. Let's get this worked out now, so we can get on with it."

The headlight beams of a car in the circular drive penetrated the window, crossing the faces of all three adults. Patrice peeked out through the sidelight.

"Wayne's here," she said.

"Good. I'll have him join us then. One more voice of reason that will put this insanity behind us."

41

Shauna sat in Wayne's truck for a whole minute before deciding to get out. Worse than the possibility that Trent would not negotiate with her was the possibility that Wayne's men would arrive with Miguel before she had tried to secure Trent's help.

Shaking, she plodded up the brick steps and rang the bell.

She'd expected to face Trent and his hideous betrayal. But it was Patrice who opened the door.

Patrice.

Confusion washed away the words she'd rehearsed for Trent. And then she saw past her stepmother to the foyer, where her uncle looked at her with deadpan eyes. Shauna's last hope fell away in a landslide of understanding. Her knees smacked the textured concrete of the porch as she collapsed, exhausted from chasing this carrot of possibility only to find, at every bend in the road, more horrible news.

They were working together.

She and Miguel would both die.

Patrice scowled. "Where's Wayne?"

Landon shoved Patrice aside and stood in the doorway, looking down at Shauna with round eyes.

So he was in on it too.

The pain of the revelation brought a tremble to her arms. She stared up at Landon's form, backlit in the door frame and blurred by fresh tears. "Why are you doing this?"

The confused expression on his face told her that he didn't understand what she meant.

"Why would you want to hurt me? And Rudy? Why would you let them do this to him?"

Landon looked over his shoulder toward Trent, who joined Landon. "Shauna, where is Wayne?" Trent asked.

Shauna couldn't speak past the knot in her throat. Landon's features set in their hard lines. He was impatient with her again. "Stop this, now. Why are you here?"

"Miguel," she managed, then swallowed to clear her throat. "You have Miguel . . ."

"Who's Miguel?"

Patrice spun on her heel, pulled Trent out of the entry, and leaned in to whisper in his ear. She stalked off toward the kitchen.

Trent returned to the door and put a hand on Landon's back. "Let's bring her inside," he said to Landon.

Inside? Panic seized her. They would take her inside and she would never come out alive!

Shauna grew hysterical. She dropped her weight against Landon's efforts to pull her up.

"No! You can't kill me!"

Landon's mouth slackened. "*Kill* you? Shauna, I would never—"

"You would do anything! Look at what the drug trial did to me. The drug trial was all you—you told them to drug me!"

Landon shot a look to Trent. "The drug trial? What did you give her?"

"You approved it because you knew it was best."

"For who, Trent? I wanted what was best for *her*."

"Really, Landon. You knew there was a risk."

"Is this kind of behavior a side effect?"

"Possibly." Trent looked back toward the kitchen.

"Shauna, listen. I want to talk with you, but you're not making any sense. You can come in and we can all sort this out together, or you can stay out here in the cold. I don't really care what you choose."

Shauna's tears dried up. There was nothing more to cry about. Nothing mattered anymore. There was no way they would let her live through the day now that she knew. She'd been a fool to cling to any hope that she could save Miguel from these monsters.

She set her jaw and let Landon pull her up. Followed him like lamb to the slaughter, through the doorway, into the marble-floored foyer.

Odd how warm his hand felt on her cold fingers. She stood under a huge crystal chandelier, numb, as Trent closed the door.

"In here," he said, and walked toward the hall.

Landon glanced at her, released her hand, and stepped after Trent. But Shauna didn't follow them. Couldn't follow them. She felt suffocated.

"Did you know he's trafficking children, Landon?"

The question came out softly, but it stopped Landon before he entered the other room.

"Black-market babies are funding your campaign," she said. "And other children. Girls."

Landon slowly turned around. Trent had stopped and now turned as well. He walked back into the round foyer, eyes expressionless again.

"Wayne defected from the Marines during the Iraq war," Shauna said, eager to say it all even if they knew it already. "He spent a year hiding in Thailand, established black-market connections while he was there. He met Trent on a flight to Canada, bartered his liaisons in exchange for Trent's political access. Trent pulled strings to wipe Wayne's military record."

Her father looked at Trent. "You told me you recruited him from Global Wellness, that he could give us a competitive edge over them."

Trent didn't bother responding. His dark gaze drilled Shauna's.

"I put my career on the line for that," Landon said. "You used *my* connections to expunge his record."

"Yes," Trent said without looking at Landon. "I did."

"Wayne's only real role at MMV was to launder funds," Shauna said, returning Trent's glare with her own. "He brought in kids from Thailand, then later from Cambodia and Indonesia. The children passed through Houston and Florida and went to American families and . . . and other parties."

"They paid MMV?" Landon's question pleaded for a denial.

"They paid artificial overseas subsidiaries of MMV," Shauna told him. "Shell companies. The company pocketed net amounts at a 75 percent rate."

"This can't be true."

"She does have some imagination, doesn't she?" Trent said.

Shauna looked at her father. His frown was so perplexed that she almost believed he hadn't known any of it. But she didn't have the stomach to embrace such a futile hope.

"I think you should go home, Shauna," Trent said. "And you, Landon, use your head. Does this sound reasonable to you?"

Landon looked at Trent, then back at Shauna. The color had drained from his face.

"Landon . . ." Sweat beaded Trent's forehead. "You can't possibly believe her."

The words reached into Shauna's chest and squeezed her heart. *No, Landon, you will never believe me, will you? Not when Patrice is burning my skin, not when I'm the target of a murder, not when I am telling you the truth.*

Landon took his daughter's hand. There was that warmth again. His eyes watered. "How many children?" Landon asked.

"Three hundred fifty a year for seven years," Shauna said. "Sixty million dollars net, nine million a year for the company. For your profit-sharing plan."

Her father's features seemed to age in seconds.

Was it possible that he . . . ?

"Patrice coordinated the placement of the infants," Shauna said.

Landon studied her with a look of such confusion and despair that Shauna wondered if she could hope in him after all. That somehow he would return to her, that he would believe her.

"Please. You have to believe me. You have to. Just this one thing." Her words came out too fast, running into each other, but she couldn't slow them down. "It's so important. I didn't make up any of it. Miguel and I found out . . . Tell me you weren't a part of this. Please. Daddy, please tell me you believe me."

Trent laid a hand on Landon's arm. "She's delusional, Landon. Send her home before this gets ugly."

"No," Landon said, shrugging Trent off.

"She's going to bungle everything."

"Shut up, Trent."

Patrice appeared and gave an object to Trent.

"Please," Shauna whispered. She squeezed Landon's hands, and his fingers brushed Miguel's ring. She saw him register it, then nudge it with his thumb.

"Miguel," she whispered. "They're going to kill Miguel. He knows everything."

"Stop," Trent said. "She's full of lies!"

"And you aren't?" Landon snapped. "Shauna may be the only one in this room who is telling the truth!"

"You'll lose everything, you fool."

"I've already lost everything. But maybe it's not too late to get my daughter back."

Shauna's eyes registered the gun in Trent's hand as it slashed through the air and crashed into Landon's temple.

"Dad!"

Her father staggered.

Trent leveled the gun at Shauna's ear. Landon shouted something.

Shauna dropped to her knees and threw her arms over her head. The gunshot filled the room.

But the detonation came from behind her, from the door. And she was not dead, not hit, not even touched.

She turned and saw two black-suited men gliding through the open door, sidearms raised.

"No one moves."

She tried to get up, but Landon's security detail would have none of it.

"Down!"

"Leave my daughter. Take *her*."

Shauna saw that her father had regained his feet and was pointing at Patrice. The men glanced at each other.

"She's at the heart of this mess."

Trent lay prone in a pool of blood on the marble floor, gun still in his outstretched hand. He'd been hit by one of Landon's men. He did not move.

Patrice was fixated on the still body. Slowly her eyes lifted, shifted to Landon, then over to the agents. "Don't be ridiculous. He was trying to—"

"Get her out of my sight!" Landon thundered.

The closest agent nodded. "If you'll come with me, ma'am."

"No."

The other agent crossed to her, grabbed her arm, and jerked her across the foyer toward the hallway. "Politeness doesn't work on this one," he said to his partner.

She went unwillingly, uttering a string of vile protests.

"You okay, sir?"

"I'm fine. Help Joe, and get the authorities out here."

The agent nodded and followed the other toward the kitchen, phone already in hand.

For a moment they faced each other, father and daughter, unsure. Then Landon extended his hand to Shauna and helped her up. Through the doorway, Shauna saw a brown SUV appear at the end of the drive, creeping toward Wayne's Chevy.

"Are you hurt?" Landon asked.

Shauna hardly heard him. Her eyes were on the SUV.

"Miguel!"

She launched herself across the foyer and had taken two steps before Landon grabbed her arm and snatched her back. His grip was so strong that she smacked into his chest.

"What are you doing?" she demanded.

"Helping you get Miguel," he whispered.

She pulled against him. "He's in that car!"

"You go and they'll bolt, Shauna. They're looking for Wayne. They see his car and think he's here."

He was right, she realized, and the knowledge intensified her fear.

"They're going to kill him!"

Landon spun Shauna to face him and gripped her by both shoulders. "No, *they are not*. Do you hear me? I will not let them." Shauna heard but did not understand. "Listen to me, Shauna. I need you to tell me where Wayne is."

"The police have him."

"Do these men know it?"

She shook her head.

Slowly, Landon released her, holding up his hands as a protective warning. "Wait here. Don't move! They see you, it's over, you understand?"

Landon snatched up the gun that Trent had struck him with. "What are you going to do? You can't go—"

"Yes!" Then he calmed and searched her eyes with his. "Yes, I can. I'm not their enemy, you are. I can stall them until the police get here."

"Your guards—"

"Would spook them as quickly as you would. I'm not supposed to be here."

He stepped up to her, put his arm around her, and pulled her close. She could smell his cologne. Irrational peace washed over her, like the love of her mother.

Like the love of God.

Landon hadn't held her this way since she was a preschooler prone to tantrums. Back then, they would end in her clinging to him while he stroked her hair until her heart settled. Now, he touched his palm against her cheek. "I'm so sorry, Shauna. So sorry." He kissed the crown of her head and rested there for a moment.

She closed her eyes, still high-strung from the confrontation and wanting not to be. He broke away from her before she was ready.

"Don't move," he said.

He tucked the gun out of sight, behind his belt, and stepped out into the dim hours of the morning.

Shauna hurried to the window, watched her father crossing the lawn in the glow of the porch lights, and prayed for Miguel. She prayed that he was alive, that they could get to him soon, that neither he nor her father would be harmed in the midst of all that was about to happen.

The SUV came to a stop, abreast with Wayne's truck. She half expected the driver to gun its engine and blast down the drive at the sight of Landon approaching. But her father was right. Wayne's men didn't see him as an immediate threat.

Landon walked up to the car and signaled for them to roll down the window.

After several seconds and a harsh tap on the door, the window slid down.

For half a minute they talked. About what, Shauna had no clue.

Landon was gesturing toward the house, perhaps suggesting the men come inside.

She saw the man in the passenger seat check out the red Chevy, then turn back to Landon and shake his head. He pointed at the house and then hooked his thumb toward the rear of the SUV as he talked to her father. He wanted Wayne to come out here?

The driver leaned forward as if to restart the engine.

Landon grabbed his door and yanked it open. The man started yelling. Landon leaned into the cab and dragged him out by the hair at the nape of his neck.

Shauna strained to hear any sign that police were on their way. What was taking so long?

Her father was familiar with firearms, as were most Texans, but the ease with which he withdrew Trent's gun from his waistband and shoved it into the driver's face surprised her.

What was he doing?

The man was begging Landon not to shoot him as he dragged him into the headlight beams at the front of the car.

The passenger was clambering out of his side and crouching low between the SUV and Wayne's truck. He slunk toward the rear.

Miguel. He would get Miguel, use him as leverage. She had to get to him first.

Shauna flew to the door and leaped out onto the porch. She jumped the brick steps before thinking that she should have fetched Landon's security detail for help.

She started screaming, hoping they would hear her.

She was halfway across the lawn in a full sprint when the first gunshot popped like ice breaking off a glacier.

Shauna stumbled. *Dad?*

God, please, please.

Landon was still standing. The driver had dropped to the ground, hands clamped over his ears, swearing a stream. Landon held his gun level between the two vehicles, aimed in the direction of the passenger. She saw smoke rising from the barrel.

Everyone was shouting. The two agents cleared the brick steps and hit the ground behind her at the same moment that she found her feet again. They bolted toward Landon.

She raced to the SUV. The passenger, screaming and clutching his bleeding leg, had collapsed at the rear tire. Shauna jumped over him. At the back, breathless, she threw open the hatch. Miguel lay in the cargo hold.

He was so pale, nearly folded in half and limp. *No no no.*

"Miguel?" She jumped in next to him and placed her hand over his heart, begging God for a rhythm. She couldn't feel anything. She tried to find a pulse in his neck—so faint! But he was breathing. Shallow.

Distant sirens sounded on River Oaks Boulevard.

He was so cold.

She lifted his head into her lap and brushed his hair with her fingers, waiting for other people to come help her do what she could not. She was crying again.

"Don't forget me," she murmured. "Please don't forget."

42

Shauna lay on a cot in Miguel's Houston hospital room, staring at the ceiling. She wasn't sure what time it was, or what day, or whether she would ever move from this spot. She didn't care whether she should shower, whether she would eat, or whether she could answer the phone if it rang again.

In four days, Miguel had shown no sign of regaining consciousness. Shauna grilled the attending physician on Miguel's condition. They had no clear picture of his mental state. He was stable and would likely survive the ordeal, but precise details would have to wait until he was alert.

Drs. Carver, Siders, and Harding and various Hill Country Medical Center Staff had been arrested at their homes as they left for work Thursday morning, for their role in falsifying and misrepresenting the clinical trials of MMV's experimental drugs. Their information was not all that useful to Miguel's doctors. Apparently it would take more than four days to sort out the truth.

Dr. Siders admitted to injecting Shauna with MDMA while she was in the emergency room.

Frank Danson was arrested in Denver Saturday when he attempted to use one of Miguel's credit cards. He was charged with Corbin's murder, but Frank's attorney planned to negotiate a reduced sentence for Frank's "assistance" in bringing Wayne Spade to justice. The Jeep had been recovered, along with the pearl-handled knife and the medications administered to Shauna.

Trent Wilde died en route to the hospital, shot clean through the heart by the agent sworn to defend the senator. After a standard review, Landon expected Joe to be reinstated.

Confiscated phone records, e-mail messages, and documents from Wayne's and Trent's computers implicated Leon Chalise in the ring. He was arrested Thursday evening, ten minutes before he was due to board a flight to Brazil.

Patrice McAllister confessed to planting MDMA in Shauna's car and apartment. She took the fifth regarding her role in the trafficking operation.

All charges against Shauna were dropped.

Wayne Spade thought he was a student at Arizona State named Wayne Marshall, late for football practice, hung over from a night of heavy drinking. His attorney was cooking up an insanity defense.

Without it, Wayne faced a possible life sentence for his leadership in the trafficking ring and laundering, in addition to a court-martial for his desertion in Iraq, and a second possible life sentence for his attempted murder of Shauna McAllister. If implicated as a coconspirator in the murder of Corbin Smith, he might face the death penalty. And he didn't remember any of it.

Landon withdrew from the presidential race Friday morning, when Scott Norris's first-scoop story hit the AP wires. Landon's MMV shares bottomed out within a half hour of his withdrawal, leaving him with too little to pay restitution to other shareholders and to employees who'd lost their fair portion of the profits. His accountant estimated it would take years to climb out of the hole. His attorney said it was too early to tell whether Landon would serve a prison sentence for his role in the records tampering, but they could hope for a censure and a minimal term.

He stepped down from his leadership of MMV's board by Friday afternoon, then resigned from his post as senator as people were leaving work early for cocktails. By Friday night, he had returned home, dismissed everyone from his staff except Pam Riley, and fallen asleep draped across the foot of his son's bed.

Thirty-six hours to lose his career, his business, his livelihood, his wife, his best friend.

All he had left were his children, just as he had more than two decades ago when Xamina died.

Shauna watched her father's humiliation without joy.

And when her own interrogation with every involved authority and a few psychologists temporarily ended late Saturday afternoon, she had taken up residence next to Miguel, collapsing on the cot, exhausted and tearful. Tear trails encrusted her hairline and neck.

She dozed on and off. It seemed she hadn't slept at all. Someone was knocking on the door, and she wished the noise into silence.

The doorknob unlatched. A blinding beam of light fell across her closed eyes, and she crossed her arm over her face as a shield.

The door closed and someone walked into the room.

She smelled her father's aftershave.

"Shauna, honey." His voice held inflections she hadn't heard from him before. Hope. Affection. Regret. With his free hand he lifted her arm off her eyes and fingered Miguel's ring.

"Shauna, come sit up with us."

For two hours Shauna sat by Miguel's side with her father, studying every line and pore of her fiancé's face, and holding his hand.

After an hour of silence, Landon said, "I went to church this morning."

Shauna took her eyes off Miguel and rediscovered her father.

"I haven't been to church since your mother died."

Shauna hadn't thought of church in years. She withdrew her hand and wiped her palm on her filthy jeans, nearly five days old now.

"The preacher was speaking out of the book of Revelation. I didn't hear anything he said but the Scripture, 'Remember the height from which you have fallen.'" He turned his eyes to Shauna. "'Repent and do the things you did at first.'

"Shauna, honey, I've forgotten so many important things, things your mother used to hold in front of me. This is an honest-to-goodness starting over for me. I hope"—he cleared his throat—"I hope you will forgive me."

Shauna stared at him, half believing as the years of hurt and rejection lifted for a moment. She wanted a new beginning with her dad. She'd wanted it all along. The words she wanted to say knotted in her throat, so she grasped his hand in hers and smiled at him until she could find her voice.

"Yes," she said, "I forgive you."

After that, neither McAllister said anything; their presence with each other said enough for the time being.

At seven o'clock, Shauna was driven out of the room by restlessness. She needed to walk off the what-ifs. What if Miguel never awoke? What if he awoke and could not remember her? What if the effects of the drugs Miguel and she had received were irreversible?

She borrowed Landon's rental car and found a mall, bought a fresh pair of pants and a blouse without trying them on, showered at his hotel, and returned to the hospital. Landon had continued to sit with Miguel in her absence. She stopped at the cafeteria on the way back to Miguel's room and shared a tuna sandwich and an apple with her father. Shauna managed about three bites.

Landon left at nine.

Shauna slept just under the surface of her awareness and woke before the sun rose. She resumed her study of Miguel's face, looking for a way to remember everything she had known about him without having to steal it. She discovered nothing.

Nothing but a growing love.

At ten, someone knocked on the door. Shauna turned, and a young woman in a candy striper's frock leaned in and whispered, "Can I get you anything? Something to drink? A blanket?"

Shauna stared. The girl was probably a mere sixteen, give or take. Her sleek black hair was pulled back into a tail, and her bronze skin glowed with the same youthfulness that radiated from her smiling eyes.

Her duotone eyes. Brown and hazel. Just like Khai's.

Shauna caught herself gawking. "I'm sorry. Your eyes. They're beautiful."

The girl giggled. "That's okay. They're a good conversation starter, you know? How many people do you know have heterochromia iridis? The way I see it, you can either make it work for you or you can be a freak. I myself prefer the former."

Shauna nodded and managed, "Actually, you look like someone I know."

"You mean the eyes? That would be amazing if I could meet them sometime. I mean, I've only met one other person in my whole life. It's genetic, you know. My dad says it means I can see all the nuances of the world."

"Smart dad."

"The smartest."

Shauna caught a look at the girl's ID badge. Amy Mitchell.

"Well, if you don't need anything I should get on."

"Thanks," Shauna said. "Maybe I'll see you again? I could introduce you to my friend."

"You bet."

Amy left the room and Shauna continued looking at the space she had occupied. There was no way to be sure she was Khai's daughter. The chances were onion-skin thin. And yet . . .

Miguel's sheets rustled. Shauna spun. He was watching her.

"Miguel."

He closed his eyes as if he had a blockbuster headache, then opened them again. He took a deep breath.

"Are you hurting? Should I get the doctor?" Shauna gripped the bedrails near his head and pulled her rolling stool closer to him.

He lifted his hand off the bed. No.

She rested her chin on her hands. Oh, she wanted to touch his face, hold his hand, kiss him! She wanted tangible evidence that he was not severely harmed.

That he remembered her. She couldn't bring herself to ask.

He turned his head toward her and took a long look at her hair, her face, her hands.

"What happened to you?" he asked.

Shauna straightened and touched her bruised face with her left hand. Tears sprang to her eyes, but not because her skin was tender.

He had forgotten.

She swallowed and forced a controlled voice. "I tripped in a stairwell." That was all she could manage.

Miguel shifted onto his side and placed his hand over her grip on the railing. A small sideways grin poked his cheek.

"No, lovely. You moved the ring. I want to know what happened."

Her relief came out in a laugh. She covered her mouth, and her tears spilled over.

"I remembered that I love you," she said.

He lifted her hand off the rail and pulled it toward him, kissed her palm. She set up a guard over her heart and mind.

"Miguel, don't risk—"

He kissed her palm harder, then placed it against his unshaven cheek and held it there.

"I don't want to hurt—"

"Shauna, I've already said you can't take anything from me that I wouldn't freely give you."

She shook her head. What she was capable of . . . even Miguel didn't know.

"Don't close yourself off to me," he said. "Don't."

"But—"

"You have to trust me."

"I trust you." But she didn't trust herself, the unknown factor in this equation.

"I'm pretty sure I got some of those drugs they gave to you." Miguel winked at her. "I can't remember my home address. Maybe we'll cancel each other out."

"I doubt—",

"I need you to shut up now."

And I need you to save me again.

Miguel lifted his hand to pull her closer to him, and Shauna dropped her defenses, willing herself to believe that the love she had for him would be greater than her mutant mind. She decided to believe that his love for her would fill the empty places in her heart because he wanted to fill them, and not because she demanded it.

She let him kiss her.

Epilogue

The view from the dock on my father's estate is beautiful today, November 13. Election Day. The sky is blue and the river is green and the air is unusually still. Lando—Dad—and I have decided to spend the day outdoors, as far from the video and radio streams as possible.

Rudy is on his chair at the end of the dock, eyes closed, face turned toward the sun. He is smiling. I can't explain it and won't ruin the moment by trying. Our father is smiling at him.

I hear Miguel's footsteps approaching behind us and turn as he descends the short hill. Dr. Ayers walks beside him, tall and graceful and ramrod straight. I still have no memory of my sessions with him, though Miguel has told me what he knows of them and assures me that of all the doctors I could trust at this time in my life, Dr. Ayers is the one.

I extend my hand to him in a greeting, and he takes it in both of his, swallowing my fingers in his wide palms. He pats my knuckles. I think I'll adopt this man to be my grandfather.

His eyes twinkle. "So tell me, Shauna, how it feels to have gotten your wish?"

"My wish?" I can't imagine what he means, but I hope he'll tell me.

"Well now. The last time we spoke, you wanted nothing more than to forget all the pain of your life. We had ourselves a little argument over that one, we did." He wags his finger to tease me, and I doubt we really argued at all.

But then a flash of an image streaks across my eyes, startling me: a blazing hot parking lot, four stories beneath a high window.

A memory?

My memory has not returned, but Miguel's memories have filled many of my gaps. In an act of trust I will never take for granted, Miguel has allowed me to learn how to access his mind without taking anything, how to look but not steal. Together we have been able to reconstruct our shared history—an effort that has led to some exceptionally beautiful kisses.

I show Dr. Ayers to a group of portable chairs we've set up near the dock.

"Who won that argument?" I ask, which sends Dr. Ayers into a fit of hooting laughter. Miguel and I exchange delighted grins and take seats beside him.

"Oh, I always win," he says when he catches his breath. "We elders are always right."

I don't know about all elders, all the time, but it's easy enough to imagine of Dr. Ayers. "Well, to answer your question," I go on, "I'm not sure exactly what I was hoping for when I wanted to forget. But I think I have a different perspective on my past now. A different idea of its value, I mean. Hurts and all."

Dr. Ayers rubs the corner of his laughing eyes, nodding. "Yes, yes. Pain or perspective," he said. "That's the choice."

"Not a very easy choice, is it?"

"Oh now, that depends."

"What do you mean?"

"You choose pain—you choose to fight it, deny it, bury it—then yes, the choice is always hard. But you choose perspective—embrace your history, give it credit for the better person it can make you, scars and all—the choice gets easier every time."

"Seems backward."

"Yes it does. But I tell you it's true. I wrestled for years with that one like Jacob wrestled with God. How else could this head of black hair have turned so white?" He points to his curls.

I settle against the back of my chair and turn my face to the sun, like Rudy. I'm not sure I agree with Dr. Ayers, but the gaping black holes that still remain in my past suggest that he is right. Again. Whatever I learned or gathered or developed from those experiences is gone forever. I have lost a part of myself in them.

Besides, the man must have at least fifty years of life on me to prove me wrong.

"So what did God tell you when you wrestled with him?"

"'Remember that you were a slave in Egypt.'"

I look up. "That's cryptic."

"Not really. It's Scripture. His people were oppressed by their enemies."

"And he wants you to keep that at the front of your mind? He wants you to stay focused on the darkest seasons in your life? How could that possibly do any good?"

Dr. Ayers folds his hands across his slim midsection and locks eyes with mine. Though the laugh lines deepen at the corners, his gaze tells me clearly that I must not miss what he is about to say.

"He wants you to remember who delivered you from that time, Shauna. That's the point of holding on to memory: delivery, not darkness."

"Perspective, not pain," I murmur.

"Now, my dear, I think you're getting it."

AFTER *KISS* COMES
BURN.

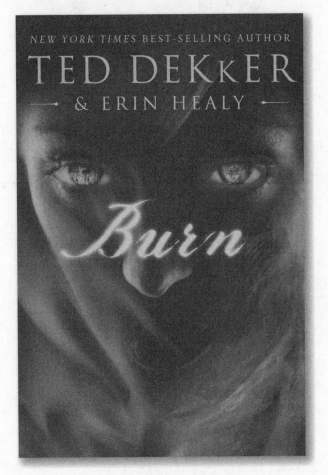

The New Novel from
Ted Dekker and Erin Healy
ARRIVES JANUARY 2010.

THE WORLD IS HARDLY READY FOR CALEB.

THOMAS NELSON, INC.
Since 1798

THE FUTURE CHANGES IN
THE BLINK OF AN EYE . . . OR DOES IT?

About the Authors

Ted Dekker is known for novels that combine adrenaline-laced stories with unexpected plot twists, unforgettable characters, and incredible confrontations between good and evil. He lives in Austin, Texas, with his wife and children. Visit teddekker.com

Erin Healy is an award-winning editor who worked with Ted Dekker on more than a dozen of his stories before their collaboration on *Kiss*. Her debut solo novel, *Never Let You Go*, will release in Spring, 2010. She and her husband, Tim, have two children. Visit erinhealy.com